Tobias Wolff was born in Alabama in 1945 and grew up in Washington State. Tobias Wolff's books include *Hunters in the Snow* and *Back in the World*, both collections of stories; *The Barracks Thief*, a short novel, and *In Pharoah's Army*, winner of the *Esquire/Volvo/Waterstone's* Non-fiction Award 1994. His memoir, *This Boy's Life*, and his most recent collection of stories, *The Night in Question*, are both available from Bloomsbury. He lives with his wife, Catherine, and their two sons in upstate New York, where he teaches at Syracuse University.

The Stories of Tobias Wolff

BLOOMSBURY

First published in Great Britain 1988
This paperback edition published 1997

The stories between 9 and 178 first appeared in one volume in 1982 as *Hunters in the Snow* published by Jonathan Cape. The stories between pages 179 and 326 first appeared in one volume in 1986 as *Back in the World* published by Jonathan Cape.

Bloomsbury Publishing Plc, 38 Soho Square, London W1D 3HB

A CIP catalogue record for this book
is available from the British Library

ISBN 0 7475 3153 6

10 9 8 7 6 5

All papers used by Bloomsbury Publishing are natural, recyclable products made from wood grown in well-managed forests. The manufacturing processes conform to the environmental regulations of the country of origin.

Typeset by Hewer Text Ltd, Edinburgh
Printed in Great Britain by Clays Ltd, St Ives plc

For Catherine

Grateful acknowledgment is made to the following publications in which the stories first appeared:
Antaeus, The Atlantic, Encounter, Esquire, Fiction Magazine, Granta, Literary Review, Macmillan's Winter Tales, Missouri Review, Ploughshares, TriQuarterly, and *Vanity Fair.*

Grateful acknowledgment is made to *Antaeus* and to *Granta* where 'The Barracks Thief' first appeared.

Contents

Next Door

I wake up afraid. My wife is sitting on the edge of my bed, shaking me. 'They're at it again,' she says.

I go to the window. All their lights are on, upstairs and down, as if they have money to burn. He yells, she screams something back, the dog barks. There is a short silence, then the baby cries, poor thing.

'Better not stand there,' says my wife. 'They might see you.' I say, 'I'm going to call the police,' knowing she won't let me.

'Don't,' she says.

She's afraid that they will poison our cat if we complain.

Next door the man is still yelling, but I can't make out what he's saying over the dog and the baby. The woman laughs, not really meaning it, '*Ha! Ha! Ha!*,' and suddenly gives a sharp little cry. Everything goes quiet.

'He struck her,' my wife says. 'I felt it just the same as if he struck me.'

Next door the baby gives a long wail and the dog starts up again. The man walks out into his driveway and slams the door.

'Be careful,' my wife says. She gets back into her bed and pulls the cover up to her neck.

The man mumbles to himself and jerks at his fly. Finally he gets it open and walks over to our fence. It's a white picket fence, ornamental more than anything else. It couldn't keep anyone out.

I put it in myself, and planted honeysuckle and bougainvillea all along it.

My wife says, 'What's he doing?'

'Shh,' I say.

He leans against the fence with one hand and with the other he goes to the bathroom on the flowers. He walks the length of the fence like that, not missing any of them. When he's through he gives Florida a shake, then zips up and heads back across the driveway. He almost slips on the gravel but he catches himself and curses and goes into the house, slamming the door again.

When I turn around my wife is leaning forward, watching me. She raises her eyebrows. 'Not again,' she says.

I nod.

'Between him and the dog it's a wonder you can get anything to grow out there.'

I would rather talk about something else. It depresses me, thinking about the flowers. They are past their prime, but still. Next door the woman is shouting. 'Listen to that,' I say.

'I used to feel sorry for her,' my wife says. 'Not any more. Not after last month.'

'Ditto,' I say, trying to remember what happened last month to make my wife not feel sorry for the woman next door. I don't feel sorry for her either, but then I never have. She yells at the baby, and excuse me, but I'm not about to get all excited over someone who treats a child like that. She screams things like '*I thought I told you to stay in your bedroom*!' and here the baby can't even talk yet.

As far as her looks, I guess you would have to say she's pretty. But it won't last. She doesn't have good bone structure. She has a soft look to her, like she has never eaten anything but doughnuts and milk shakes. Her skin is white. The baby takes after her, not that you would expect it to take after *him*, dark and hairy. Even with his shirt on you can tell that he has hair all over his back and on his shoulders, thick and springy like an Airedale's.

Now they're all going at once over there, plus they've got the stereo turned on full blast. One of those bands. 'It's the baby I feel sorry for,' I say.

My wife puts her hands over her ears. 'I can't stand another minute of it,' she says. She takes her hands away. 'Maybe there's something on TV.' She sits up. 'See who's on *Johnny Carson.*'

I turn on the television. It used to be down in the den but I brought it up here a few years ago when my wife got sick. I took care of her myself – made the meals and everything. I got to where I could change the sheets with her still in the bed. I always meant to take the television back down when my wife recovered from her illness, but I never got around to it. It sits between our beds on a little table I made. Johnny is saying something to Sammy Davis, Jr. Ed McMahon is bent over laughing. He is always so cheerful. If you were going to take a really long voyage you could do worse than bring Ed McMahon along.

My wife wants to know what else is on. '"*El Dorado*",' I read. '"Brisk adventure yarn about a group of citizens in search of the legendary city of gold." It's got two-and-a-half stars beside it.'

'Citizens of what?' my wife asks.

'It doesn't say.'

Finally we watch the movie. A blind man comes into a small town. He says that he has been to El Dorado, and that he will lead an expedition there for a share of the proceeds. He can't see, but he will call out the landmarks one by one as they ride. At first people make fun of him, but eventually all the leading citizens get together and decide to give it a try. Right away they get attacked by Apaches and some of them want to turn back, but every time they get ready the blind man gives them another landmark, so they keep riding.

Next door the woman is going crazy. She is saying things to him that no person should ever say to another person. It makes my wife restless. She looks at me. 'Can I come over?' she says. 'Just for a visit?'

I pull down the blankets and she gets in. The bed is just fine for one, but with two of us it's a tight fit. We are lying on our sides with me in back. I don't mean for it to happen but before long old Florida begins to stiffen up on me. I put my arms around my wife. I move my hands up onto the Rockies, then on down across the Plains, heading South.

'Hey,' she says. 'No Geography. Not tonight.'

'I'm sorry,' I say.

'Can't I just visit?'

'Forget it. I said I was sorry.'

The citizens are crossing a desert. They have just about run out of water, and their lips are cracked. Though the blind man has delivered a warning, someone drinks from a poisoned well and dies horribly. That night, around the campfire, the others begin to quarrel. Most of them want to go home. 'This is no country for a white man,' one says, 'and if you ask me nobody has ever been here before.' But the blind man describes a piece of gold so big and pure that it will burn your eyes out if you look directly at it. 'I ought to know,' he says. When he is finished the citizens are silent: one by one they move away and lie down on their bedrolls. They put their hands behind their heads and look up at the stars. A coyote howls.

Hearing the coyote, I remember why my wife stopped feeling sorry for the woman next door. It was a Monday evening, about a month ago, right after I got home from work. The man next door started to beat the dog, and I don't mean just smacking him once or twice. He was beating him, and he kept beating him until the dog couldn't even cry any more; you could hear the poor creature's voice breaking. Finally it stopped. Then, a few minutes later, I heard my wife say, 'Oh!' and I went into the kitchen to find out what was wrong. She was standing by the window, which looks into the kitchen next door. The man had his wife backed up against the fridge. He had his knee between her legs and she had her knee between his legs and they were kissing, really hard, not just with their lips but rolling their faces back and forth against each other. My wife could hardly speak for a couple of hours afterwards. Later she said that she would never waste her sympathy on that woman again.

It's quiet over there. My wife has gone to sleep and so has my arm, which is under her head. I slide it out and open and close my fingers, considering whether to wake her up. I like sleeping in my own bed, and there isn't enough room for the both of us. Finally I decide that it won't hurt anything to change places for one night.

I get up and fuss with the plants for a while, watering them and moving some to the window and some back. I trim the coleus, which is starting to get leggy, and put the cuttings in a glass of water on the sill. All the lights are off next door except the one in their bedroom window. I think about the life they have, and how it goes on and on, until it seems like the life they were meant to live. Everybody is always saying how great it is that human beings are so adaptable, but I don't know. A friend of mine told me that in Amsterdam, Holland, they have a whole section of town where you can see women sitting in rooms, waiting. If you want one of them you just go in and pay, and they close the drapes. This is nothing special to the people who live in Holland. In Istanbul, Turkey, my friend saw a man walking down the street with a grand piano on his back. Everyone just moved around him and kept going. It's awful, what we get used to.

I turn off the television and get into my wife's bed. A sweet, heavy smell rises off the sheets. At first it makes me dizzy but after that I like it. It reminds me of gardenias.

The reason I don't watch the rest of the movie is that I can already see how it will end. The citizens will kill each other off, probably about ten feet from the legendary city of gold, and the blind man will stumble in by himself, not knowing that he has made it back to El Dorado.

I could write a better movie than that. My movie would be about a group of explorers, men and women, who leave behind their homes and their jobs and their families – everything they have known. They cross the sea and are ship-wrecked on the coast of a country which is not on their maps. One of them drowns. Another gets attacked by a wild animal, and eaten. But the others want to push on. They ford rivers and cross an enormous glacier by dog sled. It takes months. On the glacier they run out of food and for a while there it looks like they might turn on each other, but they don't. Finally they solve their problem by eating the dogs. That's the sad part of the movie.

At the end we see the explorers sleeping in a meadow filled with white flowers. The blossoms are wet with dew and stick to their bodies, petals of columbine, clematis, blazing star, baby's breath, larkspur, iris, rue – covering them completely, turning them white so that you cannot tell one from another, man from woman, woman from man. The sun comes up. They stand and raise their arms, like white trees in a land where no one has ever been.

Hunters in the Snow

Tub had been waiting for an hour in the falling snow. He paced the sidewalk to keep warm and stuck his head out over the kerb whenever he saw lights approaching. The fall of snow thickened. Tub stood below the overhang of a building. Across the road the clouds whitened just above the rooftops, and the street lights went out. He shifted the rifle strap to his other shoulder. The whiteness seeped up the sky.

A truck slid around the corner, horn blaring, rear end sashaying. Tub moved to the sidewalk and held up his hand. The truck jumped the kerb and kept coming, half on the street and half on the sidewalk. It wasn't slowing down at all. Tub stood for a moment, still holding up his hand, then jumped back. His rifle slipped off his shoulder and clattered on the ice, a sandwich fell out of his pocket. He ran for the steps of the building. Another sandwich and a package of cookies tumbled onto the new snow. He made the steps and looked back.

The truck had stopped several feet beyond where Tub had been standing. He picked up his sandwiches and his cookies and slung the rifle and went up to the driver's window. The driver was bent against the steering wheel, slapping his knees and drumming his feet on the floorboards. He looked like a cartoon of a person laughing. 'You ought to see yourself,' the driver said. 'He looks just like a beach ball with a hat on, doesn't he? Doesn't he, Frank?'

The man beside him smiled and looked off.

'You almost ran me down,' Tub said. 'You could've killed me.'

'Come on, Tub,' said the man beside the driver. 'Be mellow. Kenny was just messing around.' He opened the door and slid over to the middle of the seat.

Tub took the bolt out of his rifle and climbed in beside him. 'I waited an hour,' he said. 'If you meant ten o'clock why didn't you say ten o'clock?'

'Tub, you haven't done anything but complain since we got here,' said the man in the middle. 'If you want to piss and moan all day you might as well go home and bitch at your kids. Take your pick.' When Tub didn't say anything he turned to the driver. 'Okay, Kenny, let's hit the road.'

Some juvenile delinquents had heaved a brick through the windshield on the driver's side, so the cold and snow funnelled right into the cab. The heater didn't work. They covered themselves with a couple of blankets Kenny had brought along and pulled down the muffs on their caps. Tub tried to keep his hands warm by rubbing them under the blanket but Frank made him stop.

They left Spokane and drove deep into the country, running along black lines of fences. The snow let up, but still there was no edge to the land where it met the sky. Nothing moved in the chalky fields. The cold bleached their faces and made the stubble stand out on their cheeks and along their upper lips. They stopped twice for coffee before they got to the woods where Kenny wanted to hunt.

Tub was for trying someplace different; two years in a row they'd been up and down this land and hadn't seen a thing. Frank didn't care one way or the other, he just wanted to get out of the goddamned truck. 'Feel that,' Frank said, slamming the door. He spread his feet and closed his eyes and leaned his head way back and breathed deeply. 'Tune in on that energy.'

'Another thing,' Kenny said. 'This is open land. Most of the land around here is posted.'

'I'm cold,' Tub said.

Frank breathed out. 'Stop bitching, Tub. Get centred.'

'I wasn't bitching.'

'Centred,' Kenny said. 'Next thing you'll be wearing a nightgown, Frank. Selling flowers out at the airport.'

'Kenny,' Frank said, 'you talk too much.'

'Okay,' Kenny said. 'I won't say a word. Like I won't say anything about a certain babysitter.'

'What babysitter?' Tub asked.

'That's between us,' Frank said, looking at Kenny. 'You keep your mouth shut.'

Kenny laughed.

'You're asking for it,' Frank said.

'Asking for what?'

'You'll see.'

'Hey,' Tub said, 'are we hunting or what?'

They started off across the field. Tub had trouble getting through the fences. Frank and Kenny could have helped him; they could have lifted up the top wire and stepped on the bottom wire, but they didn't. They stood and watched him. There were a lot of fences and Tub was puffing when they reached the woods.

They hunted for over two hours and saw no deer, no tracks, no sign. Finally they stopped by the creek to eat. Kenny had several slices of pizza and a couple of candy bars; Frank had a sandwich, an apple, two carrots, and a square of chocolate; Tub ate one hard-boiled egg and a stick of celery.

'You ask me how I want to die today,' Kenny said, 'I'll tell you burn me at the stake.' He turned to Tub. 'You still on that diet?' He winked at Frank.

'What do you think? You think I like hard-boiled eggs?'

'All I can say is, it's the first diet I ever heard of where you gained weight from it.'

'Who said I gained weight?'

'Oh, pardon me. I take it back. You're just wasting away before my very eyes. Isn't he, Frank?'

Frank had his fingers fanned out, on the stump where he'd laid his food. His knuckles were hairy. He wore a heavy wedding band and on his right pinky another gold ring with a flat face and an 'F' in what looked like diamonds. 'Tub,' he said, 'you haven't seen your own balls in ten years.'

Kenny doubled over laughing. He took off his hat and slapped his leg with it.

'What am I supposed to do?' Tub said. 'It's my glands.'

They left the woods and hunted along the creek. Frank and Kenny worked one bank and Tub worked the other, moving upstream. The snow was light but the drifts were deep and hard to move through. Wherever Tub looked the surface was smooth, undisturbed, and after a time he lost interest. He stopped looking for tracks and just tried to keep up with Frank and Kenny on the other side. A moment came when he realized he hadn't seen them in a long time. The breeze was moving from him to them; when it stilled he could sometimes hear Kenny laughing but that was all. He quickened his pace, breasting the drifts, fighting away the snow. He heard his heart and felt the flush on his face but he never once stopped.

Tub caught up with Frank and Kenny at a bend of the creek. They were standing on a log that stretched from their bank to his. Ice had backed up behind the log. Frozen reeds stuck out.

'See anything?' Frank asked.

Tub shook his head.

There wasn't much daylight left and they decided to head back towards the road. Frank and Kenny crossed the log and they started downstream, using the trail Tub had broken. Before they had gone very far Kenny stopped. 'Look at that,' he said, and pointed to some tracks going from the creek back into the woods. Tub's footprints crossed right over them. There on the bank, plain as day, were several mounds of deer shit. 'What do you think that is, Tub?' Kenny kicked at it. 'Walnuts on vanilla icing?'

'I guess I didn't notice.'

Kenny looked at Frank.

'I was lost.'

'You were lost. Big deal.'

They followed the tracks into the woods. The deer had gone over a fence half buried in drifting snow. A no hunting sign was nailed to the top of one of the posts. Frank laughed and said the son of a bitch could read. Kenny wanted to go after him but Frank said no way, the people out here didn't mess around. He thought maybe the farmer who owned the land would let them use it if they asked. Kenny wasn't so sure. Anyway, he figured that by the time they walked to the truck and drove up the road and doubled back it would be almost dark.

'Relax,' Frank said. 'You can't hurry nature. If we're meant to get that deer, we'll get it. If we're not, we won't.'

They started back towards the truck. This part of the woods was mainly pine. The snow was shaded and had a glaze on it. It held up Kenny and Frank but Tub kept falling through. As he kicked forward, the edge of the crust bruised his shins. Kenny and Frank pulled ahead of him, to where he couldn't even hear their voices any more. He sat down on a stump and wiped his face. He ate both the sandwiches and half the cookies, taking his own sweet time. It was dead quiet.

When Tub crossed the last fence into the road the truck started moving. Tub had to run for it and just managed to grab hold of the tailgate and hoist himself into the bed. He lay there, panting. Kenny looked out the rear window and grinned. Tub crawled into the lee of the cab to get out of the freezing wind. He pulled his earflaps low and pushed his chin into the collar of his coat. Someone rapped on the window but Tub would not turn around.

He and Frank waited outside while Kenny went into the farmhouse to ask permission. The house was old and paint was curling off the sides. The smoke streamed westward off the top of the chimney, fanning away into a thin grey plume. Above the ridge of the hills another ridge of blue clouds was rising.

'You've got a short memory,' Tub said.

'What?' Frank said. He had been staring off.

'I used to stick up for you.'

'Okay, so you used to stick up for me. What's eating you?'

'You shouldn't have just left me back there like that.'

'You're a grown-up, Tub. You can take care of yourself. Anyway, if you think you're the only person with problems I can tell you that you're not.'

'Is something bothering you, Frank?'

Frank kicked at a branch poking out of the snow. 'Never mind,' he said.

'What did Kenny mean about the babysitter?'

'Kenny talks too much,' Frank said. 'You just mind your own business.'

Kenny came out of the farmhouse and gave the thumbs-up and they began walking back towards the woods. As they passed the barn a large black hound with a grizzled snout ran out and barked at them. Every time he barked he slid backwards a bit, like a cannon recoiling. Kenny got down on all fours and snarled and barked back at him, and the dog slunk away into the barn, looking over his shoulder and peeing a little as he went.

'That's an old-timer,' Frank said. 'A real greybeard. Fifteen years if he's a day.'

'Too old,' Kenny said.

Past the barn they cut off through the fields. The land was unfenced and the crust was freezing up thick and they made good time. They kept to the edge of the field until they picked up the tracks again and followed them into the woods, farther and farther back toward the hills. The trees started to blur with the shadows and the wind rose and needled their faces with the crystals it swept off the glaze. Finally they lost the tracks.

Kenny swore and threw down his hat. 'This is the worst day of hunting I ever had, bar none.' He picked up his hat and brushed off the snow. 'This will be the first season since I was fifteen I haven't got my deer.'

'It isn't the deer,' Frank said. 'It's the hunting. There are all these forces out here and you just have to go with them.'

'You go with them,' Kenny said. 'I came out here to get me a deer, not listen to a bunch of hippie bullshit. And if it hadn't been for dimples here I would have, too.'

'That's enough,' Frank said.

'And you – you're so busy thinking about that little jailbait of yours you wouldn't know a deer if you saw one.'

'Drop dead,' Frank said, and turned away.

Kenny and Tub followed him back across the fields. When they were coming up to the barn Kenny stopped and pointed. 'I hate that post,' he said. He raised his rifle and fired. It sounded like a dry branch cracking. The post splintered along its right side, up towards the top. 'There,' Kenny said. 'It's dead.'

'Knock it off,' Frank said, walking ahead.

Kenny looked at Tub. He smiled. 'I hate that tree,' he said, and fired again. Tub hurried to catch up with Frank. He started to speak but just then the dog ran out of the barn and barked at them. 'Easy, boy,' Frank said.

'I hate that dog.' Kenny was behind them.

'That's enough,' Frank said. 'You put that gun down.'

Kenny fired. The bullet went in between the dog's eyes. He sank right down into the snow, his legs splayed out on each side, his yellow eyes open and staring. Except for the blood he looked like a small bearskin rug. The blood ran down the dog's muzzle into the snow.

They all looked at the dog lying there.

'What did he ever do to you?' Tub asked. 'He was just barking.'

Kenny turned to Tub. 'I hate you.'

Tub shot from the waist. Kenny jerked backwards against the fence and buckled to his knees. He folded his hands across his stomach. 'Look,' he said. His hands were covered with blood. In the dusk his blood was more blue than red. It seemed to belong to the shadows. It didn't seem out of place. Kenny eased himself onto his back. He sighed several times, deeply. 'You shot me,' he said.

'I had to,' Tub said. He knelt beside Kenny. 'Oh God,' he said. 'Frank. Frank.'

Frank hadn't moved since Kenny killed the dog.

'Frank!' Tub shouted.

'I was just kidding around,' Kenny said. 'It was a joke. Oh!' he said, and arched his back suddenly. 'Oh!' he said again, and dug his heels into the snow and pushed himself along on his head for several feet.

Then he stopped and lay there, rocking back and forth on his heels and head like a wrestler doing warm-up exercises.

Frank roused himself. 'Kenny,' he said. He bent down and put his gloved hand on Kenny's brow. 'You shot him,' he said to Tub.

'He made me,' Tub said.

'No no no,' Kenny said.

Tub was weeping from the eyes and nostrils. His whole face was wet. Frank closed his eyes, then looked down at Kenny again. 'Where does it hurt?'

'Everywhere,' Kenny said, 'just everywhere.'

'Oh God,' Tub said.

'I mean where did it go in?' Frank said.

'Here.' Kenny pointed at the wound in his stomach. It was welling slowly with blood.

'You're lucky,' Frank said. 'It's on the left side. It missed your appendix. If it had hit your appendix you'd really be in the soup.' He turned and threw up onto the snow, holding his sides as if to keep warm.

'Are you all right?' Tub said.

'There's some aspirin in the truck,' Kenny said.

'I'm all right,' Frank said.

'We'd better call an ambulance,' Tub said.

'Jesus,' Frank said. 'What are we going to say?'

'Exactly what happened,' Tub said. 'He was going to shoot me but I shot him first.'

'No sir!' Kenny said. 'I wasn't either!'

Frank patted Kenny on the arm. 'Easy does it, partner.' He stood. 'Let's go.'

Tub picked up Kenny's rifle as they walked down toward the farmhouse. 'No sense leaving this around,' he said. 'Kenny might get ideas.'

'I can tell you one thing,' Frank said. 'You've really done it this time. This definitely takes the cake.'

They had to knock on the door twice before it was opened by a thin man with lank hair. The room behind him was filled with smoke. He squinted at them. 'You get anything?' he asked.

'No,' Frank said.

'I knew you wouldn't. That's what I told the other fellow.'

'We've had an accident.'

The man looked past Frank and Tub into the gloom. 'Shoot your friend, did you?'

Frank nodded.

'I did,' Tub said.

'I suppose you want to use the phone.'

'If it's okay.'

The man in the doorway looked behind him, then stepped back. Frank and Tub followed him into the house. There was a woman sitting by the stove in the middle of the room. The stove was smoking badly. She looked up and then down again at the child asleep in her lap. Her face was white and damp; strands of hair were pasted across her forehead. Tub warmed his hands over the stove while Frank went into the kitchen to call. The man who had let them in stood at the window, his hands in his pockets.

'My friend shot your dog,' Tub said.

The man nodded without turning around. 'I should have done it myself. I just couldn't.'

'He loved that dog so much,' the woman said. The child squirmed and she rocked it.

'You asked him to?' Tub said. 'You asked him to shoot your dog?'

'He was old and sick. Couldn't chew his food any more. I would have done it myself but I don't have a gun.'

'You couldn't have anyway,' the woman said. 'Never in a million years.'

The man shrugged.

Frank came out of the kitchen. 'We'll have to take him ourselves. The nearest hospital is fifty miles from here and all their ambulances are out anyway.'

The woman knew a shortcut but the directions were complicated and Tub had to write them down. The man told them where they could find some boards to carry Kenny on. He didn't have a flashlight but he said he would leave the porch light on.

It was dark outside. The clouds were low and heavylooking and the wind blew in shrill gusts. There was a screen loose on the house and it banged slowly and then quickly as the wind rose again. They could hear it all the way to the barn. Frank went for the boards while Tub looked for Kenny, who was not where they had left him. Tub found him farther up the drive, lying on his stomach. 'You okay?' Tub said.

'It hurts.'

'Frank says it missed your appendix.'

'I already had my appendix out.'

'All right,' Frank said, coming up to them. 'We'll have you in a nice warm bed before you can say Jack Robinson.' He put the two boards on Kenny's right side.

'Just as long as I don't have one of those male nurses,' Kenny said.

'Ha ha,' Frank said. 'That's the spirit. Get ready, set, *over you go*,' and he rolled Kenny onto the boards. Kenny screamed and kicked his legs in the air. When he quieted down Frank and Tub lifted the boards and carried him down the drive. Tub had the back end, and with the snow blowing into his face he had trouble with his footing. Also he was tired and the man inside had forgotten to turn the porch light on. Just past the house Tub slipped and threw out his hands to catch himself. The boards fell and Kenny tumbled out and rolled to the bottom of the drive, yelling all the way. He came to rest against the right front wheel of the truck.

'You fat moron,' Frank said. 'You aren't good for diddly.'

Tub grabbed Frank by the collar and backed him hard up against the fence. Frank tried to pull his hands away but Tub shook him and snapped his head back and forth and finally Frank gave up.

'What do you know about fat,' Tub said. 'What do you know about glands.' As he spoke he kept shaking Frank. 'What do you know about me.'

'All right,' Frank said.

'No more,' Tub said.

'All right.'

'No more talking to me like that. No more watching. No more laughing.'

'Okay, Tub. I promise.'

Tub let go of Frank and leaned his forehead against the fence. His arms hung straight at his sides.

'I'm sorry, Tub.' Frank touched him on the shoulder. 'I'll be down at the truck.'

Tub stood by the fence for a while and then got the rifles off the porch. Frank had rolled Kenny back onto the boards and they lifted him into the bed of the truck. Frank spread the seat blankets over him. 'Warm enough?' he asked.

Kenny nodded.

'Okay. Now how does reverse work on this thing?'

'All the way to the left and up.' Kenny sat up as Frank started forward to the cab. 'Frank!'

'What?'

'If it sticks don't force it.'

The truck started right away. 'One thing,' Frank said, 'you've got to hand it to the Japanese. A very ancient, very spiritual culture and they can still make a hell of a truck.' He glanced over at Tub. 'Look, I'm sorry. I didn't know you felt that way, honest to God I didn't. You should have said something.'

'I did.'

'When? Name one time.'

'A couple of hours ago.'

'I guess I wasn't paying attention.'

'That's true, Frank,' Tub said. 'You don't pay attention very much.'

'Tub,' Frank said, 'what happened back there, I should have been more sympathetic. I realize that. You were going through a lot. I just want you to know it wasn't your fault. He was asking for it.'

'You think so?'

'Absolutely. It was him or you. I would have done the same thing in your shoes, no question.'

The wind was blowing into their faces. The snow was a moving white wall in front of their lights; it swirled into the cab through the hole in the windshield and settled on them. Tub clapped his hands and shifted around to stay warm, but it didn't work.

'I'm going to have to stop,' Frank said. 'I can't feel my fingers.'

Up ahead they saw some lights off the road. It was a tavern. Outside in the parking lot there were several jeeps and trucks. A couple of them had deer strapped across their hoods. Frank parked and they went back to Kenny. 'How you doing, partner?' Frank said.

'I'm cold.'

'Well, don't feel like the Lone Ranger. It's worse inside, take my word for it. You should get that windshield fixed.'

'Look,' Tub said, 'he threw the blankets off.' They were lying in a heap against the tailgate.

'Now look, Kenny,' Frank said, 'it's no use whining about being cold if you're not going to try and keep warm. You've got to do your share.' He spread the blankets over Kenny and tucked them in at the corners.

'They blew off.'

'Hold on to them then.'

'Why are we stopping, Frank?'

'Because if me and Tub don't get warmed up we're going to freeze solid and then where will you be?' He punched Kenny lightly in the arm. 'So just hold your horses.'

The bar was full of men in coloured jackets, mostly orange. The waitress brought coffee. 'Just what the doctor ordered,' Frank said, cradling the steaming cup in his hand. His skin was bone white. 'Tub, I've been thinking. What you said about me not paying attention, that's true.'

'It's okay.'

'No. I really had that coming. I guess I've just been a little too interested in old number one. I've had a lot on my mind. Not that that's any excuse.'

'Forget it, Frank. I sort of lost my temper back there. I guess we're all a little on edge.'

Frank shook his head. 'It isn't just that.'

'You want to talk about it?'

'Just between us, Tub?'

'Sure, Frank. Just between us.'

'Tub, I think I'm going to be leaving Nancy.'

'Oh, Frank. Oh, Frank.' Tub sat back and shook his head.

Frank reached out and laid his hand on Tub's arm. 'Tub, have you ever been really in love?'

'Well – '

'I mean *really* in love.' He squeezed Tub's wrist. 'With your whole being.'

'I don't know. When you put it like that, I don't know.'

'You haven't then. Nothing against you, but you'd know it if you had.' Frank let go of Tub's arm. 'This isn't just some bit of fluff I'm talking about.'

'Who is she, Frank?'

Frank paused. He looked into his empty cup. 'Roxanne Brewer.'

'Cliff Brewer's kid? The babysitter?'

'You can't just put people into categories like that, Tub. That's why the whole system is wrong. And that's why this country is going to hell in a rowboat.'

'But she can't be more than – ' Tub shook his head.

'Fifteen. She'll be sixteen in May.' Frank smiled. 'May fourth, three twenty-seven p.m. Hell, Tub, a hundred years ago she'd have been an old maid by that age. Juliet was only thirteen.'

'Juliet? Juliet Miller? Jesus, Frank, she doesn't even have breasts. She doesn't even wear a top to her bathing suit. She's still collecting frogs.'

'Not Juliet Miller. The real Juliet. Tub, don't you see how you're dividing people up into categories? He's an executive, she's a secretary, he's a truck driver, she's fifteen years old. Tub, this so-called babysitter, this so-called fifteen-year-old has more in her little finger than most of us have in our entire bodies. I can tell you this little lady is something special.'

Tub nodded. 'I know the kids like her.'

'She's opened up whole worlds to me that I never knew were there.'

'What does Nancy think about all this?'

'She doesn't know.'

'You haven't told her?'

'Not yet. It's not so easy. She's been damned good to me all these years. Then there's the kids to consider.' The brightness in Frank's eyes trembled and he wiped quickly at them with the back of his hand. 'I guess you think I'm a complete bastard.'

'No, Frank. I don't think that.'

'Well, you *ought* to.'

'Frank, when you've got a friend it means you've always got someone on your side, no matter what. That's the way I feel about it, anyway.'

'You mean that, Tub?'

'Sure I do.'

Frank smiled. 'You don't know how good it feels to hear you say that.'

Kenny had tried to get out of the truck but he hadn't made it. He was jackknifed over the tailgate, his head hanging above the bumper. They lifted him back into the bed and covered him again. He was sweating and his teeth chattered. 'It hurts, Frank.'

'It wouldn't hurt so much if you just stayed put. Now we're going to the hospital. Got that? Say it – I'm going to the hospital.'

'I'm going to the hospital.'

'Again.'

'I'm going to the hospital.'

'Now just keep saying that to yourself and before you know it we'll be there.'

After they had gone a few miles Tub turned to Frank. 'I just pulled a real boner,' he said.

'What's that?'

'I left the directions on the table back there.'

'That's okay. I remember them pretty well.'

The snowfall lightened and the clouds began to roll back off the fields, but it was no warmer and after a time both Frank and Tub were bitten through and shaking. Frank almost didn't make it around a curve, and they decided to stop at the next roadhouse.

There was an automatic hand-dryer in the bathroom and they took turns standing in front of it, opening their jackets and shirts and letting the jet of hot air breathe across their faces and chests.

'You know,' Tub said, 'what you told me back there, I appreciate it. Trusting me.'

Frank opened and closed his fingers in front of the nozzle. 'The way I look at it, Tub, no man is an island. You've got to trust someone.'

'Frank – '

Frank waited.

'When I said that about my glands, that wasn't true. The truth is I just shovel it in.'

'Well, Tub – '

'Day and night, Frank. In the shower. On the freeway.' He turned and let the air play over his back. 'I've even got stuff in the paper towel machine at work.'

'There's nothing wrong with your glands at all?' Frank had taken his boots and socks off. He held first his right, then his left foot up to the nozzle.

'No. There never was.'

'Does Alice know?' The machine went off and Frank started lacing up his boots.

'Nobody knows. That's the worst of it, Frank. Not the being fat, I never got any big kick out of being thin, but the lying. Having to lead a double life like a spy or a hit man. This sounds strange but I feel sorry for those guys, I really do. I know what they go through. Always having to think about what you say and do. Always feeling like people are watching you, trying to catch you at something. Never able to just be yourself. Like when I make a big deal about only having an orange for breakfast and then scarf all the way to work. Oreos, Mars Bars, Twinkies. Sugar Babies. Snickers.' Tub glanced at Frank and looked quickly away. 'Pretty disgusting, isn't it?'

'Tub. Tub.' Frank shook his head. 'Come on.' He took Tub's arm and led him into the restaurant half of the bar. 'My friend is hungry,' he told the waitress. 'Bring four orders of pancakes, plenty of butter and syrup.'

'Frank – '

'Sit down.'

When the dishes came Frank carved out slabs of butter and just laid them on the pancakes. Then he emptied the bottle of syrup, moving it back and forth over the plates. He leaned forward on his elbows and rested his chin in one hand. 'Go on, Tub.'

Tub ate several mouthfuls, then started to wipe his lips. Frank took the napkin away from him. 'No wiping,' he said. Tub kept at it. The syrup covered his chin; it dripped to a point like a goatee. 'Weigh in, Tub,' Frank said, pushing another fork across the table. 'Get down to business.' Tub took the fork in his left hand and lowered his head and started really chowing down. 'Clean your plate,' Frank said when the pancakes were gone, and Tub lifted each of the four plates and licked it clean. He sat back, trying to catch his breath.

'Beautiful,' Frank said. 'Are you full?'

'I'm full,' Tub said. 'I've never been so full.'

Kenny's blankets were bunched up against the tailgate again.

'They must have blown off,' Tub said.

'They're not doing him any good,' Frank said. 'We might as well get some use out of them.'

Kenny mumbled. Tub bent over him. 'What? Speak up.'

'I'm going to the hospital,' Kenny said.

'Attaboy,' Frank said.

The blankets helped. The wind still got their faces and Frank's hands but it was much better. The fresh snow on the road and the trees sparkled under the beam of the headlight. Squares of light from farmhouse windows fell onto the blue snow in the fields.

'Frank,' Tub said after a time, 'you know that farmer? He told Kenny to kill the dog.'

'You're kidding!' Frank leaned forward, considering. 'That Kenny.

What a card.' He laughed and so did Tub. Tub smiled out the back window. Kenny lay with his arms folded over his stomach, moving his lips at the stars. Right overhead was the Big Dipper, and behind, hanging between Kenny's toes in the direction of the hospital, was the North Star, Pole Star, Help to Sailors. As the truck twisted through the gentle hills the star went back and forth between Kenny's boots, staying always in his sight. 'I'm going to the hospital,' Kenny said. But he was wrong. They had taken a different turn a long way back.

An Episode in the Life of Professor Brooke

Professor Brooke had no real quarrel with anyone in his department, but there was a Yeats scholar named Riley whom he could not bring himself to like. Riley was flashy, so flashy that even his bright red hair seemed an affectation, and it was said that he'd had affairs with some of his students. Brooke did not as a rule give credit to these rumours, but in Riley's case he was willing to make an exception. He had once seen a very pretty girl leaving Riley's office in tears. Students did at times cry over bad grades, but this girl's misery was something else: it looked more like a broken heart than a C –.

They belonged to the same parish, and Brooke, who liked to sit in the back of the church, often saw Riley at Mass with his wife and their four red-haired children. Seeing the children and their father together, like a row of burning candles, always made Brooke feel more kindly toward Riley. Then Riley would turn to his wife or look around, and the handlebars of his unnecessarily large moustache would come into view, and Brooke would dislike him again.

The Sunday after he'd seen the girl come out of Riley's office Brooke watched him go up and take communion, then return to his seat with downcast eyes and folded hands. Was he praying, or was he trying to remember whether he'd checked his collar for stains? Where did Riley find the time, considering his tireless production of superficial articles and books, for romancing girls who had not yet mastered the English sentence, who were still experimenting with hair styles and perfumes? Did Mrs Riley know?

Brooke raised these questions with his wife after lunch, after their children had left the table. They often talked about other people's infidelities, not in a mean or superior way, but out of a sense of relief that after sixteen years they were still in love. Brooke's wife said that a crying girl didn't mean much – girls cried all the time. In her opinion Brooke should not make up his mind about Riley until he knew more. Brooke was touched by his wife's innocence and generosity, and pretended to agree.

In November the regional chapter of the Modern Language Association met in Bellingham. Professor Brooke had been invited to take part in a panel discussion on the afternoon of the second day, and though he did not enjoy literary carnivals he hoped that he might bring some sanity to the meeting. He knew the work of the other panel members and judged that there was a real and present danger of the discussion becoming a brawl.

Just before he left, Brooke had a call from Riley. Riley was scheduled to read a paper that night and his car was on the blink. Could he have a ride? 'Of course,' Brooke said, but after he hung up he complained to his wife. 'Dammit,' he said, 'I was looking forward to being alone.' It wasn't only the loss of privacy that made him cross; he and Riley had quarrelled at a tenure committee meeting the week before and he feared that Riley, who had no tact or sense of occasion, would renew the argument. Brooke did not want to fight his way to Bellingham with a man who wore powder-blue suits.

But Riley was taciturn, preoccupied. As they were leaving Seattle he asked Brooke to pull into a filling station so that he could make a telephone call. Brooke watched him in the booth, frowning at the receiver and gesticulating like a man practising a speech. When he got back in the car he wore a theatrically tormented expression and Brooke felt obliged to ask whether there was anything wrong.

'Yes,' Riley said, 'but you don't want to hear about it, believe me.' He said that he was having difficulties with the editor of his latest book.

Brooke didn't quite believe him. He wondered if it had something to do with the girl. Perhaps Riley had gotten her pregnant and was trying to dissuade her from having an abortion. 'Let me know,' he said, 'if there's anything I can do.'

'That's nice of you,' Riley said. 'You know, you remind me of a guy I knew in high school who was voted Nicest in the Class. No kidding.' He hooked his arm over the seat and smiled at Brooke in a special way he had, curling his handlebars up and showing a flash of teeth. It looked as if he had somewhere come upon the phrase 'roguish smile' and developed this expression to match it, and it drove Brooke absolutely crazy. 'Tell me,' Riley said, 'what's the worst thing you've ever done?'

'The worst thing I've ever done?'

Riley nodded, showing more teeth.

For some reason Brooke panicked: his hands got wet on the steering wheel, his knees trembled, and he couldn't think straight.

'Forget it,' said Riley after a time, and gave a little laugh, and hardly spoke again for the rest of the trip.

Brooke finally calmed down, but the question persisted. What *was* the worst thing he had ever done? One night when he was thirteen, and home alone, and had just finished off all the maraschino cherries in the refrigerator and gotten bored with sighting in the neighbours on the scope of his father's hunting rifle, he called the parents of a girl who had died of leukaemia and asked to speak to her. That same year he threw a cat off a bridge. Later, in high school, he unthinkingly used the word 'nigger' in front of a black classmate who considered Brooke his friend, and claimed that he had seduced a girl who had merely let him kiss her.

When Brooke recalled these things he felt pain – a tightening at the neck that pulled his head down and made his shoulders hunch, and a tingling in his wrists. Still, he doubted that Riley would be very impressed. Riley clearly had him down for a goody-goody. And, in a way, he was; that is, he tried to be good. When you tried to be good you ran the risk of seeming a prig, but what was the alternative? Brooke did not want to know. Yet at times he wondered if he had been too easily tamed.

The panel discussion was not a success. One of the members, a young man named Abbot from Oregon State University, had recently published a book on Samuel Johnson which attempted to define him as a poet and thinker of the Enlightenment. The thesis was so wrong-headed that Brooke had assumed it to be insincere, but this was not the case. Abbot seemed to think that his ideas did him credit, and persistently dragged them into conversations where they had no place. After one very long tirade Brooke decided to set him right and did so, he thought successfully, with few words.

'Excellent points,' said the chairwoman, a Dryden scholar from Reed College who wore sunglasses and blew smoke out of her mouth as she talked. Turning to Abbot she said, 'Is your speech finished?'

Abbot looked at her sharply, then nodded.

'Good,' the chairwoman said. 'To quote Samuel Johnson, that paradigm figure of the Enlightenment, "No one would have wished it longer."'

Abbot was crushed. His face went stiff with misery, and he sat without speaking for the rest of the discussion. Brooke felt embarrassed by the chairwoman's treatment of Abbot, not only because she was unkind but because her unkindness was so distinctly professorial.

When the panel ended he chatted with a woman he'd known in graduate school. They were joined by an athletic-looking fellow whom Brooke supposed to be one of her students until she introduced him as her husband. The disparity in their ages made Brooke fidgety and he soon drifted away.

The room where the discussion had been held was actually half of a long hall, divided by a folding partition. A meeting of some kind had just begun on the other side. All the voices were male, and Brooke guessed that they belonged to a group of scoutmasters who were holding a convention in the hotel. He stood at one end of the refreshment table and ate little sandwiches with pennants sticking out of them onto which someone had typed literary quotations about food ık. He saw Abbot at the other end, looking out over the room ıirking to himself. Brooke hoped that he would not become the kin of academic who believes that his ideas are not accepted because they are too profound and original. He went over to Abbot and showed him one of his pennants.

'What did you get?' he asked.

'Nothing,' Abbot said. 'I'm on a diet.' He stared into his coffee, the surface of which had an iridescent sheen.

'Tell me,' Brooke said, 'what are you working on now?'

Abbot drew a deep breath, put the cup down, and walked past Brooke and out of the room.

'Ouch,' said the woman on the other side of the table.

Brooke turned to her. She was striking, not beautiful, really, but very blonde and heavily made-up. 'You saw that?'

'Yes. You tried, anyway.' She reached below the table and brought up a fresh platter of sandwiches. 'Have one,' she said. 'Salami and cheese.'

'No thanks. Those quotations are hard to swallow.'

She lowered the platter, her face as red as if she'd been slapped.

Brooke turned one of the pennants with his finger. 'You did all these, didn't you?'

'Yes.'

'I'm very sorry I said that. I was just being clever.'

'It's all right.'

'I'm going to keep my mouth shut,' Brooke said. 'Every time I open it I hurt someone's feelings.'

'I didn't really understand what the panel was all about,' she said, 'but he was the one who kept interrupting all the time. I thought you were nice. I could tell, listening to you, that I would like you. But that woman. If anybody ever talked to me like that I would die. I would just die.'

She leaned towards Brooke and spoke quietly, as though imparting confidences. Her lips were unusually full and, like the Wife of Bath, she had a gap between her front teeth. Brooke was going to tell her that in Chaucer's time a gap between your teeth meant that you were a very sensual person, but he decided not to. She might take it wrong.

On the other side of the partition the scoutmasters were saying the Pledge of Allegiance.

'Where did you get all the quotes?' Brooke asked.

'From Bartlett's. It was a dumb idea.'

'No it wasn't. It was very thoughtful.' Brooke meant to end the conversation there, but the woman asked him several questions and he thought that he should ask her some questions in return. Her name was Ruth. She was a nurse at Bellingham General and had lived in the town all her life. She was unmarried. The local waiters' union, to which the caterers belonged, had gone on strike and Ruth had been asked to help out at the conference by a college teacher who belonged to her literary society.

'Literary society,' Brooke said. 'I didn't know they had them any more.'

'Oh yes,' Ruth said. 'It's the most important thing in my life.'

At that moment another woman ran up with a list of items for Ruth to collect at the hotel kitchen. As Ruth turned away she looked over her shoulder and smiled.

By this time there were several people standing in line for sandwiches. Brooke moved to make room and soon found himself in a corner with a graduate student from his university who had just completed a dreary thesis on Ruskin. 'Well,' said the student, a tall boy with a stoop, 'I guess the good doctor is turning over in his grave today.'

'What good doctor?' Brooke asked, uncomfortable with this person who had spent four years of his life reading *The Stones of Venice*.

'Doctor Johnson.'

'I don't know what you're talking about,' Brooke said.

Riley, holding several sandwiches, joined them and the student had no chance to explain. 'You really went after Abbot,' Riley said.

'I didn't intend to go after anyone.'

'You could have fooled me.'

'It was a panel,' Brooke said. 'He spoke from his point of view and I spoke from mine. That's what we were supposed to do.'

'You mean,' Riley said, 'that you spoke from the right point of view and he spoke from the wrong point of view.'

'I think so. What do you think?'

'I don't know the period as well as I should,' Riley said, 'but I thought his ideas seemed original. They were interesting enough.'

'Interesting,' Brooke said, 'in the way flat-Earth theories are interesting.'

'I envy you,' Riley said. 'You're always so sure of yourself.'

The student looked at his watch. 'Uh-oh,' he said. 'I have to be going.'

'I'm not always sure of myself,' Brooke said. 'But this time I am.'

'I wasn't just thinking of the panel.' Riley reminded Brooke of the tenure committee meeting the previous week. He wanted to know how Brooke could deny work to a woman with a sick husband and three children. He wanted to know how Brooke justified that to himself.

'We were asked to consider her professional qualifications,' Brooke said. 'She's a terrible teacher, as you very well know, and she hasn't published anything in over four years. Not even a book review.'

'It was that simple, was it?'

'It wasn't simple at all,' Brooke said. 'If there was anything I could do for her short of giving her tenure I would do it. Now if you'll excuse me I'm going out for some fresh air.'

A cold, salty breeze was blowing in off the water. The streets were empty. Brooke walked around the hotel several times, nodding to the doorman as he passed the entrance. The street lights were on, and some mineral embedded in the concrete made it glitter in a false and irritating way.

He decided that he was right and Riley wrong. But why did he feel so awful? It was ridiculous. He would have a bite to eat and drive home that very night. Riley could find another ride.

As he left the hotel restaurant Brooke saw the blonde woman – Ruth – standing in the lobby. He was about to run away but just then she looked in his direction and smiled and waved. She was plainly glad to see him and Brooke decided to say hello. Not to do so, he thought, would be rude. They sat side by side in chairs that had, for some reason, been bolted to the floor. In the chairs across from them two scoutmasters were arm-wrestling. Ruth's perfume smelled like lavender; it came over Brooke in waves.

'I called the library,' she said, 'but they didn't have either one of your books.'

'That doesn't surprise me,' Brooke said. He explained that they were too specialized to be of interest to the general public.

'I'd still like to read them,' Ruth said. 'There are people in the literary society who write things, haikus and so on, but I've never met anyone before who wrote a book, not to mention two books. Maybe,' she said, 'I can order them through a bookstore.'

'That's possible,' Brooke said, but he hoped she would not do that. His books were very difficult and she might think him pedantic.

'You know,' she said, 'I had a feeling I was going to see you tonight, either here or at the poetry reading.'

'I didn't know there was one,' Brooke said. 'Who's the poet?'

'Francis X. Dillon. Is he a friend of yours?'

'No. Why do you ask?'

'Well, you're both writers.'

'I've heard of him,' Brooke said. 'Of course.' Dillon's poetry was very popular with Brooke's younger students and with his wife's mother. Brooke had picked up one of his books in a drugstore not long ago, intrigued by a blurb on the back claiming that the poet had been translated into twenty-three languages, including Sanskrit. As he turned the pages Brooke formed the image of a guru in a darkened cell reading these same dreadful verses by no other light than that of his own mystical aura. Now he thought it would be a shame to miss seeing Dillon in person.

The room was large and overheated and so crowded that the two of them had to stand in the back. The poet was half an hour late but not one person left, even though the air was stuffy and smelled bad.

Dillon arrived and without apology began to read. He was wearing a lumberjack shirt and a loose pair of khaki pants tied at the waist with a length of rope. All of the poems were about trees. They seemed to be saying that people had a lot to learn from trees. Trees were natural and uninhibited and didn't find it necessary to build roads and factories all over the place.

The principle by which the poems were arranged eluded Brooke until, during a pause, Dillon remarked that they would now be moving up into the aspen country. Then Brooke realized that the poems were grouped according to elevation. They had begun the ascent at sea level with the coastal redwoods and they'd been climbing steadily ever since. Brooke's attention wandered until finally the audience began to applaud; he joined in, assuming that they must have reached the timberline. Dillon read as an encore a very long piece which he described as 'my other cedar poem,' and left the room without a word to anyone when he was through.

'Isn't he wonderful!' Ruth said, as they stood applauding the empty podium.

Brooke gave a nod, the best he could manage.

She was not taken in. Later, at Lord George's, the bar where Ruth had suggested they go for a drink, she asked him why he didn't like the poems. He sensed that she was close to tears.

'I did like them,' he said. 'In fact, I loved them.'

'Really?'

'Oh yes. I thought they were extraordinary.'

'So did I,' Ruth said, and began to describe her reactions to particular poems that Dillon had read. Brooke wondered why she had brought him to this place, with shields and maces and broadswords on the walls.

'Another thing I like about his poetry,' Ruth said, 'is you don't feel like killing yourself after you've read it.'

'That's true,' Brooke said. He noticed that two men at a nearby table were staring at her. They probably thought she was his wife. He could tell that they were wishing they were in his shoes.

'I went to a play last year,' Ruth said, 'a Shakespeare play, where this king gave everything away to his daughters – '

'*King Lear*.'

'That's the one. And then they turned on him and left him with nothing and gouged his best friend's eyeballs out and jumped on them. I don't understand why anybody, especially a really good writer like Shakespeare, would dream up junk like that.'

'Life,' Brooke said, 'is not always uplifting.'

'I know all about it,' Ruth said, 'believe me. But why should I rub my nose in it? I like to read about lovers. I like to read about how beautiful the mountains are, and the stars. I like to read about people taking care of injured animals and setting them free again.'

'You are very beautiful,' Brooke said.

'You don't know what I look like,' Ruth said. 'This isn't my hair. It's a wig.'

'I wasn't talking about what you look like,' Brooke said, and this was partly true.

'Hello there,' said Riley, who had come up to their table with Abbot. Both of them had their overcoats on, and Riley was doing his smile and blowing into his cupped hands. His face was white with a suggestion of blue, like milk. Brooke wondered why red-haired people went pale from the cold when others turned florid. It seemed strange. Abbot swayed back and forth in time to music only he could hear. 'We've been making the rounds,' Riley said. 'Mind if we join you?'

Ruth moved closer to Brooke, and Riley slid into the booth and immediately began talking to her in a low voice. Abbot sat next to Brooke. He was quiet at first, then he abruptly leaned against Brooke and spoke into his ear as though it were a telephone receiver. 'Been thinking about what you said today. Interesting. Very interesting. But all wrong.' He began to repeat the arguments he had made earlier that day. When the waitress brought his drink, a tomato-juice concoction, he spilled most of it down the front of his shirt. 'Can't be helped,' he said, brushing away the handkerchief Ruth held out.

Brooke turned to Riley. 'How did your paper go?'

'It was brilliant,' Abbot said. 'Brilliant beyond brilliant.'

'Thank you,' Riley said. 'It did go quite well, I think.'

'I'm sorry I missed it,' Brooke said. 'We went to the Dillon reading.'

'I've just been hearing about it,' Riley said. 'Your friend . . .'

'Ruth,' Brooke said.

'Ruth! What a beautiful name. "Whither thou goest I will go; wherever thou lodgest,"' Riley said, looking right into her face, '"there also will I lodge."'

This man is outrageous, Brooke thought, and groped under the table for Ruth's hand. He took it into his own and squeezed it. She squeezed back. What in the world am I doing? Brooke thought happily.

'Excuse me,' Abbot said. He stood, then sat again heavily and pitched face down onto the table.

'I'd say it's taps for that soldier,' Riley said.

'Would you mind taking him back to the hotel?' Brooke asked. 'I'll see Ruth home.'

Riley hesitated, and Brooke suspected that he was trying to think of a way to reverse the proposal. 'All right,' Riley said at last. 'I'll call a cab.'

At a table across the room a group of scoutmasters leaned together and sang:

> Our paddles clean and bright
> Shining like sil-ver
> Swift as the wild goose flies
> Dip, dip and swing,
> Dip, dip and swing.

When the song was ended they howled in a way they all knew and one of them did a somersault on the floor.

Brooke had intended to go back to the hotel after he'd seen Ruth to her door, but he couldn't think of the right words to say and followed her inside. There were red pillows arranged in a circle around the living room, and a fat candle in the middle of the floor. Next to the door hung a framed, blown-up photograph of three seagulls in flight with the sun behind them. Several wooden elephants, placed according to size like a growth chart, marched trunk-to-tail across the top of the bookshelf. 'I believe in being honest,' Ruth said.

'So do I,' Brooke said, thinking that she was going to tell him about a boyfriend or fiancé. He hoped so.

Ruth said nothing. Instead she brought both of her hands up to her hair and lifted it off like a hat. There was no hair underneath it, only a light down like a baby's. Ruth put the wig on a plaster bust that stood between a camel saddle and some foreign dolls on her bric-à-brac shelf. Then she faced Brooke. 'Do you mind?' she asked.

'Of course not.'

'Don't say "Of course not." It doesn't mean anything. Anyway, I've had a couple of bad experiences.'

'No, Ruth. I don't mind.' Brooke thought she looked exotic. She made him think of pictures he had seen of Frenchwomen whose heads had been shaved because they'd slept with Germans. He knew he should leave, but if he went now she would misunderstand and be hurt.

'I don't mind wearing the wig outside,' Ruth said, 'so that people won't get uncomfortable. But when I'm at home I'm going to be plain old me and that's that.' She poured each of them a glass of wine and lit the candle. 'I'm a floor person,' she said, settling on a pillow. 'If you want a chair there's one in the bedroom.'

'That's all right,' Brooke said. 'I'm a floor person too.' He tugged the knees of his trousers and sat Indian style across from her. As an afterthought he removed his suit jacket and folded it and laid it on the pillow next to him. 'There,' he said, and rubbed his hands together.

'I didn't think it would bother you,' Ruth said. 'I've noticed that creative people are usually interested in more than just looks.'

'You look fine to me,' Brooke said. 'Exotic.'

'You think so? Well, frankly, I'd rather have hair. I got pretty sick a few years ago and this is all I had left after the chemotherapy. They said it would grow back but it didn't. At least I'm still alive.' She broke a string of wax off the candle and rolled it between her hands. 'For a while there I wasn't doing too well.'

'I'm sorry,' Brooke said. 'It must have been awful.'

Ruth said that she had been just lying there, waiting for it to happen, when a friend of hers came for a visit and left a book of poems by Francis X. Dillon. 'Do you know "Sunrise near Monterey"?' she asked.

'Vaguely,' Brooke said.

'That was the first poem I read,' Ruth said. 'When I got to the end I read it again and again and I just knew I was going to live. And here I am.'

'You should write Dillon and tell him that.'

'I did. I made up a poem and sent it to him.'

'What did he say? Did he like it?'

'I don't know. I didn't want him to think that I was trying to get something out of him, so I didn't put down my address. Anyway, I started reading lots of poems and when I got out of the hospital I joined the Society.' She named the poets who mattered to her – all of them, like Dillon, the sort who make Christmas albums, whose lines appear on the bottom of inspirational posters.

'What do you do there?' Brooke asked. 'At the Society.'

'We share.'

'You lend each other books?'

'That,' Ruth said, 'and other things. Sometimes we read to each other and talk about life.'

'It sounds like an encounter group.'

'Isn't that why you write books?' Ruth asked. 'To bring people together and help them live their lives?'

Brooke did not know exactly why he had written his books. He was not sure that his motives could stand that kind of scrutiny. 'Let me hear your poem, Ruth. The one you sent Dillon.'

'All right.' She began to recite it from memory. Brooke nodded to the beat, which was forced and obvious. He barely heard the words. He was thinking that nothing he had ever thought or said could make a woman want to live again. 'That was beautiful,' he said when Ruth had finished the poem. 'How about an encore?'

'That's the only poem I ever wrote except for one other, which is pretty personal.' Ruth said that she couldn't write unless something made her do it, some really strong emotion.

'Then read something.'

She slid a book from the shelf, opened it and cleared her throat. '"Sunrise near Monterey,"' she said, 'by Francis X. Dillon.'

She glanced up at Brooke. 'Oh,' she said, 'I love how you look at me.'

'Read,' Brooke said. He forced himself to smile and shake his head in the right places. After a time he began to enjoy it, and even allowed himself to believe what it was saying: that the world was beautiful and we were beautiful, and that we could be more beautiful if we just let ourselves go – if we shouted when we wanted to shout, ran naked when we wanted to run naked, embraced when we wanted to embrace.

Riley, wearing a green jacket with a plaid tie and plaid pants, came to Brooke's room the next morning. 'You told me you wanted to get an early start,' he said. 'I hope this isn't too early for you.'

Brooke felt Riley's gaze go over his shoulder to the bed. He had considered messing it up a little, but he couldn't bring himself to do it. Now he wished he had. 'You should have called,' he said.

Riley grinned. 'I thought you might be up.'

Heartsick, Brooke said very little on the drive home. Riley talked a blue streak and didn't seem to notice. He described the troubles he was having with the university press that was bringing out his new book, and gave Brooke a lot of advice on how to deal with editors.

Riley's wife was standing at the picture window. She waved as Brooke pulled up to the house. Riley got his suitcase out of the back seat and stuck his head in the door just as Brooke was putting the car in gear. 'Listen,' he said. 'I don't know what happened last night and I don't care. As far as I'm concerned I've never heard of anyone named Ruth.'

'It wasn't like that,' Brooke said.

'It never is,' Riley said. He rapped the roof of the car with his knuckles and turned up the walk to his house.

Brooke decided not to tell his wife what he had done. In the past she had known everything about him, and it pleased him to be the man she thought him to be. Now he was different from what his wife thought, and if he were honest he would hurt her terribly. Brooke thought he had no right to do this. He would have to pretend that things were the same. He owed her that. It seemed hypocritical to him, but he could not think of a better way to settle the matter.

Without really being aware of it, Brooke saw the events of his life as forming chapters, and when he felt a chapter drawing to a close he liked to tie it up with an appropriate sentiment. Never again, he decided, would he sit in the back of the church and watch Riley. From now on he would sit in the front of the church and let Riley, knowing what he knew, watch him. He would kneel before Riley as we must all, he thought, kneel before one another.

Of course the chapter now ending for Professor Brooke was not ending for everyone else. Throughout that winter he found, in his mailbox at the university, anonymous love poems in envelopes with no return address.

And Brooke's wife, unpacking his clothes, smelled perfume on his necktie. Then she went through the laundry hamper and discovered the same heavy scent all over one of his shirts. There had to be an explanation, but no matter how long she sat on the edge of the bed and held her head in her hands and rocked back and forth she could not imagine what it might be. And her husband was so much himself that night, so merry and warm, that she felt unworthy of him. The doubt passed from her mind to her body; it became one of those flutters that stops you cold from time to time for a few years, and then goes away.

Smokers

I noticed Eugene before I actually met him. There was no way not to notice him. As our train was leaving New York, Eugene, moving from another coach into the one where I sat, managed to get himself jammed in the door between his two enormous suitcases. I watched as he struggled to free himself, fascinated by the hat he wore, a green Alpine hat with feathers stuck in the brim. I wondered if he hoped to reduce the absurdity of his situation by grinning as he did in every direction. Finally something gave and he shot into the coach. I hoped he would not take the seat next to me, but he did.

He started to talk almost the moment he sat down, and he didn't stop until we reached Wallingford. Was I going to Choate? What a coincidence – so was he. My first year? His too. Where was I from? Oregon? No shit? Way the hell and gone up in the boondocks, eh? He was from Indiana – Gary, Indiana. I knew the song, didn't I? I did, but he sang it for me anyway, all the way through, including the tricky ending. There were other boys in the coach, and they were staring at us, and I wished he would shut up.

Did I swim? Too bad, it was a good sport, I ought to go out for it. He had set a free-style record in the Midwestern conference the year before. What was my favourite subject? He liked math, he guessed, but he was pretty good at all of them. He offered me a cigarette, which I refused.

'I oughta quit myself,' he said. 'Be the death of me yet.'

Eugene was a scholarship boy. One of his teachers told him that he was too smart to be going to a regular high school and gave him a list of prep schools. Eugene applied to all of them – 'just for the hell of it' – and all of them accepted him. He finally decided on Choate because only Choate had offered him a travel allowance. His father was dead and his mother, a nurse, had three other kids to support, so Eugene didn't think it would be fair to ask her for anything. As the train came into Wallingford he asked me if I would be his roommate.

I didn't jump at the offer. For one thing, I did not like to look at Eugene. His head was too big for his lanky body, and his skin was oily. He put me in mind of a seal. Then there was the matter of his scholarship. I too was a scholarship boy, and I didn't want to finish myself off before I even got started by rooming with another, the way fat girls hung out together back home. I knew the world Eugene came from. I came from that world myself, and I wanted to leave it behind. To this end I had practised over the summer an air of secret amusement which I considered to be aristocratic, an association encouraged by English movie actors. I had studied the photographs of the boys in the prep school bulletins, and now my hair looked like their hair and my clothes looked like their clothes.

I wanted to know boys whose fathers ran banks and held Cabinet office and wrote books. I wanted to be their friend and go home with them on vacation and someday marry one of their sisters, and Eugene Miller didn't have much of a place in those plans. I told him that I had a friend at Choate with whom I'd probably be rooming.

'That's okay,' he said. 'Maybe next year.'

I assented vaguely, and Eugene returned to the problem he was having deciding whether to go out for baseball or lacrosse. He was better at baseball, but lacrosse was more fun. He figured maybe he owed it to the school to go out for baseball.

As things worked out, our room assignments were already drawn up. My roommate was a Chilean named Jaime who described himself as a Nazi. He had an enormous poster of Adolf Hitler tacked above his desk until a Jewish boy on our hall complained and the dean made him take it down. Jaime kept a copy of *Mein Kampf* beside his bed like a Gideons Bible and was fond of reading aloud from it in a German accent. He enjoyed practical jokes. Our room overlooked the entrance to the headmaster's house and Jaime always whistled at the headmaster's ancient secretary as she went home from work at night. On Alumni Day he sneaked into the kitchen and spiced up the visitors' mock turtle soup with a number of condoms, unrolled and obscenely knotted. The next day at chapel the headmaster stammered out a sermon about the incident, but he referred to it in terms so coy and oblique that nobody knew what he was talking about. Ultimately the matter was dropped without another word. Just before Christmas Jaime's mother was killed in a plane crash, and he left school and never returned. For the rest of the year I roomed alone.

Eugene drew as his roommate Talbot Nevin. Talbot's family had donated the Andrew Nevin Memorial Hockey Rink and the Andrew Nevin Memorial Library to the school, and endowed the Andrew Nevin Memorial Lecture Series. Talbot Nevin's father had driven his car to second place in the Monaco Grand Prix two years earlier, and celebrity magazines often featured a picture of him with someone like Jill St John and a caption underneath quoting one of them as saying, 'We're just good friends'. I wanted to know Talbot Nevin.

So one day I visited their room. Eugene met me at the door and pumped my hand. 'Well what do you know,' he said. 'Tab, this here's a buddy of mine from Oregon. You don't get any farther up in the boondocks than that.'

Talbot Nevin sat on the edge of his bed, threading snow-white laces through the eyes of a pair of dirty sneakers. He nodded without raising his head.

'Tab's father won some big race last year,' Eugene went on, to my discomfort. I didn't want Talbot to know that I had heard anything about him. I wanted to come to him fresh, with no possibility of his suspecting that I liked him for anything but himself.

'He didn't win. He came in second.' Talbot threw down the sneakers and looked up at me for the first time. He had china-blue eyes under lashes and brows so light you could hardly see them. His hair too was shock-white and lank on his forehead. His face had a moulded look, like a doll's face, delicate and unhealthy.

'What kind of race?' I asked.

'Grand Prix,' he said, taking off his shoes.

'That's a car race,' Eugene said.

Not to have heard of the Grand Prix seemed to me evidence of too great ignorance. 'I know. I've heard of it.'

'The guys down the hall were talking about it and they said he won.' Eugene winked at me as he spoke; he winked continuously as if everything he said was part of a ritual joke and he didn't want a tenderfoot like me to take it too seriously.

'Well, I say he came in second and I damn well ought to know.' By now Talbot had changed to his tennis shoes. He stood. 'Let's go have a weed.'

Smoking at Choate was forbidden. 'The use of tobacco in any form,' said the student handbook, 'carries with it the penalty of immediate expulsion.' Up to this moment the rule against smoking had not been a problem for me because I did not smoke. Now it was a problem, because I did not want Eugene to have a bond with Talbot that I did not share. So I followed them downstairs to the music room, where the choir practised. Behind the conductor's platform was a long, narrow closet where the robes were kept. We huddled in the far end of this closet and Talbot passed out cigarettes. The risk was great and the activity silly, and we started to giggle.

'Welcome to Marlboro Country,' I said.

'It's what's up front that counts,' Talbot answered. The joke was lame, but I guffawed anyway.

'Better keep it down,' Eugene whispered. 'Big John might hear us.'

Big John was the senior dorm master. He wore three-piece suits and soft-heeled shoes and had a way of popping up at awkward moments. He liked to grab boys by the neck, pinching the skin between his forefinger and thumb, squeezing until they cried. 'Fuck Big John,' I said.

Neither Talbot nor Eugene responded. I fretted in the silence as we finished our cigarettes. I had intended to make Eugene look timid. Had I made myself look frivolous instead?

I saw Talbot several times that week and he barely nodded to me. I decided I had made a bad impression on him. But on Friday night he came up as we were leaving the dining hall and asked me if I wanted to play tennis the next morning. I doubt that I have ever felt such complete self-satisfaction as I felt that night.

Talbot missed our appointment, however, so I dropped by his room. He was still in bed, reading. 'What's going on?' he asked, without looking up from his book.

I sat on Eugene's bed. 'I thought we might play a little tennis.'

'Tennis?' He continued reading silently for a few moments. 'I don't know. I don't feel so hot.'

'No big deal. I thought you wanted to play. We could just knock a couple of balls around.'

'Hell.' He lowered the book onto his chest. 'What time is it?'

'Nine o'clock.'

'The courts'll be full by now.'

'There's always a few empty ones behind the science building.'

'They're asphalt, aren't they?'

'Cement.' I shrugged. I didn't want to seem pushy. 'Like I said, no big deal. We can play some other time.' I stood and walked towards the door.

'Wait.' Talbot yawned without covering his mouth. 'What the hell.'

As it happened, the courts were full. Talbot and I sat on the grass and I asked him questions I already knew the answers to, like where was he from and where had he gone to school the year before and who did he have for English. At this question he came to life. 'English? Parker, the bald one. I got A's all through school and now Parker tells me I can't write. If he's such a god-damned William Shakespeare what's he teaching here for?'

We sat for a time without speaking. 'I'm from Oregon,' I said finally. 'Near Portland.' We didn't live close enough to the city to call it near, I suppose, but I assumed everyone had heard of Portland.

'Oregon.' He pondered this. 'Do you hunt?'

'I've been a few times with my father.'

'What kind of weapon do you use?'

'Marlin.'

'30–30?'

I nodded.

'Good brush gun,' he said. 'Useless over a hundred yards. Have you ever killed anything?'

'Deer, you mean?'

'Deer, elk, whatever you hunt in Oregon.'

'No.'

Talbot had killed a lot of animals, and he named them for me: deer, moose, bear, elk, even an alligator. There were more, many more.

'Maybe you can come out West and go hunting with us sometimes.'

'Where, to Oregon?' Talbot looked away. 'Maybe.'

I had not expected to be humiliated on the court. My brother, who played tennis for Oregon State, had coached me through four summers. I had a good hot serve and my brother described my net game as 'ruthless'. Talbot ran me ragged. He played a kind of tennis different from any I had ever seen. He did not sweat, not the way I did anyway, or pant, or swear when he missed a shot, or get that thin quivering smile that tugged my lips whenever I aced my opponents. He seemed hardly to notice me, gave no sign that he was competing except that twice he called shots out that appeared to me to be well short of the line. I might have been mistaken, though. After he won the second set he walked abruptly off the court and went back to where he had left our sweaters. I followed him.

'Good game,' I said.

He pulled impatiently at the sleeve of his sweater. 'I can't play on these lousy asphalt courts.'

Eugene made himself known around school. You did not wear belted jackets at Choate, or white buck shoes. Certainly you did not wear Alpine hats with feathers stuck in the brim. Eugene wore all three.

Anyone who didn't know who Eugene was found out by mid-November. *Life* magazine ran a series of interviews and pictures showing what it was like to be a student at a typical Eastern prep school. They had based their piece on research done at five schools, of which ours was one. Eugene had been interviewed and one of his remarks appeared in bold face beneath a photograph of students bent morosely over their books in evening study hall. The quotation: 'One thing, nobody at Choate ever seems to smile. They think you're weird or something if you smile. You get dumped on all the time.'

True enough. We were a joyless lot. Laughter was acceptable only in the sentimental parts of the movies we were shown on alternate Saturday nights. The one category in the yearbook to which everyone aspired was 'Most Sarcastic'. The arena for these trials of wit was the dining room, and Eugene's statements in *Life* did nothing to ease his load there.

However conspicuous Eugene may have been, he was not unpopular. I never heard anything worse about him than that he was 'weird'. He did well in his studies, and after the swimming team began to practise, the word went around that Eugene promised to put Choate in the running for the championship. So despite his hat and his eagerness and his determined grin, Eugene escaped the fate I had envisioned for him: the other students dumped on him but they didn't cast him out.

The night before school recessed for Christmas I went up to visit Talbot and found Eugene alone in the room, packing his bags. He made me sit down and poured out a glass of Hawaiian Punch which he laced with some murky substance from a prescription bottle. 'Tab rustled up some codeine down at the infirmary,' he explained. 'This'll get the old Yule log burning.'

The stuff tasted filthy but I took it, as I did all the other things that made the rounds at school and were supposed to get you off but never did, like aspirin and Coke, after-shave lotion, and Ben-Gay stuffed in the nostrils. 'Where's Talbot?'

'I don't know. Maybe over at the library.' He reached under his bed and pulled out a trunk-sized suitcase, made of cardboard but tricked up to look like leather, and began filling it with an assortment of pastel shirts with tab collars. Tab collars were another of Eugene's flings at sartorial trailblazing at school. They made me think of what my mother always told my sister when she complained at having to wear Mother's cast-off clothes: 'You never know, you might start a fashion.'

'Where are you going for Christmas?' Eugene asked.

'Baltimore.'

'Baltimore? What's in Baltimore?'

'My aunt and uncle live there. How about you?'

'I'm heading on up to Boston.'

This surprised me. I had assumed he would return to Indiana for the holidays. 'Who do you know in Boston?'

'Nobody. Just Tab is all.'

'Talbot? You're going to be staying with Talbot?'

'Yeah. And his family, of course.'

'For the whole vacation?'

Eugene said in a confidential tone, almost a whisper: 'Old Tab's got himself an extra key nobody knows about to his daddy's liquor closet. We aim to do some very big drinking. And I mean very big.'

I went to the door. 'If I don't see you in the morning, have a Merry Christmas.'

'You bet, buddy. Same to you.' Eugene grabbed my right hand in both of his. His fingers were soft and damp. 'Take it easy on those Baltimore girls. Don't do anything I wouldn't do.'

Jaime had been called home the week before by his mother's death. His bed was stripped, the mattress doubled over. All the pictures in the room had gone with him, and the yellow walls glared blankly. I turned out the lights and sat on my bed until the bell rang for dinner.

I had never met my aunt and uncle before. They picked me up at the station in Baltimore with their four children, three girls and a boy. I disliked all of them immediately. During the drive home my aunt asked me if my poor father had ever learned to cope with my mother's moods. One of the girls, Pammy, fell asleep on my lap and drooled on me.

They lived in Sherwood Park, a brick suburb several miles outside the city. My aunt and uncle went out almost every night and left me in charge of the children. This meant turning the television set on and turning it off when they had all passed out in front of it. Putting them to bed any earlier wasn't in the cards. They held on to everything – carpets, electrical cords, the legs of tables and chairs – and when that failed tried to injure themselves by scratching and gouging at their own faces.

One night I broke down. I tried to call Talbot to ask him if I could come up to Boston and stay with him. The Nevins's number was unlisted, however, and after I considered the idea again, I thought better of it.

When I returned to school my aunt and uncle wrote my father a letter which he sent on to me. They said that I was selfish and unenterprising. They had welcomed me as a son. They had opened their hearts to me, but I had taken no interest in them or in their children, my cousins, who worshipped the very ground I walked on. They cited an incident when I was in the kitchen reading and the wind blew all my aunt's laundry off the line and I hadn't so much as *asked* if I could help. I just sat there and went right on reading and eating peanuts. Finally, my uncle was missing a set of cuff links that had great sentimental value for him. All things considered, they didn't think my coming to Baltimore had worked out very well. They thought that on future vacations I would be happier somewhere else.

I wrote back to my father, denying all charges and making a few of my own.

After Christmas Talbot and I were often together. Both of us had gone out for basketball, and as neither of us was any good to the team – Talbot because of an ankle injury, me because I couldn't make the ball go through the basket – we sat together on the bench most of the time. He told me Eugene had spoiled his stepmother's Christmas by leaning back in an antique chair and breaking it. Thereafter I thought of Mrs Nevin as a friend; but I had barely a month to enjoy the alliance because in late January Talbot told me that his father and stepmother had separated.

Eugene was taken up with swimming, and I saw him rarely. Talbot and I had most of our friends among the malcontents in the school: those, like Talbot, to whom every rule gave offence; those who missed their girlfriends or their cars; and those, like me, who knew that something was wrong but didn't know what it was.

Because I was not rich my dissatisfaction could not assume a really combative form. I paddled around on the surface, dabbling in revolt by way of the stories I wrote for *off the record*, the school literary journal. My stories took place at 'The Hoatch School' and concerned a student from the West whom I referred to simply as 'the boy'.

The boy's father came from a distinguished New York family. In his early twenties, he had travelled to Oregon to oversee his family's vast lumber holdings. His family turned on him when he married a beautiful young woman who happened to be part Indian. The Indian blood was noble, but the boy's father was disowned anyway.

The boy's parents prospered in spite of this and raised a large, gifted family. The boy was the most gifted of all, and his father sent him back East to Hoatch, the traditional family school. What he found there saddened him: among the students a preoccupation with money and social position, and among the masters hypocrisy and pettiness. The boy's only friends were a beautiful young dancer who worked as a waitress in a café near the school, and an old tramp. The dancer and tramp were referred to as 'the girl' and 'the tramp'. The boy and girl were forever getting the tramp out of trouble for doing things like painting garbage cans beautiful colours.

I doubt that Talbot ever read my stories – he never mentioned them if he did – but somehow he got the idea I was a writer. One night he came to my room and dropped a notebook on my desk and asked me to read the essay inside. It was on the topic 'Why Is Literature Worth Studying?' and it sprawled over four pages, concluding as follows:

> I think Literature is worth studying but only in a way. The people of our Country should know how intelligent the people of past history were. They should appreciate what gifts these people had to write such great works of

Literature. This is why I think Literature is worth studying.

Talbot had received an F on the essay.

'Parker says he's going to put me in summer school if I flunk again this marking period,' Talbot said, lighting a cigarette.

'I didn't know you flunked last time.' I stared helplessly at the cigarette. 'Maybe you shouldn't smoke. Big John might smell it.'

'I saw Big John going into the library on my way over here.' Talbot went to the mirror and examined his profile from the corner of his eye. 'I thought maybe you could help me out.'

'How?'

'Maybe give me a few ideas. You ought to see the topics he gives us. Like this one.' He took some folded papers from his back pocket. 'Describe the most interesting person you know.' He swore and threw the papers down.

I picked them up. 'What's this? Your outline?'

'More like a rough draft, I guess you'd call it.'

I read the essay. The writing was awful, but what really shocked me was the absolute lack of interest with which he described the most interesting person he had ever known. This person turned out to be his English teacher from the year before, whose chief virtue seemed to be that he gave a lot of reading periods and didn't expect his students to be William Shakespeare and write him a novel every week.

'I don't think Parker is going to like this very much,' I said.

'Why? What's wrong with it?'

'He might get the idea you're trying to criticize him.'

'That's his problem.'

I folded up the essay and handed it back to Talbot with his notebook.

'You really think he'll give me an F on it?'

'He might.'

Talbot crumpled the essay. 'Hell.'

'When is it due?'

'Tomorrow.'

'*Tomorrow?*'

'I'd have come over before this but I've been busy.'

We spent the next hour or so talking about other interesting people he had known. There weren't many of them, and the only one who really interested me was a maid named Tina who used to beat Talbot off when she tucked him in at night and was later arrested for trying to burn the Nevins's house down. Talbot couldn't remember anything about her though, not even her last name. We finally abandoned what promise Tina held of suggesting an essay.

What eventually happened was that I got up at four-thirty next morning and invented a fictional interesting person for Talbot. This person's name was Miles and he was supposed to have been one of Talbot's uncles.

I gave the essay to Talbot outside the dining hall. He read it without expression. 'I don't have any Uncle Miles,' he said. 'I don't have any uncles at all. Just aunts.'

'Parker doesn't know that.'

'But it was supposed to be about someone interesting.' He was frowning at the essay. 'I don't see what's so interesting about this guy.'

'If you don't want to use it I will.'

'That's okay. I'll use it.'

I wrote three more essays for Talbot in the following weeks: 'Who Is Worse – Macbeth or Lady Macbeth?'; 'Is There a God?'; and 'Describe a Fountain Pen to a Person Who Has Never Seen One.' Mr Parker read the last essay aloud to Talbot's class as an example of clear expository writing and put a note on the back of the essay saying how pleased he was to see Talbot getting down to work.

In late February the dean put a notice on the bulletin board: those students who wished to room together the following year had to submit their names to him by Friday. There was no time to waste. I went immediately to Talbot's dorm.

Eugene was alone in the room, stuffing dirty clothes into a canvas bag. He came towards me, winking and grinning and snorting. 'Hey there, buddy, how they hangin'? Side-by-side for comfort or back-to-back for speed?'

We had sat across from each other at breakfast, lunch, and dinner every day now for three weeks, and each time we met he behaved as if we were brothers torn by Arabs from each other's arms and just now reunited after twenty years.

'Where's Talbot?' I asked.

'He had a phone call. Be back pretty soon.'

'Aren't you supposed to be at swimming practice?'

'Not today.'

'Why not?'

'I broke the conference butterfly record yesterday. Against Kent.'

'That's great. Congratulations.'

'And butterfly isn't even my best stroke. Hey, good thing you came over. I was just about to go see you.'

'What about?'

'I was wondering who you were planning on rooming with next year.'

'Oh, well, you know, I sort of promised this other guy.'

Eugene nodded, still smiling. 'Fair enough. I already had someone ask me. I just thought I'd check with you first. Since we didn't have a chance to room together this year.' He stood and resumed stuffing the pile of clothes in his bag. 'Is it three o'clock yet?'

'Quarter to.'

'I guess I better get these duds over to the cleaners before they close. See you later, buddy.'

Talbot came back to the room a few minutes later.

'Where's Eugene?'

'He was taking some clothes to the cleaners.'

'Oh.' Talbot drew a cigarette from the pack he kept hidden under the washstand and lit it. 'Here,' he said, passing it to me.

'Just a drag.' I puffed at it and handed it back. I decided to come to the point. 'Who are you rooming with next year?'

'Eugene.'

'*Eugene*?'

'He has to check with somebody else first but he thinks it'll be all right.' Talbot picked up his squash racket and hefted it. 'How about you?'

'I don't know. I kind of like rooming alone.'

'More privacy,' said Talbot, swinging the racket in a broad backhand.

'That's right. More privacy.'

'Maybe that South American guy will come back.'

'I doubt it.'

'You never know. His old man might get better.'

'It's his mother. And she's dead.'

'Oh.' Talbot kept swinging the racket, forehand now.

'By the way, there's something I meant to tell you.'

'What's that?'

'I'm not going to be able to help you with those essays any more.'

He shrugged. 'Okay.'

'I've got enough work of my own to do. I can't do my work and yours too.'

'I said okay. Parker can't flunk me now anyway. I've got a C+ average.'

'I just thought I'd tell you.'

'So you told me.' Talbot finished the cigarette and stashed the butt in a tin soap dish. 'We'd better go. We're gonna be late for basketball.'

'I'm not going to basketball.'

'Why not?'

'Because I don't feel like going to basketball, that's why not.'

We left the building together and split up at the bottom of the steps without exchanging another word. I went down to the infirmary to get an excuse for not going to basketball. The doctor was out and I had to wait for an hour until he came back and gave me some pills and Kaopectate. When I got back to my room the dorm was in an uproar.

I heard the story from the boys in the room next to mine. Big John had caught Eugene smoking. He had come into Eugene's room and found him there alone and smelled cigarette smoke. Eugene had denied it but Big John tore the room apart and found cigarettes and butts all over the place. Eugene was over at the headmaster's house at this moment.

They told me the story in a mournful way, as though they were really broken up about it, but I could see how excited they were. It was always like that when someone got kicked out of school.

I went to my room and pulled a chair to the window. Just before the bell rang for dinner a taxi came up the drive. Big John walked out of the dorm with two enormous cardboard suitcases and helped the driver put them in the trunk. He gave the driver some money and said something to him and the driver nodded and got back into the cab. Then the headmaster and the dean came out of the house with Eugene behind them. Eugene was wearing his hat. He shook hands with both of them and then with Big John. Suddenly he bent over and put his hands up to his face. The dean reached out and touched his arm. They stook like that for a long time, the four of them, Eugene's shoulders bucking and heaving. I couldn't watch it. I went to the mirror and combed my hair until I heard the door of the taxi bang shut. When I looked out the window again the cab was gone. The headmaster and the dean were standing in the shadows, but I could see Big John clearly. He was rocking back on his heels and talking, hands on his hips, and something he said made the headmaster laugh, not really a laugh, more like a giggle. The only thing I heard was the word 'feathers'. I figured they must be talking about Eugene's hat. Then the bell rang and the three of them went into the dining hall.

The next day I walked by the dean's office and almost went in and told him everything. The problem was, if I told the dean about Talbot he would find out about me, too. The rules didn't set forth different punishments according to the amount of smoke consumed. I even considered sending the dean an anonymous note, but I doubted if it would get much attention. They were big on doing the gentlemanly thing at Choate.

On Friday Talbot came up to me at basketball practice and asked if I wanted to room with him next year.

'I'll think about it,' I told him.

'The names have to be in by dinner time tonight.'

'I said I'll think about it.'

That evening Talbot submitted our names to the dean. There hadn't really been that much to think about. For all I know, Eugene *had* been smoking when Big John came into the room. If you wanted to get technical about it, he was guilty as charged a hundred times over. It wasn't as if some great injustice had been done.

Face to Face

She met him at a fireworks display. That part of it was funny when she thought about it later.

Virginia had been set up. Not that anyone really *meant* to set her up – but it happened that way. The boy, for example. He'd stopped asking questions like 'Where's Daddy?' 'Why doesn't Daddy want to live with us any more?' Lately, he had taken to drawing pictures instead – immature pictures considering his age – with bug-bodied figures and fat suns with long yellow rays like spokes. All the pictures showed the same thing: a man and a woman with a little boy between them. 'Ricky,' she said, 'why don't you draw someone else?' He wouldn't, though. For this and for other reasons his teacher had begun to send Virginia strange notes.

Virginia's neighbours, Ben and Alice, played their part too. Alice kept telling her that it was a blessing in disguise that her husband had taken off. 'You're free now, hon,' said Alice. 'You can find someone nice.' Virginia had to admit that her husband wasn't any great shakes. But when he left, not saying a word, it took the life out of her, and she didn't think much about going out with men. Besides, she had her hands full with the boy.

Whenever Alice talked about her smart cousin from Everett, though, Virginia found herself listening. In late June Alice told her that her cousin would be coming with them to see the fireworks display at Green Lake, and she invited Virginia and her son to join them. Virginia suspected that she had something in mind, but Alice had already told Ricky about the fireworks and he was all set to go; so she agreed.

From what Alice had told her about Robert, Virginia expected a distinguished, confident man, full of opinions and unlikely to be interested in her. Actually, he was shy. And polite. Whenever he reached for his cigarettes, he offered one to her even after she told him she didn't smoke. He was full of questions about her, though he had a way of looking off when he asked them. Robert's eyelids drooped and he had dense brown curls. A faint, acrid odour clung to him, like the smell of a newly painted room. He called Ricky 'Crazylegs' and by the time they got to Green Lake he had promised to take the boy fishing – 'As long as it's okay with your mom. Maybe she'd even like to come along,' he added.

'We'll see,' Virginia said.

Just after the fireworks started she went back to the parking lot with Robert to get some potato salad. They walked along without speaking. Finally, Virginia broke the silence.

'Alice says you went to college.'

He nodded. 'For a while, back in Michigan.'

'What did you study?'

'Math, mostly. I was going to be an engineer. I didn't finish.'

'That must be hard.'

'It was a long time ago. Grin and bear it.' He laughed.

'I mean the math must be hard.'

'It wasn't that bad. I got all B's, except for some C's.'

They got the potato salad from the car and started walking back. The only time they could really see was when a big flare or rocket went off. Robert took her arm gingerly when there were things they had to go around. Once they almost stepped on a couple lying under a blanket. Then a flare went off in descending stages with a big burst like an exclamation mark at the end, and they could see the couple moving together. Robert looked away quickly. Virginia thought that he did so because he didn't want to embarrass her by saying something about it.

'So you live in Everett,' she said.

'Just outside.'

'What do you do there?'

Robert hesitated. 'I'm a housepainter.' He turned and looked her in the face for the first time. 'Maybe I could come over for a visit sometime.'

'All the way from Everett? That would be a lot of trouble, wouldn't it?'

'I wouldn't mind,' he said.

When they got back Virginia sat down beside the boy. Ricky was lying on his back, watching the display. The boy's face changed colours with the rockets.

Robert called her often after that night. They usually went over to Alice and Ben's and drank and kidded around. When they didn't go there he took her and the boy out to the movies, once to a baseball game. He helped her with her coat, opened doors, and walked on the outside. When they parted, he would stare into her eyes and squeeze her hand with furtive, almost illicit intensity. More than a month passed before they went anywhere alone.

He took her to dinner at a place called Enrique's, where there was a violinist. Robert read the menu and told her about wines. 'I like good food,' he said. 'It's my one weakness.'

Virginia had guessed. Not that Robert was fat, exactly. More like stocky.

After dinner he took a big cigar from a metal tube and roasted the tip over the candle, all the while explaining how a really good cigar should be smoked. 'You've got to respect it,' he said, 'almost like a person.' Then he called the violinist over and had him play 'Hungarian Tears' and a couple of other numbers. The violinist closed his eyes and smiled to himself as he played. Virginia squirmed and fiddled with her napkin. She was unable to meet the eyes of the people from the other tables who looked in their direction. She stared at Robert, who stared at the tip of his cigar. He gave the violinist a twenty-dollar bill.

'Your husband – ' Robert paused – waiting, Virginia thought, for her to supply a name. She said nothing. 'How come the two of you split up?'

Virginia stared at him for a moment.

'We didn't split up. He left me.'

These were hard words. It would have been easier to say, 'Oh, we decided to take a vacation from each other.' But when people said things like that to Virginia, she felt sorry for them, and she didn't want anyone feeling sorry for her. Nevertheless she felt ashamed.

'Left you?' Robert scowled at his cigar. 'Why?'

'I don't know.'

'Where – '

'I don't know where he is.'

'Tell me about him.'

She began haltingly. Then, seeing that the stories about her husband fascinated Robert, she went on. Though he laughed in a way she didn't like, at least he laughed. So did she. Between stories, she said, 'You've been married before, haven't you?'

He nodded. 'How did you know?'

'Alice told me. What was she like?'

'Who? Florence? I don't know.' Robert stood and fumbled for his wallet. 'I'll get your coat. You want to go to the little girls' room or anything?'

They did not speak again, except politely, until he pulled up in front of her apartment building. He put his arm over the back of the seat. She tried to relax against it. He had left the engine running and the windshield wipers on.

Robert kissed her. He kissed her for a long time, and in the middle of it she opened her eyes and saw that his eyes were wide and startled. They held each other for a while. 'I was wondering,' Robert said softly.

'What?' She leaned back to look at him. 'What?'

'You think Crazylegs likes me?'

'Sure.'

'Really?'

'Really.'

'I'll bet he misses his dad.'

'Sometimes. A lot of the time.'

'A kid his age needs a father.' Robert moved abruptly, banging his elbow against the steering wheel. 'You ever been up to Vancouver?'

'To Vancouver? No.'

'I was thinking maybe the two of us could go up there this weekend. Get to know each other.'

He bent towards Virginia until they were face to face. She looked at him and wondered what he saw when he looked at her. He had stopped breathing, or so it seemed, he was so quiet. The windshield wipers went back and forth. 'All right,' she said. 'Sure. Why not?'

Their hotel was old and run-down, but they had a big room with a fireplace. Virginia bounced on the bed and said how soft it was. She didn't mean anything by it, but Robert grew silent. He adjusted the blinds. Then he took his clothes out of his suitcase and refolded them and put them in the bureau.

At dinner Robert drank a lot of wine, and whatever it was that seemed to be troubling him passed off for a while. He told Virginia about a hiking trip he had gone on that the boy might like to take sometime. She reached out and touched his hand. 'You're a good man,' she said.

He frowned.

'Is there anything the matter?' she asked.

'I suppose you want to go upstairs,' he said. He looked at Virginia.

'Not especially. Whatever you want.'

'I thought I'd have a drink at the bar. You don't have to. You're probably tired.'

'A little. A drink sounds nice, though.' Virginia thought that he wanted a nightcap, to settle him after the long drive. When he ordered his fourth whisky, she understood that he planned to make a night of it. She had the feeling that he wanted either to get rid of her or drink her under the table. 'I think I'll run along to bed,' she said finally.

'Go on. I'll be up in a minute.'

Virginia went upstairs and bathed and waited for Robert in bed. She was almost asleep when she heard Robert's key fumbling in the lock.

He tiptoed over, carrying his shoes in his hand, and stood beside the bed, looking down at her. 'Virginia?' he whispered.

She lay still. She did not reply, because she sensed he did not want her to.

Robert put his shoes under the bed and undressed quietly. He slipped between the sheets and curled up on the far side of the bed. Virginia wondered what she ought to do. Finally she decided to do nothing. He might get mad if he found out she was awake. Maybe he'd feel better in the morning. She wondered what she had done wrong.

Just after sunrise, Virginia started awake and felt Robert's hand on her breast. He was squeezing her softly. It surprised her and she looked over at him. He lay on his side, facing her, eyes closed. He moved his hand to her other breast. He squeezed there for awhile, then he threw his arm around her and pulled her close.

'Robert.'

He didn't answer. Still with his eyes closed, he began to kiss her neck. He rolled over on top ofher and wedged his legs between hers. 'Robert,' she said again, but he seemed not to hear her. He forced her legs apart.

It didn't last long, and it hurt.

Robert rolled off and turned away. A few moments later he was sighing in sleep. Virginia took a long bath. When she came out of the bathroom Robert was sitting on the edge of the bed, fully dressed, studying a map of Vancouver. He smiled at Virginia and stood up. 'Good morning.'

She dipped her head in his direction and waited. After what had happened she expected him to say something.

Instead he dropped the map and pointed towards the bathroom. 'You all through in there?'

'Yes.'

'I didn't know whether you were taking a bath or going for a swim.'

'If you wanted to get in you should have knocked.'

'Don't worry about it.' He pecked her on the cheek as he went past her.

Robert didn't come out until after she was dressed. 'Boy, you look nice,' he said, rubbing his hands together.

Virginia could not look at him. 'Just for you,' she said.

They walked around Vancouver all morning. Robert read things to her from a tourist booklet. 'It's better exercise than going on one of those buses,' he explained, 'and we won't have to put up with a bunch of people from God knows where.' They ate lunch in a cafeteria he had noticed earlier in the day, and then they went to a movie. Virginia had never been to a movie in the daytime, not since she was a little kid anyway, and it made her uneasy. Most of the people in the theatre were older men.

After he'd finished his popcorn Robert reached over and pressed Virginia's hand. Then he started to stroke the inside of her thigh.

'Please, Robert,' she whispered. 'Not here.'

He pulled away from her. 'What?'

Virginia had the idea that Robert was prepared to deny that he'd touched her. 'Nothing,' she said.

'Too bad old Crazylegs isn't with us.' Robert took a sip of his Pepsi. 'He'd get a kick out of this movie.'

'Let's go, Robert.'

'What's wrong?'

'I want to go.' She stood and walked up the aisle. She waited for him in the lobby. Robert bought another popcorn on the way out and offered some to her. She shook her head. Outside they walked up the street in the direction of a logging museum.

At dinner that night Virginia asked Robert about his marriage. She had told him more about her husband's idea of style, the high life, his own possibilities. Robert had enjoyed a certain freedom with her past and she wanted something back.

But Robert kept talking about his old girlfriends instead. 'I hope it doesn't bother you,' he said. 'It's ancient history.' They'd been nuts about him, he said, but he'd had to cut them loose because it just didn't feel right. Most of them came from rich, classy backgrounds – daughters of colonels and district attorneys.

She said, 'Tell me about your wife.'

Robert stared into his glass. 'Florence was a whore.'

'What do you mean, Robert?'

'You know.'

'No, I don't. Did she actually go out and sell herself to men? For money?'

'She was an amateur. She had to give it away.' He almost smiled at his own joke. 'I should have listened to my aunt,' he went on. 'She saw through Florence the first time they met.'

'Then why did you marry her?' Virginia hoped that he would tell her that he had married out of love.

'Had to.' He grinned. 'You know how it is.'

'Then you have a child!'

He shook his head. 'Miscarriage.'

'Where is Florence now?'

'I don't know. Still in Detroit, I guess. I don't know. I don't care.'

'Is she alone?'

'No. She managed to get this guy to marry her. Don't ask me how.'

'What guy?'

'The guy she was fooling around with.'

'There was just one? One man?'

'One that I know of.'

'But you called her a whore.'

'How come we started talking about Florence, anyway?' Robert said. 'The hell with her.' He stood. 'Come on, let's go have a drink.'

'I don't want any more to drink. You go ahead if you want.'

He walked her to the lobby, and they waited for the elevator without speaking. He moved towards her a little, his eyes on her face, and she thought he wanted to kiss her. He looked unhappy. Maybe his wife had been a whore. Virginia wanted to believe that. She moved forward slightly, ready to receive his kiss, but he suddenly looked down and rummaged in his pocket.

'Here's the key,' he said. He shuffled towards the bar, his arms dangling.

Virginia was sleeping when Robert came in. She only became aware of him when he slid on top of her. At first she didn't know where she was or what was happening. She sat up and pushed him away. She didn't remember screaming, but she might have, because Robert leaped out of bed. 'Jesus,' he said, 'what's wrong?'

'Oh, Robert.' She rubbed her eyes, trying not to cry. 'Please don't do that.'

'Don't do what?'

'Oh, God.' She covered her face.

Robert sat on the bed. 'You don't like me, do you?'

'Sure I do. I'm here, aren't I?'

'I don't mean like that. I mean in bed.'

She looked at him, hunched against the cold of the night. 'No. Not that way. Not when I'm asleep.'

He nodded grimly. 'Whatever you say.'

Neither of them slept well. Virginia could feel Robert's misery. She softened. In the morning she reached out to him and began rubbing his back. She had to do this. She rubbed his back, his neck, his shoulders. He tensed. Then he rolled over. 'Okay,' he said. He reached out for her.

'No, Robert. I want to go home.'

They said little during the drive back, until they crested a hill and saw a lake far below. 'Boy,' Robert said, 'that's really something.'

'It sure is.'

'When I used to see things like that,' he went on, 'I used to wish I had someone to see it with me.' He looked at Virginia and laughed.

She saw that he was in some pain. She touched his hand. 'I know what you mean. It's not easy, sometimes, being alone.'

'Not to complain,' he said. 'I do all right. It's different with men and women. The minute a woman gets alone she starts looking for someone.'

'So do men.'

Robert moved his hand away from Virginia's. 'Some men,' he said.

'It's natural, Robert, really. There's nothing to be ashamed of.'

He looked at her with sudden panic and she started out of herself, became enormous in her pity for him. 'Don't give up, Robert. Not just because it didn't work with me.' She wanted to say more but he had left her, gone back to his injury. She exercised her pity on him. The road slipped under the tyres. Virginia stared greedily ahead.

Poor Robert, she thought.

Passengers

Glen left Depoe Bay a couple of hours before sunup to beat the traffic and found himself in a heavy fog; he had to lean forward and keep the windshield wipers going to see the road at all. Before long the constant effort and the lulling rhythm of the wipers made him drowsy, and he pulled into a gas station to throw some water in his face and buy coffee.

He was topping off the tank, listening to the invisible waves growl on the beach across the road, when a girl came out of the station and began to wash the windshield. She had streaked hair and wore knee-length, high-heeled boots over her blue jeans. Glen could not see her face clearly.

'Lousy morning for a drive,' she said, leaning over the hood. Her blue jeans had studs poking through in different patterns and when she moved they blinked in the light of the sputtering yellow tubes overhead. She threw the squeegee into a bucket and asked Glen what kind of mileage he got.

He tried to remember what Martin had told him. 'Around twenty-five per,' he said.

She looked the car up and down as if she were thinking of buying it from him.

Glen held out Martin's credit card but the girl laughed and said she didn't work there.

'Actually,' she said, 'I was kind of wondering which way you were headed.'

'North,' Glen said. 'Seattle.'

'Hey,' she said. 'What a coincidence. I mean that's where I'm going, too.'

Glen nodded but he didn't say anything. He had promised not to pick up any hitchhikers; Martin said it was dangerous and socially irresponsible, like feeding stray cats. Also Glen was a little browned off about the way the girl had come up to him all buddy-buddy, when really she just wanted something.

'Forget it,' she said. 'Drive alone if you want. It's your car, right?' She smiled and went back into the station office.

After Glen paid the attendant he thought things over. The girl was not dangerous – he could tell by how tight her jeans were that she wasn't carrying a gun. And if he had someone to talk to there wouldn't be any chance of dozing off.

The girl did not seem particularly surprised or particularly happy that Glen had changed his mind. 'Okay,' she said, 'just a sec.' She stowed her bags in the trunk, a guitar case and a laundry sack tied at the neck like a balloon, then cupped her hands around her mouth and yelled, 'Sunshine! Sunshine!' A big hairy dog ran out of nowhere and jumped up on the girl, leaving spots of mud all over the front of her white shirt. She clouted him on the head until he got down and then pushed him into the car. 'In back!' she said. He jumped onto the back seat and sat there with his tongue hanging out.

'I'm Bonnie,' the girl said when they were on the road. She took a brush out of her purse and pulled it through her hair with a soft ripping noise.

Glen handed her one of his business cards. 'I'm Glen,' he said.

She held it close to her face and read it out loud. 'Rayburn Marine Supply. Are you Rayburn?'

'No. Rayburn is my employer.' Glen did not mention that Martin Rayburn was also his room-mate and the owner of the car.

'Oh,' she said, 'I see, here's your name in the corner. Marine Supply,' she repeated. 'What are you, some kind of defence contractors?'

'No,' Glen said. 'We sell boating supplies.'

'That's good to hear,' Bonnie said. 'I don't accept rides from defence contractors.'

'Well, I'm not one,' Glen said. 'Mostly we deal in life jackets, caps, and deck furniture.' He named the towns along the coast where he did business, and when he mentioned Eureka, Bonnie slapped her knee.

'All right!' she said. She said that California was her old stomping ground. Bolinas and San Francisco.

When she said San Francisco Glen thought of a high-ceilinged room with sunlight coming in through stained-glass windows, and a lot of naked people on the floor flopping all over each other like seals. 'We don't go that far south,' he said. 'Mendocino is as far as we go.' He cracked the window a couple of inches; the dog smelled like a sweater just out of mothballs.

'I'm really beat,' Bonnie said. 'I don't think I slept five straight minutes last night. This truck driver gave me a ride up from Port Orford and I think he must have been a foreigner. Roman fingers, ha ha.'

The fog kept rolling in across the road. Headlights from passing cars and trucks were yellow and flat as buttons until they were close; then the beams swept across them and lit up their faces. The dog hung his head over the back of the seat and sighed heavily. Then he put his paws up alongside his ears. The next time Glen looked over at him the dog was hanging by its belly, half in front and half in back. Glen told Bonnie that he liked dogs but considered it unsafe to have one in the front seat. He told her that he'd read a story in the paper where a dog jumped onto an accelerator and ran a whole family off a cliff.

She put her hand over the dog's muzzle and shoved hard. He tumbled into the back seat and began noisily to clean himself. 'If everybody got killed,' Bonnie said, 'how did they find out what happened?'

'I forget,' Glen said.

'Maybe the dog confessed,' Bonnie said. 'No kidding, I've seen worse evidence than that hold up in court. This girlfriend of mine, the one I'm going to stay with in Seattle, she got a year's probation for soliciting and you know what for? For smiling at a guy in a grocery store. It's a hell of a life, Glen. What's that thing you're squeezing, anyway?'

'A tennis ball.'

'What do you do that for?'

'Just a habit,' Glen said, thinking that it would not be productive to discuss with Bonnie his performance at golf. Being left-handed, he had a tendency to pull his swing and Martin had suggested using the tennis ball to build up his right forearm.

'This is the first time I've ever seen anyone squeeze a tennis ball,' Bonnie said. 'It beats me how you ever picked up a habit like that.'

The dog was still cleaning himself. It sounded awful. Glen switched on the tape deck and turned it up loud.

'Some station!' Bonnie said. 'That's the first time I've heard 101 Strings playing "76 Trombones".'

Glen told her that it was a tape, not the radio, and that the song was 'Oklahoma!' All of Martin's tapes were instrumental – he hated vocals – but it just so happened that Glen had a tape of his own in the glove compartment, a Peter Paul and Mary. He said nothing to Bonnie about it because he didn't like her tone.

'I'm going to catch some zees,' she said after a time. 'If Sunshine acts cute just smack him in the face. It's the only thing he understands. I got him from a cop.' She rolled up her denim jacket and propped it under her head. 'Wake me up,' she said, 'if you see anything interesting or unusual.'

The sun came up, a milky presence at Glen's right shoulder, whitening the fog but not breaking through it. Glen began to notice a rushing sound like water falling hard on pavement and realized that the road had filled up with cars. Their headlights were bleached and wan. All the drivers, including Glen, changed lanes constantly.

Glen put on 'Exodus' by Ferrante and Teicher, Martin's favourite. Martin had seen the movie four times. He thought it was the greatest movie ever made because it showed what you could do if you had the will. Once in a while Martin would sit in the living room by himself with a bottle of whiskey and get falling-down drunk. When he was halfway there he would yell Glen's name until Glen came downstairs and sat with him. Then Martin would lecture him on various subjects. He often repeated himself, and one of his favourite topics was the

Jewish people, which was what he called the Jews who died in the camps. He made a distinction between them and the Israelis. This was part of his theory.

According to Martin the Jewish people had done the Israelis a favour by dying out; if they had lived they would have weakened the gene pool and the Israelis would not have had the strength or the will to take all that land away from the Arabs and keep it.

One night he asked whether Glen had noticed anything that he, Martin, had in common with the Israelis. Glen admitted that he had missed the connection. The Israelis had been in exile for a long time, Martin said; he himself, while in the Navy, had visited over thirty ports of call and lived at different times in seven of the United States before coming home to Seattle. The Israelis had taken a barren land and made it fruitful; Martin had taken over a failing company and made it turn a profit again. The Israelis defeated all their enemies and Martin was annihilating his competition. The key, Martin said, was in the corporate gene pool. You had to keep cleaning out the deadwood and bringing in new blood. Martin named the deadwood who would soon be cleaned out, and Glen was surprised; he had supposed a few of the people to be, like himself, new blood.

The fog held. The ocean spray gave it a sheen, a pearly colour. Big drops of water rolled up the windshield, speckling the grey light inside the car. Glen saw that Bonnie was not a girl but a woman. She had wrinkles across her brow and in the corners of her mouth and eyes, and the streaks in her hair were real streaks – not one of these fashions as he'd first thought. In the light her skin showed its age like a coat of dust. She was old, not *old* old, but old; older than him. Glen felt himself relax, and realized that for a moment there he had been interested in her. He squinted into the fog and drove on with the sensation of falling through a cloud. Behind Glen the dog stirred and yelped in his dreams.

Bonnie woke up outside Olympia. 'I'm hungry,' she said, 'let's score some pancakes.'

Glen stopped at a Denny's. While the waitress went for their food

Bonnie told Glen about a girlfriend of hers, not the one in Seattle but another one, who had known the original Denny. Denny, according to her girlfriend, was mighty weird. He had made a proposition. He would set Bonnie's girlfriend up with a place of her own, a car, clothes, the works; he wanted only one thing in return. 'Guess what,' Bonnie said.

'I give up,' Glen said.

'All right,' Bonnie said, 'you'd never guess it anyway.' The proposition, she explained, had this price tag: her girlfriend had to invite different men over for dinner, one man at a time, at least three days a week. The restaurateur didn't care what happened after the meal, had no interest in this respect either as participant or observer. All he wanted was to sit under the table while they ate, concealed by a floor-length tablecloth.

Glen said that there had to be more to it than that.

'No sir,' Bonnie said. 'That was the whole proposition.'

'Did she do it?' Glen asked.

Bonnie shook her head. 'She already had a boyfriend, she didn't need some old fart living under her table.'

'I still don't get it,' Glen said, 'him wanting to do that. What's the point?'

'The point?' Bonnie looked at Glen as if he had said something comical. 'Search me,' she said.

Bonnie went at her food – a steak, an order of pancakes, a salad and two wedges of lemon meringue pie – and did not speak again until she had eaten everything but the steak, which she wrapped in a place mat and stuck in her purse. 'I have to admit,' she said, 'that was the worst meal I ever ate.'

Glen went to the men's room and when he came out again the table was empty. Bonnie waved him over to the door. 'I already paid,' she said, stepping outside.

Glen followed her across the parking lot. 'I was going to have some more coffee,' he said.

'Well,' she said, 'I'll tell you straight. That wouldn't be a good idea right now.'

'In other words you didn't pay.'

'Not exactly.'

'What do you mean, "not exactly"?'

'I left a tip,' she said. 'I'm all for the working girl but I can't see paying for garbage like that. They ought to pay us for eating it. It's got cardboard in it, for one thing, not to mention about ten million chemicals.'

'What's got cardboard in it?'

'The batter. Uh-oh, Sunshine's had a little accident.'

Glen looked into the back seat. There was a big stain on the cover. 'Godalmighty,' Glen said. The dog looked at him and wagged his tail. Glen turned the car back on to the road; it was too late to go back to the restaurant, he'd never be able to explain. 'I noticed,' he said, 'you didn't leave anything on your plate, considering it was garbage.'

'If I hadn't eaten it, they would have thrown it out. They throw out pieces of butter because they're not square. You know how much food they dump every day?'

'They're running a business,' Glen said. 'They take a risk and they're entitled to the profits.'

'I'll tell you,' Bonnie said. 'Enough to feed the population of San Diego. Here, Sunshine.' The dog stood with his paws on the back of the seat while Bonnie shredded the steak and put the pieces in his mouth. When the steak was gone she hit the dog in the face and he sat back down.

Glen was going to ask Bonnie why she wasn't afraid of poisoning Sunshine but he was too angry to do anything but steer the car and squeeze the tennis ball. They could have been arrested back there. He could just see himself calling Martin and saying that he wouldn't be home for dinner because he was in jail for walking a cheque in East Jesus. Unless he could get that seat cleaned up he was going to have to tell Martin about Bonnie, and that wasn't going to be any picnic, either. So much for trying to do favours for people.

'This fog is getting to me,' Bonnie said. 'It's really boring.' She started to say something else, then fell silent again. There was a truck just ahead of them; as they climbed a gentle rise the fog thinned and Glen could make out the logo on the back – WE MOVE FAMILIES NOT JUST

FURNITURE – then they descended into the fog again and the truck vanished. 'I was in a sandstorm once,' Bonnie said, 'in Arizona. It was really dangerous but at least it wasn't boring.' She pulled a strand of hair in front of her eyes and began picking at the ends. 'So,' she said, 'tell me about yourself.'

Glen said there wasn't much to tell.

'What's your wife's name?'

'I'm not married.'

'Oh yeah? Somebody like you, I thought for sure you'd be married.'

'I'm engaged,' Glen said. He often told strangers that. If he met them again he could always say it hadn't worked out. He'd once known a girl who probably would have married him but like Martin said, it didn't make sense to take on freight when you were travelling for speed.

Bonnie said that she had been married for the last two years to a man in Santa Barbara. 'I don't mean married in the legal sense,' she said. Bonnie said that when you knew someone else's head and they knew yours, that was being married. She had ceased to know his head when he left her for someone else. 'He wanted to have kids,' Bonnie said, 'but he was afraid to with me, because I had dropped acid. He was afraid we would have a werewolf or something because of my chromosomes. I shouldn't have told him.'

Glen knew that the man's reason for leaving her had nothing to do with chromosomes. He had left her because she was too old.

'I never should have told him,' Bonnie said again. She made a rattling sound in her throat and put her hands up to her face. First her shoulders and then her whole body began jerking from side to side.

'All right,' Glen said, 'all right.' He dropped the tennis ball and began patting her on the back as if she had hiccups.

Sunshine uncoiled from the back seat and came scrambling over Glen's shoulder. He knocked Glen's hand off the steering wheel as he jumped onto his lap, rooting for the ball. The car went into a broadside skid. The road was slick and the tyres did not scream. Bonnie stopped jerking and stared out the window. So did Glen. They watched the fog whipping along the windshield as if they were at a movie. Then the car began to spin. When they came out of it Glen watched the yellow lines shoot away from the hood and realized that they were sliding backwards in the wrong lane of traffic. The car went on this way for a time, then it went into another spin and when it came out it was pointing in the right direction though still in the wrong lane. Not far off Glen could see weak yellow lights approaching, bobbing gently like the running lights of a ship. He took the wheel again and eased the car off the road. Moments later a convoy of logging trucks roared out of the fog, airhorns bawling; the car rocked in the turbulence of their wake.

Sunshine jumped into the back seat and lay there, whimpering. Glen and Bonnie moved into each other's arms. They just held on, saying nothing. Holding Bonnie, and being held by her, was necessary to Glen.

'I thought we were goners,' Bonnie said.

'They wouldn't even have found us,' Glen said. 'Not even our shoes.'

'I'm going to change my ways,' Bonnie said.

'Me too,' Glen said, and though he wasn't sure just what was wrong with his ways, he meant it.

'I feel like I've been given another chance,' Bonnie said. 'I'm going to pay back the money I owe, and write my mother a letter, even if she is a complete bitch. I'll be nicer to Sunshine. No more shoplifting. No more – ' Just then another convoy of trucks went by and though Bonnie kept on talking Glen could not hear a word. He was thinking they should get started again.

Later, when they were back on the road, Bonnie said that she had a special feeling about Glen because of what they had just gone through. 'I don't mean boy-girl feelings,' she said. 'I mean – do you know what I mean?'

'I know what you mean,' Glen said.

'Like there's a bond,' she said.

'I know,' Glen said. And as a kind of celebration he got out his Peter Paul and Mary and stuck it in the tape deck.

'I don't believe it,' Bonnie said. 'Is that who I think it is?'

'Peter Paul and Mary,' Glen said.

'That's who I thought it was,' Bonnie said. 'You like that stuff?'

Glen nodded. 'Do you?'

'I guess they're all right. When I'm in the mood. What else have you got?'

Glen named the rest of the tapes.

'Jesus,' Bonnie said. She decided that what she was really in the mood for was some peace and quiet.

By the time Glen found the address where Bonnie's girlfriend lived, a transients' hotel near Pioneer Square, it had begun to rain. He waited in the car while Bonnie rang the bell. Through the window of the door behind her he saw a narrow ladder of stairs; the rain sliding down the windshield made them appear to be moving upward. A woman stuck her head out the door; she nodded constantly as she talked. When Bonnie came back her hair had separated into ropes. Her ears, large and pink, poked out between strands. She said that her girlfriend was out, that she came and went at all hours.

'Where does she work?' Glen asked. 'I could take you there.'

'Around,' Bonnie said. 'You know, here and there.' She looked at Glen and then out the window. 'I don't want to stay with her,' she said, 'not really.'

Bonnie went on talking like that, personal stuff, and Glen listened to the raindrops plunking off the roof of the car. He thought he should help Bonnie, and he wanted to. Then he imagined bringing Bonnie home to Martin and introducing them; Sunshine having accidents all over the new carpets; the three of them eating dinner while Bonnie talked, interrupting Martin, saying the kinds of things she said.

When Bonnie finished talking, Glen explained to her that he really wanted to help out but that it wasn't possible.

'Sure,' Bonnie said, and leaned back against the seat with her eyes closed.

It seemed to Glen that she did not believe him. That was ungrateful of her and he became angry. 'It's true,' he said.

'Hey,' Bonnie said, and touched his arm.

'My room-mate is allergic to dogs.'

'Hey,' Bonnie said again. 'No problem.' She got her bags out of the trunk and tied Sunshine's leash to the guitar case, then came around the car to the driver's window. 'Well,' she said, 'I guess this is it.'

'Here,' Glen said, 'in case you want to stay somewhere else.' He put a twenty-dollar bill in her hand.

She shook her head and tried to give it back.

'Keep it,' he said. 'Please.'

She stared at him. 'Jesus,' she said. 'Okay, why not? The price is right.' She looked up and down the street, then put the bill in her pocket.

'I didn't mean – ' Glen said.

'Wait,' Bonnie said. 'Sunshine! Sunshine!'

Glen looked behind him. Sunshine was running up the street after another dog, pulling Bonnie's guitar case behind him. 'Nuts,' Bonnie said, and began sprinting up the sidewalk in the rain, cursing loudly. People stopped to watch, and a police car slowed down. Glen hoped that the officers hadn't noticed them together. He turned the corner and looked back. No one was following him.

A few blocks from home Glen stopped at a gas station and tried without success to clean the stain off the seat cover. On the floor of the car he found a lipstick and a clear plastic bag with two marijuana cigarettes inside, which he decided had fallen out of Bonnie's purse during the accident.

Glen knew that the cigarettes were marijuana because the two engineers he'd roomed with before moving in with Martin had smoked it every Friday night. They would pass joints back and forth and comment on the quality, then turn the stereo on full blast and listen with their eyes closed, nodding in time to the music and now and then smiling and saying 'Get down!' and 'Go for it!' Later on they would strip the refrigerator, giggling as if the food belonged to someone else, then watch TV with the sound off and make up stupid dialogue. Glen suspected they were putting it on; he had taken puffs a couple of times and it didn't do anything for him. He almost threw the marijuana away but finally decided to hang on to it. He thought it might be valuable.

* * *

Glen could barely eat his dinner that night; he was nervous about the confession he had planned, and almost overcome by the smell of Martin's after-shave. Glen had sniffed the bottle once and the lotion was fine by itself, but for some reason it smelled like rotten eggs when Martin put it on. He didn't just use a drop or two, either; he drenched himself, slapping it all over his face and neck with the sound of applause. Finally Glen got his courage up and confessed to Martin over coffee. He had hoped that the offence of giving Bonnie a ride would be cancelled out by his honesty in telling about it, but when he finished Martin hit the roof.

For several minutes Martin spoke very abusively to Glen. It had happened before and Glen knew how to listen without hearing. When Martin ran out of abuse he began to lecture.

'Why didn't she have her own car?' he asked. 'Because she's used to going places free. Some day she's going to find out that nothing's free. You could have done anything to her. *Anything.* And it would have been her fault, because she put herself in your power. When you put yourself in someone else's power you're nothing, nobody. You just have to accept what happens.'

After he did the dishes Glen unpacked and sat at the window in his room. Horns were blowing across the sound. The fog was all around the house, thickening the air; the breath in his lungs made him feel slow and heavy.

He wondered what it really felt like, being high. He decided to try it; this time, instead of just a few puffs, he had two whole marijuana cigarettes all to himself. But not in his room – Martin came in all the time to get things out of the closet, plant food and stationery and so on, and he might smell it. Glen didn't want to go outside, either. There was always a chance of running into the police.

In the basement, just off the laundry room, was another smaller room where Martin kept wood for the fireplace. He wouldn't be going in there for another two or three months, when the weather turned cold. Probably the smell would wear off by that time; then again, maybe it wouldn't. What the hell, thought Glen.

He put on his windbreaker and went into the living room where Martin was building a model aeroplane. 'I'm going out for a while,' he said. 'See you later.' He walked down the hall and opened the front door. 'So long!' he yelled, then slammed the door shut so Martin would hear, and went down the stairs into the basement.

Glen couldn't turn on the lights because then the fan would go on in the laundry room; the fan had a loud squeak and Martin might hear it. Glen felt his way along the wall and stumbled into something. He lit a match and saw an enormous pile of Martin's shirts, all of them white, waiting to be ironed. Martin only wore cotton because wash 'n' wear gave him hives. Glen stepped over them into the wood room and closed the door. He sat on a log and smoked both of the marijuana cigarettes all the way down, holding in the smoke the way he'd been told. Then he waited for it to do something for him but it didn't. He was not happy. Glen stood up to leave, but at that moment the fan went on in the room outside so he sat down again.

He heard Martin set up the ironing board. Then the radio came on. Whenever the announcer said something Martin would talk back. 'First the good news,' the announcer said. 'We're going to get a break tomorrow, fair all day with highs in the seventies.' 'Who cares?' Martin said. The announcer said that peace-seeking efforts had failed somewhere and Martin said, 'Big deal.' A planeload of athletes had been lost in a storm over the Rockies. 'Tough tittie,' said Martin. When the announcer said that a drug used in the treatment of cancer had been shown to cause demented behaviour in laboratory rats, Martin laughed.

There was music. The first piece was a show tune, the second a blues number sung by a woman. Martin turned it off after a couple of verses. 'I can sing better than that,' he said. Substituting da-da-dum for the words, he brought his voice to a controlled scream, not singing the melody but cutting across the line of it, making fun of the blues.

Glen had never heard a worse noise. It became part of the absolute darkness in which he sat, along with the bubbling sigh of the iron and the sulphurous odour of Martin's after-shave and the pall of smoke that filled his little room. He tried to reckon how many shirts might be in that pile. Twenty, thirty. Maybe more. It would take forever.

Maiden Voyage

Twice the horn had sounded, and twice Howard had waved and shouted dumb things at the people below; now he was tired and they still hadn't left the dock. But he waved again anyway, doing his best, when the horn went off a third time.

The boat began to glide out of its slip. Nora leaned against Howard, fanning the air with a long silk scarf. On the dock below, their daughter held up a printed cardboard sign she had brought along for the occasion: HAPPY GOLDEN ANNIVERSARY MOM AND DAD. As the boat picked up speed she dropped the sign and kept pace beside the hull, running and yelling up at them with her hands cupped in front of her mouth. Howard worried. She had been a stupid girl and now she was a stupid woman, perfectly capable of running off the end of the pier. But she stopped finally, and grew smaller and smaller until Howard could barely make her out from the rest of the crowd. He stopped waving and turned to Nora. 'I'm cold. Look at that sky. You said it was going to be warm.'

Nora glanced up at the clouds. They were steely grey like the water below. 'The brochure said this was an ideal time of year in these waters. Those were the exact words.'

'These waters my foot.' Howard gave her the look. The look was enough now, he didn't have to say anything else. Howard walked towards the steps leading to their cabin. Nora followed, quoting from the brochure.

Paper banners hung from wall to wall: 'Welcome Aboard the *William S. Friedman*,' 'Happy Sailing – To Those in the Throes of Love from Those in the Business of Love.' The cabin was bright with fruit and flowers; on the door hung two interlocking life preservers in the shape of hearts.

'Help me to the bathroom, Howard. I'm afraid to walk the way the floor keeps tilting.'

'You don't have your sea legs yet.' Howard took Nora's arm and led her to the door in the corner. 'This is the head. And the floor is called the deck. If we have to be on this boat for a week you might just as well get it right.' He closed the door behind her and stared around the cabin.

There was a big brass latch on the wall. Howard jiggled it and finally slipped it free and the bed fell out on top of him. It took him by surprise and almost knocked him down but he kept his footing and managed to push the bed back into the wall. Then he read the barometer and opened and closed the drawers. The upper drawers contained several bars of soap in miniature packets. Howard slipped a few in his pocket and opened the porthole and stuck his head out. Other people had their heads stuck out too. He battened the porthole and read the barometer again, then picked up the intercom.

'Testing,' he said. 'One two three four testing. Night Raider this is Black Hawk. Testing.'

A voice crackled from the speaker. 'Steward here.'

'It's me. Howard. Just testing. Over and out.'

Nora came back into the cabin and made her way to the couch. 'It's too small in there. I couldn't breathe.'

'I could have told you this wouldn't be any palace.'

'I feel awful. I bet I look awful too.'

Nora's face had gone white. The burst veins in her cheeks and along her upper lip stood out like notations on a map. Her eyes glittered feverishly behind her spectacles. Sick, she looked more than ever like Harry Truman, for whom Howard had not voted.

He sat beside Nora and took her hand. 'You look all right.'

'Do I really?'

'What'd I just say?' He let go of her hand. 'Why do you always think about what you look like?'

'That's not true. I don't.'

Howard paced the cabin. 'Goddam boat.'

'I thought it would be nice, just the two of us.'

A knock came at the door and a man stuck his head in, a large square head divided by a pencil-line moustache. 'Our Golden Couple,' he said, smiling. 'I'm Bill Tweed, your social director.' His body followed his head into the cabin. 'I want to extend a real warm welcome aboard from all of us here on the *Friedman*. I guess you know this is our maiden voyage. Ever been to sea?'

Howard nodded. 'World War Two. Before your time, I guess.' He gestured towards the porthole. 'You could have walked all the way from New York to Paris on top of German submarines. They got three of our ships. Saw it myself.' Howard had been sure they would get him too. He had been sure of it all the way across and never slept at night for knowing it. When the war ended and he got on another ship to come back home he knew that somewhere out there was a German who hadn't gotten the word. His German. Howard had a sense of things catching up with him.

Tweed handed Howard a pamphlet. 'We here on the *Friedman* feel that our business is your pleasure. Just read this over and let us know what you're interested in. We have a number of special programmes for our senior sailors. Can you both walk?'

Howard just stared. 'Yes,' Nora said.

'Wonderful. That's a real help.' He ran his forefinger across his moustache and made a notation against his clipboard. 'A few more questions. Your age, Mr Lewis?'

'I was seventy-five years old on April first. April Fool's Day.'

'"Young", Dad – seventy-five years young. We here on board the *Friedman* don't know the word "old". We don't believe in it. Just think of yourself as three twenty-five-year-olds. And you, Mrs Lewis?'

'I'm seventy-eight.'

'Ah. December-May. Any children?'

'Two. Sharon and Clifford.'

'The poor man's riches. Happy the man who has his quiver full of them. Their occupations?'

Howard handed Nora the pamphlet. 'Clifford is in jail.'

Tweed, still scribbling, looked up from the clipboard. 'I'm so sorry. Of course this is all confidential.'

Nora scowled at Howard. 'Are you married, Mr Tweed?'

'Indeed I am. Married to the single life. My mother keeps telling me I should take a wife but I haven't decided yet whose wife I'm going to take.' He winked at Howard and pocketed his pen. 'Well, then, until dinner. You'll be interested to know who your tablemates will be. Ron and Stella Speroni. Newlyweds from Delaware. Ever been to Delaware?'

'On the train once,' said Howard. 'Didn't get off.'

'A real nice state. Intimate. Anyway, I'm sure that Ron and Stella can learn a lot about love from you, seeing you've piled up a hundred years of it between you.' Smiling at his arithmetic he closed the door.

'Whatever gave you that idea?' said Nora. 'Telling him Clifford was in jail.'

Howard spent most of the dinner talking to Ron. Ron reminded him of a horse. He had a long face and muddy brown eyes and when he laughed his upper lip curled up over his teeth. He worked in his father's jewellery store in Wilmington. They specialized in synthetic diamonds and Ron was willing to bet that Howard couldn't tell the difference between their product and the real McCoy. He had Stella take off the tiara she wore, an intricate silver band dense with stones, and handed it to Howard.

'Go on,' he said. 'If you can tell the difference you can have it.'

Howard turned the tiara over a couple of times, then scraped it along the side of a water glass.

'No fair,' Ron said, snatching it away. 'I already told you it was synthetic.' He stared at his wife constantly as he talked. Stella had platinum hair going brown at the roots and long black fingernails.

She didn't say much; most of the time she sat with her chin cupped in her hand, gazing around at the other tables and scraping her fingernails back and forth over the linen tablecloth. Ron had met her in the shop. She came in to have some earrings converted and one thing led to another. 'She's an incredible person,' Ron said. 'You ought to see her with kids.'

After dinner the waiters moved all the tables out of the centre of the room and the band started to warm up. Tweed walked out to the middle of the dance floor holding a microphone attached to a long wire. The room fell silent.

'Tonight,' Tweed said, 'we have with us what you might call the summer and winter, the Alpha and Omega of human love. Let's hear it for Ron and Stella Speroni, married three days this very afternoon, and for Mom and Dad Lewis, who celebrated their Golden Anniversary last Wednesday.' Everyone clapped.

'We here on the *Friedman* have a special place for our senior sailors. To those who are afraid of time I say: what tastes better than old wine or old cheese? And where the art of love is concerned (Tweed paused) we all know that old wood gives off the most heat.' Everyone laughed. Nora sent a smile around the room. Howard cracked his knuckles under the table. Stella grinned at him and he looked away. Then Ron and Nora and Stella all stood together and he stood too and found himself dancing with Stella. He held her awkwardly as the music began, not knowing what to say and not wanting to look down at all the faces looking up at him.

Stella spoke first. 'You've got strong hands.' She ran a black fingernail across his palm. 'You're very passionate. Look.' She traced a crease running from his wrist to the base of his forefinger.

'Probably comes from my grandfather. He had fourteen kids. He was still grinding them out in his sixties.'

'I have the same thing.' Stella showed him her own palm. Her scent was overwhelming. 'When were you born?'

'April first. April Fool's Day.'

'Aries. The Ram.' Howard could see the dark glimmer of gold in her back teeth.

'I don't know about any rams. I guess I do all right.'

'People like us shouldn't get married. We have too much passion for just one person.'

'Marrying Nora was the smartest thing I ever did.'

'Ron and I have an open marriage.'

Howard turned this over for a moment. He felt adventurous. 'So do me and Nora.'

'Wow, think of that.' Stella stepped backwards. 'You were ahead of your time. You really were.'

'Well, like the man says – you only live once.'

'Me and Ron figure that's the best way of dealing with the problem. You know, instead of sneaking around and all that stuff. Ron is very understanding.'

The music stopped and everyone applauded and Howard led Stella back to the table. He and Nora watched people dance for a while but she wouldn't talk to him and he could tell she was mad about something. Finally she got up and walked outside. He followed and stood silently beside her, leaning against the rail. The rolling swells had flattened out but a mist had fallen over the ship like a screen. Howard reached out and touched Nora's arm. She stiffened.

'Don't touch me.'

Howard drew his arm back.

'I know who you're thinking about,' Nora said.

'All right. Who am I thinking about?'

'Miriam Selby.'

Howard stared over the side of the ship. 'She does look like Miriam, I'll grant you. Can't see where that's any fault of mine.'

'You don't love me. You never have.'

'There you are,' said a voice behind them. 'Sneaking off already, eh? And unchaperoned. We'll have to see about this.' Tweed stepped closer. 'How did you get on with the Speronis?'

'Nice couple,' Nora said. 'Attractive.'

'Youth.' Tweed shook his head. 'A once-in-a-lifetime experience. I just wanted to remind you about the costume party tomorrow night.'

'But we don't have any costumes.'

'Don't worry, Mom. We provide everything. Well then. You two behave yourselves.'

Howard leaned against the rail, watching Tweed move along the deck until he disappeared into the mist.

'Howard, I'm sorry.'

He took Nora's hand.

'Do you love me?' she said.

'Sure. Sure I do.'

'You never say so.' Nora waited but Howard didn't answer. 'It's all right,' she said, leaning against him; 'it doesn't matter.' Howard put his arm around her and stared down over the railing, watching the water, black as oil, slide along the hull of the boat.

When the horn gave the alarm – HAHOOGA HAHOOGA HAHOOGA – Howard came awake knowing that his German had found him. He got out of bed and put on his robe and went out into the companionway. The passage was choked with people asking each other what the horn meant. Just then one of the ship's attendants came through and told everyone not to worry and to go back to bed. Someone had brought a hot plate aboard and left it plugged in and it had started a small fire. Howard was about to go back in the cabin when Ron Speroni came up to him. He wore pyjama tops over striped tuxedo trousers.

'Excuse me, Mr Lewis. Have you seen Stella?'

'No. Why?'

'I just thought maybe you had.'

'You share the same cabin, don't you?'

Speroni nodded. 'She went up on deck for some fresh air. When I woke up after that whistle went off she still wasn't back.'

'When did she go out?'

'About eleven.'

'That was three hours ago.'

'I know.' Speroni looked down at his bare feet. His toes were long and hairy and curled like a monkey's. Howard decided to help him.

'Let's take a look around. Maybe she fell asleep up on deck.'

They went topside and walked along the rail, peering at the rows of empty deck chairs by the misty glow of the running lights. Then, as they approched the stern, a man's voice came to them, fruity, disembodied, chuckling portentously. They looked around. They saw nothing. Then came the woman's voice, murmuring and low, suddenly breaking into laughter unmistakably Stella's.

The voices came from the lifeboat hanging across the stern. Speroni leaned forward, trembling slightly, his arms rigid at his sides, his eyes fixed on the darkness above the boat. Howard reached out and took him by the elbow. Speroni turned to him, his mouth twitching, and Howard felt him yield. He walked Speroni around the bow to the other side of the boat. Under the lights Speroni's cheeks shone like wet pavement. Howard looked out over the water.

'She didn't fall overboard,' Speroni said. 'She's safe. That's the main thing.'

Howard nodded.

'Don't get the wrong idea. Stella's very moral, really.'

'I'm sure she is.'

'You ought to see her with kids.'

'I was thinking,' Howard said, 'maybe this is a stage she's going through.'

'Maybe.' Speroni rubbed at his eyes with the back of his sleeve. 'I'm cold. Coming down?'

'Later. You go on ahead.'

Speroni took a couple of steps, then turned. 'You really think this is a stage she's going through?'

'Could be.'

'That's what I think, too. I just wouldn't want you to get the wrong impression. Stella's a beautiful person. Very spiritual.'

The mist was lifting. A few stars began to appear, blinking remotely. Howard wondered what Aries looked like. He heard voices and footsteps and Stella's laugh and looked up. 'Hello, Stella. Mr Tweed.'

Tweed looked up and down the deck. 'Evening, Dad. Stargazing, are you? We're never too old for dreams.' He held his watch up to his face. 'It's late,' he said. 'I'll wish you goodnight.'

'Hi, Howard.' Stella leaned on the railing. 'Bill's a real card but a little bit of him goes a long way, if you know what I mean. So what brings you up here at this hour?'

'Just getting some fresh air.'

'Look – the stars are out. Don't you wish you could reach out and pick them like flowers?'

'I hadn't thought of it.'

'Life. That's the way life is to me, Howard. You keep picking things until you get the one thing that really matters. Tell me about your great love.'

'My great love?'

'How did you meet her?' Stella did a pirouette, one hand held aloft. 'Was it at a dance? What was she wearing?'

'Me and Nora were friends since we were kids.'

'Not Nora, Howard. She's your wife.'

'That's what I'm saying.'

'Come on, Howard. Anyone can see she's not your great love. What did she look like, Howard?'

Howard glanced at Stella, then stared back over the railing. 'Nora's been good to me. Marrying Nora was the smartest thing I ever did.'

'What did she call you, Howard?'

'It don't last, the other thing. You can't trust it.'

'What did she call you?'

Howard scratched his wrist. 'Sunshine.'

'Sunshine. That's beautiful, Howard. That's really beautiful. I'll bet that's what you were, too. Just for her.'

'You can't trust it.'

'So what? What else is there?'

'There's a lot else. A lot.'

'But what?'

'Don't you think you ought to be with Ron instead of tearing around up here? There's certain considerations, you know, like people's feelings.'

'Considerations? No thanks, Howard. That's what they make cages out of.' Stella stepped back and gave Howard's arm a friendly squeeze. 'Don't you go and get stuffy on me, now. I know you.'

Howard went to the costume party as a buccaneer. A sort of gentleman pirate. Actually the costume was that of an eighteenth-century squire – ruffled shirt front, brocade jacket, and kneepants with buckled shoes – but Nora had made him an eyepatch and Tweed lent him the captain's ceremonial sword. Nora came as Venus. She wore a flowing toga and Tweed gave her some plastic leaves to weave into her hair. He said they gave the costume a Greek accent.

They had their own table. The Speronis sat across the room, Stella wearing her tiara and below it a low-cut peasant girl's smock with billowing sleeves. Ron had on a Confederate officer's uniform from the Civil War. He looked unhappy.

After dinner the room went dark. A few moments later red shafts of light shot out from the corners and began moving over the dance floor. Someone played a long mounting roll on a snare drum. A white spotlight blazed out on the middle of the floor and Tweed stepped into it.

'Friends, before we go any further I just wonder if we couldn't all take a moment and think about why we're here. I'm not talking about old Sol up there, who was kind enough to come out and give us a big smile today. I'm not even talking about our excellent cuisine, painstakingly prepared for us courtesy of Monsieur and Madame Grimes.'

The spotlight moved over to the door of the kitchen. The cooks waved and smiled and the spotlight raced back to Tweed, who held up his arms for silence. The spotlight jerked to the right and Tweed sidestepped back into focus. 'I'm talking about what really brings us here – I'm talking about love. That's right, love. A word you don't hear much these days but I for one am not ashamed to say it – and to say it again – LOVE! And I'll bet you're not either. L-O-V-E – LOVE!'

A few people joined in. 'Love,' they said.

'All together! Come on now, let them hear you all the way back home. L-O-V-E – '

'LOVE!' everyone shouted.

'Now your hearts are talking. That's it – love, the artillery of heaven. We here on the *Friedman* like to believe that love still calls the shots in this battered and bruised old world of ours. And we think we can prove it. Because if two individuals can stack up a century of love between them, well, as far as I personally am concerned the smartalecks will just have to go home and think of something else to try and make us give up on. Because we're sure as heck not going to give up on love. You know who I'm talking about. Let's hear it for Mom and Dad Lewis. Let's hear it for a hundred years of love!'

The sound of clapping filled the room. Howard covered his unpatched eye as it filled with hot silver light. Someone was tugging at his arm.

'Stand up!' Nora hissed.

Howard stood up. Nora was smiling and bowing, the green plastic leaves in her hair bobbing up and down. Howard groped behind him for his chair but Nora clamped down even harder on his arm.

The spotlight returned to Tweed. 'Maybe we can persuade these two fine individuals to say a word to us. How about it, Mom and Dad? How did you do it?'

Howard shrank back but Nora pulled him along. He let her lead him to the middle of the room, unsettled by her forcefulness.

Nora took the microphone. She smiled, her spectacles glittering in the spotlight: 'Girls, don't ever let yourselves get run down and go to pieces. A little exercise every day. Don't ever let the sun set on a quarrel.' She chuckled and looked at Howard. 'And don't be afraid to stand up and give your man what for every once in a while.' She ducked her head at the applause.

Howard took the microphone. He stared at it as if it were something he was being asked to eat. 'Nothing to it,' he said. 'You just go from day to day and before you know it fifty years are up.' He tried to think of something else to say but he couldn't. That was all there was. He frowned at the microphone, the silence building as it dropped slowly to his side.

Tweed started another round of clapping. 'Thank you,' he said, retrieving the microphone. He nodded in the direction of the bandstand. A single clarinet began to play 'The Anniversary Waltz'. The spotlight mellowed.

Howard understood that he was expected to dance with Nora. As he took her hand the boat plunged into a swell and the deck pitched. Nora stumbled but caught herself. Howard thought they should probably be talking to each other.

'You're getting your sea legs,' he said.

Nora moved close to him, pressed her cheek to his. His unpatched eye ached. Howard turned slowly around to escape Stella's grin, and the winking of her tiara in the moving red light.

Worldly Goods

Davis and his dinner partner were waiting for a taxi one night when she saw a pinball arcade across the street. She insisted they play a few games before going home and when Davis reminded her that it was getting late she said, 'Oh, don't be such an old fuddy-duddy.' Though he did not see the woman again, that remark bothered him.

Not long afterwards he was looking at secondhand cars and saw, in the back of the lot, a powerful automobile just like one his best friend had owned when they were boys; the same make, even the same year. The salesman admired it with Davis for a moment, then tried to interest him in a newer car, an ugly grey sedan with lots of trunk room. Suddenly Davis felt angry. He went back to the first car, worked the gears for a while, then bought it and drove it home.

That Saturday Davis took the car out to Long Island. On the highway he passed a similar model, a few years older, and he and the other driver honked at each other.

The next morning Davis decided to show the car to some people he knew from back home. He had been an usher at their wedding, and when he first came to town he had stayed with them for a few months while he was looking for a place of his own.

There was a peep-hole in the door and after Davis rang the bell he smiled at it. He heard whispers. 'I wish you'd called,' the husband said as he opened the door.

The apartment smelled sour, and dirty ashtrays were stacked on the end tables next to half-empty glasses with limp slices of lemon floating in them. The husband was mute, the wife nervously chatty. Davis wondered why they had not invited him to the party.

'I bought a car,' Davis said.

'You're kidding,' the wife said. 'I didn't even know you could drive.'

'It's right outside,' Davis said.

They laughed when they saw it. The husband stood on the sidewalk with his arms folded, smiling and shaking his head. 'Hot dog!' said the wife. 'If anybody else told me this baby belonged to you I would never believe them. Not in a million years.'

Before long Davis began to wish he hadn't bought the car. It was not in good condition. Patches of rust showed through the paint, and the engine was filthy and out of phase. Gasoline went through it like pork through a duck. Richie, the boy across the street, offered to fix it up but Davis thought that he had already carried things far enough. 'I'll think about it,' he said, really intending to drive the car the way it was until it fell apart.

Soon after he bought the car Davis collided with a Japanese compact. He had been moving forward and the compact had been backing up. The cars came together with an awful grinding sound. Davis had seen few women as tall as the one who emerged from the compact, and as she uncoiled from her seat he had the sense of watching a biological process.

Together they circled the cars. His, tanklike, had bellied up on her trunk, folding it like an accordion. She had punched out his headlight and crumpled his right fender. 'I should have stayed home today,' the woman said. She was wearing yellow designer sunglasses and her hair was covered with a yellow scarf. She had bony wrists and her knees, fully exposed beneath the hem of her blue dress, were also bony. As she spoke she chipped away methodically at a ridge of paint on the trunk of the compact, using her fingernails like tools. 'I'll probably get all the blame,' she said. 'You know how they always talk about women drivers.'

'Don't worry,' Davis said, 'it wasn't all your fault. I should have been paying closer attention.'

'Oh, but they'll claim it's my fault in the end,' she said bitterly.

Davis thought that one of them should call the police; perhaps they could make some assignment of guilt. He called from a grocery store, watching the woman as he talked. She sat in his car, crying. When he joined her again Davis tried to comfort her by pointing out that though her car was damaged she herself was not. 'That's the important thing,' he said.

'Not to my husband.' She looked at her watch. 'I can't wait any longer.'

'The police should be here soon.'

'But I have a business meeting. I mustn't be late. I *can't* be late.'

'We really should be here when the police come,' Davis said. Then, thinking her business meeting a fabrication, he added: 'There's nothing to be afraid of.'

'My husband beats me,' she said, 'when I don't make enough money.' She insisted that it was not necessary for both of them to wait for the police, that they had only to report the accident to their insurance companies. Finally Davis agreed, and they exchanged names and licence numbers. Before the women left she gave Davis a brochure with her card attached. He backed his machine off hers and she drove away, tyres squealing under the pressure of collapsed metal. Davis glanced through the brochure while he waited for the police. 'Clara!' it said on the cover: 'Concepts For Spacious Living.' There was a picture of a woman, not Clara, sitting in a chrome chair on an Oriental rug in the middle of an otherwise empty barn.

The claims adjuster wore a silver whistle around his neck. When he noticed Davis staring at it he explained that it was for muggers. 'Last month alone,' he said, 'there were three robberies on my street. Incidents is what the police call them, but you lose your money just the same. I don't know, maybe it's all this busing – the you-know-whats are taking over. But here I am telling you, a Southerner. You have personally seen all this yourself.'

Davis did not take to the suggestion that he had anything in common with this man, or to the implication that by virtue of being from the South he was bound to extend hospitality to other people's hatreds. 'I wouldn't know,' he said. 'I've been here a long time.'

'Far be it from me to cast racial slurs,' the adjuster said. 'You don't have to tell me where that leads to. Not a day goes by that I don't say "Live and let live!" But these people will take your wallet and shoot you in the head.' The adjuster leaned forward. 'I see that I am offending you. Forgive me. But when I walk in the street at night I hear noises. That's why I said those things. Fear. I admit it, I'm afraid.'

Davis recited the facts of the accident and the adjuster took them down on a form, writing in long, rhythmic strokes. Davis read the cartoons under the glass desk top while he waited for the adjuster to catch up. In one cartoon the judge was questioning a woman with her arm in a sling. 'How far,' the judge asked, 'have you been able to raise your arm since the accident?' Frowning with pain, the woman raised her hand shoulder-high. 'And how far could you raise it *before* the accident?' Brightly she held her hand above her head. Another cartoon showed three gypsies leaning together and shedding tears while the one in the middle sawed at a violin. 'Oh, *do* tell us your story!' the caption said.

'This is good,' the adjuster said when Davis had finished. 'This is very good. If they get funny we will eat them alive.' He pushed a card across the desk. 'Here is our doctor. The sooner you see him the better.'

'I have my own doctor. Anyway I feel fine. We didn't really crash, just sort of bumped.'

'Today you feel fine, okay. But what about next year? I have seen a lot of cervical sprain in my time and I can tell you it is no laughing matter.'

'You mean whiplash?'

'Cervical sprain is I believe what they say in the medical business.'

Davis would never be able to claim that he had whiplash. It was too public. People made jokes about it. 'I feel fine,' he said again, and pushed the card back. The adjuster put it away with a shrug and gave Davis the report to sign. Davis read it through, shaking his head.

'You've completely twisted my words around,' he said. 'You make it seem like a hit-and-run.'

'Show me where I said hit-and-run. I did not say any such thing. You told me she left the scene of the accident and that is what I said, no more.'

'But I told her she could leave.'

'You told her she could leave. Oh boy. I don't care what you told her, she should not have left the scene of the accident and that is the whole point.'

'I know what you want,' Davis said. 'You want to throw the blame on her so the other company has to pay everything.'

'No!' the adjuster said. 'I am only trying to protect you. Maybe she will try to make money out of this – it happens every day.'

'You even make it sound as if the accident were her fault.'

'You were driving at a lawful rate of speed and she backed into you is what I have there. Legally speaking she is at fault.'

'All I want,' Davis said, 'is for you to write down what happened the way I tell it to you. I was there and you weren't.'

The adjuster shook his head and sighed as he made up the new form. 'Terrible,' he said. 'This leaves you with no protection.'

Davis signed it and handed it back. 'That's all right. It's the truth.'

'Maybe, but I know a mistake when I see one. So be it. We will need two estimates.'

Davis was going into a drugstore a block from the insurance company when he heard someone calling him. It was the adjuster. He had been running. His face was streaming and the whistle bounced on his chest. He looked like a coach. 'Listen,' he said, 'I've been thinking maybe I insulted you.'

'You didn't insult me.'

'Then let me buy you a cup of coffee. Or a Coke, whatever.'

Davis was not due at work for another half hour, and simply did not have the energy to lie to the man. So he sat at the counter and sipped an iced tea and listened to the adjuster tell about the Southern friends he had had in the Marine Corps. It surprised Davis to hear that he had been a Marine, and he probably wouldn't have believed it if the adjuster had not taken from his wallet several photographs and spread them across the counter-top.

'This is Johnny Lee,' the adjuster said, stabbing his finger at one of the soldiers in a group picture. 'Related to the great general, Robert E. Lee. Every night we would sit up, the two of us, and talk about life. We had different philosophies but we were like brothers.' He put the photographs away, looking hard at each one as he did so.

Davis's cup was empty but he pulled on the straw, making a commotion so the adjuster would know he was ready to leave.

'What happened in the office today,' the adjuster said, 'I was doing my job, I was trying to help.'

'I understand that,' Davis said, standing up. Together they walked outside.

'It wasn't lies,' the adjuster said, 'not the way you thought. That is how we make out an accident report – for protection. But I know you don't see it like that. You are a Southern gentleman.'

'I was brought up in the South.'

'Down there you have all that tradition. Honour. Up here – ' he swept his hand around – 'all they know is grab. Well,' the adjuster stepped back, 'I won't detain you.' He said this in a formal way and gave a slight bow which he evidently thought to be courtly. Davis attributed the gesture to some movie the adjuster had seen with belles and gallants and pillared houses.

A man who worked with Davis recommended Leo the Lion so he took the car there for an estimate. Leo the Lion was a perfectly made, very small man. His mechanic's overalls were tailored to nip in at the waist and flare at the legs. His top two buttons were undone. He paid no attention to Davis when Davis told him that all he wanted was the dents pounded out and the headlight replaced. Instead he made Davis get down and look at the underside of the fender. It was crusted and black. There were wires everywhere. Davis tugged at his trousers, trying to keep the cuffs off the floor.

'See?' Leo the Lion said. 'The metal's just about rusted through. We start banging on that and it'll fall apart.' He turned and walked towards his office. Davis got to his feet and followed. There was a lion painted in velvet over the desk. A large stuffed lion was seated on one of the chairs and another peered out from behind the dusty leaves of a philodendron.

Leo the Lion took several manuals down from the shelves and made calculations. He showed them to Davis.

'Nine hundred dollars,' Davis said. 'That seems very high. Why do you have to repaint the whole car?'

'Because when we find another fender it's going to be a different colour. We can't match the colour you've got, they don't make it any more. That's why.' He put the manuals away. Then he explained to Davis that he might not be able to do the job at all. Cars like that were rare and it wouldn't be easy to locate a fender for it. But his computer was plugged in to salvage yards all over the country, so if anybody could do it he could.

'Nine hundred dollars,' Davis said.

'You can probably get it done cheaper if you look around,' Leo the Lion said. 'I wouldn't vouch for the work, though. That car's cherry except for the fender. It's a classic. People are investing in classics these days. They put them on blocks and run the engine once a week, then take them to rallies.'

Davis folded the estimate sheet and said that he would be in touch, thinking that no way was he going to spend nine hundred dollars getting a fender fixed. As he drove away he saw another shop up the street and took the car in there. The mechanic told him it wasn't worth the trouble and offered to take it off his hands for three hundred dollars.

'It's worth more than that,' Davis said. 'How much to fix it?'

'Twelve hundred dollars.'

'That's a lot of money.'

The mechanic laughed. He monkeyed around with the figures and brought the total down to a thousand. He explained the difficulties he would have repairing the car. 'Oh, all right,' he said suddenly, as though Davis had been trying to beat him down, and made up another estimate for seven hundred dollars. 'That's my absolute bottom price,' he said. 'I can't do it for less and come out ahead.'

As Davis was leaving the shop the mechanic ran towards the car, waving a piece of paper. Davis assumed that he had come up with another set of figures. 'You forgot this,' the mechanic said, and pushed the first estimate through the window. Seeing that Davis did not understand, he explained how Davis could make himself an easy five hundred. He spoke with an angry kind of patience, the way people back home spoke to Negroes who couldn't follow simple instructions. Davis was furious. He crumpled the paper and threw it out of the window. For a time he considered reporting the man to an appropriate agency but decided against it. He would look like a whiner, and anyway he had no real proof.

A few days later the adjuster called Davis at work. 'I trust this is not a busy time for you,' he said.

Actually this was the busiest part of the day, but Davis did not wish to seem rude so he said nothing.

'Hello?' the adjuster said.

'I'm here,' Davis said. 'Did you get the estimates?'

'I did indeed receive your estimates only yesterday by the mail.'

'They seemed high to me. If you like I'll get some more.'

The adjuster was not calling about the estimates. A more important matter had come up which he thought he should not discuss over the telphone. Davis agreed to drop in later. When he hung up his mouth was dry and his pulse racing. He knew that guilty people felt like this and decided to have the adjuster withdraw his claim that very day.

'That will not be possible at this time,' the adjuster said when Davis advised him of his intentions. 'This woman has filed a claim against you which if she wins is going to cost a lot.' He slid a form across the desk and when Davis had read it he asked, 'Do you understand?'

'No.'

'What she is saying is you ran into her because you were not watching where you were going and also you were driving at an illegal rate of speed.'

'But that's not true!'

'She is claiming three thousand dollars in damages.'

Davis thought that was absurd, but the adjuster did not find it so. 'She is not saying anything about personal injury, thank God. It would be a mess. I could tell you stories.'

Davis closed his eyes.

'She is saying you told her, quote unquote: "Don't worry, it wasn't your fault, I wasn't paying attention."' The adjuster looked over the top of the paper. 'Which is a complete falsehood of course.'

'Not exactly.'

The adjuster lowered the paper. 'You told her this?'

'Not those exact words,' Davis said. 'It meant nothing, I was just being polite.' He looked down at the desk, at a cartoon of a man standing in front of a jury and displaying an empty sleeve where his right arm should have been. From behind, the outline of his missing arm was clear beneath the jacket, and his hand poked out below. 'That's the truth,' Davis said.

'Polite! Oh boy!' The adjuster laughed, then stopped and peered closely at Davis. 'Forgive me,' he said, 'but you don't look so hot. You feel okay? You want some water?'

'I'm all right,' Davis said.

'Come on, I'll buy you an iced tea. The other day I talked, now it's your turn.'

'I have to get back to work,' Davis said. 'What are we going to do?'

'What I told you before. You say she backed up without looking and hit you and left the scene of the accident. None of this stuff about you told her she could go. No more polite. This is time for impolite.'

'That would contradict the first report I gave you.'

'What report?' The adjuster took a form out of his desk and began tearing it into long shreds. 'What report?' he repeated.

'You didn't turn it in?'

'You want a miracle? You want me to turn in what does not exist? So – you have a sense of humour, you're smiling.'

Richie, the boy from across the street, came over with a friend. 'I can fix that light for you,' he said. 'Fifty dollars. It won't look like much but you'll be legal.' His friend stood behind him staring at the car. Rust was gathering in the folds of the metal. 'Thirty for the light,' said Richie, 'twenty for labour.' The boy with him suddenly flipped over on his back and crawled under the car.

'I don't know,' Davis said. 'I'm considering having it done right.'

'That'll cost you. It's not going to be easy, finding parts for this, but I guess you won't have to sweat the bucks, you can put the screws to your insurance company. It'd be worth it, fixing this car up. I can do it if you want. I'll give you a good price.'

Davis could see nothing of the boy under the car except the soles of his shoes. One was brown and the other was black. He had no idea what the boy could be doing under there. 'I'll take it into consideration,' Davis said.

Richie kicked his friend's shoes and the boy rolled out from underneath the car. 'I can give you an estimate,' Richie said importantly. 'Just let me know.'

'Where are you going to find the parts?'

Richie and his friend looked at each other and grinned.

Davis tried to read after dinner that night but the story made no sense to him. He could not understand why the people did what they did or said what they said. Finally he decided to visit his friends from home.

They were doing the dishes when Davis arrived. He watched TV in the living room and when they joined him he told them all about the accident, about Clara and the adjuster and the crooked mechanic. What should he do?

The wife yawned. 'Search me,' she said. 'I've never been in an accident.'

She went to bed and her husband got up and began tidying the room. 'I'm not impressed with this display of virtue,' he said. 'If you really want to do something worthwhile why didn't you help us with the dishes? In the five months you stayed here with us you never once offered to wash the dishes.'

He followed Davis to the door. 'Nothing is good enough for you,' he said. 'When you were looking at apartments they were always too big or too small, too far from work or too close to the traffic. It doesn't take anybody five months to find an apartment. And when we took you to parties you acted bored. Oh, what the hell. I'm sorry!' He shouted down the stairs: 'Call me tomorrow!'

The thing to do, Davis thought, was to sit down and reason with Clara. She had seemed ridiculous to him but not dishonest. Probably her adjuster had gotten to her, or her husband. He could imagine how someone like her might get confused trying to do both the right thing and the pleasing thing.

He considered calling Clara, but her husband might answer and hang up, a strange man asking for his wife. Davis knew that somewhere there was someone capable of jealousy over Clara, and it was just possible that she had married him. Finally he copied down the address from the brochure and drove there.

Davis parked across the street. The houses in this neighbourhood were very expensive, which irritated him. What could people like that, who could afford to live in such a house, possibly want with another three thousand dollars?

A long shadow passed across the drapes in the front window. It might have been Clara or it might have been her husband. To marry someone as tall as Clara, and beat her, you would have to be big – really big. But it was not this consideration that kept Davis in his car. He was thinking that he shouldn't go around like a child, without keeping his eyes open, without thinking twice about everything. He ought to have learned that by now. If he got out of his car and went up to Clara's door, they would find a way of using his honesty against him as they had used his good manners against him. He pitied her and he pitied himself.

Oh Clara, he thought, why can't we tell the truth?

After Davis got the cheque he took the car down to Leo the Lion. The other man was cheaper but Davis thought he would cut corners. Richie was too young and inexperienced and probably wouldn't have the right tools. Davis did not care for the way Leo the Lion swaggered but he took it as a sign of pride, and in his experience proud people did good work.

When Davis went down to pick it up he was surprised at how beautiful the car was. People on the shop floor whistled when Leo the Lion drove it up from the basement parking lot. The colour was brighter than Davis had thought from the sample book, brighter than he would have wished, but everyone else seemed to like it.

'The lock on the passenger side is broken,' Leo the Lion said. 'The brakes aren't good for more than another five thousand miles. She runs fine, though.' He sent Davis off with a small stuffed lion and a bumper sticker – 'Treat Yourself to a Leo Today.'

The motor had been cleaned and fine-tuned, and Davis noticed the difference immediately. The car was faster, more responsive. The engine made a throaty, bubbling sound and banged like a pistol whenever he down-shifted. On his way home a bunch of boys pulled up next to Davis at a red light. Their car had wide tyres and was raised in back. The driver gunned his engine several times. Davis fed his own engine a little gas to keep it turning over and it popped loudly. The boys started yelling things at him, not mean but playful. Davis stared straight ahead. When the light changed the other car laid rubber, and the boys in the back seat looked over their shoulders at him.

The adjuster called one last time. He called Davis at home, and Davis resented it. 'Listen,' the adjuster said, 'I am very intuitive and I have this picture of you brooding all the time. You have to remember that up here is different from down there. Down there you can do things right. You have honour, what you call the gentleman code.'

'It's the same there as here,' Davis said. 'It's no different anywhere.'

'You got scrunched,' the adjuster said, 'and you got paid for getting scrunched, which seems to me fair.'

'I agree,' Davis said.

'Which also calls for a celebration,' the adjuster said, who then astonished Davis by inviting him to dinner on the following Wednesday. 'You will like my wife,' said the adjuster. 'She is very interesting with a degree in music. Do you enjoy music?'

'Not especially,' Davis said, though he did.

'No matter. With my wife you can talk about anything and she can talk right back. She cooks the old way. In twenty years cooking like this will be a memory, only a memory.'

Davis thought that he could very well imagine the kinds of things he would be expected to put in his mouth. He told the adjuster that he was busy on Wednesday and when the adjuster suggested Thursday, he said that he was busy that night as well. 'You will find that my wife and me are flexible,' the adjuster said. 'Whatever you say will be fine with us. You name it. You say when.'

Davis could not speak. The silence gathered and he could not think of anything to say to break it with.

'Correct me,' the adjuster said, 'but maybe you would rather not come.'

Davis switched the receiver to his left hand.

'I hope,' the adjuster went on, 'this is not because you hold against me anything I have done.'

'No, it's nothing you've done,' Davis said, and thought: it's what you are.

'What I did, I was trying to help.'

'I know.'

'I am inviting you to break bread, I am inviting you to a *banquet*, and all the time you are thinking: "He made me lie, he made me go against my honour." That is the way it has always been with you people. There you have the whole story. Listen, such pure people like you should not get into accidents.' The adjuster went on and on; the complaint seemed old, a song, a chant, the truth of it not in the words but in the tone itself. Finally he stopped, and apologized, and Davis said that there was no need. He thanked the adjuster for his help and hung up.

On Sunday morning he went to the corner for a newspaper and when he came back he saw that the hood of his car was open. One boy was leaning over the engine and another was sitting in the front seat with the door open. The radio was on. 'Hey, you kids!' Davis yelled, and they looked up. The one under the hood was Richie. 'I didn't know it was you,' Davis said, coming up to them.

'I see you had it fixed,' Richie said. 'How much it put you back?'

Davis named a price three hundred dollars less than what he had paid, not wanting to look like a sucker. Apparently even this figure was not low enough. 'Jeez,' said the boy in the front seat, and rolled his eyes.

'What the hell.' Richie closed the hood harder than was necessary. 'As long as it wasn't your money.'

Davis had the lock fixed but still he worried. There were quite a few souped-up cars in the neighbourhood and he had to stop himself from going to the window when one of them started up outside or passed in the street. He heard them in his sleep. Often they entered his dreams. This went on for weeks after the car was stolen.

One night, in a prankish and suicidal mood, the thieves drove Davis's car up and down the street at a terrific speed. Davis stirred in recognition; his dream changed, delivered him to a flat and lonely stretch of road outside Shreveport. He was in the old car with his friend. A half-empty bottle rolled on the seat between them. His friend had the pedal pushed to the floor: the white line trembled like a blown thread between the lights, and the tall roadside pines ticked by like fenceposts. They were singing, heads thrown back and teeth bared.

The thieves were singing too. They turned at the end of the block and made another pass down the street. Outside Davis's window they shifted down, and the engine detonated. Davis bolted up from sleep, hand over breast, as if his own heart had misfired.

Wingfield

When we arrived at the camp they pulled us off the buses and made us do push-ups in the parking lot. The asphalt was hot and tar stuck to our noses. They made fun of our clothes and took them away from us. They shaved our heads until little white scars showed through, then filled our arms with boots and belts and helmets and punctured them with needles.

In the middle of the night they came to our barracks and walked up and down between us as we stood by our bunks. They looked at us. If we looked at them they said, 'Why are you looking at me?' and made us do push-ups. If you didn't act right they made your life sad.

They divided us into companies, platoons, and squads. In my squad were Wingfield and Parker and seven others. Parker was a wise guy, my friend. I never saw anything get him down except malaria. Wingfield, before the military took responsibility for him, had been kept alive somewhere in North Carolina. When he was in a condition to talk his voice oozed out of him thick and slow and sweet. His eyes when he had them open were the palest blue. Most of the time they were closed.

He often fell asleep while he polished his boots, and once while he was shaving. They ordered him to paint baseboards and he curled up in the corner and let the baseboards take care of themselves. They found him with his head resting on his outstretched arm, his mouth open; a string of paint had dried between the brush and the floor.

In the afternoons they showed us films: from these we learned how to maintain our jeeps, how to protect our teeth from decay, how to treat foreigners, and how to sheathe ourselves against boils, nervous disorders, madness, and finally the long night of the blind. The foreigners wore shiny suits and carried briefcases. They smiled as they directed our soldiers to their destinations. They would do the same for us if we could remember how to ask them questions. As we repeated the important phrases to ourselves we could hear the air whistling in and out of Wingfield's mouth, rattling in the depths of his throat.

Wingfield slept as they showed us how our weapons worked, and what plants we could browse on if we got lost or ran out of food. Sometimes they caught him and made him stand up; he would smile shyly, like a young girl, and find something to lean against, and go back to sleep. He slept while we marched, which other soldiers could do; but other soldiers marched straight when they were supposed to turn and turned when they were supposed to march straight. They marched into trees and ditches and walls, they fell into holes. Wingfield could march around corners while asleep. He could sing the cadence and double-time at port arms without opening his eyes. You had to see it to believe it.

At the end of our training they drove us deep into the woods and set our company against another. To make the numbers even they gave the other side six of our men, Wingfield among them. He did not want to go but they made him. Then they handed out blank ammunition and coloured scarves, blue for us and red for them.

The presence of these two colours made the woods dangerous. We tiptoed from bush to bush, crawled on our stomachs through brown needles under the stunted pines. The bark of the trees was sweating amber resin but you couldn't stop and stare. If you dawdled and daydreamed you would be taken in ambush. When soldiers with red scarves walked by we hid and shot them from behind and sent them to the parking lot, which was no longer a parking lot but the land of the dead.

A wind sprang up, bending and shaking the trees; their shadows lunged at us. Then darkness fell over the woods, sudden as a trap closing. Here and there we saw a stab of flame and heard a shot, but soon this scattered firing fell away. We pitched tents and posted guards; sat in silence and ate food from cans, cold. Our heartbeats echoed in our helmets.

Parker threw rocks. We heard them thumping the earth, breaking brittle branches as they fell. Someone yelled at him to stop, and Parker pointed where the shout came from.

Then we blackened our faces and taped our jingling dog tags, readied ourselves to raid. We slipped into the darkness as though we belonged there, like shadows. Gnats swarmed, mosquitos stung us but we did not slap; we were that stealthy. We went on until we saw, not far ahead, a fire. A fire! The fools had made a fire! Parker put his hand over his mouth and shook his head from side to side, signifying laughter.

We only had to find the guards to take the camp by surprise. I found one right away, mumbling and exclaiming in his sleep, his rifle propped against a tree. It was Wingfield. With hatred and contempt and joy I took him from behind, and as I drew it across his throat I was wishing that my finger was a knife. Twisting in my arms, he looked into my black face and said, 'Oh my God,' as though I was no impostor but Death himself.

Then we stormed the camp, firing into the figures lumped in sleeping bags, firing into the tents and into the shocked white faces at the tent flaps. It was exactly the same thing that happened to us a year and three months later as we slept beside a canal in the Mekong Delta, a few kilometres from Ben Tré.

We were sent home on leave when our training ended, and when we regrouped, several of us were missing, sick or AWOL or sent overseas to fill the ranks of units picked clean in the latest fighting. Wingfield was among them. I never saw him again and I never expected to. From now on his nights would be filled with shadows like me, and against such enemies what chance did Wingfield have?

Parker got malaria two weeks before the canal attack, and was still in the hospital when it happened. When he got out they sent him to another unit. He wrote letters to me but I never answered them.

They were full of messages for people who weren't alive any more, and I thought it would be a good thing if he never knew this. Then he would lose only one friend instead of twenty-six. At last the letters stopped and I did not hear from him again for nine years, when he knocked on my door one evening just after I'd come home from work.

He had written my parents, he explained, and they had told him where I was living. He said that he and his wife and daughter were just passing through on their way to Canada, but I knew better. There were other ways to go than this and travellers always took them. He wanted an accounting.

Parker's daughter played with my dogs and his wife cooked steaks in the barbecue pit while we drank beer and talked and looked each other over. He was still cheerful, but in a softer, slower way, like a jovial uncle of the boy he'd been. After we ate we lay on the blanket until the bugs got to our ankles and the child began to whine. Parker's wife carried the dishes into the house and washed them while we settled on the steps. The light from the kitchen window laid a garish patch upon the lawn. Things crawled towards it under the grass. Parker asked the question he'd come to ask and then sat back and waited while I spoke name after name into the night. When I finished he said, 'Is that all? What about Washington?'

'I told you. He got home all right.'

'You're sure about that?'

'Of course I'm sure.'

'You ought to get married,' Parker said, standing up. 'You take yourself too seriously. What the hell, right?'

Parker's daughter was lying on the living-room floor next to my golden retriever, who growled softly in his sleep as Parker lifted the girl and slung her over his shoulder. His wife took my arm and leaned against me as we walked out to the car. 'I feel so comfortable with you,' she said. 'You remind me of my grandfather.'

'By the way,' Parker said, 'do you remember Wingfield?'

'He was with that first bunch that got sent over,' I said. 'I don't think he made it back.'

'Who told you that?'

'Nobody. I just don't think he did.'

'You're wrong. I saw him.' Parker shifted the girl to his other shoulder. 'That's what I was going to tell you. I was in Charlotte six months ago and I saw him in the train station, sitting on a bench.'

'You didn't.'

'Oh yes I did.'

'How was he? What did he say?'

'He didn't say anything. I was in a hurry and he looked so peaceful I just couldn't bring myself to wake him up.'

'But it was definitely him?'

'It was Wingfield all right. He had his mouth open.'

I waved at their car until it made the turn at the end of the street. Then I rummaged through the garbage and filled the dogs' bowls with the bones and gristle Parker's wife had thrown away. As I inspected the dishes she had washed the thought came to me that this was a fussy kind of thing for a young man to do.

I opened a bottle of wine and went outside. The coals in the cooking pit hissed and flushed as the wind played over them, pulling away the smoke in tight spirals. I sensed the wings of the bats above me, wheeling in the darkness. Like a soldier on leave, like a boy who knows nothing at all, like a careless and go-to-hell fellow I drank to them. Then I drank to the crickets and locusts and cicadas who purred so loudly that the earth itself seemed to be snoring. I drank to the snoring earth, to the closed eye of the moon, to the trees that nodded and sighed: until, already dreaming, I fell back upon the blanket.

In the Garden of the North American Martyrs

When she was young, Mary saw a brilliant and original man lose his job because he had expressed ideas that were offensive to the trustees of the college where they both taught. She shared his views, but did not sign the protest petition. She was, after all, on trial herself – as a teacher, as a woman, as an interpreter of history.

Mary watched herself. Before giving a lecture she wrote it out in full, using the arguments and often the words of other, approved writers, so that she would not by chance say something scandalous. Her own thoughts she kept to herself, and the words for them grew faint as time went on; without quite disappearing they shrank to remote, nervous points, like birds flying away.

When the department turned into a hive of cliques, Mary went about her business and pretended not to know that people hated each other. To avoid seeming bland she let herself become eccentric in harmless ways. She took up bowling, which she learned to love, and founded the Brandon College chapter of a society dedicated to restoring the good name of Richard III. She memorized comedy routines from records and jokes from books; people groaned when she rattled them off, but she did not let that stop her, and after a time the groans became the point of the jokes. They were a kind of tribute to Mary's willingness to expose herself.

In fact no one at the college was safer than Mary, for she was making herself into something institutional, like a custom, or a mascot – part of the college's idea of itself.

Now and then she wondered whether she had been too careful. The things she said and wrote seemed flat to her, pulpy, as though someone else had squeezed the juice out of them. And once, while talking with a senior professor, Mary saw herself reflected in a window: she was leaning towards him and had her head turned so that her ear was right in front of his moving mouth. The sight disgusted her. Years later, when she had to get a hearing aid, Mary suspected that her deafness was a result of always trying to catch everything everyone said.

In the second half of Mary's fifteenth year at Brandon the provost called a meeting of all faculty and students to announce that the college was bankrupt and would not open its gates again. He was every bit as much surprised as they; the report from the trustees had reached his desk only that morning. It seemed that Brandon's financial manager had speculated in some kind of futures and lost everything. The provost wanted to deliver the news in person before it reached the papers. He wept openly and so did the students and teachers, with only a few exceptions – some cynical upperclassmen who claimed to despise the education they had received.

Mary could not rid her mind of the word 'speculate'. It meant to guess, in terms of money to gamble. How could a man gamble a college? Why would he want to do that, and how could it be that no one stopped him? To Mary, it seemed to belong to another time; she thought of a drunken plantation owner gaming away his slaves. She applied for jobs and got an offer from a new experimental college in Oregon. It was her only offer so she took it.

The college was in one building. Bells rang all the time, lockers lined the hallways, and at every corner stood a buzzing water fountain. The student newspaper came out twice a month on mimeograph paper which felt wet. The library, which was next to the band room, had no librarian and no books.

The countryside was beautiful, though, and Mary might have enjoyed it if the rain had not caused her so much trouble. There was something wrong with her lungs that the doctors couldn't agree on, and couldn't cure; whatever it was, the dampness made it worse. On rainy days condensation formed in Mary's hearing aid and shorted it out. She began to dread talking with people, never knowing when she would have to take out her control box and slap it against her leg.

It rained nearly every day. When it was not raining it was getting ready to rain, or clearing. The ground glinted under the grass, and the light had a yellow undertone that flared up during storms.

There was water in Mary's basement. Her walls sweated, and she had found toadstools growing behind the refrigerator. She felt as though she were rusting out, like one of those old cars people thereabouts kept in their front yards, on pieces of wood. Mary knew that everyone was dying, but it did seem to her that she was dying faster than most.

She continued to look for another job, without success. Then, in the fall of her third year in Oregon, she got a letter from a woman named Louise who'd once taught at Brandon. Louise had scored a great success with a book on Benedict Arnold and was now on the faculty of a famous college in upstate New York. She said that one of her colleagues would be retiring at the end of the year and asked whether Mary would be interested in the position.

The letter surprised Mary. Louise thought of herself as a great historian and of almost everyone else as useless; Mary had not known that she felt differently about her. Moreover, enthusiasm for other people's causes did not come easily to Louise, who had a way of sucking in her breath when familiar names were mentioned, as though she knew things that friendship kept her from disclosing.

Mary expected nothing, but sent a résumé and a copy of her book. Shortly after that Louise called to say that the search committee, of which she was chairwoman, had decided to grant Mary an interview in early November. 'Now don't get your hopes *too* high,' Louise said.

'Oh, no,' Mary said, but thought: Why shouldn't I hope? They would not go to the bother and expense of bringing her to the college if they weren't serious. And she was certain that the interview would go well. She would make them like her, or at least give them no cause to dislike her.

She read about the area with a strange sense of familiarity, as if the land and its history were already known to her. And when her plane left Portland and climbed easterly into the clouds, Mary felt like she was going home. The feeling stayed with her, growing stronger when they landed. She tried to describe it to Louise as they left the airport at Syracuse and drove towards the college, an hour or so away. 'It's like *déjà vu*,' she said.

'*Déjà vu* is a hoax,' Louise said. 'It's just a chemical imbalance of some kind.'

'Maybe so,' Mary said, 'but I still have this sensation.'

'Don't get serious on me,' Louise said. 'That's not your long suit. Just be your funny, wisecracking old self. Tell me now – honestly – how do I look?'

It was night, too dark to see Louise's face well, but in the airport she had seemed gaunt and pale and intense. She reminded Mary of a description in the book she'd been reading, of how Iroquois warriors gave themselves visions by fasting. She had that kind of look about her. But she wouldn't want to hear that. 'You look wonderful,' Mary said.

'There's a reason,' Louise said. 'I've taken a lover. My concentration has improved, my energy level is up, and I've lost ten pounds. I'm also getting some colour in my cheeks, though that could be the weather. I recommend the experience highly. But you probably disapprove.'

Mary didn't know what to say. She said that she was sure Louise knew best, but that didn't seem to be enough. 'Marriage is a great institution,' she added, 'but who wants to live in an institution?'

Louise groaned. 'I know you,' she said, 'and I know that right now you're thinking "But what about Ted? What about the children?" The fact is, Mary, they aren't taking it well at all. Ted has become a nag.' She handed Mary her purse. 'Be a good girl and light me a cigarette, will you? I know I told you I quit, but this whole thing has been very hard on me, very hard, and I'm afraid I've started again.'

They were in the hills now, heading north on a narrow road. Tall trees arched above them. As they topped a rise Mary saw the forest all around, deep black under the plum-coloured sky. There were a few lights and these made the darkness seem even greater.

'Ted has succeeded in completely alienating the children from me,' Louise was saying. 'There is no reasoning with any of them. In fact, they refuse to discuss the matter at all, which is very ironical because over the years I have tried to instil in them a willingness to see things from the other person's point of view. If they could just *meet* Jonathan I know they would feel differently. But they won't hear of it. Jonathan,' she said, 'is my lover.'

'I see,' Mary said, and nodded.

Coming around a curve they caught two deer in the headlights. Mary could see them tense as the car went by. 'Deer,' she said.

'I don't know,' Louise said, 'I just don't know. I do my best and it never seems to be enough. But that's enough about me – let's talk about you. What did you think of my latest book?' She squawked and beat her palms on the steering wheel. 'Seriously, though, what about you? It must have been a real shockeroo when good old Brandon folded.'

'It was hard. Things haven't been good but they'll be a lot better if I get this job.'

'At least you have work,' Louise said. 'You should look at it from the bright side.'

'I try.'

'You seem so gloomy. I hope you're not worrying about the interview, or the class. Worrying won't do you a bit of good. Be happy.'

'Class? What class?'

'The class you're supposed to give tomorrow, after the interview. Didn't I tell you? *Mea culpa*, hon, *mea maxima culpa*. I've been uncharacteristically forgetful lately.'

'But what will I do?'

'Relax,' Louise said. 'Just pick a subject and wing it.'

'Wing it?'

'You know, open your mouth and see what comes out. Extemporize.'

'But I always work from a prepared lecture.'

'All right. I'll tell you what. Last year I wrote an article on the Marshall Plan that I got bored with and never published. You can read that.'

Parroting what Louise had written seemed wrong to Mary, at first; then it occurred to her that she had been doing the same kind of thing for many years, and that this was not the time to get scruples. 'Thanks,' she said. 'I appreciate it.'

'Here we are,' Louise said, and pulled into a circular drive with several cabins grouped around it. In two of the cabins lights were on; smoke drifted straight up from the chimneys. 'The college is another two miles thataway.' Louise pointed down the road. 'I'd invite you to stay at my house, but I'm spending the night with Jonathan and Ted is not good company these days. You would hardly recognize him.'

She took Mary's bags from the trunk and carried them up the steps of a darkened cabin. 'Look,' she said, 'they've laid a fire for you. All you have to do is light it.' She stood in the middle of the room with her arms crossed and watched as Mary held a match under the kindling. 'There,' she said. 'You'll be snugaroo in no time. I'd love to stay and chew the fat but I can't. You just get a good night's sleep and I'll see you in the morning.'

Mary stood in the doorway and waved as Louise pulled out of the drive, spraying gravel. She filled her lungs, to taste the air: it was tart and clear. She could see the stars in their figurations, and the vague streams of light that ran among the stars.

She still felt uneasy about reading Louise's work as her own. It would be her first complete act of plagiarism. It would change her. It would make her less – how much less, she did not know. But what else could she do? She certainly couldn't 'wing it'. Words might fail her, and then what? Mary had a dread of silence. When she thought of silence she thought of drowning, as if it were a kind of water she could not swim in.

'I want this job,' she said, and settled deep into her coat. It was cashmere and Mary had not worn it since moving to Oregon, because people there thought you were pretentious if you had on anything but a Pendleton shirt or, of course, raingear. She rubbed her cheek against the upturned collar and thought of a silver moon shining through bare black branches, a white house with green shutters, red leaves falling in a hard blue sky.

* * *

Louise woke her a few hours later. She was sitting on the edge of the bed, pushing at Mary's shoulder and snuffling loudly. When Mary asked her what was wrong she said, 'I want your opinion on something. It's very important. Do you think I'm womanly?'

Mary sat up. 'Louise, can this wait?'

'No.'

'Womanly?'

Louise nodded.

'You are very beautiful,' Mary said, 'and you know how to present yourself.'

Louise stood and paced the room. 'That son of a bitch,' she said. She came back and stood over Mary. 'Let's suppose someone said I have no sense of humour. Would you agree or disagree?'

'In some things you do. I mean, yes, you have a good sense of humour.'

'What do you mean, "in some things"? What kind of things?'

'Well, if you heard that someone had been killed in an unusual way, like by an exploding cigar, you would think that was funny.'

Louise laughed.

'That's what I mean,' Mary said.

Louise went on laughing. 'Oh, Lordy,' she said. 'Now it's my turn to say something about you.' She sat down beside Mary.

'Please,' Mary said.

'Just one thing,' Louise said.

Mary waited.

'You're trembling,' Louise said. 'I was just going to say – oh, forget it. Listen, do you mind if I sleep on the couch? I'm all in.'

'Go ahead.'

'Sure it's okay? You've got a big day tomorrow.' She fell back on the sofa and kicked off her shoes. 'I was just going to say, you should use some liner on those eyebrows of yours. They sort of disappear and the effect is disconcerting.'

Neither of them slept. Louise chain-smoked cigarettes and Mary watched the coals burn down. When it was light enough that they could see each other Louise got up. 'I'll send a student for you,' she said. 'Good luck.'

The college looked the way colleges are supposed to look. Roger, the student assigned to show Mary around, explained that it was an exact copy of a college in England, right down to the gargoyles and stained-glass windows. It looked so much like a college that moviemakers sometimes used it as a set. *Andy Hardy Goes to College* had been filmed there, and every fall they had an Andy Hardy Goes to College Day, with raccoon coats and goldfish-swallowing contests.

Above the door of the Founder's Building was a Latin motto which, roughly translated, meant 'God helps those who help themselves'. As Roger recited the names of illustrious graduates Mary was struck by the extent to which they had taken this precept to heart. They had helped themselves to railroads, mines, armies, states; to empires of finance with outposts all over the world.

Roger took Mary to the chapel and showed her a plaque bearing the names of alumni who had been killed in various wars, all the way back to the Civil War. There were not many names. Here too, apparently, the graduates had helped themselves. 'Oh yes,' Roger said as they were leaving, 'I forgot to tell you. The communion rail comes from some church in Europe where Charlemagne used to go.'

They went to the gymnasium, and the two hockey rinks, and the library, where Mary inspected the card catalogue, as though she would turn down the job if they didn't have the right books. 'We have a little more time,' Roger said as they went outside. 'Would you like to see the power plant?'

Mary wanted to keep busy until the last minute, so she agreed.

Roger led her into the depths of the service building, explaining things about the machine, which was the most advanced in the country. 'People think the college is really old-fashioned,' he said, 'but it isn't. They let girls come here now, and some of the teachers are women. In fact, there's a statute that says they have to interview at least one woman for each opening. There it is.'

They were standing on an iron catwalk above the biggest machine

Mary had ever beheld. Roger, who was majoring in Earth Sciences, said that it had been built from a design pioneered by a professor in his department. Where before he had been gabby Roger now became reverent. It was clear that for him this machine was the soul of the college, that the purpose of the college was to provide outlets for the machine. Together they leaned against the railing and watched it hum.

Mary arrived at the committee room exactly on time for her interview, but the room was empty. Her book was on the table, along with a water pitcher and some glasses. She sat down and picked up the book. The binding cracked as she opened it. The pages were smooth, clean, unread. Mary turned to the first chapter, which began, 'It is generally believed that . . .' How dull, she thought.

Nearly twenty minutes later Louise came in with several men. 'Sorry we're late,' she said. 'We don't have much time so we'd better get started.' She introduced Mary to the men, but with one exception the names and faces did not stay together. The exception was Dr Howells, the department chairman, who had a porous blue nose and terrible teeth.

A shiny-faced man to Dr Howell's right spoke first. 'So,' he said, 'I understand you once taught at Brandon College.'

'It was a shame that Brandon had to close,' said a young man with a pipe in his mouth. 'There is a place for schools like Brandon.' As he talked the pipe wagged up and down.

'Now you're in Oregon,' Dr Howells said. 'I've never been there. How do you like it?'

'Not very much,' Mary said.

'Is that right?' Dr Howells leaned towards her. 'I thought everyone liked Oregon. I hear it's very green.'

'That's true,' Mary said.

'I suppose it rains a lot,' he said.

'Nearly every day.'

'I wouldn't like that,' he said, shaking his head. 'I like it dry. Of course it snows here, and you have your rain now and then, but it's a *dry* rain. Have you ever been to Utah?

There's a state for you. Bryce Canyon. The Mormon Tabernacle Choir.'

'Dr Howells was brought up in Utah,' said the young man with the pipe.

'It was a different place altogether in those days,' Dr Howells said. 'Mrs Howells and I have always talked about going back when I retire, but now I'm not so sure.'

'We're a little short on time,' Louise said.

'And here I've been going on and on,' Dr Howells said. 'Before we wind things up, is there anything you want to tell us?'

'Yes. I think you should give me the job.' Mary laughed when she said this, but no one laughed back, or even looked at her. They all looked away. Mary understood then that they were not really considering her for the position. She had been brought here to satisfy a rule. She had no hope.

The men gathered their papers and shook hands with Mary and told her how much they were looking forward to her class. 'I can't get enough of the Marshall Plan,' Dr Howells said.

'Sorry about that,' Louise said when they were alone. 'I didn't think it would be so bad. That was a real bitcheroo.'

'Tell me something,' Mary said. 'You already know who you're going to hire, don't you?'

Louise nodded.

'Then why did you bring me here?'

Louise began to explain about the statute and Mary interrupted. 'I know all that. But why me? Why did you pick *me*?'

Louise walked to the window. She spoke with her back to Mary. 'Things haven't been going very well for old Louise,' she said. 'I've been unhappy and I thought you might cheer me up. You used to be so funny, and I was sure you would enjoy the trip – it didn't cost you anything, and it's pretty this time of year with the leaves and everything. Mary, you don't know the things my parents did to me. And Ted is no barrel of laughs either. Or Jonathan, the son of a bitch. I deserve some love and friendship but I don't get any.' She turned and looked at her watch. 'It's almost time for your class. We'd better go.'

'I would rather not give it. After all, there's not much point, is there?'

'But you *have* to give it. That's part of the interview.' Louise handed Mary a folder. 'All you have to do is read this. It isn't much, considering all the money we've laid out to get you here.'

Mary followed Louise down the hall to the lecture room. The professors were sitting in the front row with their legs crossed. They smiled and nodded at Mary. Behind them the room was full of students, some of whom had spilled over into the aisles. One of the professors adjusted the microphone to Mary's height, crouching down as he went to the podium and back as though he would prefer not to be seen.

Louise called the room to order. She introduced Mary and gave the subject of the lecture. But Mary had decided to wing it after all. Mary came to the podium unsure of what she would say; sure only that she would rather die than read Louise's article. The sun poured through the stained glass onto the people around her, painting their faces. Thick streams of smoke from the young professor's pipe drifted through a circle of red light at Mary's feet, turning crimson and twisting like flames.

'I wonder how many of you know,' she began, 'that we are in the Long House, the ancient domain of the Five Nations of the Iroquois.'

Two professors looked at each other.

'The Iroquois were without pity,' Mary said. 'They hunted people down with clubs and arrows and spears and nets, and blowguns made from elder stalks. They tortured their captives, sparing no one, not even the little children. They took scalps and practised cannibalism and slavery. Because they had no pity they became powerful, so powerful that no other tribe dared to oppose them. They made the other tribes pay tribute, and when they had nothing more to pay the Iroquois attacked them.'

Several of the professors began to whisper. Dr Howells was saying something to Louise, and Louise was shaking her head.

'In one of their raids,' Mary said, 'they captured two Jesuit priests, Jean de Brébeuf and Gabriel Lalement. They covered Lalement with pitch and set him on fire in front of Brébeuf. When Brébeuf rebuked them they cut off his lips and put a burning iron down his throat. They hung a collar of red-hot hatchets around his neck, and poured boiling water over his head. When he continued to preach to them they cut strips of flesh from his body and ate them before his eyes. While he was still alive they scalped him and cut open his breast and drank his blood. Later, their chief tore out Brébeuf's heart and ate it, but just before he did this Brébeuf spoke to them one last time. He said – '

'That's enough!' yelled Dr Howells, jumping to his feet. Louise stopped shaking her head. Her eyes were perfectly round.

Mary had come to the end of her facts. She did not know what Brébeuf had said. Silence rose up around her; just when she thought she would go under and be lost in it she heard someone whistling in the hallway outside, trilling the notes like a bird, like many birds.

'Mend your lives,' she said. 'You have deceived yourselves in the pride of your hearts, and the strength of your arms. Though you soar aloft like the eagle, though your nest is set among the stars, thence I will bring you down, says the Lord. Turn from power to love. Be kind. Do justice. Walk humbly.'

Louise was waving her arms. 'Mary!' she shouted.

But Mary had more to say, much more; she waved back at Louise, then turned off her hearing aid so that she would not be distracted again.

Poaching

Wharton was a cartoonist, and a nervous man – 'highstrung', he would have said. Because of his occupation and his nerves he required peace, but in Vancouver he didn't get much of that. His wife, Ellen, was deficient in many respects, and resented his constructive criticism. She took it personally. They bickered, and she threatened to leave him. Wharton believed that she was having an affair. George, their son, slouched around the house all day and paid no attention when Wharton described all the sports and hobbies that an eleven-year-old boy ought to be interested in.

Wharton dreamed of a place in the country where George would be outside all day, making friends and hiking, and Ellen would have a garden. In his dream Wharton saw her look up and smile as he came towards her.

He sometimes went camping for a few days when things got bad at home. On one of these trips he saw a large piece of land that the government was selling and decided to buy it. The property was heavily wooded, had a small pond surrounded by birch trees, and a good sturdy building. The building needed some work, but Wharton thought that such a project would bring them all together.

When he told Ellen about it she said, 'Are you kidding?'

'I've never been more serious,' Wharton said. 'And it wouldn't hurt you to show a little enthusiasm.'

'No way,' Ellen said. 'Count me out.'

Wharton went ahead and arranged the move. He was sure that when the moment came, Ellen would go with them. He never lost this conviction, not even when she got a job and had a lawyer draw up separation papers. But the moment came and went, and finally Wharton and George left without her.

They had been on the land for almost a year when Wharton began to hear shots from beyond the meadow. The shooting woke him at dawn and disturbed him at his work, and he couldn't make up his mind what to do. He hoped that it would just stop. The noise had begun to wake George, and in his obsessive way he would not leave off asking questions about it. Also, though he seldom played there, George had developed a sense of injury at being kept out of the woods. Ellen was coming up for a visit – her first – and she would make a stink.

The shooting continued. It went on for two weeks, three weeks, well past Easter. On the morning of the day Ellen was supposed to arrive Wharton heard two shots, and he knew he had to do something. He decided to go and talk to his neighbour Vernon. Vernon understood these things.

George caught Wharton leaving the house and asked if he could go play with his friend Rory.

'Absolutely not,' Wharton said, and headed up the path towards the road. The ground was swollen and spongy with rain. The fenceposts had a black and soggy look, and the ditches on either side of the road were loud with the rushing of water. Wharton dodged mudholes, huffing a little, and contemplated Rory.

To help George make friends during the previous summer Wharton had driven him to a quarry where the local children swam. George splashed around by himself at one end and pretended that he was having a fine old time, as his eyes ticked back and forth to the motion of the other children flying from bank to bank on the rope swing, shouting 'Banzai!' when they let go and reached out to the water.

One afternoon Wharton built a fire and produced hot dogs for the children to roast. He asked their names and introduced George. He told them that they should feel free to come and visit George whenever they liked. They could swim in the pond, or play hide-and-seek in the woods. When they had eaten they thanked him and went back to their end of the quarry while George went back to his. Wharton considered rounding them up for a nature walk, but he never got around to it. A few days before the weather turned too cold for swimming George caught a garter snake in the rushes by the bank, and another boy came over to take a look. That night George asked if he could sleep over at Rory's.

'Who's Rory?'

'Just a guy.'

Rory eventually came to their house for a reciprocal visit. Wharton did not think that he was an acceptable friend for George. He would not meet Wharton's eye, and had a way of laughing to himself. Rory and George whispered and giggled all night, and a few days later Wharton found several burnt matches in George's room which George would not account for. He hoped that the boy would enlarge his circle of friends when school began, but this never happened. Wharton fretted about George's shyness. Friends were a blessing and he wanted George to have many friends. In Wharton's opinion, George's timidity was the result of his being underdeveloped physically. Wharton advised him to take up weight lifting.

Over the mountains to the east a thin line of clouds was getting thicker. Wharton felt a growing dampness in the air as he turned into his neighbour's gate.

He disliked having to ask Vernon for favours or advice, but at times he had no choice. Twice during the winter his car had slipped off the icy, unbanked road, and both times Vernon had pulled him out. He showed Wharton how to keep the raccoons out of his garbage, and how to use a chain saw. Wharton was grateful, but he suspected that Vernon had begun to think of himself as his superior.

He found Vernon in the yard, loading five-gallon cans into the back of his truck. This pleased Wharton. He would not have to go into the dirty, evil-smelling house. Vernon had rented most of the place out to a commune from Seattle, and Wharton was appalled at their sloth and resolute good cheer. He was further relieved not to have to go inside, because he wished to avoid one of the women. They had kept company for a short, unhappy time during the winter; the situation was complicated, and Wharton already had enough to keep him busy for the day.

'Well howdy there,' Vernon said. 'And how's every little thing down at the lower forty?'

Wharton noticed that Vernon always countrified his speech when he was around. He guessed that Vernon did it to make him feel like a city slicker. Wharton had heard him talk to other people and he sounded normal enough. 'Not so good,' he said, and lifted one of the cans.

Vernon took it from him very firmly and slid it down the bed of the truck. 'You got to use your back hoisting these things,' he said. He slammed the tailgate shut and yanked the chain through the slots. The links rattled like bolts in a can. He took a rag out of his back pocket and blew his nose. 'What's the trouble?'

'Someone's been shooting on my land.'

'What do you mean, shooting? Shooting what?'

'I don't know. Deer, I suppose.'

Vernon shook his head. 'Deer have all headed back into the high country by now.'

'Well, whatever. Squirrels. Rabbits. The point is that someone has been hunting in the woods without asking my permission.'

'It isn't any of us,' Vernon said. 'I can tell you that much. There's only one rifle in this house and nobody goes near it but me. I wouldn't trust that load of fruitcakes with an empty water pistol.'

'I didn't think it was you. It just occurred to me that you might have some idea who it could be. You know the people around here.'

Vernon creased his brow and narrowed his eyes to show, Wharton supposed, that he was thinking. 'There's one person,' he said finally. 'You know Jeff Gill from up the road?'

Wharton shook his head.

'I guess you wouldn't have met him at that. He keeps to himself. He's pretty crazy, Jeff Gill. You know that song "I'm My Own Grandpaw"?

Well, Jeff Gill is his own uncle. The Gills,' he said, 'are a right close family. You want me to call down there, see what's going on?'

'I would appreciate that.'

Wharton waited outside, leaning against an empty watering trough. The breeze rippled puddles and blew scraps of paper across the yard. Somewhere a door creaked open and shut. He tried to count the antlers on the front of the barn but gave up. There were over a hundred pairs of them, bleached and silvered by the sun. It was a wonder there were any deer left in the province. Over the front door of the house there were more antlers, and on the porch a set of suitcases and a steamer trunk. Apparently someone was leaving the commune. If so, it would not be the first defection.

Vernon's tenants had had a pretty awful winter. Factions developed over the issues of child care and discipline, sleeping arrangements, cooking, shovelling snow, and the careless use of someone's Deutschegrammophon records. According to Wharton's lady friend, Vernon had caused a lot of trouble. He made fun of the ideals of the commune with respect to politics, agriculture, religion, and diet, and would not keep his hands off the women. It got to where they were afraid to go out to the woodshed by themselves. Also, he insisted on calling them Hare Krishnas, which they were not.

Wharton's friend wanted to know why, if Vernon couldn't be more supportive of the commune, he had rented the house to them in the first place? And if he hated them so much how come he stayed on in the master bedroom?

Wharton knew the answer to the first question and could guess the answer to the second. Vernon's father had been a wild man and died owing twelve years' back taxes. Vernon needed money. Wharton imagined that he stayed on himself because he had grown up in the house and could not imagine living anywhere else.

Vernon came back into the yard carrying a rifle. Wharton could smell the oil from ten feet away. 'I couldn't get anybody down at the Gills,' Vernon said. 'Phone's been disconnected. I talked to a guy I knew who works with Jeff, and he says Jeff hasn't been at the mill in over a month. Thinks he's went somewhere else.' Vernon held out the rifle. 'You know how to work this?'

'Yes,' Wharton said.

'Why don't you keep it around for awhile. Just till things get sorted out.'

Wharton did not want the rifle. As he had told George when George asked for a B-B gun, he believed that firearms were a sign of weakness. He reached out and took the thing, but only because Vernon would feel slighted if he refused it.

'Wow,' George said when he saw the rifle. 'Are you going to shoot the sniper?'

'I'm not going to shoot anybody,' Wharton said. 'And I've told you before, the word is poacher, not sniper.'

'Yeah, poacher. Where did you get the gun?'

Wharton looked down at his son. The boy had been sawing up and nailing together some scrap lumber. He was sweating and his skin had a flush on it. How thin he was! You would think he never fed the boy, when in fact he went out of his way to prepare wholesome meals for him. Wharton had no idea where the food went, unless, as he suspected, George was giving his lunches to Rory. Wharton began to describe to George the difference between a rifle and a gun but George was not interested. He would be perfectly content to use his present vocabulary for the next eighty years.

'When I was your age,' he said, 'I enjoyed acquiring new words and learning to use them correctly.'

'I know, I know,' George said, then mumbled something under his breath.

'What was that?'

'Nothing.'

'You said something. Now what did you say?'

George sighed. 'Jeez.'

Wharton was going to point out that if George wished to curse he should do so forthrightly, manfully, but he stopped himself. George was not a man, he was a boy, and boys should not be hounded all the time. They should be encouraged. Wharton nodded at the tangle of lumber and congratulated George on doing something both physical and creative. 'What is it?' he asked.

'A lair,' George said. 'For a wolf.'

'I see,' Wharton said. 'That's good.' He nodded again and went inside. As he locked the rifle away – he didn't really know how to work it – Wharton decided that he should let George see his lighter side more often. He was capable of better conversation than reminders that 'okay' was not a word, that it was prudent not to spend all one's allowance the same day, or that chairs were for sitting in and floors for walking on. Just the other day the plumber had come in to unclog the kitchen sink and he had laughed at several things Wharton had said.

For the rest of the morning Wharton sketched out episodes for his old bread-and-butter strip. This was about a trapper named Pierre who, in the course of his adventures, passed along bits of homespun philosophy and wilderness lore, such as how to treat frostbite and corns, and how to take bearings so that you would not end up walking in circles. The philosophy was anti-materialist, free-thinking stuff, much like the philosophy of Wharton's father, and over the years it had become obnoxious to him. He was mortally tired of the Trapper and his whole bag of tricks, his smugness and sermonizing and his endless cries of 'Mon Dieu!' and 'Sacre Bleu!' and 'Ze ice, she ees breaking up!' Wharton was more interested in his new strip, *Ulysses*, whose hero was a dog searching for his master in the goldfields of the Yukon. Pierre still paid the bills, though, and Wharton could not afford to pull the plug on him.

There was no shooting from the woods, and Wharton's concentration ran deep. He worked in a reverie, and when he happened to look at his watch he realized that he was supposed to have picked up his wife ten minutes earlier. The station was an hour away.

Ellen kept after Wharton all the way home in her flat, smoky voice. She had old grievances and she listed them, but without anger, as if they bored her: his nagging, his slovenliness, his neglect of her. Oh, she didn't mind waiting around bus stations for an hour now and then. But he *always* kept her waiting. Why? Did he want to humiliate her? Was that it?

'No,' Wharton said. 'I just lost track of the time.' The other charges she had brought against him were true and he did not challenge them.

'If there's one thing I can't stand,' Ellen said, 'it's this suffering-in-silence, stiff-upper-lip crap.'

'I'm sorry,' Wharton said.

'I know you are. That doesn't change anything. Oh, look at the little colts and fillies!'

Wharton glanced out the window. 'Actually,' he said, 'those are ponies. Shetlands.'

She didn't answer.

It rained hard, then cleared just before they came up the drive to the house. Ellen got out of the car and looked around sceptically. In the distance the mountains were draped with thick coils of cloud, and closer up in the foothills the mist lay among the treetops. Water ran down the trunks of the trees and stood everywhere. Wharton picked up Ellen's bags and walked towards the house, naming wildflowers along the path.

'I don't know what you're trying to prove,' Ellen said, 'living out in the middle of no goddam where at all.' She saw George and shouted and waved. He dropped the board he was hammering and ran to meet her. She knelt on the wet glass and hugged him, pinning his arms to his side. He tried to hug back but finally gave up and waited, looking over Ellen's shoulder at Wharton. Wharton picked up his bags again. 'I'll be in the house,' he said, and continued up the path, his boots making a sucking noise in the mud.

'House?' Ellen said when she had come inside. 'You call this a house? It's a barn or something.'

'Actually,' Wharton said, 'it's a converted stable. The government used to keep mules here.'

'I'm all for simple living but God Almighty.'

'It's not so bad. We're getting along just fine, aren't we, George?'

'I guess so.'

'Why don't you show Mother your room?'

'Okay.' George went down the passageway. He waited outside,

holding the door like an usher. Ellen looked inside and nodded. 'Oh, you set up a cot for me. Thank you, George.'

'Dad set it up. I'll sleep there and you can have the bed if you want.'

Wharton showed her what was left to see of the house. She hated it. 'You don't even have any pictures on the walls!' she said. He admitted that the place lacked warm touches. In the summer he would throw on a coat of paint, maybe buy some curtains. When they came down from the loft where Wharton worked Ellen took a package from her suitcase and gave it to George.

'Well, George,' Wharton said, 'what do you say?'

'Thank you,' George said, not to Ellen but to Wharton.

'Go ahead and open it,' Wharton said.

'For Christ's sake,' Ellen said.

It was a book, *The World of Wolves*. 'Jeez,' George said. He sat down on the floor and began thumbing through the pictures.

How could Ellen have guessed at George's interest in wolves? She had an instinct for gifts the way other people had an instinct for finding the right words to say. The world of things was not alien and distasteful to her as it was to Wharton. He despised his possessions with some ostentation; those who gave him gifts went away feeling as if they'd made Wharton party to a crime. He knew that over the years he had caused Ellen to be shy of her own generosity.

'Why don't you read in your bedroom, George? The light here is terrible.'

'He can stay,' Ellen said.

'Okay,' George said, and went down the hall, not lifting his eyes from the page.

'That wasn't as expensive as it looks,' Ellen said.

'It was a fine gift,' Wharton said. 'Wolves are one of George's obsessions these days.'

'I got it for a song,' Ellen said. She put a cigarette in her mouth and began to rummage through her purse. Finally she turned her bag upside down and dumped it all over the floor. She poked through the contents, then looked up. 'Have you got a match?'

'No. You'll have to light it from the stove.'

'I suppose you've quit.' She said this as though it were an accusation.

'I still enjoy one every now and then,' Wharton said.

'Did you read what that doctor said who did the postmortem on Howard Hughes?' asked Ellen, returning from the kitchen. 'He said, "Howard Hughes had lungs just like a baby." I almost cried when I read that, it made me so nostalgic for when I was young. I'd hate to think what my lungs look like, not to mention my liver and God knows what else.' She blew out some smoke and watched it bitterly as it twisted through a slant of light.

'Howard Hughes never let anyone touch him or come close to him,' Wharton said. 'That's not your style.'

'What do you mean by that?'

'Only that there's always a certain risk when we get close – '

'You didn't mean that. You think I've got this big love life going. What a laugh.'

'Well, you did.'

'I don't want to get into that,' Ellen said. 'Let's just say I like to be appreciated.'

'I appreciated you.'

'No. You thought you were too good for me.'

Wharton denied this without heat. During most of their marriage he *had* imagined that he was too good for Ellen. He had been wrong about that and now look at the mess he had made. He stood abruptly, but once he was on his feet he could not think of anything to do, so he sat again.

'What's the point, anyway?' Ellen asked, waving her hand around. 'Living in a stable, for God's sake, wearing those boots and that dumb hat.'

'I was wearing the boots because the ground is muddy and the hat because my head gets cold.'

'Who are you trying to kid? You wear the hat because you think it makes you look like Pierre the Trapper. Ees true, no?'

'You've made your point, Ellen. You don't like the house

and you don't like me. Actually, I'm not even sure why you came.'

'Actually,' she said, 'I came to see my son.'

'I don't understand why you couldn't wait until June. That's only two more months and you'll have him all summer. According to the terms – '

Ellen snorted. 'According to the terms,' she said. 'Come off it.'

'Let me finish. I don't have to grant you visiting privileges. This is a courtesy visit. Now if you can't stop finding fault with everything you can leave, and the sooner the better.'

'I'll leave tomorrow,' Ellen said.

'Suit yourself.'

Ellen bent suddenly in her chair. Piece by piece, she picked up the things she'd emptied onto the floor and replaced them in her purse. Then she stood and walked down the passageway to George's room, moving with dignity as if concealing drunkenness, or a limp.

At dinner George announced his intention to acquire a pet wolf. Wharton had entertained a similar fancy at George's age, and the smile he gave his son was addressed to the folly of both their imaginations. George took it as encouragement and pressed on. There was, he said, a man in Sinclair who had two breeding pairs of timber wolves. George knew for sure that a litter was expected any day now.

Wharton wanted to let George down lightly. 'They're probably not real wolves,' he said. 'More likely they're German shepherds, or huskies, or a mix.'

'These are real wolves all right,' George said.

'How can you be sure?' Ellen asked. 'Have you seen them?'

'No, but Rory has.'

'Who is Rory?'

'Rory is an acquaintance of George's.' Wharton said, 'and Rory does not have the last word on every subject, at least not in this house.'

'Rory is my friend,' George said.

'All right,' Wharton said, 'I'm willing to accept Rory's testimony that those are real wolves. What I will not accept is the idea of bringing a wild animal into the house.'

'They're not wild. Rory says – '

'Rory again!'

'– Rory says that they're just as tame as dogs, only smarter.'

'George, be reasonable. A wolf is a killing machine. It needs to kill in order to survive. There's nothing wrong with that, but a wolf belongs in the wild, not on a chain or locked up in a cage somewhere.'

'I wouldn't lock him up. He'd have a lair.'

'A lair? Is that what you're building?'

George nodded. 'I told you.'

'George,' Ellen said, 'why don't you think about a nice dog? Wolves really are very dangerous animals.'

George did not want a nice dog. He was willing to admit that wolves were dangerous, but only to the enemies of their friends. This carried him to his last argument, which he played like a trump: a wolf was just exactly what they needed to help them get rid of the sniper.

'Sniper?' Ellen said. 'What sniper?'

'He means poacher,' Wharton said. 'George, I'm at the end of my patience. A wolf belongs with other wolves, not with people. I don't approve of this habit of turning wild animals into pets. Now please drop the subject. And stop playing with your food.'

'What poacher?' Ellen asked.

'I'm not hungry,' George said.

'Then leave the table.'

George went to his room and slammed the door.

'What poacher?'

'Someone has been doing some shooting on the property. It's nothing serious.'

'There's someone running around out there with a gun and you say it isn't serious?'

'This used to be public land. I want people to feel like they can use it.'

'But this is your home!'

'Ellen – '

'What have you done about it? You haven't done anything at all, have you?'

'No,' Wharton said, and got up and left the room. On his way outside he stopped to talk to George. The boy was sitting on the floor, sorting through some junk he kept in a cigar box. 'Son,' Wharton said, 'I'm sorry if I was short with you at dinner.'

'It's okay,' George said.

'I'm not just being mean,' Wharton said. 'A mature wolf can weigh over a hundred and fifty pounds. Think what would happen if it turned on you.'

'He wouldn't turn on me. He would protect me.' George shook the box. 'He would love me.'

Wharton had intended to go for a walk but decided it was too slippery underfoot. He sat on the front steps instead, hunched down in his coat. The moon was racing through filmy clouds, melting at the edges. The wind had picked up considerably, and Wharton could hear trees creaking in the woods beyond. Gradually the sky lowered and it began to rain. Ellen came out and told Wharton that he had a phone call.

It was the woman from the commune. She was going to be leaving the next day and wanted to come up to say goodbye. Wharton told her that this was not possible just now. The woman was obviously hurt. She had once accused Wharton of not valuing her as a person and he wanted to show that this was not true. 'Look,' he said, 'let me take you to the station tomorrow.'

'Forget it.'

Wharton insisted and finally she agreed. Only after he hung up did Wharton realize that he might have Ellen along as well. There was just one bus out on Sunday.

Ellen and George were lying on the floor, reading the book together. Ellen patted the place beside her. 'Join us?' Wharton shook his head. They were getting on fine without him; he had no wish to break up such a cosy picture. Still restless, he went up to the loft and worked. It was very late when he finished. He took off his boots at the foot of the ladder and moved as quietly as he could past George's bedroom.

When he turned on the light in his own room he saw that Ellen was in his bed. She covered her eyes with her forearm. The soft flesh at the base of her throat fluttered gently with her breathing.

'Did you really want me to stay with George?'

'No,' Wharton said. He dropped his clothes on top of the chest that served as dresser and chair. Ellen drew the covers back for him and he slid in beside her.

'Who was that on the phone?' she asked. 'Have you got a little something going?'

'We saw each other a few times. The lady is leaving tomorrow.'

'I'm sorry. I hate to think of you all alone out here.'

Wharton almost said, 'Then stay!' but he caught himself.

'There's something I've got to tell you,' Ellen said, raising herself on an elbow. 'Jesus, what a look.'

'What have you got to tell me?'

'It isn't what you're thinking.'

'You don't know what I'm thinking.'

'The hell I don't.' She sank back onto her side. 'I'm leaving Vancouver,' she said. 'I'm not going to be able to take George this summer.'

Ellen explained that she did not feel comfortable living alone in the city. She hated her job and the apartment was too small. She was going back to Victoria to see if she couldn't find something better there. She hated to let George down, but this was a bad time for her.

'Victoria? Why Victoria?' Ellen had never spoken well of the place. According to her the people were all stuffed shirts and there was nothing to do there. Wharton could not understand her and said so.

'Right now I need to be someplace I feel at home.' That brought Ellen to another point. She was going to need money for travel and to keep body and soul together until she found another job.

'Whatever I can do,' Wharton said.

'I knew you'd help.'

'I guess this means you don't have to go back tomorrow.'

'No. I guess not.'

'Why don't you stay for a week? It would mean a lot to George.'

'We'll see.'

Wharton turned off the light, but he could not sleep for the longest time. Neither could Ellen; she kept turning and arranging herself. Wharton wanted to reach out to her but he wouldn't have felt right about it, so soon after lending her money.

George woke them in the morning. He sat on the edge of the bed, pale and trembling.

'What's wrong, sweetie?' Ellen asked, and then they heard a shot from the woods. She looked at Wharton. Wharton got out of bed, dressed quickly, and went outside.

He knew it was Jeff Gill, had known so the moment he heard the man's name. It sounded familiar, as things to come often did. He even knew what Jeff Gill would look like: short and wiry, with yellow teeth and close-set, porcine eyes. He did not know why Jeff Gill hated him but he surely did, and Wharton felt that in some way the hatred was justified.

It was raining, not hard but drearily. The air had a chill on it and as he circled the house Wharton walked into the mist of his own breathing. Two swallows skimmed the meadow behind the house, dipping and wheeling through the high grass. They did not break their pattern as he walked by them, yellow rubber boots glistening, and passed into the shadow of the tall trees.

He realized that he had not been in these woods for almost a month. He had been afraid to walk in his own land. He still was.

There were still clumps of snow lying everywhere, grey and crystalline and impacted with brown needles. The branches of pine and fir and spruce were tipped with sweet new growth. Stirred by the rain, the soil gave off an acid smell, like a compost heap. Wharton stepped under a sugar pine to catch his breath and scrape some of the mud off his boots. They were so heavy he could hardly lift them.

He heard another shot; it came from the direction of the pond and seemed to crash beside him. 'Listen!' Wharton yelled. 'I've got a rifle too and I'll use it! Go away!' Wharton thought that he was capable of doing what he said, if he had brought the weapon and had known how to work it. He had felt foolish and afraid for so long that he was becoming dangerous.

He walked towards the pond. The banks were ringed with silver birches and he leaned against one of these. The brown water bristled with splashing raindrops. He caught a motion on the surface of the pond, a rippling triangle like an arrowhead with a dark spot at its point. Wharton assumed that it was a duck and stepped out on a small jetty to get a better look.

Suddenly the creature raised its head and stared at Wharton. It was a beaver, swimming on its back. Its gaze was level and unblinking. Its short front legs were folded over its gently rounded belly, reminding Wharton of a Hogarth engraving of an English clubman after a meal. The beaver lowered its head into the pond and then its belly disappeared and its paddle-like tail swung in a wide arc and cracked flat against the surface of the water. The birches around the pond squeezed the sound and made it sharp and loud, like a rifle going off.

Wharton turned and went back to the house and explained everything to Ellen and George. He made breakfast while they dressed, and afterwards they all walked down to the pond to look at the beaver. Along the way Wharton slipped and fell and when he tried to stand he fell again. Ellen told him that he ought to take a roll in the mud every day, that it would be the making of him.

George reached the bank first and shouted, 'I see him! I see him!'

The beaver was old and out of place. A younger beaver had driven him away from his lodge, and during the thaw he had followed a seasonal stream, now gone dry, up to the pond.

When Vernon heard about the beaver he took his rifle back and went to the pond and shot him. Wharton was outraged, but Vernon insisted that the animal would have destroyed the birches and fouled the bottom of the pond, killing the plants and turning the water stagnant. George's biology teacher agreed.

Ellen left at the end of the week. She and Wharton wrote letters, and sometimes, late at night, she called him. They had good talks but they never lived together again. A few days after she left, George's friend

Rory turned on him and threw his books and one of his shoes out the schoolbus window, with the help of another boy more to his liking.

But Wharton, standing in the warm rain with his family that morning, did not know that these things would come to pass. Nor did he know that the dog Ulysses would someday free him from the odious Trapper Pierre, or that George would soon – too soon – put on muscle and learn to take care of himself. The wind raised small waves and sent them slapping up against the jetty, so that it appeared to be sliding forward like the hull of a boat. Out in the pond the beaver dove and surfaced again. It seemed to Wharton, watching him move in wide circles upon the water, that the creature had been sent to them, that they had been offered an olive branch and were not far from home.

The Liar

My mother read everything except books. Advertisements on buses, entire menus as we ate, billboards; if it had no cover it interested her. So when she found a letter in my drawer that was not addressed to her she read it. 'What difference does it make if James has nothing to hide?' – that was her thought. She stuffed the letter in the drawer when she finished it and walked from room to room in the big empty house, talking to herself. She took the letter out and read it again to get the facts straight. Then, without putting on her coat or locking the door, she went down the steps and headed for the church at the end of the street. No matter how angry and confused she might be, she always went to four o'clock Mass and now it was four o'clock.

It was a fine day, blue and cold and still, but Mother walked as though into a strong wind, bent forward at the waist with her feet hurrying behind in short, busy steps. My brother and sisters and I considered this walk of hers funny and we smirked at one another when she crossed in front of us to stir the fire, or water a plant. We didn't let her catch us at it. It would have puzzled her to think that there might be anything amusing about her. Her one concession to the fact of humour was an insincere, startling laugh. Strangers often stared at her.

While Mother waited for the priest, who was late, she prayed. She prayed in a familiar, orderly, firm way: first for her late husband, my father, then for her parents – also dead. She said a quick prayer for my father's parents (just touching base; she had disliked them) and finally for her children in order of their ages, ending with me. Mother did not consider originality a virtue and until my name came up her prayers were exactly the same as on any other day.

But when she came to me she spoke up boldly. 'I thought he wasn't going to do it any more. Murphy said he was cured. What am I supposed to do now?' There was reproach in her tone. Mother put great hope in her notion that I was cured. She regarded my cure as an answer to her prayers and by way of thanksgiving sent a lot of money to the Thomasite Indian Mission, money she had been saving for a trip to Rome. She felt cheated and she let her feelings be known. When the priest came in, Mother slid back on the seat and followed the Mass with concentration. After communion she began to worry again and went straight home without stopping to talk to Frances, the woman who always cornered Mother after Mass to tell about the awful things done to her by Communists, devil-worshippers, Rosicrucians. Frances watched her go with narrowed eyes.

Once in the house, Mother took the letter from my drawer and brought it into the kitchen. She held it over the stove with her fingernails, looking away so that she would not be drawn into it again, and set it on fire. When it began to burn her fingers she dropped it in the sink and watched it blacken and flutter and close upon itself like a fist. Then she washed it down the drain and called Dr Murphy.

The letter was to my friend Ralphy in Arizona. He used to live across the street from us but he had moved. Most of the letter was about a tour we, the junior class, had taken of Alcatraz. That was all right. What got Mother was the last paragraph where I said that she had been coughing up blood and the doctors weren't sure what was wrong with her, but that we were hoping for the best.

This wasn't true. Mother took pride in her physical condition, considered herself a horse: 'I'm a regular horse,' she would reply when people asked about her health. For several years now I had been saying unpleasant things that weren't true and this habit of mine irked

Mother greatly, enough to persuade her to send me to Dr Murphy, in whose office I was sitting when she burned the letter. Dr Murphy was our family physician and had no training in psychoanalysis but he took an interest in 'things of the mind', as he put it. He had treated me for appendicitis and tonsillitis and Mother thought that he could put the truth into me as easily as he took things out of me, a hope Dr Murphy did not share. He was basically interested in getting me to understand what I did, and lately he had been moving towards the conclusion that I understood what I did as well as I ever would.

Dr Murphy listened to Mother's account of the letter, and what she had done with it. He was curious about the wording I had used and became irritated when Mother told him she had burned it. 'The point is,' she said, 'he was supposed to be cured and he's not.'

'Margaret, I never said he was cured.'

'You certainly did. Why else would I have sent over a thousand dollars to the Thomasite mission?'

'I said that he was responsible. That means that James knows what he's doing, not that he's going to stop doing it.'

'I'm sure you said he was cured.'

'Never. To say that someone is cured you have to know what health is. With this kind of thing that's impossible. What do you mean by curing James, anyway?'

'You know.'

'Tell me anyway.'

'Getting him back to reality, what else?'

'Whose reality? Mine or yours?'

'Murphy, what are you talking about? James isn't crazy, he's a liar.'

'Well, you have a point there.'

'What am I going to do with him?'

'I don't think there's much you can do. Be patient.'

'I've been patient.'

'If I were you, Margaret, I wouldn't make too much of this. James doesn't steal, does he?'

'Of course not.'

'Or beat people up or talk back.'

'No.'

'Then you have a lot to be thankful for.'

'I don't think I can take any more of it. That business about leukaemia last summer. And now this.'

'Eventually he'll outgrow it, I think.'

'Murphy, he's sixteen years old. What if he doesn't outgrow it? What if he just gets better at it?'

Finally Mother saw that she wasn't going to get any satisfaction from Dr Murphy, who kept reminding her of her blessings. She said something cutting to him and he said something pompous back and she hung up. Dr Murphy stared at the receiver. 'Hello,' he said, then replaced it on the cradle. He ran his hand over his head, a habit remaining from a time when he had hair. To show that he was a good sport he often joked about his baldness, but I had the feeling that he regretted it deeply. Looking at me across the desk, he must have wished that he hadn't taken me on. Treating a friend's child was like investing a friend's money.

'I don't have to tell you who that was.'

I nodded.

Dr Murphy pushed his chair back and swivelled it around so he could look out the window behind him, which took up most of the wall. There were still a few sailboats out on the Bay, but they were all making for shore. A woolly grey fog had covered the bridge and was moving in fast. The water seemed calm from this far up, but when I looked closely I could see white flecks everywhere, so it must have been pretty choppy.

'I'm surprised at you,' he said. 'Leaving something like that lying around for her to find. If you really have to do these things you could at least be kind and do them discreetly. It's not easy for your mother, what with your father dead and all the others somewhere else.'

'I know. I didn't mean for her to find it.'

'Well.' He tapped his pencil against his teeth. He was not convinced professionally, but personally he may have been. 'I think you ought to go home now and straighten things out.'

'I guess I'd better.'

'Tell your mother I might stop by, either tonight or tomorrow. And James – don't underestimate her.'

While my father was alive we usually went to Yosemite for three or four days during the summer. My mother would drive and Father would point out places of interest, meadows where boom towns once stood, hanging trees, rivers that were said to flow upstream at certain times. Or he read to us; he had that grown-ups' idea that children love Dickens and Sir Walter Scott. The four of us sat in the back seat with our faces composed, attentive, while our hands and feet pushed, pinched, stomped, goosed, prodded, dug, and kicked.

One night a bear came into our camp just after dinner. Mother had made a tuna casserole and it must have smelled to him like something worth dying for. He came into the camp while we were sitting around the fire and stood swaying back and forth. My brother Michael saw him first and elbowed me, then my sisters saw him and screamed. Mother and Father had their backs to him but Mother must have guessed what it was because she immediately said, 'Don't scream like that. You might frighten him and there's no telling what he'll do. We'll just sing and he'll go away.'

We sang 'Row Row Row Your Boat' but the bear stayed. He circled us several times, rearing up now and then on his hind legs to stick his nose into the air. By the light of the fire I could see his doglike face and watch the muscles roll under his loose skin like rocks in a sack. We sang harder as he circled us, coming closer and closer. 'All right,' Mother said, 'enough's enough.' She stood abruptly. The bear stopped moving and watched her. 'Beat it,' Mother said. The bear sat down and looked from side to side. 'Beat it,' she said again, and leaned over and picked up a rock.

'Margaret, don't,' my father said.

She threw the rock hard and hit the bear in the stomach. Even in the dim light I could see the dust rising from his fur. He grunted and stood to his full height. 'See that?' Mother shouted: 'He's filthy. Filthy!' One of my sisters giggled. Mother picked up another rock. 'Please, Margaret,' my father said. Just then the bear turned and shambled away. Mother pitched the rock after him. For the rest of the night he loitered around the camp until he found the tree where we had hung our food. He ate it all. The next day we drove back to the city. We could have bought more supplies in the valley, but Father wanted to go and would not give in to any argument. On the way home he tried to jolly everyone up by making jokes, but Michael and my sisters ignored him and looked stonily out the windows.

Things were never easy between my mother and me, but I didn't underestimate her. She underestimated me. When I was little she suspected me of delicacy, because I didn't like being thrown into the air, and because when I saw her and the others working themselves up for a roughhouse I found somewhere else to be. When they did drag me in I got hurt, a knee in the lip, a bent finger, a bloody nose, and this too Mother seemed to hold against me, as if I arranged my hurts to get out of playing.

Even things I did well got on her nerves. We all loved puns except Mother, who didn't get them, and next to my father I was the best in the family. My speciality was the Swifty – '"You can bring the prisoner down," said Tom condescendingly.' Father encouraged me to perform at dinner, which must have been a trial for outsiders. Mother wasn't sure what was going on, but she didn't like it.

She suspected me in other ways. I couldn't go to the movies without her examining my pockets to make sure I had enough money to pay for the ticket. When I went away to camp she tore my pack apart in front of all the boys who were waiting in the bus outside the house. I would rather have gone without my sleeping bag and a few changes of underwear, which I had forgotten, than be made such a fool of. Her distrust was the thing that made me forgetful.

And she thought I was cold-hearted because of what happened the day my father died and later at his funeral. I didn't cry at my father's funeral, and showed signs of boredom during the eulogy, fiddling around with the hymnals. Mother put my hands into my lap and I left them there without moving them as though they were things I was holding for someone else. The effect was ironical and she resented it. We had a sort of reconciliation a few days later after I closed my eyes at school and refused to open them. When several teachers and then the principal failed to persuade me to look at them, or at some reward they claimed to be holding, I was handed over to the school nurse, who tried to pry the lids open and scratched one of them badly. My eye swelled up and I went rigid. The principal panicked and called Mother, who fetched me home. I wouldn't talk to her, or open my eyes, or bend, and they had to lay me on the back seat and when we reached the house Mother had to lift me up the steps one at a time. Then she put me on the couch and played the piano to me all afternoon. Finally I opened my eyes. We hugged each other and I wept. Mother did not really believe my tears, but she was willing to accept them because I had staged them for her benefit.

My lying separated us, too, and the fact that my promises not to lie any more seemed to mean nothing to me. Often my lies came back to her in embarrassing ways, people stopping her in the street and saying how sorry they were to hear this or that. No one in the neighbourhood enjoyed embarrassing Mother, and these situations stopped occurring once everybody got wise to me. There was no saving her from strangers, though. The summer after Father died I visited my uncle in Redding and when I got back I found to my surprise that Mother had come to meet my bus. I tried to slip away from the gentleman who had sat next to me but I couldn't shake him. When he saw Mother embrace me he came up and presented her with a card and told her to get in touch with him if things got any worse. She gave him his card back and told him to mind his own business. Later, on the way home, she made me repeat what I had said to the man. She shook her head. 'It's not fair to people,' she said, 'telling them things like that. It confuses them.' It seemed to me that Mother had confused the man, not I, but I didn't say so. I agreed with her that I shouldn't say such things and promised not to do it again, a promise I broke three hours later in conversation with a woman in the park.

It wasn't only the lies that disturbed Mother; it was their morbidity.

This was the real issue between us, as it had been between her and my father. Mother did volunteer work at Children's Hospital and St Anthony's Dining Hall, collected things for the St Vincent de Paul Society. She was a lighter of candles. My brother and sisters took after her in this way. My father was a curser of the dark. And he loved to curse the dark. He was never more alive than when he was indignant about something. For this reason the most important act of the day for him was the reading of the evening paper.

Ours was a terrible paper, indifferent to the city that bought it, indifferent to medical discoveries – except for new kinds of gases that made your hands fall off when you sneezed – and indifferent to politics and art. Its business was outrage, horror, gruesome coincidence. When my father sat down in the living room with the paper Mother stayed in the kitchen and kept the children busy, all except me, because I was quiet and could be trusted to amuse myself. I amused myself by watching my father.

He sat with his knees spread, leaning forward, his eyes only inches from the print. As he read he nodded to himself. Sometimes he swore and threw the paper down and paced the room, then picked it up and began again. Over a period of time he developed the habit of reading aloud to me. He always started with the society section, which he called the parasite page. This column began to take on the character of a comic strip or a serial, with the same people showing up from one day to the next, blinking in chiffon, awkwardly holding their drinks for the sake of Peninsula orphans, grinning under sunglasses on the deck of a ski hut in the Sierras. The skiers really got his goat, probably because he couldn't understand them. The activity itself was inconceivable to him. When my sisters went to Lake Tahoe one winter weekend with some friends and came back excited about the beauty of the place, Father calmed them right down. 'Snow,' he said, 'is overrated.'

Then the news, or what passed in the paper for news: bodies unearthed in Scotland, former Nazis winning elections, rare animals slaughtered, misers expiring naked in freezing houses upon mattresses stuffed with thousands, millions; marrying priests, divorcing actresses, high-rolling oilmen building fantastic mausoleums in honour of a favourite horse, cannibalism. Through all this my father waded with a fixed and weary smile.

Mother encouraged him to take up causes, to join groups, but he would not. He was uncomfortable with people outside the family. He and my mother rarely went out, and rarely had people in, except on feast days and national holidays. Their guests were always the same, Dr Murphy and his wife and several others whom they had known since childhood. Most of these people never saw each other outside our house and they didn't have much fun together. Father discharged his obligations as host by teasing everyone about stupid things they had said or done in the past and forcing them to laugh at themselves.

Though Father did not drink, he insisted on mixing cocktails for the guests. He would not serve straight drinks like rum-and-Coke or even Scotch-on-the-rocks, only drinks of his own devising. He gave them lawyerly names like 'The Hanging Judge', 'The Ambulance Chaser', 'The Mouthpiece', and described their concoction in detail. He told long, complicated stories in a near-whisper, making everyone lean in his direction, and repeated important lines; he also repeated the important lines in the stories my mother told, and corrected her when she got something wrong. When the guests came to the ends of their own stories he would point out the morals.

Dr Murphy had several theories about Father, which he used to test on me in the course of our meetings. Dr Murphy had by this time given up his glasses for contact lenses, and lost weight in the course of fasts which he undertook regularly. Even with his baldness he looked years younger than when he had come to the parties at our house. Certainly he did not look like my father's contemporary, which he was.

One of Dr Murphy's theories was that Father had exhibited a classic trait of people who had been gifted children by taking an undemanding position in an uninteresting firm. 'He was afraid of finding his limits,' Dr Murphy told me: 'As long as he kept stamping papers and making out wills he could go on believing that he didn't *have* limits.' Dr Murphy's fascination with Father made me uneasy, and I felt traitorous listening to him. While he lived, my father would never have submitted himself for analysis; it seemed a betrayal to put him on the couch now that he was dead.

I did enjoy Dr Murphy's recollections of Father as a child. He told me about something that happened when they were in the Boy Scouts. Their troop had been on a long hike and Father had fallen behind. Dr Murphy and the others decided to ambush him as he came down the trail. They hid in the woods on each side and waited. But when Father walked into the trap none of them moved or made a sound and he strolled on without even knowing they were there. 'He had the sweetest look on his face,' Dr Murphy said, 'listening to the birds, smelling the flowers, just like Ferdinand the Bull.' He also told me that my father's drinks tasted like medicine.

While I rode my bicycle home from Dr Murphy's office Mother fretted. She felt terribly alone but she didn't call anyone because she also felt like a failure. My lying had that effect on her. She took it personally. At such times she did not think of my sisters, one happily married, the other doing brilliantly at Fordham. She did not think of my brother Michael, who had given up college to work with runaway children in Los Angeles. She thought of me. She thought that she had made a mess of her family.

Actually she managed the family well. While my father was dying upstairs she pulled us together. She made lists of chores and gave each of us a fair allowance. Bedtimes were adjusted and she stuck by them. She set regular hours for homework. Each child was made responsible for the next eldest, and I was given a dog. She told us frequently, predictably, that she loved us. At dinner we were each expected to contribute something, and after dinner she played the piano and tried to teach us to sing in harmony, which I could not do. Mother, who was an admirer of the von Trapp family, considered this a character defect.

Our life together was more orderly, healthy, while Father was dying than it had been before. He had set us rules to follow, not much different really than the ones Mother gave us after he got sick, but he had administered them in a fickle way. Though we were supposed to get an allowance we always had to ask him for it and then he would give us too much because he enjoyed seeming magnanimous. Sometimes he punished us for no reason, because he was in a bad mood. He was apt to decide, as one of my sisters was going out to a dance, that she had better stay home and do something to improve herself. Or he would sweep us all up on a Wednesday night and take us ice-skating.

He changed after he learned about the cancer, and became more calm as the disease spread. He relaxed his teasing way with us, and from time to time it was possible to have a conversation with him which was not about the last thing that had made him angry. He stopped reading the paper and spent time at the window.

He and I became close. He taught me to play poker and sometimes helped me with my homework. But it wasn't his illness that drew us together. The reserve between us had begun to break down after the incident with the bear, during the drive home. Michael and my sisters were furious with him for making us leave early and wouldn't talk to him or look at him. He joked: though it had been a grisly experience we should grin and bear it – and so on. His joking seemed perverse to the others, but not to me. I had seen how terrified he was when the bear came into the camp. When Mother started pitching rocks I thought he was going to bolt. I understood – I had been frightened too. The others took it as a lark after they got used to having the bear around, but for Father and me it got worse through the night. I was glad to be out of there, grateful to Father for getting me out. I saw that his jokes were how he held himself together. So I reached out to him with a joke: '"There's a bear outside," said Tom intently.' The others turned cold looks on me. They thought I was sucking up. But Father smiled.

When I thought of other boys being close to their fathers I thought of them hunting together, tossing a ball back and forth, making birdhouses in the basement, and having long talks about girls, war, careers. Maybe the reason it took us so long to get close was that I had this idea. It kept getting in the way of what we really had, which was a shared fear.

Towards the end Father slept most of the time and I watched him. From below, sometimes, faintly, I heard Mother playing the piano.

Occasionally he nodded off in his chair while I was reading to him; his bathrobe would fall open then, and I would see the long new scar on his stomach, red as blood against his white skin. His ribs all showed and his legs were like cables.

I once read in a biography of a great man that he 'died well'. I assume the writer meant that he kept his pain to himself, did not set off false alarms, and did not too much inconvenience those who were to stay behind. My father died well. His irritability gave way to something else, something like serenity. In the last days he became tender. It was as though he had been rehearsing the scene, that the anger of his life had been a kind of stage fright. He managed his audience – us – with an old trouper's sense of when to clown and when to stand on his dignity. We were all moved, and admired his courage, as he intended we should. He died downstairs in a shaft of late afternoon sunlight on New Year's Day, while I was reading to him. I was alone in the house and didn't know what to do. His body did not frighten me but immediately and sharply I missed my father. It seemed wrong to leave him sitting up and I tried to carry him upstairs to the bedroom but it was too hard, alone. So I called up my friend Ralphy across the street. When he came over and saw what I wanted him for he started crying but I made him help me anyway. A couple of hours later Mother got home and when I told her that Father was dead she ran upstairs, calling his name. A few minutes later she came back down. 'Thank God,' she said, 'at least he died in bed.' This seemed important to her and I didn't tell her otherwise. But that night Ralphy's parents called. They were, they said, shocked at what I had done and so was Mother when she heard the story, shocked and furious. Why? Because I had not told her the truth? Or because she had learned the truth, and could not go on believing that Father had died in bed? I really don't know.

'Mother,' I said, coming into the living room, 'I'm sorry about the letter.'

She was arranging wood in the fireplace and did not look at me or speak for a moment. Finally she finished and straightened up and brushed her hands. She stepped back and looked at the fire she had laid. 'That's all right,' she said. 'Not bad for a consumptive.'

'Mother, I'm sorry.'

'Sorry? Sorry you wrote it or sorry I found it?'

'I wasn't going to mail it. It was a sort of joke.'

'Ha ha.' She took up the whisk broom and swept bits of bark into the fireplace, then closed the drapes and settled on the couch. 'Sit down,' she said. She crossed her legs. 'Listen, do I give you advice all the time?'

'Yes.'

'I do?'

I nodded.

'Well, that doesn't make any difference. I'm supposed to. I'm your mother. I'm going to give you some more advice, for your own good. You don't have to make all these things up, James. They'll happen anyway.' She picked at the hem of her skirt. 'Do you understand what I'm saying?'

'I think so.'

'You're cheating yourself, that's what I'm trying to tell you. When you get to be my age you won't know anything at all about life. All you'll know is what you've made up.'

I thought about that. It seemed logical.

She went on. 'I think maybe you need to get out of yourself more. Think more about other people.'

The doorbell rang.

'Go see who it is,' Mother said. 'We'll talk about this later.'

It was Dr Murphy. He and Mother made their apologies and she insisted that he stay for dinner. I went to the kitchen to fetch ice for their drinks, and when I returned they were talking about me. I sat on the sofa and listened. Dr Murphy was telling Mother not to worry. 'James is a good boy,' he said. 'I've been thinking about my oldest, Terry. He's not really dishonest, you know, but he's not really honest either. I can't seem to reach him. At least James isn't furtive.'

'No,' Mother said, 'he's never been furtive.'

Dr Murphy clasped his hands between his knees and stared at them. 'Well, that's Terry. Furtive.'

Before we sat down to dinner Mother said grace; Dr Murphy bowed his head and closed his eyes and crossed himself at the end, though he had lost his faith in college. When he told me that, during one of our meetings, in just those words, I had the picture of a raincoat hanging by itself outside a dining hall. He drank a good deal of wine and persistently turned the conversation to the subject of his relationship with Terry. He admitted that he had come to dislike the boy. He used the word 'dislike' with relish, like someone on a diet permitting himself a single potato chip. 'I don't know what I've done wrong,' he said abruptly, and with reference to no particular thing. 'Then again maybe I haven't done anything wrong. I don't know what to think any more. Nobody does.'

'I know what to think,' Mother said.

'So does the solipsist. How can you prove to a solipsist that he's not creating the rest of us?'

This was one of Dr Murphy's favourite riddles, and almost any pretext was sufficient for him to trot it out. He was a child with a card trick.

'Send him to bed without dinner,' Mother said. 'Let him create that.'

Dr Murphy suddenly turned to me. 'Why do you do it?' he asked. It was a pure question, it had no object beyond the satisfaction of his curiosity. Mother looked at me and there was the same curiosity in her face.

'I don't know,' I said, and that was the truth.

Dr Murphy nodded, not because he had anticipated my answer but because he accepted it. 'Is it fun?'

'No, it's not fun. I can't explain.'

'Why is it all so sad?' Mother asked. 'Why all the diseases?'

'Maybe,' Dr Murphy said, 'sad things are more interesting.'

'Not to me,' Mother said.

'Not to me, either,' I said. 'It just comes out that way.'

After dinner Dr Murphy asked Mother to play the piano. He

particularly wanted to sing 'Come Home Abbie, the Light's on the Stair'.

'That old thing,' Mother said. She stood and folded her napkin deliberately and we followed her into the living room. Dr Murphy stood behind her as she warmed up. Then they sang 'Come Home Abbie, the Light's on the Stair', and I watched him stare down at Mother intently, as if he were trying to remember something. Her own eyes were closed. After that they sang 'O Magnum Mysterium'. They sang it in parts and I regretted that I had no voice, it sounded so good.

'Come on, James,' Dr Murphy said as Mother played the last chords. 'These old tunes not good enough for you?'

'He just can't sing,' Mother said.

When Dr Murphy left, Mother lit the fire and made more coffee. She slouched down in the big chair, sticking her legs straight out and moving her feet back and forth. 'That was fun,' she said.

'Did you and Father ever do things like that?'

'A few times, when we were first going out. I don't think he really enjoyed it. He was like you.'

I wondered if Mother and Father had had a good marriage. He admired her and liked to look at her; every night at dinner he had us move the candlesticks slightly to right and left of centre so he could see her down the length of the table. And every evening when she set the table she put them in the centre again. She didn't seem to miss him very much. But I wouldn't really have known if she did, and anyway I didn't miss him all that much myself, not the way I had. Most of the time I thought about other things.

'James?'

I waited.

'I've been thinking that you might like to go down and stay with Michael for a couple of weeks or so.'

'What about school?'

'I'll talk to Father McSorley. He won't mind. Maybe this problem will take care of itself if you start thinking about other people.'

'I do.'

'I mean helping them, like Michael does. You don't have to go if you don't want to.'

'It's fine with me. Really. I'd like to see Michael.'

'I'm not trying to get rid of you.'

'I know.'

Mother stretched, then tucked her feet under her. She sipped noisily at her coffee. 'What did that word mean that Murphy used? You know the one?'

'Paranoid? That's where somebody thinks everyone is out to get him. Like that woman who always grabs you after Mass – Frances.'

'Not paranoid. Everyone knows what that means. Solipsist.'

'Oh. A solipsist is someone who thinks he creates everything around him.'

Mother nodded and blew on her coffee, then put it down without drinking from it. 'I'd rather be paranoid. Do you really think Frances is?'

'Of course. No question about it.'

'I mean really *sick*?'

'That's what paranoid *is*, is being sick. What do you think, Mother?'

'What are you so angry about?'

'I'm not angry.' I lowered my voice. 'I'm not angry. But you don't believe those stories of hers, do you?'

'Well, no, not exactly. I don't think she knows what she's saying, she just wants someone to listen. She probably lives all by herself in some little room. So she's paranoid. James, we should pray for her. Will you remember to do that?'

I nodded. I thought of Mother singing 'O Magnum Mysterium', saying grace, praying with easy confidence, and it came to me that her imagination was superior to mine. She could imagine things as coming together, not falling apart. She looked at me and I shrank; I knew exactly what she was going to say. 'Son,' she said, 'do you know how much I love you?'

The next afternoon I took the bus to Los Angeles. I looked forward to the trip, to the monotony of the road and the empty fields by the roadside. Mother walked with me down the long concourse. The station was crowded and oppressive. 'Are you sure this is the right bus?' she asked at the loading platform.

'Yes.'

'It looks so old.'

'Mother – '

'All right.' She pulled me against her and kissed me, then held me an extra second to show that her embrace was sincere, not just like everyone else's, never having realized that everyone else does the same thing. I boarded the bus and we waved at each other until it became embarrassing. Then Mother began checking through her handbag for something. When she had finished I stood and adjusted the luggage over my seat. I sat and we smiled at each other, waved when the driver gunned the engine, shrugged when he got up suddenly to count the passengers, waved again when he resumed his seat. As the bus pulled out my mother and I were looking at each other with plain relief.

I had boarded the wrong bus. This one was bound for Los Angeles but not by the express route. We stopped in San Mateo, Palo Alto, San Jose, Castroville. When we left Castroville it began to rain, hard; my window would not close all the way, and a thin stream of water ran down the wall onto my seat. To keep dry I had to stay away from the wall and lean forward. The rain fell harder. The engine of the bus sounded as though it were coming apart.

In Salinas the man sleeping beside me jumped up but before I had a chance to change seats his place was taken by an enormous woman in a print dress, carrying a shopping bag. She took possession of her seat and spilled over onto half of mine, backing me up to the wall. 'That's a storm,' she said loudly, then turned and looked at me. 'Hungry?' Without waiting for an answer she dipped into her bag and pulled out a piece of chicken and thrust it at me. 'Hey, by God,' she hooted, 'look at him go to town on that drumstick!' A few people turned and smiled. I smiled back around the bone and kept at it. I finished that piece and she handed me another, and then another. Then she started handing out chicken to the people in the seats near us.

Outside of San Luis Obispo the noise from the engine grew suddenly louder and just as suddenly there was no noise at all. The driver pulled off to the side of the road and got out, then got on again dripping wet. A few moments later he announced that the bus had broken down and they were sending another bus to pick us up. Someone asked how long that might take and the driver said he had no idea. 'Keep your pants on!' shouted the woman next to me. 'Anybody in a hurry to get to L.A. ought to have his head examined.'

The wind was blowing hard around the bus, driving sheets of rain against the windows on both sides. The bus swayed gently. Outside the light was brown and thick. The woman next to me pumped all the people around us for their itineraries and said whether or not she had ever been where they were from or where they were going. 'How about you?' She slapped my knee. 'Parents own a chicken ranch? I hope so!' She laughed. I told her I was from San Francisco. 'San Francisco, that's where my husband was stationed.' She asked me what I did there and I told her I worked with refugees from Tibet.

'Is that right. What do you do with a bunch of Tibetans?'

'Seems like there's plenty of other places they could've gone,' said a man in front of us. 'Coming across the border like that. We don't go there.'

'What do you do with a bunch of Tibetans?' the woman repeated.

'Try to find them jobs, locate housing, listen to their problems.'

'You understand that kind of talk?'

'Yes.'

'Speak it?'

'Pretty well. I was born and raised in Tibet. My parents were missionaries over there.'

Everyone waited.

'They were killed when the Communists took over.'

The big woman patted my arm.

'It's all right,' I said.

'Why don't you say some of that Tibetan?'

'What would you like to hear?'

'Say "The cow jumped over the moon."' She watched me, smiling, and when I finished she looked at the others and shook her head. 'That was pretty. Like music. Say some more.'

'What?'

'Anything.'

They bent towards me. The windows suddenly went blind with rain. The driver had fallen asleep and was snoring gently to the swaying of the bus. Outside the muddy light flickered to pale yellow, and far off there was thunder. The woman next to me leaned back and closed her eyes and then so did all the others as I sang to them in what was surely an ancient and holy tongue.

Coming Attractions

Jean was alone in the theatre. She had seen the customers out, locked the doors, and zipped up the night's receipts in the bank deposit bag. Now she was taking a last look around while she waited for her boss to come back and drive her home.

Mr Munson had left after the first show to go ice skating at the new mall on Buena Vista. He'd been leaving early for almost a month now and at first Jean thought he was committing adultery against his wife, until she saw him on the ice one Saturday afternoon while she was out shoplifting with her girlfriend Kathy. They stopped by the curved window that ran around the rink and watched Mr Munson crash into the wall several times. 'Fat people shouldn't skate,' Kathy said, and they walked on.

Most nights Mr Munson came back to the theatre around eleven. This was the latest he had ever been. It was almost twelve o'clock.

Someone had left an orange scarf on one of the seats in the back row. Under the same seat lay a partially eaten hambone and a bottle of hot sauce. The hambone still looked like what it was, an animal's leg, and when she saw it Jean felt weak. She picked up the scarf and left the food for Mr Munson to deal with. If he said anything about it she would just play dumb. She put the scarf in the lost-and-found bag and walked towards the front of the theatre, glancing from side to side to scan the length of the rows.

Halfway down the aisle Jean found a pair of sunglasses. They were Guccis. She dropped them in the bag and tried to forget about them, as if she were a regular honest person who did not steal lost items and everything else that wasn't bolted down, but Jean knew that she was going to keep the sunglasses and this knowledge made her resistance feel ridiculous. She walked a few rows farther, then gave a helpless shrug as if someone were watching and took the sunglasses out of the bag. They didn't fit. Her face was too narrow for them, her nose too thin. They made everything dim and kept slipping down, but Jean left them on as she worked her way towards the front of the theatre.

In the first row on the right, near the wall, Jean saw a coat draped over one of the seats. She moved along the row to pick it up. Then she stopped and took off the sunglasses, because she had decided to believe that the coat was not a coat, but a dead woman wearing a coat. A dead woman all by herself in a theatre at midnight.

Jean closed her eyes and made a soft whimpering noise like a dreaming dog makes. It sounded phony to her, so she stopped doing it; she opened her eyes and walked back along the row and up the aisle towards the lobby.

Jean put the lost-and-found bag away, then stood by the glass entrance doors and watched the traffic. She leaned forward as each new line of cars approached, looking through her own reflected face for Mr Munson's Toyota. The glass grew so foggy from her breath that Jean could barely see through it. She became aware of her breathing, how shallow and fast it was. The game with the coat had scared her more than she'd meant it to. Jean watched some more cars go by. Finally she turned away and crossed the lobby to Mr Munson's office.

Jean locked the office door behind her, but the closed door made her feel trapped. She unlocked the door again and left it open. From Mr Munson's desk she could see the Coke machine and a row of posters advertising next week's movie. The desk top was empty except for the telephone and a picture of Mrs Munson standing beside a snowdrift back where the Munsons used to live – Minnesota or Wisconsin. Mrs Munson had on a parka, and she was pointing at the top of the drift to show how tall it was.

The snow made Jean think of her father.

It was quiet in the office. Jean laid her head on her crossed arms and closed her eyes. Almost at once she opened them again. She sat up and pulled the telephone across the desk and dialled her father's number. It was three hours later there and he was a heavy sleeper, so she let the phone ring for a long time. At first she held the receiver tight against her ear. Then she laid it down on the desk and listened to it until she heard a voice. Jean picked up the receiver again. It was her stepmother, Linda, saying 'Hello? . . . Hello? . . . Hello? . . .' Jean would have hung up on her but she heard the fear in Linda's voice like an echo of her own, and she couldn't do it. 'Hello,' she said.

'Hello? Who is this, please?'

'Jean,' Jean murmured.

'Gee-Gee? Is this Gee-Gee?'

'It's me,' Jean said.

'It's you,' Linda said. 'My God, you gave me a fright.'

'I'm sorry.'

'What time is it out there?'

'Twelve. Ten past twelve.'

'It's three o'clock in the morning here, lambchop. We're later than you are.'

'I know.'

'I just wondered if maybe you thought we were earlier. Wow, just hang on till I get myself together.' A moment later Linda said, 'There. Pulse normal. All systems go. So where are you, anyway?'

'At work.'

'That's right, your dad told me you had a job. Gee-Gee with a job! You're just turning into a regular little grown-up, aren't you?'

'I guess,' Jean said.

'Well, I think that's just super.'

Jean nodded.

'I'm big on people doing for themselves,' Linda said. 'Fifteen isn't too young. I started work when I was twelve and I haven't stopped since.'

'I know,' Jean said.

Linda laughed. 'Christ almighty, the jobs I've had. I could tell you stories.'

Jean smiled politely into the receiver. She caught herself doing it and made a face.

'I guess you want to talk to old grumpy bear,' Linda said.

'If that's okay.'

'I hope it isn't bad news. You're not preggers, are you?'

'No.'

'How about your brother?'

'Tucker isn't pregnant either,' Jean said. 'He hasn't started dating yet.'

Linda laughed again. 'I didn't mean *that*. I meant how *is* he?'

'Tucker's doing fine.'

'And your mom?'

'She's fine too. We're all fine.'

'That's great,' Linda said, 'because you know how your dad is about bad news. He's just not set up for it. He's more of a good news person.'

Jean gave Linda the finger. She mashed it against the mouthpiece, then said, 'Right.' And Linda *was* right. Jean knew that, knew she wouldn't have said anything even if her father had come to the telephone except how great she was, and how great Tucker and her mom were, because telling him anything else would be against the rules. 'Everyone's fine,' Jean repeated. 'I just had this urge to talk to him, that's all.'

'Sure you did,' Linda said. 'Don't think he doesn't get the same urge sometimes.'

'Tell him hi,' Jean said. 'Sorry I woke you up.'

'That's what we're here for, dumpling. I'll see if I can get him to write you. He keeps meaning to, but letters are hard for him. He likes to be more hands-on with people. Still, I'll see what I can do, okay? You take care now.'

Jean smashed the phone down and yelled 'Fool!' She leaned violently back in the chair and crossed her legs. 'Stupid hag,' she said. 'Vegetable.'

She went on like this until she couldn't think of anything else.

Then she called her mother's apartment. Tucker answered the phone. 'Tucker, what are you doing up?' Jean asked.

'Nothing,' Tucker said. 'You're supposed to be home. Mom said you'd be home now.'

'And you're supposed to be in bed,' Jean told him. She heard a woman's voice shrieking, then two gunshots and a blare of music. 'I can't believe you're still up,' Jean said. 'Let me speak to Mom.'

'What?'

'Let me speak to Mom.'

'She's not here,' Tucker said. 'Jean, know what?'

Jean closed her eyes.

'There's a bicycle in the swimming pool,' Tucker said. 'In the deep end. Under the diving board. Mr Fox told me I could keep it if we get it out. It's red,' he added.

'Tucker, where's Mom? I want to talk to her.'

'She went out with Uncle Nick.'

'Where?'

Tucker didn't answer.

'Where did they go, Tucker?'

Tucker still didn't answer. Jean heard the sound of police sirens and squealing tyres, and knew that he was watching the television again. He'd forgotten all about her. She screamed his name into the receiver. 'What?' he said.

'Where are the grown-ups?'

'I don't know. Jean, are you coming home now?'

'In a few minutes. Go to bed, Tucker.'

'Okay,' he said. Then he said, 'Bye,' and hung up.

Jean got the telephone book out of the desk, but she could not remember Nick's last name. His number was probably lying around the apartment somewhere; in fact she knew it was, she had seen it, on her mom's bedside table or stuck to the refrigerator with a magnet. But if she asked Tucker to look for it he would get all confused and start crying.

Jean stood and went to the doorway. A jogger wearing phosphorescent stripes ran past the lobby window. The Coke machine gave a long rattling shudder, then went off with a sigh. Jean felt hungry. She got herself a package of Milk Duds from the refreshment counter and carried them back to Mr Munson's office, where she chewed mouthful after mouthful until her jaws were tired. Jean put the rest of the Milk Duds in her purse with the sunglasses. Then she took out the telephone book and looked for the name of her English teacher, Mr Hopkins. Mr Hopkins also taught Driver's Ed and Kathy said that he had practically climbed on top of her when they were doing parallel parking. Jean hated him for that. How could someone recite poetry the way Mr Hopkins did and still want Kathy?

His number wasn't in the book. Jean kept flipping through the pages. She chose a name and dialled the number and a man answered right away. In a soft voice he said, 'Yes.' Not 'Yes?' but 'Yes,' as if he'd been expecting this call.

'Mr Love,' Jean said, 'have I got news for you.'

'Who is this?' he asked. 'Do you know what time it is?'

'The news just came in. We thought you'd want to hear it right away. But if you wish to refuse the call all you have to do is say so.'

'I'm not sure I understand,' Mr Love said.

'Do you wish to refuse the call, Mr Love?'

He did not answer right away. Then he said, 'Don't tell me I won something.'

'Won something? Mr Love, that is the understatement of the century.'

'Just a minute,' he said. 'I have to get my glasses.'

'This *is* Mr Love, I assume?' Jean asked when he returned to the telephone.

'Yes, ma'am. One and the same.'

'We can't be too careful,' Jean told him. 'We're not talking about a bunch of steak knives here.'

'I've never won anything before,' Mr Love said. 'Just spelling bees. When I was a kid I could spell the paint off the walls.'

'I guess I've got you on the edge of your seat,' Jean said.

Mr Love laughed.

'You sound like a nice person,' Jean said. 'Where are you from?'

Mr Love laughed again. 'You're deliberately tying me up in knots.'

Jean said, 'We have a few standard questions we like to ask.' She took the sunglasses from her purse and slipped them on. She leaned back and looked up at the ceiling. 'We like to get acquainted with our winners.'

'You've got me in a state,' Mr Love said. 'All right, here goes. Born and raised in Detroit. Joined the navy after Pearl Harbor. Got my discharge papers in San Diego, June 'forty-six, and moved up here a couple weeks later. Been here ever since. That's about it.'

'Good. So far so good. Age, Mr Love?'

'Sixty-one.'

'Marital status?'

'No status at all. I'm a single man.'

'Do you mean to say, Mr Love, that you have lived more than half a century and never entered into holy matrimony?'

Mr Love was silent for a moment. Then he said, 'Come on now – what's all this about?'

'One more question, Mr Love. Then we'll talk prizes.'

Mr Love said nothing, but Jean could hear him breathe.

She picked up the photograph of Mrs Munson and laid it face down on the desk. 'Here's the question, Mr Love. I lie and steal and sleep around. What do you think about that?'

'Ah,' Mr Love said. 'So I didn't win anything.'

'Well, sir, no. I have to say no.'

He cleared his throat and said, 'I don't follow.'

'It's a prank,' Jean told him. 'I'm a prankster.'

'I understand that. I just don't see the point. What's the point?'

Jean let the question pass.

'Well, you're not the first to make a fool out of me,' Mr Love said, 'and I suppose you won't be the last.'

'I don't actually sleep around,' Jean said.

He said, 'You need to learn some concern for other people. Do you go to church?'

'No, sir. Sometimes back home we used to, but not here. Only once on Easter. The priest didn't even give a sermon. All he did was play a tape of a baby being born, with whale songs in the background.' Jean waited for Mr Love's reaction. He didn't seem to have one. 'I don't actually sleep around,' Jean repeated. 'Just with one of my teachers. He's married,' she added.

'Married!' Mr Love said. 'That's terrible. How old are you?'

'He thinks I'm brilliant,' Jean said. 'Brilliant and seductive. He kept staring at me in class. The next thing I knew he was writing poems on the back of my essays, and that's how it started. He's hopelessly in love with me but I couldn't care less. I'm just playing him along.'

'God in heaven,' Mr Love said.

'I'm awful to him. Absolutely heartless. I make fun of him in front of my friends. I do imitations of him. I even do imitations of him in bed, all the sounds he makes and everything. I guess you could say I'm just totally out of control. Don't ask me to tell you where it is, but I have this tattoo that says X-RATED. It's my motto. That and "Live fast, die young". Whenever I'm doing something really depraved I always say "Live fast, die young". I probably will too.'

'I'm at a loss,' Mr Love said. 'I wish I knew what to do here.'

He was quiet.

'Say something,' Jean told him. 'Bawl me out.'

'I don't know you. I don't even know your name. I might be of some help if I knew your name.'

'Fat chance,' Jean said.

'Then I just don't know what to say.'

Jean heard the snapping of the lock in the lobby door. 'Adieu,' she said, and hung up. She took the sunglasses off and put them in her purse, then stood and walked around the desk in time to see Mr Munson swinging towards the office between a pair of crutches, one plaster-bound foot held cocked behind him. There was a bandage across his forehead. 'Don't say a word,' he told Jean. 'I don't want to talk about it.' Mr Munson lurched past her into the office. 'Just a little difficulty on the ice,' he said bitterly. 'Just a little taste of the old Munson karma.' He took the bank deposit bag from the drawer where Jean kept it for him, unzipped it, leaned forward on the crutches, and shook the money onto the desk top. 'Here,' he said. Without looking up, Mr Munson held out a five to Jean. 'There's a cab waiting out front.'

'A cab?'

'Do you expect me to drive in this condition? Look at me, for Christ's sake. I'm a mess.'

'You don't look that bad,' Jean told him.

'I look like the goddamn *Spirit of 'Seventy-six* or something,' Mr Munson said. He lowered himself into the chair and propped his crutches against the desk. 'I used to be good,' he said, 'I mean really good.' He raised his eyes to Jean. 'I'm nice to you, aren't I? I don't yell at you when you screw up. I don't say anything when you sneak your little friend in. You shouldn't look at me like that,' he said. 'You should try to look sorry.'

Tucker was asleep on the floor in front of the television. Jean opened the Hide-a-Bed and managed to get him into his pyjamas and between the covers without waking him up. Then she ransacked her mother's room for Nick's telephone number. She didn't find it, but she did find a new letter from her father. Jean sat on the bed and read the letter through, scowling at the sugary words he used, sometimes repeating them in a sarcastic tone. They still wrote each other love letters, her mother and father, but they had no right to; not now, not after what they'd done. It was disgusting.

Jean went to her own room. She read *Silas Marner* for a while, then got undressed and stood in front of the mirror. She studied herself. She turned and glanced coldly over her shoulder.

Jean faced the mirror again and practised looking sad but brave. Then she got the sunglasses out of her purse and put them on, along with one of the blouses she'd stolen at Bullock's last weekend. She switched off all the lights except the swag lamp above her desk, so that she looked as if she were standing under a streetlight. The blouse hung halfway down her bare thighs. Jean turned the wide collar up, and lowered her eyelids, and let her mouth fall open a little. 'I think of you all the time,' she whispered, reciting her father's words, 'every day and every night, dearest love, only love of my life.' Jean moved her shoulders sinuously to make the sequins shimmer. 'Dearest sackbutt,' she said. 'Dearest raisinbrain.' She pursed her lips and made her eyelids flutter.

Tucker yelled something from the next room.

Jean went to the doorway. 'Go to sleep, Tucker.'

'I want Mom,' Tucker said.

Jean took the sunglasses off. Tucker was sitting up in bed, looking wildly around as if he didn't know where he was. Jean walked across the room and sat down beside him. 'Mom'll be home in a minute.' Tucker's hair was sticking up all over, and Jean began to smooth it down. 'You want a glass of water?'

'I want Mom.'

'Listen, Tucker.' Jean kept combing back his hair with her fingers. 'Listen, tomorrow is going to be a really special day but it won't come unless you go to sleep.'

He looked around the room again, then back at Jean. 'Special how?'

'You'll see.'

'You mean when I wake up?'

'Right, but first you have to go to sleep.' Jean pushed against Tucker as she stroked his hair, and at last he relented and lay down again.

'Promise?' he said.

'Promise.'

When Tucker was asleep Jean got up and went outside. She leaned against the door, her skin bristling with cold, and looked around at the other apartments. All of them were dark. Jean hugged herself and padded along the rough wooden walkway, down the steps to the courtyard.

The pool lights were still on so that nobody would fall in and sue. Still hugging herself, Jean tested the water with one foot. It was icy. Mrs Fox must have turned off the heat. That was just like her, to turn the heat on in the summer and turn it off in the winter. Stupid witch. It wasn't even her money. Jean sniffed and rubbed her arms and stuck her foot in the water again, this time past the ankle. Again she looked at the dark windows all around. Then she peeled off the blouse, tossed it behind her, and jumped in.

Jean's heart clenched when she hit the water. She kicked herself back up, gasping for air, and grabbed the ladder. Tremors twitched across her shoulders. Her toes curled painfully, then went numb. Jean held to the ladder and waited for the numbness to spread. She looked up. A plane was moving slowly across the sky. Jean timed her breathing to the blinking of its lights, and when she had calmed herself she took a series of deeper and deeper breaths until she had the one she wanted. Then she pushed off and dove towards the glowing red triangle at the bottom of the pool.

Her eyes ached. That was all she felt. Jean closed her fingers around the handlebars and tried to scissor-kick the bicycle up with her, but when she had it halfway to the surface it seemed to take on weight, and she had to let it go. It settled to the bottom without a sound, sending only a dull shock up through the water. Jean filled her lungs and went back under. She took hold of the handlebars again. She dragged the bike along the tiles to the side of the pool, where she went into a crouch and shoved away hard from the bottom. Kicking furiously, clawing the water with her free hand, Jean rose slowly towards the gleaming chrome of the ladder and just managed to grab the second rung as the bike began to pull her back down.

She let out the last of her air.

The bike was getting heavy. Jean brought her knees up and got her feet on the lowest rung. She rested a moment. Then she moved her free hand to the rail and began to straighten her legs, pushing herself up towards the light flashing on the surface just above her. She felt her mouth start to open. *No*, she thought, but her mouth opened anyway and Jean was choking when her head broke through to air. She coughed out the water in her throat and then gagged on the chlorine aftertaste until she almost puked. Her eyes burned.

Jean climbed the ladder to where she could work her hips over the edge of the pool and slide forward a bit. She let go of the rail and wiped her face. Her other arm was dead, but she knew the bike was still there because she could feel its weight in her shoulders and back. In a little while she would pull it out. No problem – just as soon as she got herself back together. But until then she couldn't do a thing but lie with her cheek on the cement, and blink her eyes, and savour the cold air that passed through her.

The Missing Person

Father Leo started out with the idea of becoming a missionary. He'd read a priest's account of his years among the Aleuts and decided that this was the life for him – trekking from trapper's hut to Indian village, a dog for company, sacramental wine in his knapsack, across snowfields that gleamed like sugar. He knew it would be hard. He would suffer things he could not imagine in that polar solitude. But it was the life he wanted, a life full of risk among people who needed him and were hungry for what he had to give.

Shortly before his ordination he asked to be sent to Alaska. The diocese turned down his request. The local parishes were short of priests and their needs came first. Father Leo was assigned to a parish in West Seattle, where the pastor took an immediate dislike to him and put him on what he called 'crone duty' – managing rummage sales, bingo, the Legion of Mary, and visiting sick parishioners in the hospital. Father Leo worked hard at everything he put his hand to. He hoped that the old priest would notice and begin to soften towards him, but that never happened.

He stayed on in the parish. The old priest kept going, though his mind had begun to wander and he could not walk without a stick. He repeated his sermons again and again. There was one story he told at least once a month, about an Irishman who received a visitation from his mother the night after her death, a visit that caused him to change his whole life. He told the story with a brogue, and it went on forever.

The parishioners didn't seem to mind. More of them came every year, and they kept the old priest busy from morning to night. He liked to say that he didn't have time to die. One night he said it at dinner and Father Leo thought, *Make time.*

Finally the old priest did die. Father Leo collected his papers for the diocese and found copies of several reports the old priest had made on him. They were all disparaging, and some of them were untrue. He sat on the floor and read them through carefully. Then he put them down and rubbed his eyes. It was the first warm night of the year. The window was open. A moth fluttered against the screen.

Father Leo was surprised at what he'd found. He couldn't understand why the old priest had hated him. But the more he thought about it, the less strange it seemed. Father Leo had been in love once, before entering the seminary, and remembered the helplessness of it. There had been no reason for him to be in love with the girl; she was no better than other girls he knew, and apart from loving her he didn't like her very much. Still, he probably would have married her if he had not felt even greater helplessness before his conviction that he should become a priest. She was desolate when he told her what he was planning to do, to the point that he nearly changed his mind. Then she lost interest. A few months later she married another man.

Vocation was a mystery, love was a mystery, and Father Leo supposed that hatred was a mystery. The old priest had been pulled under by it. That was a shame, but Father Leo knew better than to ponder its meaning for him.

A monsignor from the chancery was named to succeed the old priest. Father Leo brooded. He began to fear that he would never get his own parish, and for the first time he considered leaving the priesthood, as most of his friends from the seminary had done. But he never got very far with this thought, because he could not imagine himself as anything other than what he was.

The monsignor asked Father Leo to stay on and teach religion in the parish elementary school. Father Leo agreed. At the end of their interview the monsignor asked if there were any hard feelings.

'Not at all,' Father Leo said, and smiled. That night, driving back to the rectory from a visit with his sister, Father Leo began to shake. He was shaking so badly that he pulled onto the shoulder of the road, where he pounded his fist on the dashboard and yelled, 'No hard feelings! No hard feelings!'

But he came to like teaching. His students were troubled and cruel to each other but they were still curious about things that mattered: what they should believe in, how they should live. They paid attention to what Father Leo said, and at these moments he felt glad to be where he was.

Every couple of years or so the diocese sent out new books to religion teachers. Father Leo found the changes confusing and stopped trying to keep up. When the books came in he put them on a shelf and forgot about them. That was how he got fired. His classes were inspected by a priest in the education office that sent the books, and afterwards Father Leo received a summons. He went before a committee. After they questioned him, the chairman sent a letter to the monsignor saying that Father Leo's ideas were obsolete and peculiar. The committee suggested that he be replaced.

The monsignor took Father Leo out to dinner at a seafood house and explained the situation to him. The suggestion of the committee was actually a directive, he said. The monsignor had no choice in the matter. But he had been calling around and had found an open position, if Father Leo was interested. Mother Vincent at Star of the Sea needed a new chaplain. Their last chaplain had married one of the nuns. It so happened, the monsignor said, looking into his wine, swirling it gently, that he had done several favours for Mother Vincent in his days at the chancery. In short, if Father Leo wanted the position he could have it. The monsignor lit a cigarette and looked out the window, over the water. Gulls were diving for scraps.

He seemed embarrassed and Father Leo knew why. It was a job for an old priest, or one recovering from something: sickness, alcohol, a breakdown.

'Where will I live?' he asked.

'At the convent,' the monsignor said.

Something had gone wrong at Star of the Sea. It was an unhappy place. Some of the sisters were boisterous, and their noise made the silence of the others seem that much deeper. Coming upon these sad, silent nuns in the corridor or in the grounds, Father Leo felt a chill. It was like swimming into a cold pocket in a lake.

Several nuns had left the order. Others were thinking of it. They came to Father Leo and complained about the noise and confusion. They couldn't understand what was happening. Father Leo told them what he told himself: Be patient. But the truth was that his own patience had begun to give out.

He was supposed to be spiritual adviser to the convent. Many of the nuns disregarded him, though. They went their own way. The director of novices described herself as a 'Post-Christian' and at Easter sent out cards showing an Indian god ascending to the clouds with arms waving out of his sides like a centipede's. Some held jobs in town. The original idea had been for the nuns to serve the community in some way, but now they did what they wanted to do. One was a disc jockey.

The rowdy nuns ran around together and played pranks. Their jokes were good-natured but often in bad taste, and they didn't know when to stop. A couple of them had stereos and played weird music at night. The hallways echoed with their voices.

They called Father Leo 'Padre' or just 'Pod'. When he walked past them they usually made some crack or asked a cute question. They made racy jokes about Jerry, the fellow Mother Vincent had hired to raise funds. They were always laughing about something.

One evening Father Leo went to Mother Vincent's office and told her, again, that the convent was in trouble. This was his third visit that month and she made it plain that she was not glad to see him. She neither rose to meet him nor invited him to sit down. While he talked she gazed out the open window and rubbed the knuckles of her huge hands. Father Leo could see that she was listening to the crickets, not to him, and he lost heart.

Mother Vincent was strong, but old and drifting. She had no idea what was going on downstairs. Her office and rooms were on the top floor of the building, separate from the others, and her life took place even farther away than that. She lived in her dream of what the convent was. She believed that it was a perfect song, all voices tuned, sweet and cool and pure, rising and falling in measure. Her strength had hardened around that dream. It was more than Father Leo could contend with.

He broke off, though he hadn't finished what he had come to say. She went on staring out the window at the darkness.

'Father,' she said, 'I wonder if you are happy with us.'

He waited.

'Because if you are not happy at Star of the Sea,' she went on, 'the last thing I would want to do is keep you here.' She looked at him. She said, 'Is there anywhere else you want to be?'

Father Leo took her meaning, or thought he did. She meant, Is there anywhere else that would have you? He shook his head.

'Of course you hear complaints,' she said. 'You will always hear complaints. Every convent has its sob-sister element. Myself, I would trade ten wilting pansies for one Sister Gervaise any day. High spirits. A sense of fun. You need a sense of fun in this life, Father.'

Mother Vincent drew her chair up to the desk. 'If you don't mind my saying so, Father,' she said, 'you are inclined to take yourself too seriously. You think too much about your own problems. That's because you don't have enough to keep you busy here.' She put her hands on the desk top and folded them together. She said that she had a suggestion to make. Jerry, her fund-raiser, needed some help. The convent could not afford to hire another man but she saw no reason why Father Leo couldn't pitch in. It would be good for him. It would be good for everyone.

'I've never done any fund-raising before,' Father Leo said. But later that night, back in his room, he began to like the idea. It meant that he would meet new people. He would be doing something different.

Most of all, it meant that he would be getting out every day, away from this unhappy place.

Father Leo had coffee with Jerry a few mornings later. Though the weather was warm, Jerry had on a three-piece suit which he kept adjusting. He was nearly as tall as Father Leo but much thicker. There were lines across the front of his vest where the buttons strained. Rings sparkled on his thick, blunt fingers as he moved his hands over the sheets of paper he'd spread on the table. The papers were filled with figures showing what the convent's debts were, and how fast they were growing.

Father Leo hadn't known any of this. It came as a surprise to him that they could owe so much – that it was allowed. He studied the papers. He felt good bending over the table with Jerry, the smell of coffee rising up from the mug in his hand.

'That's not all of it,' Jerry said. 'Not by a long shot. Let me show you what we're actually looking at here.' He took Father Leo on a tour. He pointed out the old pipes, the warped window frames, the cracked foundations. He dug at the crumbling mortar in the walls and even pulled out a brick. He turned a flashlight on pools of scummy water in the vast basement. At the end of the tour Jerry added everything up – debts, operating expenses, and the cost of putting the physical plant back in shape.

Father Leo looked at the figures. He whistled.

'I've seen worse,' Jerry said. 'Our Lady of Perpetual Help was twice as bad as this, and I had them in the black in two years. It's easy. You go where the money is and you bring the money back.'

They were standing beside an empty greenhouse with most of the windows broken out. Shards of glass glittered at their feet. It had rained earlier and now everything seemed unnaturally bright: the grass, the blue of the sky, the white sails of the boats on Puget Sound. The sun was at Father Leo's back, shining into Jerry's face. Jerry squinted as he talked. Father Leo saw that there were little scars under his eyes. His nose was puffy.

'I should tell you,' Father Leo said. 'I've never raised funds before.'

'Nothing to it,' Jerry said. 'But first you have to make up your mind whether you really want the money. You ask yourself, Is it worth going after or isn't it? Then, if the answer is yes, you go after it.' He looked at Father Leo. 'So what is it? Yes or no?'

'Yes,' Father Leo said.

'All right! That's the big step. The rest is easy. You don't mess around. You don't get hung up on details. You do whatever you have to do and keep going. It's the only way. The question is, can you work like that?' Jerry brushed some brick dust off his jacket. He straightened his vest. He looked down at his shoes, then at Father Leo.

'I think so,' Father Leo said.

'You have to be a gunslinger,' Jerry said. 'No doubts. No pity.'

'I understand,' Father Leo said.

'All right,' Jerry said. 'Just so you know how I work. My philosophy.' He pulled a flask from his jacket pocket, drank from it, and held it out to Father Leo. 'Go on,' he said. Father Leo took it. The flask was silver, half-covered with leather, and engraved with initials below the neck. They weren't Jerry's initials. The liquor burned. Father Leo became aware of the sun on the back of his neck, the sighing of the trees. They each had another drink, then Jerry put the flask away. 'Cognac,' he said. 'Napoleon's brand. So, what do you think? Partners?'

'Partners,' Father Leo said.

'Bueno,' Jerry said. He slapped his leg and brought his hand up like a pistol. 'Okay,' he said. 'Let's ride.'

The plan was for Father Leo to go with Jerry and watch how he approached potential donors. Then, once he got the hang of it, he could go out on his own. Jerry coached him on the way to their first interview. He said that the big thing was to make it personal. Nobody wanted to hear about old furnaces. You had to do your homework, you had to know your man – in this case, your woman. Here they had a lady who went to Lourdes every year. She'd been to Lourdes more than twenty times. That meant she had a special interest in crippled people. She had a big heart and she had money. Going to France wasn't like going to Mexico.

The woman was standing at the door when they arrived. Father Leo followed Jerry up the walk, moving slowly, because Jerry had assumed what appeared to be a painful limp. He had endless trouble with the steps but refused the woman's help. 'I can manage,' he said. 'There's plenty worse off than me. I just think of them and it's easy.'

Jerry did all the talking when they got inside. Now and then the woman looked over at Father Leo, but he would not meet her eyes. Jerry was describing a number of projects that Star of the Sea had developed for the handicapped, all of them imaginary. He implied that most of the nuns were devoted to this particular work and that he himself had been rescued by their efforts. Jerry's voice cracked. He looked away for a moment, then went on. When he finished, the woman served tea and wrote out a cheque.

Not everyone they visited gave them money. One old man laughed in their faces when Jerry told him that the convent had been built on orders from the Blessed Mother, and that she was taking a personal interest in the fund drive. When the old man stopped laughing he threw them out. 'You must take me for an idiot,' he said.

Not everyone gave, but most people did. Jerry would say anything. He said that the convent helped orphans, lepers, Navahos, earthquake victims, even pandas and seals. There was no end to what he would do.

Jerry had a saying: 'If you want the apples, you have to shake the tree.'

Father Leo knew that he should disapprove of Jerry's methods, but he didn't. That is, he felt no disapproval. The people they visited lived in Broadmoor and Windermere. They had plenty of money, too much money. It was good for them to share it. Anyway, Jerry was a performer, not a liar. Lying was selfish, furtive, low. What Jerry did was reckless and grand, for a good cause.

Father Leo did not want to go out on his own. He would never be able to carry on the way Jerry did in front of complete strangers. Besides, he was having the time of his life. Jerry called him 'Slim', and he liked that. He liked getting into Jerry's big car and driving through the convent gate with no idea what would happen that day. He looked forward to the lunches they ate downtown – club sandwiches, fruit platters, big salads covered with diced cheese and ham. Then the coffee afterwards, and one of Jerry's stories about his days in the navy. Father Leo came to need these pleasures, most of all the pleasure of watching Jerry have it his way with people who were used to having it their way.

As it happened they did not split up after all. Jerry tallied their take for the month and decided that they should stick together. The receipts were almost double the average. He said that as a team they were unbeatable. He had the blarney and Father Leo had the collar, which Jerry called 'The Persuader'.

They would go on as before. Father Leo's job was just to sit there. He didn't have to say anything. If someone should look at him in a questioning way, all he had to do was close his eyes. No nodding. No murmuring.

'We'll rake it in,' Jerry said, and they did.

When they finished their rounds, Jerry and Father Leo usually had a drink at a fern bar on the wharf. They sat in a booth and Jerry told stories about his life. He'd sold cars and worked as a private detective. For two years he had been a professional fighter. He had been everywhere and seen everything. In Singapore he had witnessed a murder, one man shooting another man right in the face. 'Just like you'd shoot a can,' Jerry said. Later he'd heard the men were brothers. He had seen men make love to each other on board ship. In Dakar he'd watched a woman with knobs where her arms should have been paint pictures of sailors, take their money, and give change all with the toes of her feet. He had seen children chained to a wall, for sale.

So he said. Father Leo did not believe all the stories Jerry told him. Roughly speaking, he believed about half of what he heard. That was fine with him. He didn't mind having his leg pulled. He thought it was the sort of thing men did in lumber camps and on ships – sitting around, swapping lies.

Just before Thanksgiving they had a meeting with a vice president of Boeing. The man wore sunglasses during the interview. It was hard to tell what he was thinking. Father Leo guessed that he was trying to keep his temper, because in his opinion Jerry had chosen the wrong line to follow. Jerry was going on about missiles and bombers and instruments of destruction. He suggested that the man had a lot to make amends for. Father Leo wanted to get out. When Jerry was through, the vice president sat there behind his desk and stared at them. He said nothing. Father Leo became uncomfortable, then angry. This was obviously some technique the vice president used to bully his subordinates. 'You ought to be ashamed of yourself,' he said. The vice president suddenly bent over. He buried his face in the crook of his arm. 'You don't know the half of it,' he said. His shoulders began to jerk.

Jerry looked at Father Leo and gave the thumbs-up. He went around the desk and stood behind the man. 'There, there,' he said.

The vice president stopped crying. He took off his sunglasses and wiped his eyes. 'I needed that,' he said. 'By God, I needed that.' He went into the adjoining room and came back with a plastic garbage bag. It was full of money, but he would not let Jerry count it in the office or give him a receipt. He insisted that the gift remain anonymous. As he showed them out of the office, he took Father Leo by the sleeve. 'Pray for me,' he said.

They counted the money in the car. It came to seven thousand dollars, all in twenties. Jerry locked it in the trunk and they went to the fern bar to celebrate. Jerry's cheeks were red and they grew redder as he drank cognac after cognac. Father Leo did not try to keep up with him, but he drank more than usual and became a little giddy. Now and then the young people at the bar turned and smiled at him. He could see that they were thinking, *What a jolly priest!* That was all right. He wanted to look like someone with good news, not like someone with bad news.

Jerry held up his glass. 'The team,' he said, and Father Leo said, 'The team.' They toasted each other. 'I'll tell you what,' Jerry said. 'We have a bonus coming, and I'm going to see that we get it if I have to break Vincent's arm.' When Father Leo asked what kind of a bonus Jerry had in mind, Jerry said, 'How about Thanksgiving in Vegas?'

'Las Vegas?'

'You bet. We're riding a streak. We've made plenty for Vincent, why shouldn't we make a little for ourselves?'

Father Leo knew that Mother Vincent would never agree, so he said, 'Sure. Why not?' and they touched glasses again.

'Slim, you're something,' Jerry said. 'You're really something.' He shook his head. 'You're as bad as I am.'

Father Leo smiled.

Jerry said, 'I'm going to tell you something I've never told anyone before. Maybe I shouldn't even tell you.' He lit a cigar and blew smoke at the ceiling. 'Hell with it,' he said. He leaned forward. In a low voice he told Father Leo that Jerry was not his real name. Royce, his last name, was also made up. He'd taken it from Rolls-Royce, his favourite car.

It happened like this. He had been selling insurance in San Diego a few years back and some of his clients complained because they didn't get the benefits he had promised them. It was his own fault. He had overdone it, laid it on too thick. He would be the first to admit that. Anyway, he'd had to change names. There was no choice, not if he wanted to keep working and stay out of jail. The worst of it was that his wife left town with their son. He hadn't seen them since, had no idea where they were. That hurt. But in some ways, looking back on it, he thought that it was for the best. They didn't get along and she was holding him back. Always criticizing. If she'd had her way he'd still be in the navy, pulling down a hundred and forty dollars a month. 'She loved it,' he said. 'So did I, at least for a while. We were just kids. We didn't know from Adam.'

Jerry looked at the people in the next booth, then at Father Leo. He said, 'Do you want to know what my real name is?'

Father Leo nodded. But just when Jerry was about to speak he interrupted. 'Maybe you'd better not tell me,' he said. 'It's probably not such a good idea.'

Jerry looked disappointed. Father Leo felt bad, but he didn't want that kind of power, the power to send a man to jail. He was also afraid that Jerry would start wondering about him all the time, whether he could be trusted, whether he would tell. It would spoil everything.

They sat for a while without talking. Father Leo knew that it was his turn. He should open up and talk about himself for a change. But there was nothing to tell. He had no stories. Not one.

Outside the window it was raining. Cars went past with a hissing sound. Father Leo said, 'Jerry?' His throat felt scratchy. He did not know what he would say next.

Jerry moved in his seat and looked at him.

'You've got to keep this to yourself,' Father Leo said.

Jerry pulled his thumb and forefinger across his lips as if he were closing a zipper. 'It stops here,' he said.

'All right,' Father Leo said. He took a sip from his drink. Then he started talking. He said that when he was a senior in high school he had been waiting for a bus when he heard someone scream across the road. He ran over and saw a woman on her knees, hanging on to the belt of a man with a purse in his hand. The man turned and kicked the woman in the face. 'I guess I went berserk,' Father Leo said. The next thing he knew, the police were dragging him off the man's body. The man was dead. Father Leo said that they'd had to pry his fingers off the man's throat, one by one.

'Jesus,' Jerry said. 'Is that the reason you became a priest?'

Father Leo looked out the window. 'One of the reasons,' he said.

'Jesus,' Jerry said again. He looked young and amazed, wide-eyed as he must have been years ago, before his name was Jerry. His eyes were watery; when he tried to smile, his mouth wouldn't hold the shape. He reached out and squeezed Father Leo's shoulder. He squeezed it again, then got up and went to the bar.

Oh, no, Father Leo thought. What have I done?

Jerry came back with fresh drinks. He sat down and slid one over to Father Leo. His eyes were still misty. 'Vegas,' he said, and raised his glass.

'Vegas,' Father Leo said.

Mother Vincent gave them the bonus. Thanksgiving weekend in Las Vegas, all expenses paid – air fare, hotel, meals, and a hundred dollars apiece in gambling coupons. The trip was arranged at discount by a nun who worked as a travel agent.

'Something is going to happen,' Jerry told Father Leo as their plane banked over the desert. 'I feel it. Something big. We're going to come home with gold in our saddle-bags. Hey, don't laugh,' he said. 'Don't ever laugh about that.'

'I can't help it,' Father Leo said.

'Be serious, Slim. We are two serious hombres on a roll and we are about to bust this town wide open. We'll never work again. It is written.' He leaned past Father Leo and looked down at the cluster of lights that turned below them in the darkness.

There was a commotion in the hotel lobby when they arrived. A woman was yelling that her room had been broken into. Two men in fringed leather jackets tried to soothe her and finally managed to lead her to an office behind the registration desk, where she began to yell again. Father Leo could hear every word from where he stood in line. He picked up the room keys and meal coupons and gambling chips, and turned around just in time to see Jerry win twelve dollars at one of the quarter slots by the Hertz counter. The coins slid out of the machine onto the tile floor with a steady ringing sound and rolled in every direction. Jerry got down on his hands and knees and crawled after them. Nobody paid any attention except a red-haired man in silver pants who went over to Jerry and touched his shoulder, then hurried away.

They ate dinner at the hotel, the only place where their coupons were good. Jerry spent his winnings on a bottle of wine, to celebrate. He couldn't get over it – a jackpot the first time around. 'Figure the odds on that,' he said. 'It's an omen. It means we can't lose.'

'I'm not much of a gambler,' Father Leo said. It was true. He had never won a bet in his life. The chips they'd been given were negotiable and he intended to cash them in just before he left and buy his sister something nice for Christmas, something he would not usually be able to afford. For now they were squirrelled away in the bottom of his suitcase.

'Who's talking about gambling?' Jerry said. 'I'm talking about fate. You know what I mean.'

'I guess I don't,' Father Leo said. 'Not really.'

'Sure you do. What about the guy you killed? It was fate that put you there. It was fate that you became a priest.'

Father Leo saw how the lie had grown. It had taken on a meaning and the meaning was false. He felt tired of himself. He said, 'Jerry, it isn't true.'

'What isn't true?'

'I never killed anyone.'

Jerry smiled at him. 'Come off it.'

'I've never even been in a fight,' Father Leo said.

Jerry leaned forward. 'Look,' he said, 'you shouldn't feel guilty about it. It was that kind of a situation. I would have done the same thing in your shoes. That's what I told Sister Gervaise.'

'No,' Father Leo said. 'You didn't.'

'Don't worry,' Jerry said. 'She promised not to tell anyone. The thing is, she made a smart remark about you and I wanted to set her straight. It worked, too. She went white as a ghost. She looked about ready to haemorrhage. You should have seen her.'

'She's a gossip,' Father Leo said. 'She'll tell everyone. She'll tell Mother Vincent.'

'I made her promise,' Jerry said. 'She gave her word.'

'So did you.'

Jerry put a coupon on the table. He ground out his cigar. 'This conversation isn't going anywhere,' he said. 'What's done is done. We're in Get Rich City now, and it's time to start raking it in.'

There was a small casino on the other side of the lobby. Jerry suggested that they start there. He sat down at the blackjack table. Father Leo moved up and watched the play. He was pretending to study Jerry's tactics, but none of it made any sense to him. He could only think of Sister Gervaise turning white. He felt as if he must be turning white himself. 'I'm going upstairs,' he told Jerry. 'I'll be back in a little while.'

Father Leo sat on the balcony outside his room. In the courtyard below there was a turquoise pool lit by underwater lights. He gripped the armrests of his chair. He could not stop thinking of Sister Gervaise, stricken and pale. What was he supposed to do? He couldn't have Mother Vincent and the others believing that he had killed a man. It would terrify them. On the other hand, he didn't want them to think that he went around telling crazy lies about himself.

In its own way, that was just as bad. He put his head in his hands. He couldn't think. Finally he gave up and went back downstairs.

Another man had taken Jerry's place at the blackjack table. Father Leo couldn't find Jerry at any of the other tables and he wasn't at the bar or in the lobby. On the chance that he'd gone to his room, Father Leo called upstairs on the house phone. There was no answer. He went outside and stood under the awning beside the doorman.

A greyhound wearing a sweater and pulling an old woman behind him stopped and lifted his leg over a small border of flowers in front of the hotel. While the dog peed, the woman glared at the doorman. He clasped his white-gloved hands behind his back and looked up at the sky.

Along the street coloured lights flashed names and pictures. Farther down was a sign that must have been twenty feet high, showing a line of chorus girls in cowboy boots and bikinis. Every so often they kicked their legs this way and that. They were smiling, and each tooth was a little light. People spilled over into the street, moving in different directions. They shouted back and forth and ignored the cars that honked at them.

'Thanksgiving,' the doorman said. Then he said something that Father Leo couldn't hear because of the noise.

There was no point in looking for Jerry in that crowd. Father Leo went back inside and took a seat at the bar. From the bar he could keep an eye on both the lobby and the casino. He sipped at his drink and glanced around. A muscular-looking girl with tattooed snakes coiling up her bare arms was poking out numbers on a punchboard. Two pudgy Indian men wearing identical Hawaiian shirts sat silently side by side. At the end of the bar a small, red-haired woman was emptying her purse and spreading its contents in front of her. She dipped her hand into her purse with the predatory crispness of a robin driving its beak into the ground, and Father Leo found himself watching her to see what she came up with. At last she found what she was after – cigarettes – and lit one. She pursed her lips and blew out a long stream of smoke. Then she noticed that Father Leo was looking at her. She looked back at him. Father Leo gave a little nod, and lowered his eyes. Soon afterwards he finished his drink and left the bar.

Father Leo sat in the lobby for an hour, reading newspapers. Every time someone came in he looked up. When he felt himself getting sleepy he went to the desk and talked to the clerk. Jerry had left his key, but no message. 'That's strange,' Father Leo said. He walked across the lobby to the elevator. The red-haired woman from the bar was standing inside, holding the door for him. 'What floor?' she asked.

'Five. Thank you.'

'Coincidence,' she said. 'That's my floor too.' She and Father Leo stared at each other's reflections in the mirrored wall. She was about his age, older than he'd thought. There were wrinkles around her mouth. He saw that she was badly sunburned except for a white circle around each eye. He could almost feel the heat coming off her pink skin. She was tapping one foot.

'Been here long?' she asked.

He shook his head. The elevator stopped and they got out. She walked beside him down the corridor. 'I flew in two days ago,' she said. 'I don't mind telling you I've been having a ball.' When Father Leo put his key into the lock she read the number on his door. 'Five-fifteen. That's easy to remember. I always leave work at five-fifteen. I could leave at five but I like it when everyone's gone. I like to just sit and look out the window. It's so peaceful.'

'Good night,' Father Leo said. She was still talking when he closed the door. He sat for a time on his balcony. There were high palms around the pool, and overhead a bright crescent moon. Father Leo thought of a band of marauders camped by a well in the desert, roasting a lamb over a spitting fire, the silver moon reflected in the chasing of their long inlaid rifles. Veiled women moving here and there in silence, doing as they were told.

Before he went to bed Father Leo called the desk. Jerry's key was still on its hook.

'It's only twelve-thirty,' the clerk said. 'You could try later.'

Father Leo turned out the lights. He was staring at it when he thought he heard a sound at the door. He sat up. 'Who's there?' he called. When no one answered he said, 'Jerry?' The sound did not come again.

On his way to breakfast the next morning Father Leo stopped by the front desk. Jerry still hadn't come in. Father Leo left a message – 'I'm in the coffee shop' – and when he finished eating he changed it to 'Went out. Be back soon.'

Though it was just after eleven, the street was already jammed with people. A dry breeze blew, bearing a faint smell that made Father Leo think of the word *sage*. Off in the distance purple mountains floated on a shimmering lake of blue. The sidewalk glowed.

For the rest of the morning Father Leo searched the casinos. He thought that Jerry might have wandered in and got caught up in one of those games that went on forever. But he didn't see him, or if he saw him he didn't recognize him. That was possible. There were so many people. Bent over their machines, faces fixed and drained by the hot lights, they all began to look the same to Father Leo. He couldn't tell who he was looking at and it wore him out to try. At two o'clock he went back to the hotel, intending to search the casinos again after he'd eaten lunch.

He sat at the counter and watched the crowd move past outside. It was noisy in the coffee shop, which was full of Japanese men in business suits. They all wore cowboy hats and string ties with roadrunner clasps. At the back of the room a bunch of them were playing slot machines. There weren't enough machines to go around so they took turns, standing behind each other in little lines. One of them hit a jackpot and all the others, including those at the tables, stopped talking and applauded.

'If it isn't five-fifteen.' The red-haired woman from the night before sat down at the next stool and offered Father Leo a package of Salems with one cigarette sticking halfway out. He shook his head. She slid the cigarette from the pack, tapped it once on the counter top, and put it in the ashtray. 'For later,' she said. 'I can't smoke on an empty stomach.' Her face had turned the colour of brick. It was painful for Father Leo to look at her and to think of how hot and tight her skin must feel, and how it must hurt her to keep smiling the way she did.

'By the way,' she said, 'I'm Sandra.'

Father Leo did not want to know this woman's name and he did not want her to know his name. But she kept waiting. 'Slim,' he said.

'Then you must be a Westerner.'

He nodded. 'Seattle and thereabouts.'

She said, 'I met a fellow in the casino named Will. In Chicago you just don't hear names like that. Will and Slim. It's so different. I'm talking too much, aren't I?'

'Not at all,' Father Leo said.

The waitress took Sandra's order and slipped Father Leo's bill under his plate. He picked it up and looked at it.

'Let me treat you to a refill,' Sandra said, pointing at his coffee cup.

He stood. 'No thanks,' he said. 'I've got to be going. Much obliged.'

Father Leo left another message for Jerry and went upstairs to his room. He thought he would lie down for a while before making another tour of the casinos. When he stepped inside he saw that his suitcase was open, though he could remember closing it. On the table next to the suitcase a cigarette was coming apart in a glass of water.

He knelt and went through the suitcase. He sat back for a moment, caught his breath, and searched the suitcase again. The chips were gone. Father Leo flushed the cigarette down the toilet and dropped the glass in the waste basket. He could feel the blood pulse in his temples, its beat strong and uneven, surprising him and shaking him as if he were hollow. He sat on the bed. The hollowness spread downwards into his chest and legs. When he stood he rose up and up. He saw his shoes side by side on the rug, a long way below. He walked over to the balcony door and back. Then he began to talk to himself.

The things Father Leo said didn't make any sense. They were only noises. He kept pacing the room. He struck himself over the heart. He gripped his shirt in both hands and tore it open to his waist. He struck himself again. Back and forth he walked.

The sounds he made grew soft and distant, then stopped. Father Leo stood there. He looked down at the front of his shirt. One button was missing. Another hung by a thread. The room was hot and still smelled of the thief's cigarette. Father Leo slid open the glass door and went out onto the balcony. The desert was hidden by casinos but he could feel it all around him and taste its dryness in the breeze. The breeze ruffled the surface of the pool below, breaking the sun's reflection. The broken light glittered on the water.

When the desk clerk saw Father Leo coming, he shook his head. Father Leo walked up to him anyway. 'No message?'

'Not a thing,' the desk clerk said. He went back to his magazine.

Father Leo had meant to report the theft, but now he didn't see the point. The police would come and make him fill out a lot of forms. They would ask him questions; he felt uneasy about that, about explaining his presence in Las Vegas.

For the rest of the afternoon he went up and down the street, looking for Jerry. Once he thought he saw him going into a casino but it turned out to be somebody else. Father Leo returned to the hotel. He didn't feel like going back to his room, so he bought a copy of *Time* and went out to the pool.

Two young girls were doing cannonballs off the diving board. Father Leo tried to read an article about the creation of the universe but he couldn't keep his mind on it. After a time he gave up and watched the girls, who sensed his attention. They began to show off. First they did swan dives. Then one of them tried a flip. She hit the water with a loud crack, flat on her stomach. Father Leo started out of his chair, but she seemed to be all right. She pulled herself up the ladder and left the courtyard, crying. Her friend walked carefully out to the end of the board, turned around, bounced twice, and executed a perfect backward flip. Then she walked away from the pool, feet slapping on the wet cement.

'Coincidence,' Sandra said. 'Looks like we've got the pool to ourselves.' She was standing beside the next chair, looking down at him. She stepped out of her high-heeled clogs and took off her robe.

'You shouldn't be out here,' Father Leo said. 'Not with that burn of yours.'

'This is my last day,' she said. 'I wanted to catch the sunset.'

Father Leo looked up. The sun was just touching the roof of the hotel across from them. It looked like another sign.

Sandra sat down and took a bottle of baby oil out of her tote bag. She rubbed the oil along her arms and across her chest, under the halter of her bathing suit. Then she raised her legs one at a time and slowly oiled them until they glistened. They were deep red. 'So,' she said, 'where's your wife?'

'I'm not married.'

'Me neither,' she said.

Father Leo closed his magazine and sat up.

'What shows have you been to?' she asked.

'None.'

'You should go,' she said. 'The dancers are so beautiful. I don't think I've ever seen such beautiful men and women in my whole life. Do you like to dance?'

Father Leo shook his head.

Sandra drew her legs up. She rested her chin between her knees. 'What do you like?'

Father Leo was about to say 'I like peace and quiet,' but he stopped himself. She was lonely. There was no reason to hurt her feelings. 'I like to read,' he said. 'Music. Good music, not weird music. Eating in restaurants. Talking to friends.'

'Me too,' Sandra said. 'Those are the same things I like.' She lowered the back of the deck chair and rolled onto her stomach. She rubbed baby oil over her shoulders, then held the bottle out towards Father Leo. 'Could you give me a hand?' she said.

He saw that she wanted him to oil her back, which looked swollen and painful, glowing in the little sun that was left. 'I'm afraid I can't do that,' he said.

'Oh,' she said. She put the bottle down. 'Sorry I asked.'

'I'm a priest,' he said.

'That's a new one,' she said, not looking at him. 'A priest named Slim.'

'Slim is my nickname,' he said.

'Sure,' she said. 'Your nickname. What kind of priest are you, anyway?'

Father Leo began to explain but she cut him off. 'You're no priest,' she said. She sat up and began stuffing things into her tote bag – lighter, cigarettes, baby oil, sunglasses. She put her robe on and stepped into her clogs. 'If you were a priest, you wouldn't have let me go on like I did. You wouldn't have let me make a fool of myself.' She stood there, looking down at him. 'What are you, anyway?'

'I came here with a friend,' Father Leo said. 'He's been gone ever since last night. I don't have any idea where he is. This isn't a very good explanation,' Father Leo added. 'I'm a little confused right now.'

'I don't know what you are,' she said, 'but if you come near me again I'll scream.'

Father Leo thought of calling the police, but he was afraid that if they did find Jerry they would discover his real name and put him in prison. He looked up the numbers of all the hospitals in town. There were seven. None of them had a Jerry Royce registered, but at Desert Springs the nurse who took the call said that on the previous night they had admitted a John Doe with what she called a 'sucking chest wound'. Father Leo asked for a description of the man, but she did not have his file and the line to Intensive Care was busy. 'It's always busy,' she told him. 'If you're in town, the simplest thing is to just come over.'

But when Father Leo arrived at Intensive Care, he discovered that the John Doe was dead. He had died that afternoon and they had sent his body to the morgue. Father Leo put his hands on the desk. 'The morgue?' he said.

The nurse nodded. 'We have a picture. Would you like to see it?'

'I guess I'd better,' Father Leo said. He was afraid to look at the picture but he didn't feel ready for a trip to the morgue. The nurse opened a folder and took out a large glossy photograph and handed it to him. The face was that of a boy with narrow features. His eyes were open, staring without defiance or shyness into the blaze of the flash. Father Leo knew that the boy had died before the picture was taken. He gave the picture back.

The nurse looked at it. 'Not your friend?' she asked.

He shook his head. 'What happened?'

'He was stabbed.' She put the folder away.

'Did they catch the person who did it?'

'Probably not,' she said. 'We get over a hundred murders a year in town.'

On his way back to the hotel Father Leo watched the crowd through the window of the cab. A group of sailors ran across the street. The one in front was throwing coins over his shoulder and the rest were jumping for them. Signs flashed. People's faces pulsed with reflected light.

Father Leo bent forward. 'I just heard that you get over a hundred murders a year in town. Is that true?'

'I suppose it's possible,' the cabby said. 'This place has its drawbacks, all right. But Utica's a damn sight worse. They've got almost two feet of snow right now and there's more on the way.'

At half-past two in the morning Jerry called. He was sorry about the mix-up, but he could explain everything. It turned out that while Father Leo was upstairs that first night Jerry had met a fellow on his way to a poker game outside town. It was a private game. The players were rich and there was no limit. They'd had to leave right away, so Jerry wasn't able to tell Father Leo. And after he got there he'd had no chance to call. The game was that intense. Incredible amounts of money had changed hands. It was still going on; he'd just broken off to catch a few winks and let Father Leo know that he wouldn't be going back to Seattle the next morning. He couldn't, not now. Jerry had lost every penny of his own savings, the seven thousand dollars from the man at Boeing, and some other cash he had held back. 'I feel bad,' he said. 'I know this is going to put you in an awkward position.'

'I think you ought to come home,' Father Leo said. 'We can work this thing out.'

'They'll throw the book at me,' Jerry said.

'No, they won't. I won't let them.'

'Get serious. Vincent'll have me for dinner.'

'She doesn't have to know it was you,' Father Leo said. 'I'll tell her I took it.'

Jerry didn't answer right away. Finally he said, 'She'd never believe you.'

'Why not? She already thinks I'm a killer.'

Jerry laughed. 'Slim, you're something. Thanks, but no thanks. I still have four hundred left. I've been down further than that and bounced back. I'm just getting warmed up.'

'Jerry, listen.'

'Haven't you ever had the feeling that you're bound to win?' Jerry asked. 'Like you've been picked out and you'll get taken care of no matter what?'

'Sure,' Father Leo said, 'I've had that feeling. It doesn't mean a damn thing.'

'That's what you say. I happen to feel differently about it.'

'For God's sake, Jerry, use your head. Come home.'

But it was no good. Jerry said goodbye and hung up. Father Leo sat on the edge of the bed. The telephone rang again. He picked it up and said, 'Jerry?'

It wasn't Jerry, though. It was Sandra. 'I'm sorry if I woke you up,' she said.

'Sandra,' he said. 'What on earth do you want?'

'Are you really a priest?' she asked.

'What kind of a question is that? What do you mean by calling me at this hour?' Father Leo knew that he had every right to be angry, but he wasn't, not really. The sound of his own voice, fussy and peevish, embarrassed him. 'Yes,' he said.

'Oh, thank God. I'm so frightened.' He waited.

'Someone's been trying to get into my room,' she said. 'At least I think they have. I could have been dreaming,' she added.

'You should call the police.'

'I already thought of that,' she said. 'What would they do? They'd come in and stand around and then they'd go away. And there I'd be.'

'I don't know how I could help,' Father Leo said.

'You could stay.'

'My friend still isn't back,' Father Leo said. 'We have to leave tomorrow morning and I should be here in case he calls. What if you were dreaming?'

'Please,' she said.

Father Leo slammed his fist into the pillow. 'Of course,' he said. 'Of course, I'll be right there.'

After Sandra unlocked the door she told Father Leo to wait a second. Then she called, 'Okay. Come on in.' She was wearing a blue nightgown. She slid into bed and pulled the covers up to her waist. 'Please don't look at me,' she said. 'And in case you wondered, I'm not making this up. I'm not that desperate for company.'

There were two beds in the room, with a night table in between. Father Leo sat at the foot of the other bed. He looked at her. Her face was red and puffy. She had white stuff on her nose.

'I'm a sight,' she said.

'You should have that burn looked at when you get home.'

She shrugged. 'It's going to peel whatever I do. In a couple of weeks I'll be back to normal.' She tried to smile and gave it up. 'I thought I'd at least come home with a tan. This has been the worst vacation. It's been one thing after another.' She picked at the covers. 'My second night here I lost over three hundred dollars. Do you know how long it takes me to save three hundred dollars?'

'This is an awful place,' Father Leo said. 'I don't know why anybody comes here.'

'That's no mystery,' Sandra said.

'The whole thing is fixed,' Father Leo said.

Sandra shrugged. 'That doesn't matter.'

Father Leo went over to the sliding glass door. He opened it and stepped out onto the balcony. The night was cold. A mist hung over the glowing blue surface of the pool.

'You'll catch your death out there,' Sandra called.

Father Leo went back inside and closed the door. He was restless. The room smelled of coconut oil.

'I have a confession to make,' Sandra said. 'It wasn't a coincidence when I came out to the pool today. I saw you down there.'

Father Leo sat in the chair next to the TV. He rubbed his eyes. 'Did somebody really try to break into the room?'

'I thought so,' Sandra said. 'Can't you tell I'm scared?'

'Yes,' he said.

'Then what difference does it make?'

'None,' Father Leo said.

'This has been the worst vacation,' Sandra said. 'I won't tell you all the things that happened to me. Let's just say the only good thing that's happened to me is meeting you.'

'This is a terrible place,' Father Leo said. 'It's dangerous, and everything is set up so you can't win.'

'Some people win,' she said.

'That's the theory. I haven't seen any winners. Do you mind if I use your phone?'

Sandra smoked and watched Father Leo while he talked to the desk clerk. Jerry had not called back. Father Leo left Sandra's room number and hung up.

'You told him you were here?' she said. 'I wonder what he'll think.'

'He can think whatever he wants to think.'

'He probably isn't thinking anything,' Sandra said. 'I'll bet he's seen it all.'

Father Leo nodded. 'I wouldn't be surprised.'

'It's strange,' she said. 'Usually, when I'm about to go home from a vacation, I get excited – even if I've had a great time. This year I just feel sad. How about you? Are you looking forward to going home?'

'Not much,' Father Leo said.

'Why not? What's it like where you live?'

Father Leo thought of the noise in the refectory, Sister Gervaise shrieking at one of her own wisecracks. Then he saw her face go white as she listened to the lie he'd told Jerry. It would be all over the convent by now, and there was no way to undo it. When you heard a story like that it became the truth about the person it was spoken of. Denials would only make it seem more true.

He would have to live with it. And that meant that everything was going to change. He saw how it would be. The hallways empty at night and quiet. The sisters falling silent as he walked past them, their eyes downcast.

'What are you smiling at?' Sandra asked.

He shook his head. 'Nothing. Just a thought.'

Sandra stubbed her cigarette out. 'The way I've been acting, you must think I'm completely pathetic. I just want you to know that I'm not.'

'I never thought that,' Father Leo said.

'Yeah, yeah. You'll say anything to keep me quiet.'

Father Leo made sounds of denial.

'I'm not a pathetic person,' Sandra said. 'I have a life. It's just that with one thing and another I was feeling low, and you struck a chord.'

'You don't know me, Sandra.'

'Not in the usual way, maybe. But I recognize you, the kind of person you are. Intelligent. Kind. Gallant.'

'Gallant,' Father Leo said.

Sandra nodded. 'You're here, aren't you?' A group of people went past the door, talking loudly. When it was quiet again, Sandra said, 'Is it okay if I ask you a personal question?'

'I guess so,' Father Leo said. 'Sure. Why not?'

'Do you think you could love me? If the circumstances were changed?'

'The circumstances aren't going to change,' Father Leo said.

'I understand that. I understand that absolutely. But speaking in a hypothetical way, do you think you could? Don't worry about hurting my feelings – I'm just curious.'

Hypothetically, Father Leo supposed it was possible for him to love anyone. But she didn't really mean that. He thought about it. 'Yes,' he said.

'What for? What is it about me that you would love if you loved me?' She clasped her arms around her knees, and watched him.

'It's hard to put into words,' Father Leo said.

Sandra said, 'You don't have to.' She shook another cigarette out of the pack, stared at it, and put it down on the night table.

'I like the way you talk,' Father Leo said. Straight out – just what's on your mind.'

She nodded. 'I do that, all right. Let the chips fall where they may.'

'Your spirit,' Father Leo said. 'Coming here all alone the way you did.'

'I got a good deal on the trip.'

'So did I,' Father Leo said.

They both laughed.

'I thought of going home early,' Sandra said, 'but once I start something I have to finish it. I have to take it to the end and see how it turns out, even if it turns out awful.'

'I know what you mean,' Father Leo said. 'I'm the same way.'

'So what else do you like about me?'

'How friendly you are. The way you listen.'

She leaned back against the pillow.

'Your eyes.'

'My eyes? Really?'

'You have beautiful eyes.'

Father Leo went on. He did not think, he just listened to himself. His voice made a cool sound in the stuffy room. After a time Sandra whispered, 'You won't leave, will you?'

'I'll be right here,' he said.

She slept. Father Leo turned off the lights and moved his chair in front of the door. He sat and listened. Every so often, faintly, he heard the elevator open at the end of the hall. He listened for sounds in the corridor. Several people went by Sandra's door. Nobody stopped.

The only sounds in the room were his own and Sandra's breathing; hers ragged, his deep, almost silent.

After a few hours of this he began to drift. Finally he caught himself dozing off, and went outside onto the balcony. A few stars still glimmered. The breeze stirred the fronds of the palm trees. The palms were black against the purple sky. The moon was white.

Father Leo stood against the railing, chilled awake by the breeze. A car honked, a small sound in the silence. He listened for it to come again but it didn't, and the silence seemed to grow. Again he felt the desert all around him. He thought of a coyote loping home with a rabbit dangling from its mouth, yellow eyes aglow.

Father Leo rubbed his arms. The cold began to get to him and he went back inside.

The walls turned from blue to grey. A telephone started ringing in the room above. There were heavy steps.

Sandra turned. She said something in her sleep. Then she turned again.

'It's all right,' Father Leo said. 'I'm here.'

Say Yes

They were doing the dishes, his wife washing while he dried. He'd washed the night before. Unlike most men he knew, he really pitched in on the housework. A few months earlier he'd overheard a friend of his wife's congratulate her on having such a considerate husband, and he thought, *I try*. Helping out with the dishes was a way he had of showing how considerate he was.

They talked about different things and somehow got on the subject of whether white people should marry black people. He said that all things considered, he thought it was a bad idea.

'Why?' she asked.

Sometimes his wife got this look where she pinched her brows together and bit her lower lip and stared down at something. When he saw her like this he knew he should keep his mouth shut, but he never did. Actually it made him talk more. She had that look now.

'Why?' she asked again, and stood there with her hand inside a bowl, not washing it but just holding it above the water.

'Listen,' he said, 'I went to school with blacks and I've worked with blacks and lived on the same street with blacks and we've always gotten along just fine. I don't need you coming along now and implying that I'm a racist.'

'I didn't imply anything,' she said, and began washing the bowl again, turning it around in her hand as though she were shaping it.

'I just don't see what's wrong with a white person marrying a black person, that's all.'

'They don't come from the same culture as we do. Listen to them sometime – they even have their own language. That's okay with me, I *like* hearing them talk' – he did; for some reason it always made him feel happy – 'but it's different. A person from their culture and a person from our culture could never really *know* each other.'

'Like you know me?' his wife asked.

'Yes. Like I know you.'

'But if they love each other,' she said. She was washing faster now, not looking at him.

Oh boy, he thought. He said, 'Don't take my word for it. Look at the statistics. Most of those marriages break up.'

'Statistics.' She was piling dishes on the drainboard at a terrific rate, just swiping at them with the cloth. Many of them were greasy, and there were flecks of food between the tines of the forks. 'All right,' she said, 'what about foreigners? I suppose you think the same thing about two foreigners getting married.'

'Yes,' he said, 'as a matter of fact I do. How can you understand someone who comes from a completely different background?'

'Different,' said his wife. 'Not the same, like us.'

'Yes, different,' he snapped, angry with her for resorting to this trick of repeating his words so that they sounded crass, or hypocritical. 'These are dirty,' he said, and dumped all the silverware back into the sink.

The water had gone flat and grey. She stared down at it, her lips pressed tight together, then plunged her hands under the surface. 'Oh!' she cried, and jumped back. She took her right hand by the wrist and held it up. Her thumb was bleeding.

'Ann, don't move,' he said. 'Stay right there.' He ran upstairs to the bathroom and rummaged in the medicine chest for alcohol, cotton, and a Band-Aid. When he came back down she was leaning against the refrigerator with her eyes closed, still holding her hand. He took the hand and dabbed at her thumb with the cotton. The bleeding had stopped. He squeezed it to see how deep the wound was and a single drop of blood welled up, trembling and bright, and fell to the floor. Over the thumb she stared at him accusingly. 'It's shallow,' he said. 'Tomorrow you won't even know it's there.' He hoped that she appreciated how quickly he had come to her aid. He'd acted out of concern for her, with no thought of getting anything in return, but now the thought occurred to him that it would be a nice gesture on her part not to start up that conversation again, as he was tired of it. 'I'll finish up here,' he said. 'You go and relax.'

'That's okay,' she said. 'I'll dry.'

He began to wash the silverware again, giving a lot of attention to the forks.

'So,' she said, 'you wouldn't have married me if I'd been black.'

'For Christ's sake, Ann!'

'Well, that's what you said, didn't you?'

'No, I did not. The whole question is ridiculous. If you had been black we probably wouldn't even have met. You would have had your friends and I would have had mine. The only black girl I ever really knew was my partner in the debating club, and I was already going out with you by then.'

'But if we had met, and I'd been black?'

'Then you probably would have been going out with a black guy.' He picked up the rinsing nozzle and sprayed the silverware. The water was so hot that the metal darkened to pale blue, then turned silver again.

'Let's say I wasn't,' she said. 'Let's say I am black and unattached and we meet and fall in love.'

He glanced over at her. She was watching him and her eyes were bright. 'Look,' he said, taking a reasonable tone, 'this is stupid. If you were black you wouldn't be you.' As he said this he realized it was absolutely true. There was no possible way of arguing with the fact that she would not be herself if she were black. So he said it again: 'If you were black you wouldn't be you.'

'I know,' she said, 'but let's just say.'

He took a deep breath. He had won the argument but he still felt cornered. 'Say what?' he asked.

'That I'm black, but still me, and we fall in love. Will you marry me?'

He thought about it.

'Well?' she said, and stepped close to him. Her eyes were even brighter. 'Will you marry me?'

'I'm thinking,' he said.

'You won't, I can tell. You're going to say no.'

'Let's not move too fast on this,' he said. 'There are lots of things to consider. We don't want to do something we would regret for the rest of our lives.'

'No more considering. Yes or no.'

'Since you put it that way – '

'Yes or no.'

'Jesus, Ann. All right. No.'

She said, 'Thank you,' and walked from the kitchen into the living room. A moment later he heard her turning the pages of a magazine. He knew that she was too angry to be actually reading it, but she didn't snap through the pages the way he would have done. She turned them slowly, as if she were studying every word. She was demonstrating her indifference to him, and it had the effect he knew she wanted it to have. It hurt him.

He had no choice but to demonstrate his indifference to her. Quietly, thoroughly, he washed the rest of the dishes. Then he dried them and put them away. He wiped the counters and the stove and scoured the linoleum where the drop of blood had fallen. While he was at it, he decided, he might as well mop the whole floor. When he was done the kitchen looked new, the way it looked when they were first shown the house, before they had ever lived here.

He picked up the garbage pail and went outside. The night was clear and he could see a few stars to the west, where the lights of the town didn't blur them out. On El Camino the traffic was steady and light, peaceful as a river. He felt ashamed that he had let his wife get him into a fight. In another thirty years or so they would both be dead. What would all that stuff matter then? He thought of the years they had spent together and how close they were and how well they knew each other, and his throat tightened so that he could hardly breathe. His face and neck began to tingle. Warmth flooded his chest.

He stood there for a while, enjoying these sensations, then picked up the pail and went out the back gate.

The two mutts from down the street had pulled over the garbage can again. One of them was rolling around on his back and the other had something in its mouth. When they saw him coming they trotted away with short, mincing steps. Normally he would heave rocks at them, but this time he let them go.

The house was dark when he came back inside. She was in the bathroom. He stood outside the door and called her name. He heard bottles clinking, but she didn't answer him. 'Ann, I'm really sorry,' he said. 'I'll make it up to you, I promise.'

'How?' she asked.

He wasn't expecting this. But from a sound in her voice, a level and definite note that was strange to him, he knew that he had to come up with the right answer. He leaned against the door. 'I'll marry you,' he whispered.

'We'll see,' she said. 'Go on to bed. I'll be out in a minute.'

He undressed and got under the covers. Finally he heard the bathroom door open and close.

'Turn off the light,' she said from the hallway.

'What?'

'Turn off the light.'

He reached over and pulled the chain on the bedside lamp. The room went dark. 'All right,' he said. He lay there, but nothing happened. 'All right,' he said again. Then he heard a movement across the room. He sat up but he couldn't see a thing. The room was silent. His heart pounded the way it had on their first night together, the way it still did when he woke at a noise in the darkness and waited to hear it again – the sound of someone moving through the house, a stranger.

The Poor Are Always With Us

The trouble with owning a Porsche is that there is always some little thing wrong with it. This time it was a sticky brake pedal. Russell had planned a trip for Easter weekend, so he left work early on Friday afternoon and drove up to Menlo Park to have Bruno, his mechanic, take a look at the car. Bruno was an Austrian. The wall behind his desk was covered with diplomas, most written in German, congratulating him on his completion of different courses in Porsche technology. Bruno's office overlooked the bay where he and his assistant worked on the cars, both of them wearing starched white smocks and wielding tools that glittered like surgical instruments.

When Russell pulled into the garage, Bruno was alone. He looked up, waved, and bent back down under the hood of a vintage green Speedster. Russell walked around the Speedster a couple of times, then watched over Bruno's shoulder as Bruno traced the wiring with a flashlight whose thin silver beam looked as solid as a knitting needle.

'So?' Bruno asked. After Russell described the trouble he was having, Bruno grunted and said, 'Sure sure. No sweat, old bean.' He said that he would get to it as soon as he was done with the Speedster – forty-five minutes, maybe an hour. Russell could wait or pick it up on Monday.

Russell told him he would wait.

There were two men in Bruno's office. They glanced at Russell when he came in, then went on talking above the noise of a radio on Bruno's desk that was playing music from the 1950s. Russell couldn't help listening to them. They were friends; he could tell that by the way they kept insulting each other. They never let up, especially the bigger of the two, a black guy who wore sunglasses and a safari jacket and popped his knuckles steadily. Whenever the white guy got off a good line the black guy would grin and shake his head and get off a better one. Twice Russell laughed out loud, and after the second time the white guy turned and stared at him. He had red-rimmed eyes that bulged as if some pressure inside him were forcing them out. His skin was tight-looking, drawn so severely over the bones of his face that even now, unsmiling as he was, his teeth showed. He stared at Russell and said, 'Little pitchers have big ears.'

Russell looked down at the rug. He tried to mind his own business after that, until the two men began to talk about someone from Russell's company who had recently been arrested for selling information on a new computer to the Japanese. Russell had met the man once, and from what these two fellows were saying he gathered that they had both worked with him at Hewlett-Packard a few years back. Russell knew he should keep his mouth shut, but he decided to say something. He had followed the case and had strong opinions about it. Mostly, though, he just wanted to join in the conversation.

'We all got our price,' the black guy was saying. 'Shit, they'd put every one of us in stir if they could read our minds for an hour. Any hour,' he added.

'As if everybody else in this town isn't doing something just as bad,' the white guy said. 'As bad or worse. Bunch of piglets. They're just burned up because he got to the trough before they did.'

'I see it differently,' Russell said. 'I think they should lock him up and throw away the key. He sold out the people who worked with him and trusted him. He sold out his team. As far as I'm concerned he's a complete write-off.'

The white guy fixed his eyes on Russell and said, 'Groves, who is this weenie?'

'Now, now,' Groves said.

'I swear to God,' the white guy said. He pushed himself out of his chair and went to the window overlooking the garage, coming down hard on the heels of his boots as he walked. He stood there, hands clenched into fists, and when he turned away Russell saw that his upper teeth were almost entirely exposed. He squinted at Russell. 'A complete write-off,' he said. 'How old are you, anyway?'

Groves popped a knuckle. 'Easy does it,' he said. 'Lighten up there, Dave.'

Russell didn't know any Daves, but this one had something against him. 'Twenty-two,' he said, adding a year.

'Well then, I guess you know it all. From the lofty perspective of your twenty-two years.'

'I don't know it all,' Russell said. 'I know the difference between right and wrong, though.' *I hardly ever talk like this*, Russell wanted to add. *You should hear me with my friends back home.*

The pants Dave wore looked too small for him, and now he made them look even smaller by jamming his hands into the back pockets. 'Go away,' he said to Russell. 'Go away and come back later, okay?'

'Easy does it,' Groves said again. He put a small silver bong on Bruno's desk and began to stuff it with brown marijuana from a sandwich bag. 'Peace pipe,' he said. He lit up and passed the bong to Russell. Russell took a bit and held it out to Dave, but Dave kept his hands in his pockets. Russell put the bong back down on Bruno's desk. He wished that he had refused it too.

'While we're on the subject,' Dave said, 'is there anybody else you want to write off?'

'Unbelievable,' Groves said, turning up the volume on the radio. "Runaround Sue." Man, I haven't heard "Runaround Sue" in about eighty years.'

Dave looked gloomily out the window. 'Is that your Targa?' he asked. Without waiting for Russell to answer, he said, 'How do you rate a Targa? Graduation present from Pop?'

'I bought it myself,' Russell said.

Dave asked Russell where he worked, and when Russell told him, he said, 'That outfit. Nothing but Jap spies and boy wonders. I swear to God they'll be hiring them out of first grade next.'

'I do dearly love a Porsche,' Groves said. 'There isn't anything I wouldn't do to get me a Porsche.'

Dave said, 'Why don't you buy one?'

'Ask my wife.'

'Which wife?'

'You see my problem,' Groves said. He fired up the bong again and offered it to Russell. 'Go on, child, go on,' he insisted when Russell shook his head, and kept pushing it at him until Russell took another hit. Russell held the smoke in his mouth, then blew it out and said, 'Gracias. That's righteous weed.'

'Righteous!' Dave said. He grinned at Groves, who bent over and made a sound like air escaping from a balloon. Groves began to drum his feet on the floor. 'Gracias!' Dave said, and Groves threw his head back and howled.

Bruno came into the office carrying a clipboard. 'You chaps,' he said. 'Always laughing.' He sat down at the desk and started punching away at a pocket calculator.

Groves said, 'Oh Lord. Lord Lord Lord.' He pushed up his sunglasses and rubbed his eyes.

Bruno tore a sheet off the clipboard. 'Seventy-two fifty,' he said to Dave.

'Catch you tomorrow,' Dave said.

'Better now,' Bruno told him. 'Tomorrow something bad might happen.'

Dave slowly counted out the money. He was putting his wallet in his pocket when Groves pointed at him and said, 'Name that tune!'

'"Turn Me Loose",' Dave said. 'Kookie Byrnes. Nineteen fifty-eight.'

'Fabian,' Russell said.

'What do *you* know?' Dave said. 'You weren't even born when this song came out.'

Russell said, 'It's Fabian. I'll bet you anything. I'll bet you my car.'

Dave studied Russell for a moment. 'Boy, you do bad things to me, you know that? Okay,' he said. 'My Speedster against your Targa.'

Russell turned to Bruno. 'You heard that.'

'Get your papers,' Bruno said.

Russell had his in his wallet. Dave's were in the glove compartment of the Speedster. While he was down in the garage getting them, Groves stood up and began to walk around the office. 'I don't fucking believe this,' he said. Dave came back and handed the papers to Bruno, and they all waited for the song to end. But when it ended, two more songs played back to back: 'My Prayer' and 'Duke of Earl'. Then the DJ came on and gave the names of the recording artists.

'Nuts,' Dave said. Then, to Russell, 'You little weenie.'

The whole thing caught Bruno on his funnybone. He laughed until tears came to his eyes. 'You crazy chaps,' he said. 'You crazy, crazy chaps.'

Russell agreed to let Dave bring the car over to his apartment later that afternoon. He had legal title now; if Dave didn't show up, Russell could have him arrested for grand theft auto. Bruno was the one who made this point. Still laughing. Bruno got his camera out of the desk and took several pictures of the Speedster to keep as souvenirs of the event.

Russell waited alone in the office while Bruno put the Targa right; then he drove home and ate a sandwich beside the pool in the courtyard of his apartment building. He had the place to himself. All the other tenants were still at work, and none of them had children. Some owned dogs, but they'd been trained not to bark, so the courtyard was quiet except for the sigh of traffic from Page Mill Road and the tick of palm fronds above the chair where Russell sat.

He hated to think of giving the Speedster back. He wanted to keep it, and he could give himself reasons for keeping it, reasons that made sense. But all of them sounded like lies to Russell – the kind of lies you tell yourself when you already know the truth. The truth was that he'd been certain Fabian was the singer, and certain that Dave would take his bet. He had smoked marijuana in the middle of the afternoon like some kind of junior high dropout, and lied about his age, and generally made a fool of himself. Then, because his feelings were hurt, he had goaded a man into gambling away his car.

That was how the truth looked to Russell, and it had nothing to do with his dream of being a magnanimous person, open-hearted and fair. Of course, not everyone would see it this way. Russell knew that most people would think he was being fussy.

Russell lived alone now, but when he first arrived in town he had roomed with a fellow from his company, an MIT graduate whose ambition was to make a bundle in a hurry, invest it, and then become a composer. He wrote moody violin pieces, which he sometimes played for Russell. Russell thought that they sounded great and that his room-mate was a genius. But his room-mate was also a swinger. He had girls in the apartment every weekend and sometimes even during the week, different girls, and one night he and Russell got into an argument about it. Russell hadn't said anything up to then but his room-mate knew that he disapproved. He wanted to know why. Russell told him that it seemed cheap. His room-mate said, 'You're completely uptight, that's your problem,' and walked away, but he ran back a moment later yelling that nobody, but nobody, called him cheap and got away with it. He waved his long white hands in Russell's face and said, 'How would you like a knuckle sandwich?' Russell apologized, and apologized again the next morning, and after that the two of them lived together on exquisitely polite terms.

Russell moved out at the end of the month. For a long time afterwards, until he got used to living alone, he made up conversations with his old room-mate in which he laid bare his soul, and was understood and forgiven. 'Listen,' Russell would say, 'I know you think I'm uptight because I don't sleep around or do many drugs or party a lot. But I'm not uptight, I'm really not. I just don't want to end up like Teddy Wells. I don't want to end up fifty years old and getting my sixth divorce and wearing gold chains and putting half my salary up my nose and collecting erotic art and cruising El Camino for teenagers.'

And Russell's room-mate would answer, 'I never looked at it that way before, but I see what you mean and you're absolutely right.'

Russell just wanted to keep his bearings, that was all. It was easy to lose your bearings when you were three thousand miles from home and making more money than you needed, almost twice as much as your own father made after thirty years of teaching high school math. 'I'm just getting started,' Russell would say. 'I'm doing the best I can!'

And his room-mate would answer, 'Of course. Of course.'

Dave brought the Speedster by at five-thirty, half an hour later than he'd promised. Russell was waiting outside the apartment building when Dave drove up. A dark-haired woman in an old station wagon pulled in behind the Speedster and sat there with the engine running. Dave rolled his window down. 'Did you call the heat yet?' he asked.

'I knew you'd come,' Russell said. He smiled, but Dave did not smile back.

'That's funny,' Dave said. 'A throw-away-the-key guy like you, I figured you'd have my picture in the post office by now.' He got out and closed the door gently. 'Here,' he said, and tossed Russell the keys. 'What are you going to do with it? Sell it?' He looked at the car, then back at Russell.

'No,' Russell said. 'Listen – '

Dave said, 'You listen.' He crossed the strip of grass to the sidewalk where Russell stood. Russell felt the man's hatred and took a step backwards. The woman in the station wagon revved the engine. Dave stopped and looked back at her, then put his hands in his pockets as he had done earlier that day. Russell understood the gesture now: it was what Dave did with his hands to keep them from doing something else.

'I wish this hadn't happened,' Russell said.

Though Dave was a couple of inches shorter than Russell, he seemed to be examining him from a height. 'You're nothing special,' he said. 'You might think you have ideas, but you don't. No one has had an actual idea in this business for about five years. You want to know how I got the Speedster?' When Russell didn't answer, he said: 'I'll tell you. They gave it to me for an idea I had, actually a lot of ideas put together. They just handed me the keys and told me where it was parked and that was that. No speeches or anything. No plaque. Everything was understood.'

The woman in the station wagon revved the engine again. Dave ignored her. He said, 'You little snots think you're on the cutting edge but all you're doing is just sweeping up, collecting our stuff. The work's been done. You're just a bunch of janitors.'

'That's not true,' Russell said.

'You're a janitor,' Dave repeated. 'No way in hell do you rate a car like that. A car like that is completely out of your class.' He took a quarter from his pocket and said, 'Flip me for it.'

'Flip you? Flip you for what?'

Dave looked down the street where the woman sat watching them. 'The wagon,' he said.

'Come on,' Russell said. 'What kind of deal is that?'

Dave flipped the quarter. 'Call it.'

'This is baloney,' Russell said. Then, because he was afraid of Dave and wanted to be done with him, he said, 'What the hell. All right. Tails.'

'Tails it is,' Dave said, and threw the coin into Russell's face. It struck him below the eye and fell to the sidewalk. Dave walked back to the station wagon. He knocked on the window, and when the woman rolled it down he reached past her, turned off the engine, and dropped the keys into the gutter.

'Hey,' she said.

'Get out,' Dave told her, and held the door open until she obeyed him. She was thin and pale. She had liquid brown eyes like a deer's eyes, and like a deer she looked restlessly around her as if unsure of everything.

'I'll send Groves over with the papers,' Dave said. He turned and started down the street towards Page Mill Road. The woman watched him walk away, then looked at Russell.

'I'm sorry,' he said. 'It wasn't my idea.'

'Oh no,' she said. 'Wait a minute. Dave!' she called, but Dave kept walking and didn't look back. 'Don't go anywhere,' she told Russell. 'Just wait here, okay?' She took a couple of steps and gave a loud scream. Then she broke into a run, stopping once to scream again – no words, only the pure sound rising between the tiled roof-tops into the cloudless blue sky.

Russell ate dinner at a Chinese place near the freeway. When he got home, he found Groves leaning back in one of the chairs by the side of the pool. The woman who managed the building was sitting beside him. She was a widow from Michigan. The other tenants complained about her because she was snoopy and enforced all the rules. In the eight months since Russell moved in he had never seen her smile, but when he stepped into the courtyard she was laughing.

'That's gospel,' Groves said. 'I swear.'

She laughed again.

It was dark but Groves still had his sunglasses on. His hands were folded behind his head. When he saw Russell, he pointed one foot at him and said, 'Here come de champ.'

'Sorry I made you wait,' Russell said. 'I didn't know you'd be coming tonight.'

'See?' Groves said. 'I'm no perpetrator.' He pushed himself up from the chair and said to Russell, 'Emma here thought I was a perpetrator.'

'No I didn't!' she said.

Groves laughed. 'That's cool. Everybody gets one mistake.' He clapped his hand on Russell's shoulder. 'Champ, we got to talk.'

Russell led Groves up the stairs and along the walkway to his apartment. Groves followed him inside and looked around. 'What's this number?' he asked. 'You in training to be a monk or something?'

'I just moved in a while ago,' Russell said.

'No pictures, no sounds, no box,' Groves went on. 'No nothing. You sure you live here?' He took an envelope from his pocket and dropped it on the counter that divided the living room from the kitchen. 'Candygram from Dave,' he said. 'Crazy Dave. Champ, we got a problem.' Groves began to pace the small room, deliberately at first, then faster and faster, wheeling like a cat in a cage, the unbuckled straps of his safari jacket swinging at his sides. 'We got a priority situation here,' he said, 'because you just got yourself all tied up in something you don't understand, and what you don't understand is my man Dave isn't in *no* condition to go laying off his automobiles at this point in time. He isn't what we say *competent*, you dig? What we're talking about here is some serious post-Vietnam shit. I mean serious head problems.'

Without slowing down, Groves lit a cigarette. 'What we've got here is a disturbed veteran. We've got a man who's been on the big march through the valley of the shadow of death, you follow me? I'm talking about Khe Sanh, champ. The Pit. Here's how it went down. Dave's company is sitting out on the perimeter or whatever and the Cong come pouring over, you with me? There's mortars going off and all that shit and rifles and whatever, and a whole bunch of Dave's friends, I mean his special dudes, get shot up. I mean they're hanging out there on the wire and so on. Now my man Dave, he's been hit too but what he does, he crawls out there anyway and drags his buddies in. All of them. Even the dead ones. And all the time old Charlie Cong is just *raining* on him. I mean he's got holes in places you never even *heard* of.'

Groves shook his head. 'Two years in the hospital, champ. Two years all wrapped up like some kind of horror movie, and then what do they do? They give him the Congressional Medal of Honor and say, Sayonara, sucker. He don't think straight anymore, that's not their problem, right?'

Groves walked around the counter. He ran water on the butt of his cigarette and dropped it in the sink. 'What I'm saying is, you got any self-respect you don't go ripping no automobiles off of no disturbed veterans with the Congressional fucking Medal of Honor. That's what I'm saying here tonight.'

Groves leaned forward against the counter and smiled at Russell. 'Child,' he said, 'why don't you just give the man his cars back?'

'My name is Russell. And I don't believe that story. I don't believe that Dave was even in Vietnam.'

'Damn!' Groves said. 'Where's your imagination?' He took his sunglasses off, laid them on the counter, and began to rub his eyes in a way that made Russell think they were causing him pain – slowly, with his fingertips. 'I don't know,' he said. 'All right. Let's take it again. We're talking about Dave.'

Russell nodded.

'Dave's a good head,' Groves went on. 'I admit he's not that great with the general public, but he's okay. Lots of smarts, too. I mean, I'm smart, but Dave is *smart*. It used to be just about everybody in town wanted a piece of him. Dave was centrefold material for a while there, but nowadays things just keep messing up on him. It's like the well went dry. Happens to plenty of people. It could happen to you. I mean you might be coming up with sweet stuff today but there's no law says it's got to be there tomorrow, and just maybe it won't be. You ought to think about that.'

'I do,' Russell said.

'Now his wife's gone and left him. No concern of yours, but Lord, what a business.'

'I tried to give the car back to him,' Russell said. 'He didn't give me a chance. He wouldn't even let me talk.'

Groves laughed.

'It wasn't funny,' Russell said. 'I've had the willies all night. He really scared me, Groves. That's why I can't give him the car back now. I'd always wonder if I did it just because I was afraid of him. I wouldn't ever feel right about it.'

Groves said, 'Russell, I never saw no eighty-year-old man looked like you before.'

'What I'm going to do is give the Speedster to you,' Russell said. 'Then you can give it to Dave. That's something I can live with. But I'm going to keep the station wagon,' Russell added. 'I won that fair and square.'

'Well, now,' Groves said. He seemed about to go on, but finally he just shook his head and looked down at the counter.

Russell had the papers in his pocket. He spread them out. 'How do I write your name?' he asked.

'Just like it sounds. Groves. Tom Groves.' As Russell took the cap from his pen, Groves said, in a quiet voice, 'Make that Thomas B. Groves, Junior.'

Russell never saw Groves again, but from time to time he felt a coldness on his back and looked around to find Dave watching him from another line in the market where he shopped, or through the window of the bank where he kept his money. Dave never said anything, never accused, but Russell began to think that he was being followed and that a showdown was soon to come. He tried to prepare himself for it. There were times at night and even at work when Russell made angry faces, and shook his head, and glared at things without seeing them as he rehearsed again and again the proofs of his own decency. This went on for almost a year.

Then, in April, he saw Dave on El Camino. Russell had parked in the customer lot of a liquor store and was waiting for his date to come out with some wine for a party they were going to. He was sitting there, watching the cars go by, when he caught sight of Dave standing on the kerb across the road. Russell felt sure that Dave had not seen him, because Dave was giving all his attention to the traffic. He swung his head back and forth as the cars rushed past him, looking, Russell supposed, for a chance to cross. Sometimes the line of cars heading north would thin out, and sometimes the line heading south, but never both together. There was no light nearby and no pedestrian crossing, because on El Camino there were no pedestrians. You never saw anyone on foot.

Dave went on waiting for a break to come. Twice he stepped into the road as if to test his luck, but both times he changed his mind and turned back. Russell watched for Dave to bare his teeth and scream and shake his fists. Nothing like this happened. He stood there and waited for his chance, leaning into the road a little as he looked each way. His face was calm. He accepted this situation, saw nothing outrageous in it – nothing to make him go home and come back with a gun and shoot every driver on the road.

Finally Dave spotted an opening and made a run for it. He moved heavily but for all he was worth, knees flying high, arms flailing the air, and Russell's heart went out to the man. At that moment he would have given Dave everything he had – his money, his car, his job, everything – but what was the point? It didn't make sense trying to help Dave, because Dave couldn't be helped. Whatever Russell gave him he would lose. It just wasn't in the cards for him to have anything.

When Dave reached the kerb he stopped and caught his breath. Then he started south in the direction of Mountain View. Russell watched him walk past the parking lot, watched him until he disappeared from sight. The low sun burned in the windows of a motel down the street. Above the motel roof-top, against the blue sky, hung a faint white haze like the haze of chalk dust on the blue suit Russell's father wore to school. Blurred shapes of cars flashed back and forth. Russell felt a little lost, and thought, *I'm on El Camino.* He was on El Camino. Just a short drive down the road some people were having a party, and he was on his way there.

Sister

There was a park at the bottom of the hill. Now that the leaves were down Marty could see the exercise stations and part of a tennis court from her kitchen window, through a web of black branches. She took another doughnut from the box on the table and ate it slowly, watching the people at the exercise stations: two men and a woman. The woman was doing leg-raises. The men were just standing there. Though the day was cold one of the men had taken his shirt off, and even from this distance Marty was struck by the deep brown colour of his skin. You hardly ever saw great tans like that on people around here, not even in summer. He had come from somewhere else.

She went into the bedroom and put on a running suit and an old pair of Adidas. The seams were giving out but her other pair was new and their whiteness made her feet look big. She took off her glasses and put her contacts in. Tears welled up under the lenses. For a few moments she lost her image in the mirror; then it returned and she saw the excitement in her face, the eagerness. *Whoa*, she thought. She sat there for a while, feeling the steady thump of the stereo in the apartment overhead. Then she rolled a joint and stuck it in the pocket of her sweatshirt.

A dog barked at Marty as she walked down the hallway. It barked at her every time she passed its door and it always took her by surprise, leaving her fluttery and breathless. The dog was a big shepherd whose owners were gone all the time. She heard it barking all the way down the corridor until she reached the door and stepped outside.

It was late afternoon and cold, so cold she could see her breath. As always on Sunday the street was dead quiet, except for the skittering of leaves on the sidewalk as the breeze swept through them and ruffled the cold-looking pools of water from last night's rain. With the trees bare, the sky seemed vast. Two dark clouds drifted overhead, and in the far distance an angle of geese flew across the sky. Honkers, her brother called them. Right now he and his buddies would be banging away at them from one of the marshes outside town. By nightfall they'd all be drunk. She smiled, thinking of that.

Marty did a couple of knee-bends and headed towards the park, forcing herself to walk against the urge she felt to run. She considered taking a couple of hits off the joint in her pocket but decided against it. She didn't want to lose her edge.

The woman she'd seen at the exercise station was gone, but the two men were still there. Marty held back for a while, did a few more knee-bends and watched some boys playing football on the field behind the tennis courts. They couldn't have been more than ten or eleven but they moved like men, hunching up their shoulders and shaking their wrists as they jogged back to the huddle, grunting when they came off the line as if their bodies were big and weighty. You could tell that in their heads they had a whole stadium of people watching them. It tickled her. Marty watched them run several plays, then she walked over to the exercise stations.

When she got there she had a shock. Marty recognized one of the men, and she was so afraid he would recognize her that she almost turned around and went home. He was a regular at the Kon-Tiki. A few weeks earlier he had taken notice of Marty and they'd matched daiquiris for a couple of hours and things looked pretty good. Then she went out to the car to get this book she'd been describing to him, a book about Edgar Cayce and reincarnation, and when she got back he was sitting on the other side of the room with someone else. He hadn't left anything for the drinks, so she got stuck with the bar bill. And her lighter was missing. The man's name was Jack. When she saw him leaning against the chin-up station she didn't know what to do. She wanted to vanish right into the ground.

But he seemed not to remember her. In fact, he was the one who said hello. 'Hey there,' he said.

She smiled at him. Then she looked at the tan one and said, 'Hi.'

He didn't answer. His eyes moved over her for a moment, and he looked away. He'd put on a warm-up jacket with a hood but left the zipper open nearly to his waist. His chest was covered with little curls of glistening golden hair. The other one, Jack, had on faded army fatigues with dark patches where the insignia had been removed. He needed a shave. He was holding a quart bottle of beer.

The two men had been talking when she walked up but now they were silent. Marty felt them watching her as she did her stretches. They had been talking about sex, she was sure of that. What they'd been saying was still in the air somehow, with the ripe smell of wet leaves and the rain-soaked earth. She took a deep breath.

Then she said, 'You didn't get that tan around here.' She kept rocking back and forth on her knuckles but looked up at him.

'You bet your buns I didn't,' he said. 'The only thing you get around here is arthritis.' He pulled the zipper of his jacket up and down. 'Hawaii. Waikiki Beach.'

'Waikiki,' Jack said. 'Bikini-watching capital of the world.'

'Brother, you speak true,' the tan one said. 'They've got this special breed over there that they raise just to walk back and forth in front of you. They ought to parachute about fifty of them into Russia. Those old farts in the Kremlin would go out of their skulls. We could just walk in and take the place over.'

'They could drop a couple on this place while they're at it,' Jack said.

'Amen.' The tan one nodded. 'Make it four – two apiece.'

'Aloha,' Marty said. She rolled over on her back and raised her feet a few inches off the ground. She held them there for a moment, then lowered them. 'That's all the Hawaiian I know,' she said. 'Aloha and Maui Zowie. They grow some killer weed over there.'

'For sure,' the tan one said. 'It's God's country, sister, and that's a fact.'

Jack walked up closer. 'I know you from somewhere,' he said.

Oh no, Marty thought. She smiled at him. 'Maybe,' she said. 'What's your name?'

'Bill,' he said.

Right, Marty wanted to say. *You bet, Jack.*

Jack looked down at her. 'What's yours?'

She raised her feet again. 'Elizabeth.'

'Elizabeth,' he repeated, slowly, so that it struck Marty how beautiful the name was.

'I guess not,' he said.

She lowered her feet and sat up. 'A lot of people look like me.'

He nodded.

Just then something flew past Marty's head. She jerked to one side and threw her hands up in front of her face. She gave a shudder and looked around. 'Jesus,' she said.

'Sorry!' someone shouted.

'Goddam Frisbees,' Jack said.

'It's all right,' Marty told him, and waved at the man who'd thrown it. She turned and waved again at another man some distance behind her, who was wiping the Frisbee on his shirt. He waved back.

'Frisbee freaks,' Jack said. 'I'm sick of them.' He lifted the bottle and drank from it, then held it out to Marty. 'Go on,' he told her.

She took a swig. 'There's more than beer in here,' she said.

Jack shrugged.

'What's in here?' she asked.

'Secret formula,' he answered. 'Go for two. You're behind.'

Marty looked at the bottle, then drank again and passed it to the other man. Even his fingers were brown. He wore a thick wedding band and a gold chain-link bracelet. She held on to the bottle for an extra moment, long enough for him to notice and give her a look; then she let go. The hood of his jacket fell back as he tilted his head to drink. Marty saw that he was nearly bald. He had parted his hair just above one ear and swept it sideways to cover the skin on top, which was even darker than the rest of him.

'What's your name?' she asked.

Jack answered for him. 'His name is Jack,' he said.

The tan one laughed. 'Brother,' he said, 'you are too much.'

'You aren't from around here,' she said. 'I would have seen you.'

He shook his head. 'I was running and I ended up here.'

Jack said, 'Don't hog the fuel, Jack,' and made a drinking motion with his hand.

The tan one nodded. He took a long pull and wiped his mouth and passed the bottle to Jack.

Marty stood and brushed off her warm-ups. 'Hawaii,' she said. 'I've always wanted to go to Hawaii. Just kick back for about three weeks. Check out the volcanoes. Do some mai tais.'

'Get leis,' Jack said.

All three of them laughed.

'Well,' she said. She touched her toes a couple of times.

Jack kept laughing.

'Hawaii's amazing,' said the other man. 'Anything goes.'

'Stop talking about Hawaii,' Jack told him. 'It makes me cold.'

'Me too,' Marty said. She rubbed her hands together. 'I'm always cold. When I come back, I just hope I come back as a native of some place warm. California, maybe.'

'Right,' Jack said. 'Bitchin' Cal,' but there was something in his voice that made her look over at him. He was studying her. She could tell that he was trying to place her again, trying to recall where he'd met her. She wished she hadn't made that remark about coming back. That was what had set him off. She wasn't even sure she actually believed in it – believed that she was going to return as a different entity later on, someone new and different. She had serious doubts, sometimes.

'So,' she said, 'do you guys know each other?'

Jack stared at her a moment longer, then nodded. 'All our lives,' he said.

The tan one shook his head and laughed. 'Too much,' he said.

'We're inseparable,' Jack said. 'Aren't we, Jack?'

The tan one laughed again.

'Is that right?' Marty asked him. 'Are you inseparable?'

He pulled the zipper of his jacket up and down, hiding and then revealing the golden hairs on his chest, though not in a conscious way. His cheeks puffed out and his brow thickened just above his eyes, so that his face seemed heavier. He looked at her and said, 'I guess we are. For the time being.'

'That's fine,' she said. 'That's all right.' That was all right, she thought. She could call Jill, Jill was always up for a party, and if Jill was out or had company then she'd think of something else. It would work out.

'Okay,' she said, but before she could say anything else someone yelled 'Heads up!' and they all looked around. The Frisbee was coming straight at them. Marty felt her body tighten. 'Got it,' she said, and balanced herself for the catch. Suddenly the breeze gusted and the Frisbee seemed to stop cold, a quivering red line, and then it jerked upwards and flew over their heads and past them. She ran after it, one arm raised, gathering herself to jump, but it stayed just out of reach and finally she gave up.

The Frisbee flew a short distance farther, then fell to the sidewalk and skidded halfway across the street. Marty scooped it up and flipped it back into the park. She stood there, wanting to laugh but completely out of breath. Too much weed, she thought. She put her hands on her knees and rocked back and forth. It was quiet. Then, from up the hill, she heard a low rumble that grew steadily louder, and a few seconds later a big white car came around the corner. Its tyres squealed and then went silent as the car slid through a long sheet of water lying in the road. It was moving sideways in her direction. She watched it come. The car cleared the water and the tyres began to squeal again but it kept sliding, and Marty saw the faces inside getting bigger and bigger. There was a girl staring at her from the front window. The girl's mouth was open, her arms braced against the dashboard. Then the tyres caught and the car shot forward, so close that Marty could have reached out and touched the girl's cheek as they went past.

The car fish-tailed down the street. It ran a stop sign at the corner and turned left back up the hill, coughing out bursts of black exhaust.

Marty turned towards the park and saw the two men looking at her. They were looking at her as if they had seen her naked, and that was how she felt – naked. She had nearly been killed and now she was an embarrassment, like someone in need. She wasn't welcome in the park.

Marty crossed the street and started up the hill towards her apartment building. She felt as if she were floating, as if there were nothing to her. She passed a grey cat curled up on the hood of a car. There was smoke on the breeze and the smell of decay. It seemed to Marty that she drifted with the smoke through the yellow light, over the dull grass and the brown clumps of leaves. In the park behind her a boy called football signals, his voice perfectly distinct in the thin cold air.

She climbed the steps to the building but did not go inside. She knew that the dog would bark at her, and she didn't think she could handle that right now.

She sat on the steps. From somewhere nearby a bird cried out in a hoarse, ratcheting voice like chain being jerked through a pulley. Marty did some breathing exercises to get steady, to quiet the fluttering sensation in her shoulders and knees, but she could not calm herself. A few minutes ago she had nearly been killed and now there was nobody to talk to about it, to see how afraid she was and tell her not to worry, that it was over now. That everything was going to be all right. And Marty understood that there was never going to be anyone to tell her these things. She had no idea why this should be so; it was just something she knew.

The sun was going down. Marty couldn't see it from where she sat, but the windows of the house across the street had turned crimson, and the breeze was colder. A broken kite flapped in a tree. Marty fingered the joint in her pocket but left it there; she felt empty and clean, and did not want to lose the feeling.

She watched the sky darken. Her brother and his friends would be coming off the marsh about now, flushed with cold and drink, their dogs running ahead through the reeds and the tall grass. When they reached the car they'd compare birds and pass a bottle around, and after the bottle was empty they'd head for the nearest bar. Do boilermakers.

Stuff themselves with pickled eggs and jerky. Throw dice from a leather cup. And outside in the car the dogs would be waiting, ears pricked for the least sound, sometimes whimpering to themselves but mostly silent, tense, and still, watching the bright door the men had closed behind them.

Soldier's Joy

On Friday Hooper was named driver of the guard for the third night that week. He had recently been broken in rank again, this time from corporal to PFC, and the first sergeant had decided to keep Hooper's evenings busy so that he would not have leisure to brood. That was what the first sergeant told Hooper when Hooper came to the orderly room to complain.

'It's for your own good,' the first sergeant said. 'Not that I expect you to thank me.' He moved the book he'd been reading to one side of his desk and leaned back. 'Hooper, I have a theory about you,' he said. 'Want to hear it?'

'I'm all ears, Top,' Hooper said.

The first sergeant put his boots up on the desk and stared out the window to his left. It was getting on towards five o'clock. Work details had begun to return from the rifle range and the post laundry and the brigade commander's house, where Hooper and several other men were excavating a swimming pool without aid of machinery. As the trucks let them out they gathered on the barracks steps and under the dead elm beside the mess hall, their voices a steady murmur in the orderly room where Hooper stood waiting for the first sergeant to speak.

'You resent me,' the first sergeant said. 'You think you should be sitting here. You don't know that's what you think because you've totally sublimated your resentment, but that's what it is all right, and that's why you and me are developing a definite conflict profile. It's like you have to keep fucking up to prove to yourself that you don't really care. That's my theory. You follow me?'

'Top, I'm way ahead of you,' Hooper said. 'That's night school talking.'

The first sergeant continued to look out the window. 'I don't know,' he said. 'I don't know what you're doing in my army. You've put your twenty years in. You could retire to Mexico and buy a peso factory. Live like a dictator. So what are you doing in my army, Hooper?'

Hooper looked down at the desk. He cleared his throat but said nothing.

'Give it some thought,' the first sergeant said. He stood and walked Hooper to the door. 'I'm not hostile,' he said. 'I'm prepared to be supportive. Just think nice thoughts about Mexico, okay? Okay, Hooper?'

Hooper called Mickey and told her he wouldn't be coming by that night after all. She reminded him that this was the third time in one week, and said that she wasn't getting any younger.

'What am I supposed to do?' Hooper asked. 'Go AWOL?'

'I cried three times today,' Mickey said. 'I just broke down and cried, and you know what? I don't even know why. I just feel bad all the time anymore.'

'What did you do last night?' Hooper asked. When Mickey didn't answer he said, 'Did Briggs come over?'

'I've been inside all day,' Mickey said. 'Just sitting here. I'm going out of my tree.' Then, in the same weary voice, she said, 'Touch it, Hoop.'

'I have to get going,' Hooper said.

'Not yet. Wait. I'm going into the bedroom. I'm going to pick up the phone in there. Hang on, Hoop. Think of the bedroom. Think of me lying on the bed. Wait, baby.'

There were men passing by the phone booth. Hooper watched them and tried not to think of Mickey's bedroom but now he could think of nothing else. Mickey's husband was a supply sergeant with a taste for quality. The walls of the bedroom were knotty pine he'd derailed en route to some colonel's office. The brass lamps beside the bed were made from howitzer casings. The sheets were parachute silk. Sometimes, lying on those sheets, Hooper thought of the men who had drifted to earth below them. He was no great lover, as the women he went with usually got around to telling him, but in Mickey's bedroom Hooper had turned in his saddest performances and always when he was most aware that everything around him was stolen. He wasn't exactly sure why he kept going back. It was just something he did, again and again.

'Okay,' Mickey said. 'I'm here.'

'There's a guy waiting to use the phone,' Hooper told her.

'Hoop, I'm on the bed. I'm taking off my shoes.'

Hooper could see her perfectly. He lit a cigarette and opened the door of the booth to let the smoke out.

'Hoop?' she said.

'I told you, there's a guy waiting.'

'Turn around then.'

'You don't need me,' Hooper said. 'All you need is the telephone. Why don't you call Briggs? That's what you're going to do after I hang up.'

'I probably will,' she said. 'Listen, Hoop, I'm not really on the bed. I was just pulling your chain. I thought it would make me feel better but it didn't.'

'I knew it,' Hooper said. 'You're watching the tube, right?'

'Somebody just won a saw,' Mickey said.

'A saw?'

'Yeah, they drove up to this man's house and dumped a truckload of logs in his yard and gave him a chainsaw. This was his fantasy. You should see how happy he is, Hoop. I'd give anything to be that happy.'

'Maybe I can swing by later tonight,' Hooper said. 'Just for a minute.'

'I don't know,' Mickey said. 'Better give me a ring first.'

After Mickey hung up Hooper tried to call his wife but there was no answer. He stood there and listened to the phone ringing. At last he put the receiver down and stepped outside the booth, just as they began to sound retreat over the company loudspeaker. With the men around him Hooper came to attention and saluted. The record was scratchy, but, as always, the music caused Hooper's mind to go abruptly and perfectly still. He held his salute until the last note died away, then broke off smartly and walked down the street towards the mess hall.

The officer of the day was Captain King from Headquarters Company. Captain King had also been Officer of the Day on Monday and Tuesday nights, and Hooper was glad to see him again because Captain King was too lazy to do his own job or to make sure that the guards were doing theirs. He stayed in the guardhouse and left everything up to Hooper.

Captain King had grey hair and a long, greyish face. He was a West Point graduate with twenty-eight years of service behind him, just trying to make it through another two years so he could retire at three-quarters pay. All his classmates were generals or at least bird colonels but he himself had been held back for good reasons, many of which he admitted to Hooper their first night together. It puzzled Hooper at first, this officer telling him about his failures to perform, his nervous breakdowns and Valium habit, but finally Hooper understood: Captain King regarded him, a PFC with twenty-one years' service, as a comrade in dereliction, a disaster like himself with no room left for judgment against anyone.

The evening was hot and muggy. Little black bats swooped overhead as Captain King made his way along the rank of men drawn up before the guardhouse steps. He objected to the alignment of someone's belt buckle. He asked questions about the chain of command but gave no sign as to whether the answers he received were right or wrong. He inspected a couple of rifles and pretended to find something amiss with each of them, though it was clear that he hardly knew one end from the other, and when he reached the last man in the line he began to deliver a speech. He said that he had never seen such sorry troops in his life. He asked how they expected to stand up to a determined enemy.

On and on he went. Captain King had delivered the same speech on Monday and Tuesday, and when Hooper recognized it he lit another cigarette and sat down on the running board of the truck he'd been leaning against.

The sky was grey. It had a damp, heavy look and it felt heavy too, hanging close overhead, nervous with rumblings and small flashes in the distance. Just sitting there made Hooper sweat. Beyond the guardhouse a stream of cars rushed along the road to Tacoma. From the officers' club farther up the road came the muffled beat of rock music, which was almost lost, like every other sound of the evening, in the purr of crickets that rose up everywhere and thickened the air like heat.

When Captain King had finished talking he turned the men over to Hooper for transportation to their posts. Two of them, both privates, were from Hooper's company and these he allowed to ride with him in the cab of the truck while everybody else slid around in back. One was a cook named Porchoff, known as Porkchop. The other was a radio operator named Trac who had managed to airlift himself out of Saigon during the fall of the city by hanging from the skids of a helicopter. That was the story Hooper had heard, anyway, and he had no reason to doubt it; he'd seen the slopes pull that trick plenty of times, though few of them were as young as Trac must have been then – eight or nine at the most. When Hooper tried to picture his son Wesley at the same age doing that, hanging over a burning city by his fingertips, he had to smile.

But Trac didn't talk about it. There was nothing about him to suggest his past except perhaps the deep, sickle-shaped scar above his right eye. To Hooper there was something familiar about this scar. One night, watching Trac play the video game in the company rec room, he was overcome with the certainty that he had seen Trac before somewhere – astride a water buffalo in some reeking paddy or running alongside Hooper's APC with a bunch of other kids all begging money, holding up melons or a bag full of weed or a starving monkey on a stick.

Though Hooper had the windows open, the cab of the truck smelled strongly of aftershave. Hooper noticed that Trac was wearing orange Walkman earphones under his helmet liner. They were against regulations but Hooper said nothing. As long as Trac had his ears plugged he wouldn't be listening for trespassers and end up blowing his rifle off at some squirrel cracking open an acorn. Of all the guards only Porchoff and Trac would be carrying ammunition, because they had been assigned to the battalion communications centre where there was a tie-in terminal to the division mainframe computer. The theory was that an intruder who knew his stuff could get his hands on highly classified material. That was how it had been explained to Hooper. Hooper thought it was a load of crap. The Russians knew everything anyway.

Hooper let out the first two men at the PX and the next two at the parking lot outside the main officers' club, where lately there'd been several cars vandalized. As they pulled away, Porchoff leaned over Trac and grabbed Hooper's sleeve. 'You used to be a corporal,' he said.

Hooper shook Porchoff's hand loose. He said, 'I'm driving a truck, in case you didn't notice.'

'How come you got busted?'

'None of your business.'

'I'm just asking,' Porchoff said. 'So what happened, anyway?'

'Cool it, Porkchop,' said Trac. 'The man doesn't want to talk about it, okay?'

'Cool it yourself, fuckface,' Porchoff said. He looked at Trac. 'Was I addressing you?'

Trac said, 'Man, you must've been eating some of your own food.'

'I don't believe I was addressing you,' Porchoff said. 'In fact, I don't believe that you and me have been properly introduced. That's another thing I don't like about the army, the way people you haven't been introduced to feel perfectly free to get right into your face and unload whatever shit they've got in their brains. It happens all the time. But I never heard anyone say "cool it" before. You're a real phrasemaker, fuckface.'

'That's enough,' Hooper said.

Porchoff leaned back and said, 'That's enough,' in a falsetto voice. A few moments later he started humming to himself.

Hooper dropped off the rest of the guards and turned up the hill towards the communications centre. There were chokeberry bushes along the gravel drive, with white blossoms going grey in the dusky light. Gravel sprayed up under the tyres and rattled against the floorboards of the truck. Porchoff stopped humming. 'I've got a cramp,' he said.

Hooper pulled up next to the gate and turned off the engine. He looked over at Porchoff. 'Now what's your problem?' he said.

'I've got a cramp,' Porchoff repeated.

'For Christ's sake,' Hooper said. 'Why didn't you say something before?'

'I did. I went on sick call but the doctor couldn't find it. It keeps moving around. It's here now.' Porchoff touched his neck. 'I swear to God.'

'Keep track of it,' Hooper told him. 'You can go on sick call again in the morning.'

'You don't believe me,' Porchoff said.

The three of them got out of the truck. Hooper counted out the ammunition to Porchoff and Trac, and watched as they loaded their clips. 'That ammo's strictly for show,' he said. 'Forget I even gave it to you. If you run into a problem, which you won't, use the phone in the guard shack. You can work out your own shifts.' Hooper opened the gate and locked the two men inside. They stood watching him, faces in shadow, black rifle barrels poking over their shoulders. 'Listen,' Hooper said, 'nobody's going to break in here, understand?'

Trac nodded. Porchoff just looked at him.

'Okay,' Hooper said. 'I'll drop by later. Me and the captain.' Hooper knew that Captain King wasn't about to go anywhere, but Trac and Porchoff didn't know that. Hooper behaved better when he thought he was being watched and he supposed that the same was true of other people.

Hooper climbed back inside the truck and started the engine. He gave the V sign to the men at the gate. Trac gave the sign back and turned away. Porchoff didn't move. He stayed where he was, fingers laced through the wire. He looked about ready to cry. 'Damn,' Hooper said, and hit the gas. Gravel clattered in the wheel wells. When Hooper reached the main road a light rain began to fall, but it stopped before he'd even turned the wipers on.

Hooper and Captain King sat on adjacent bunks in the guardhouse, which was empty except for them and a bat that was flitting back and forth among the dim rafters. As on Monday and Tuesday nights, Captain King had brought along an ice chest filled with little bottles of Perrier water. From time to time he tried pressing one on Hooper, but Hooper declined. His refusals made Captain King apologetic. 'It's not a class thing,' Captain King said, looking at the bottle in his hand. 'I don't drink this stuff because I went to the Point or anything like that.' He leaned down and put the bottle between his bare feet. 'I'm allergic to alcohol,' he said. 'Otherwise I'd probably be an alcoholic. Why not? I'm everything else.' He smiled at Hooper.

Hooper lay back and clasped his hands behind his head and stared up at the mattress above him. 'I'm not much of a drinker myself,' he said. He knew that Captain King wanted him to explain why he refused the Perrier water but there was really no reason in particular.

'I drank eggnog one Christmas when I was a kid and it almost killed me,' Captain King said. 'My arms and legs swelled up to twice their normal size. The doctors couldn't get my glasses off because my skin was all puffed up around them. You know the way a tree will grow around a rock. It was like that. A few months later I tried beer at some kid's graduation party and the same thing happened. Pretty strange, eh?'

'Yes sir,' Hooper said.

'I used to think it was all for the best. I have an addictive personality and you can bet your bottom dollar I would have been a problem drinker. No question about it. But now I wonder. If I'd had one big weakness like that maybe I wouldn't have had all these little pissant weaknesses I ended up with. I know that sounds like bull-pucky, but look at Alexander the Great. Alexander the Great was a boozer. Did you know that?'

'No sir,' Hooper said.

'Well, he was. Read your history. So was Churchill. Churchill drank a bottle of cognac a day. And of course Grant. You know what Lincoln said when someone complained about Grant's drinking?'

'Yes sir. I've heard the story.'

'He said, "Find out what brand he uses so I can ship a case to the rest of my generals." Is that the way you heard it?'

'Yes sir.'

Captain King nodded. 'I'm all in,' he said. He stretched out and assumed exactly the position Hooper was in. It made Hooper uncomfortable. He sat up and put his feet on the floor.

'Married?' Captain King asked.

'Yes sir.'

'Kids?'

'Yes sir. One. Wesley.'

'Oh my God, a boy,' Captain King said. 'They're nothing but trouble, take my word for it. They're programmed to hate you. It has to be like that, otherwise they'd spend their whole lives moping around the house, but just the same it's no fun when it starts. I have two and neither of them can stand me. Haven't been home in years. Breaks my heart. Of course I was a worse father than most. How old is your boy?'

'Sixteen or seventeen,' Hooper said. He put his hands on his knees and looked at the floor. 'Seventeen. He lives with my wife's sister in San Diego.'

Captain King turned his head and looked at Hooper. 'Sounds like you're not much of a dad yourself.'

Hooper began to lace his boots up.

'I'm not criticizing,' Captain King said. 'At least you were smart enough to get someone else to do the job.' He yawned. 'I'm whipped,' he said. 'You need me for anything? You want me to make the rounds with you?'

'I'll take care of things, sir,' Hooper said.

'Fair enough.' Captain King closed his eyes. 'If you need me just shout.'

Hooper went outside and lit a cigarette. It was almost midnight, well past the time appointed for inspecting the guards. As he walked towards the truck mosquitoes droned around his head. A breeze was rustling the treetops, but on the ground the air was hot and still.

Hooper took his time making the rounds. He visited all the guards except Porchoff and Trac, and found everything in order. There were no problems. He started down the road towards the communications centre but when he reached the turn-off he kept his eyes dead ahead and drove past. Warm, fragrant air rushed into his face from the open window. The road ahead was empty. Hooper leaned back and mashed the accelerator. The engine roared. He was moving now, really moving, past darkened barracks and bare flagpoles and bushes whose flowers blazed up in the glare of the headlights. Hooper grinned. He felt no pleasure but he grinned and pushed the truck as hard as it would go.

Hooper slowed down when he left the post. He was AWOL now. Even if he couldn't find it in him to care much about that, he saw no point in calling attention to himself.

Drunk drivers were jerking their cars back and forth between lanes. Every half-mile or so a police car with flashing lights had someone stopped by the roadside. Other police cars sat idling behind billboards. Hooper stayed in the right lane and drove slowly until he reached his turn, then he gunned the engine again and raced down the pitted street that led to Mickey's house. He passed a bunch of kids sitting on the hood of a car with cans of beer in their hands. The car door was open and Hooper had to swerve to miss it. As he went by he heard a blast of music.

When he reached Mickey's block Hooper turned off the engine. The truck coasted silently down the street, and again Hooper became aware of the sound of crickets. He stopped on the shoulder across from Mickey's house and sat listening. The thick, pulsing sound seemed to grow louder every moment. Hooper drifted into memory, his cigarette dangling unsmoked, burning its way towards his fingers. At the same instant he felt the heat of the ember against his skin Hooper was startled by another pain, the pain of finding himself where he was. It left him breathless for a moment. Then he roused himself and got out of the truck.

The windows were dark. Mickey's Buick was parked in the driveway beside another car that Hooper didn't recognize. It didn't belong to her husband and it didn't belong to Briggs. Hooper glanced around at the other houses, then walked across the street and ducked under the hanging leaves of the willow tree in Mickey's front yard. He knelt there, holding his breath to hear better, but there was no sound but the sound of the crickets and the rushing of the big air conditioner Mickey's husband had taken from a helicopter hangar. Hooper saw no purpose in staying under the tree, so he got up and walked over to the house. He looked around again, then went into a crouch and began to work his way along the wall. He rounded the corner of the house and was starting up the side towards Mickey's bedroom when a circle of light burst around his head and a woman's voice said, 'Thou shalt not commit adultery.'

Hooper closed his eyes. There was a long silence. Then the woman said, 'Come here.'

She was standing in the driveway of the house next door. When Hooper came up to her she stuck a pistol in his face and told him to raise his hands. 'A soldier,' she said, moving the beam of light up and down his uniform. 'All right, put your hands down.' She snapped the light off and stood watching Hooper in the flickering blue glow that came from the open door behind her. Hooper heard a dog bark twice and a man say, 'Remember – nothing is too good for your dog. It's "Ruff ruff" at the sign of the double R.' The dog barked twice again.

'I want to know what you think you're doing,' the woman said.

Hooper said, 'I'm not exactly sure.' He saw her more clearly now. She was thin and tall. She wore glasses with black frames, and she had on a white dress of the kind girls called 'formals' when Hooper was in high school – tight around the waist and flaring stiffly at the hip, breasts held in hard-looking cups. Shadows darkened the hollows of her cheeks. Under the flounces of the dress her feet were big and bare.

'I know what you're doing,' she said. She pointed the pistol, an Army .45, at Mickey's house. 'You're sniffing around that whore over there.'

Someone came to the door behind the woman. A deep voice called out, 'Is it him?'

'Stay inside, Dads,' the woman answered. 'It's nobody.'

'It's him!' the man shouted. 'Don't let him talk you out of it again! Do it while you've got the chance, sweetie pie.'

'What do you want with that whore?' the woman asked Hooper. Before he could answer, she said, 'I could shoot you and nobody would say boo. I'm within my rights.'

Hooper nodded.

'I don't see the attraction,' she said. 'But then I'm not a man.' She made a laughing sound. 'You know something? I almost did it. I almost shot you. I was that close, but then I saw the uniform.' She shook her head. 'Shame on you. Where is your pride?'

'Don't let him talk,' said the man in the doorway. He came down the steps, a tall white-haired man in striped pyjamas. 'There you are, you sonofabitch,' he said. 'I'll dance on your grave.'

'It isn't him, Dads,' the woman said sadly. 'It's someone else.'

'So he says,' the man snapped. He started down the driveway, hopping from foot to foot over the gravel. The woman handed him the flashlight and he turned it on in Hooper's face, then moved the beam slowly down to his boots. 'Sweetie pie, it's a soldier,' he said.

'I told you it wasn't him,' the woman said.

'But this is a terrible mistake,' the man said. 'Sir, I'm at a loss for words.'

'Forget it,' Hooper told him. 'No hard feelings.'

'You are too kind,' the man said. He reached out and shook Hooper's hand. 'You're alive,' he said. 'That's what counts.' He nodded towards the house. 'Come have a drink.'

'He has to go,' the woman said. 'He was looking for something and he found it.'

'That's right,' Hooper told him. 'I was just on my way back to base.'

The man gave a slight bow with his head. 'To base with you, then. Good night, sir.'

Hooper and the woman watched him make his way back to the

house. When he was inside the woman turned to Hooper. 'Why are you still here?' she asked angrily. 'Go back to your post.'

Captain King was still asleep when Hooper returned to the guardhouse. His thumb was in his mouth and he made little noises as he sucked it. Hooper lay in the next bunk with his eyes open. He was still awake at four in the morning when the telephone began to ring.

It was Trac calling from the communications centre. He said that Porchoff was threatening to shoot himself and threatening to shoot Trac if Trac tried to stop him. 'This dude is mental,' Trac said. 'You get me out of here and I mean now.'

'We'll be right there,' Hooper said. 'Just give him lots of room. Don't try to grab his rifle or anything.'

'Fat fucking chance,' Trac said. 'Man, you know what he called me? He called me a gook. I hope he wastes himself. I don't need no assholes with loaded guns declaring war on me, man.'

'Just hang tight,' Hooper told him. He hung up and went to wake Captain King, because this was a mess and he wanted it to be Captain King's mess and Captain King's balls that got busted if anything went wrong. He walked over to Captain King and stood looking down at him. Captain King's thumb had slipped out of his mouth but he was still making sucking noises and pursing up his lips. Hooper decided not to wake him after all. Captain King would probably refuse to come anyway, but if he did come he would screw things up for sure. Just the sight of him was enough to make somebody start shooting.

A light rain had begun to fall. The road was empty except for one jeep going the other way. Hooper waved at the two men in front as they went past, and they both waved back. Hooper felt a surge of friendliness towards them. He followed their lights in his mirror until they vanished behind him.

Hooper parked the truck halfway up the drive and walked the rest of the distance. The rain was falling harder now, tapping steadily on the shoulders of his poncho. Sweet, almost unbreathable smells rose from the earth. He walked slowly, gravel crunching under his boots. When he reached the gate a voice to his left said, 'Shit, man, you took your time.' Trac stepped out of the shadows and waited as Hooper tried to get the key into the lock. 'Come on, man,' Trac said. He knelt with his back to the fence and swung the barrel of his rifle from side to side.

'Got it,' Hooper said. He took the lock off and Trac pushed open the gate. 'The truck's down there,' Hooper told him. 'Just around the turn.'

Trac stood close to Hooper, breathing quick shallow breaths and shifting from foot to foot. His face was dark under the hood of his glistening poncho. 'You want this?' he asked. He held out his rifle.

Hooper looked at it. He shook his head. 'Where's Porchoff?'

'Around back,' Trac said. 'There's some picnic benches out there.'

'All right,' Hooper said. 'I'll take care of it. Wait in the truck.'

'Shit, man, I feel like shit,' Trac said. 'I'll back you up, man.'

'It's okay,' Hooper told him. 'I can handle it.'

'I never cut out on anybody before,' Trac said. He shifted back and forth.

'You aren't cutting out,' Hooper said. 'Nothing's going to happen.'

Trac started down the drive. When he disappeared around the turn Hooper kept watching to make sure he didn't double back. A stiff breeze began to blow, shaking the trees, sending raindrops rattling down through the leaves. Thunder rumbled far away.

Hooper turned and walked through the gate into the compound. The forms of shrubs and pines were dark and indefinite in the slanting rain. Hooper followed the fence to the right, squinting into the shadows. When he saw Porchoff hunched over the picnic table he stopped and called out to him, 'Hey, Porchoff! It's me – Hooper.'

Porchoff raised his head.

'It's just me,' Hooper said, following his own voice towards Porchoff, showing his empty hands. He saw the rifle lying on the table in front of Porchoff. 'It's just me,' he repeated, monotonously as he could. He stopped beside another picnic table ten feet or so from the one where Porchoff sat, and lowered himself onto the bench. He looked over at Porchoff. Neither of them spoke for a while. Then Hooper said, 'Okay, Porchoff, let's talk about it. Trac tells me you've got some kind of attitude problem.'

Porchoff didn't answer. Raindrops streamed down his helmet onto his shoulders and dripped steadily past his face. His uniform was soggy and dark, plastered to his skin. He stared at Hooper and said nothing. Now and then his shoulders jerked.

'Are you gay?' Hooper asked.

Porchoff shook his head.

'Well then, what? You on acid or something? You can tell me, Porchoff. It doesn't matter.'

'I don't do drugs,' Porchoff said. It was the first time he'd spoken. His voice was calm.

'Good,' Hooper said. 'I mean at least I know I'm talking to you and not to some fucking chemical. Now listen up, Porchoff – I don't want you turning that rifle on me. Understand?'

Porchoff looked down at the rifle, then back at Hooper. He said, 'You leave me alone and I'll leave you alone.'

'I've already had someone throw down on me once tonight,' Hooper said. 'I'd just as soon leave it at that.' He reached under his poncho and took out his cigarette case. He held it up for Porchoff to see.

'I don't use tobacco,' Porchoff said.

'Well I do,' Hooper said. He shook out a cigarette and bent to light it. 'Hey,' he said. 'All right. One match.' He put the case back in his pocket and cupped the cigarette under the picnic table to keep it dry. The rain was falling lightly now in fine, fitful gusts like spray. The clouds had gone the colour of ash. Misty grey light was spreading through the sky. Hooper saw that Porchoff's shoulders twitched constantly now, and that his lips were blue and trembling. 'Put your poncho on,' Hooper told him.

Porchoff shook his head.

'You trying to catch pneumonia?' Hooper asked. He smiled at Porchoff. 'Go ahead, boy. Put your poncho on.'

Porchoff bent over and covered his face with his hands. Hooper realized that he was crying. He smoked his cigarette and waited for Porchoff to stop, but Porchoff kept crying and Hooper grew impatient. He said, 'What's all this crap about you shooting yourself?'

Porchoff rubbed at his eyes with the heels of his hands. 'Why shouldn't I?' he asked.

'Why shouldn't you? What do you mean, why shouldn't you?'

'Why shouldn't I shoot myself? Give me a reason.'

'No. But I'll give you some advice,' Hooper said. 'You don't run around asking why shouldn't I shoot myself. That's decadent, Porchoff. Now do me a favour and put your poncho on.'

Porchoff sat shivering for a moment. Then he took his poncho off his belt, unrolled it, and began to pull it over his head. Hooper considered making a grab for the rifle but held back. There was no need, he was home free now. People who were going to blow themselves away didn't come in out of the rain.

'You know what they call me?' Porchoff said.

'Who's they, Porchoff?'

'Everyone.'

'No. What does everyone call you?'

'Porkchop. *Porkchop*.'

'Come on,' Hooper said. 'What's the harm in that? Everyone gets called something.'

'But that's my *name*,' Porchoff said. 'That's *me*. It's got so even when people use my real name I hear Porkchop. All I can think of is this big piece of meat. And that's what they're seeing, too. You can say they aren't, but I know they are.'

Hooper recognized some truth in this, a lot of truth, in fact, because when he himself said Porkchop that was what he saw: a porkchop.

'I hurt all the time,' Porchoff said, 'but no one believes me. Not even the doctors. You don't believe me either.'

'I believe you,' Hooper said.

Porchoff blinked. 'Sure,' he said.

'I believe you,' Hooper repeated. He kept his eyes on the rifle. Porchoff wasn't going to waste himself but the rifle still made Hooper uncomfortable. He was about to ask Porchoff to give it to him but decided to wait a little while. The moment was wrong somehow.

Hooper pushed back the hood of his poncho and took off his fatigue cap. He glanced up at the pale clouds.

'I don't have any buddies,' Porchoff said.

'No wonder,' Hooper said. 'Calling people gooks, making threats. Let's face it, Porchoff, your personality needs some upgrading.'

'But they won't give me a chance,' Porchoff said. 'All I ever do is cook food. I put it on their plates and they make some crack and walk on by. It's like I'm not even there. So what am I supposed to act like?'

Hooper was still gazing up at the clouds, feeling the soft rain on his face. Birds were starting to sing in the woods beyond the fence. He said, 'I don't know, Porchoff. It's just part of this rut we're all in.' Hooper lowered his head and looked over at Porchoff, who sat hunched inside his poncho, shaking as little tremors passed through him. 'Any day now,' Hooper said, 'everything's going to change.'

'My dad was in the National Guard back in Ohio,' Porchoff said. 'He's always talking about the great experiences he and his buddies used to have, camping out and so on. Nothing like that ever happens to me.' Porchoff looked down at the table, then looked up and said, 'How about you? What was your best time?'

'My best time,' Hooper said. He thought of telling Porchoff some sort of lie but the effort of making things up was beyond him and the memory Porchoff wanted was close at hand. For Hooper it was closer than the memory of home. In truth it was a kind of home. It was where he went to be back with his friends again, and his old self. It was where Hooper drifted when he was too low to care how much lower he'd be when he drifted back, and lost it all again. 'Vietnam,' he said.

Porchoff just looked at him.

'We didn't know it then,' Hooper said. 'We used to talk about how when we got back in the world we were going to do this and we were going to do that. Back in the world we were going to have it made. But ever since then it's been nothing but confusion.' Hooper took the cigarette case from his pocket but didn't open it. He leaned forward on the table.

'Everything was clear,' he said. 'You learned what you had to know and you forgot the rest. All this chickenshit. You didn't spend every living minute of the day thinking about your own sorry-ass little self. Am I getting laid enough? What's wrong with my kid? Should I insulate the fucking house? That's what does it to you, Porchoff. Thinking about yourself. That's what kills you in the end.'

Porchoff had not moved. In the grey light Hooper could see Porchoff's fingers spread before him on the tabletop, white and still as if they had been drawn there in chalk. His face was the same colour.

'You think you've got problems, Porchoff, but they wouldn't last five minutes in the field. There's nothing wrong with you that a little search-and-destroy wouldn't cure.' Hooper paused, smiling to himself, already deep in the memory. He tried to bring it back for Porchoff, tried to put it into words so that Porchoff could see it too, the beauty of that life, the faith so deep that in time you were not separate men anymore, but part of each other.

But the words came hard. Hooper saw that Porchoff did not understand, and then he realized that what he was trying to describe was love, and that it couldn't be done. Still smiling, he said, 'You'll see, Porchoff. You'll get your chance.'

Porchoff stared at Hooper. 'You're crazy,' he said.

'We're all going to get another chance,' Hooper said. 'I can feel it coming. Otherwise I'd take my walking papers and hat up. You'll see. All you need is a little contact. The rest of us too. Get us out of this rut.'

Porchoff shook his head and murmured, 'You're really crazy.'

'Let's call it a day,' Hooper said. He stood and held out his hand. 'Give me the rifle.'

'No,' Porchoff said. He pulled the rifle closer. 'Not to you.'

'There's no one here but me,' Hooper said.

'Go get Captain King.'

'Captain King is asleep.'

'Then wake him up.'

'No,' Hooper said. 'I'm not going to tell you again, Porchoff, give me the rifle.' Hooper walked towards him but stopped when Porchoff picked the weapon up and pointed it at his chest. 'Leave me alone,' Porchoff said.

'Relax,' Hooper told him. 'I'm not going to hurt you.' He held out his hand again.

Porchoff licked his lips. 'No,' he said. 'Not you.'

Behind Hooper a voice called out, 'Hey! Porkchop! Drop it!'

Porchoff sat bolt upright. 'Jesus,' he said.

'It's Trac,' Hooper said. 'Put the rifle down, Porchoff – now!'

'Drop it!' Trac shouted.

'Oh Jesus,' Porchoff said and stumbled to his feet with the rifle still in his hands. Then his head flapped and his helmet flew off and he toppled backwards over the bench. Hooper's heart leaped as the shock of the blast hit him. Then the sound went through him and beyond him and into the trees and the sky, echoing on in the distance like thunder. Afterwards there was silence. Hooper took a step forward then sank to his knees and lowered his forehead to the wet grass. He spread his fingers through the grass beside his head. The rain fell around him with a soft whispering sound. A bluejay squawked.

Hooper heard the swish of boots through the grass behind him. He pushed himself up and sat back on his heels and drew a deep breath.

'You okay?' Trac said.

Hooper nodded.

Trac walked on to where Porchoff lay. He said something in Vietnamese, then looked back at Hooper and shook his head.

Hooper tried to stand but went to his knees again.

'You need a hand?' Trac asked.

'I guess so,' Hooper said.

Trac came over to Hooper. He slung his rifle and bent down and the two men gripped each other's wrists. Trac's skin was dry and smooth, his bones as small as a child's. This close, he looked more familiar than ever. 'Go for it,' Trac said. He tensed as Hooper pulled himself to his feet and for a moment afterwards they stood facing each other, swaying slightly, hands still locked on one another's wrists. 'All right,' Hooper said. Each of them slowly loosened his grip.

In a soft voice, almost a whisper, Trac said, 'They gonna put me away?'

'No,' Hooper said. He walked over to Porchoff and looked down at him. He immediately turned away and saw that Trac was still swaying, and that his eyes were glassy. 'Better get off those legs,' Hooper said. Trac looked at him dreamily, then unslung his rifle and leaned it against the picnic table farthest from Porchoff. He sat down and took his helmet off and rested his head on his crossed forearms.

The wind had picked up again, carrying with it the whine of distant engines. Hooper fumbled a cigarette out of his case and smoked it down, staring towards the woods, feeling the rain stream down his face and neck. When the cigarette went out Hooper dropped it, then picked it up again and field-stripped it, crumbling the tobacco around his feet so that no trace of it remained. He put his cap back on and raised the hood of his poncho. 'How's it going?' he said to Trac.

Trac looked up. He began to rub his forehead, pushing his fingers in little circles above his eyes.

Hooper sat down across from him. 'We don't have a whole lot of time,' he said.

Trac nodded. He put his helmet on and looked over at Hooper.

'All right, son,' Hooper said. 'Let's get our story together.'

Desert Breakdown, 1968

Krystal was asleep when they crossed the Colorado. Mark had promised to stop for some pictures, but when the moment came he looked over at her and drove on. Krystal's face was puffy from the heat blowing into the car. Her hair, cut short for summer, hung damp against her forehead. Only a few strands lifted in the breeze. She had her hands folded over her belly and that made her look even more pregnant than she was.

The tyres sang on the metal grillwork of the bridge. The river stretched away on both sides, blue as the empty sky. Mark saw the shadow of the bridge on the water with the car running through the girders, and the glint of water under the grillwork. Then the tyres went silent. *California*, Mark thought, and for a time he felt almost as good as he had expected to feel.

But it soon passed. He had broken his word, and he was going to hear about it when Krystal woke up. He almost turned the car around. But he didn't want to have to stop, and hoist Hans up on his shoulders, and watch Krystal point that camera at him again. By now Krystal had hundreds of pictures of Mark, Mark with Hans on his shoulders standing in front of canyons and waterfalls and monumental trees and the three automobiles they'd owned since coming Stateside.

Mark did not photograph well. For some reason he always looked discouraged. But those pictures gave the wrong idea. An old platoon sergeant of Mark's had an expression he liked to use – 'free, white, and twenty-one'. Well, that was an exact description of Mark. Everything was in front of him. All he needed was an opening.

Two hawks wheeled overhead, their shadows immense on the baking grey sand. A spinning funnel of dust moved across the road and disappeared behind a billboard. The billboard had a picture of Eugene McCarthy on it. McCarthy's hair was blowing around his head. He was grinning. The caption below said, 'A Breath of Fresh Air'. You could tell this was California because in Arizona a McCarthy billboard would last about five minutes. This one had bullet holes in it, but in Arizona someone would have burned it down or blown it up. The people there were just incredibly backward.

In the distance the mountains were bare and blue. Mark passed exit signs for a town called Blythe. He considered stopping for some gas, but there was still half a tank and he did not want to risk waking Krystal or Hans. He drove on into the desert.

They would make Los Angeles by dinnertime. Mark had an army buddy there who'd offered to put them up for as long as they wanted to stay. There was plenty of room, his buddy had said. He was house-sitting for his parents while they made up their minds whether to get divorced or not.

Mark was sure he'd find something interesting in Los Angeles. Something in the entertainment field. He had been in plays all through high school and could sing pretty well. But his big talent was impersonation. He could mimic anybody. In Germany he had mimicked a Southern fellow in his company so accurately that after a couple of weeks of it the boy asked to be transferred to another unit. Mark knew he'd gone overboard. He laid off and in the end the boy withdrew his request for transfer.

His best impersonation was his father, Dutch. Sometimes, just for fun, Mark called his mother and talked to her in Dutch's slow, heavy voice, rolling every word along on treads, like a tank. She always fell for it. Mark would go on until he got bored, then say something like, 'By the way, Dottie, we're bankrupt'. Then she would catch on and laugh. Unlike Dutch, she had a sense of humour.

A truck hurtled past. The sound of the engine woke Hans, but Mark reached into the back and rubbed the satin edge of the baby blanket against Hans's cheek. Hans put his thumb in his mouth. Then he stuck his rear end in the air and went back to sleep.

The road shimmered. It seemed to float above the desert floor. Mark sang along with the radio, which he had been turning up as the signal grew weaker. Suddenly it blared. He turned it down, but he was too late. Hans woke up again and started fussing. Mark rubbed his cheek with the blanket. Hans pushed Mark's arm away and said, 'No!' It was the only word he knew. Mark glanced back at him. He'd been sleeping on a toy car and the wheels had left four red dents on the side of his face. Mark stroked his cheek. 'Pretty soon,' he said, 'pretty soon, Hansy,' not meaning anything in particular but wanting to sound confident, upbeat.

Krystal was awake now too. For a moment she didn't move or say anything. Then she shook her head rapidly from side to side. 'So hot,' she said. She held up the locket-watch around her neck and looked at Mark. He kept his eyes on the road. 'Back from the dead,' he said. 'Boy, you were really out.'

'The pictures,' she said. 'Mark, the pictures.'

'There wasn't any place to stop,' he said.

'But you promised.'

Mark looked at her, then back at the road. 'I'm sorry,' he said. 'There'll be other rivers.'

'I wanted that one,' Krystal said, and turned away. Mark could tell that she was close to tears. It made him feel tired. 'All right,' he said. 'Do you want me to go back?' He slowed the car to prove he meant it. 'If that's what you want just say the word.'

She shook her head.

Mark sped up.

Hans began to kick the back of the seat. Mark didn't say anything. At least it was keeping Hans busy and quiet. 'Hey, gang,' Mark said. 'Listen up. I've got ten big ones that say we'll be diving into Rick's pool by six o'clock.'

Hans gave the seat a kick that Mark felt clear through to his ribs.

'Ten big ones,' Mark said. 'Any takers?' He looked over at Krystal and saw that her lips were trembling. He patted the seat beside him. She hesitated, then slid over and leaned against him, as he knew she would. Krystal was not one to hold a grudge. He put his arm around her shoulder.

'So much desert,' she said.

'It's something, all right.'

'No trees,' she said. 'At home I could never imagine.'

Hans stopped kicking. Then, without warning, he grabbed Mark's ears. Krystal laughed and pulled him over the seat onto her lap. He immediately arched his back and slid down to the floor, where he began to tug at the gear shift.

'I have to stop,' Krystal said. She patted her belly. 'This one likes to sit just so, here, on my bladder.'

Mark nodded. Krystal knew the English words for what Dottie had always been content to call her plumbing, and when she was pregnant she liked to describe in pretty close detail what went on in there. It made Mark queasy.

'Next chance we get,' he said. 'We're low anyway.'

Mark turned off at an exit with one sign that said GAS. There was no mention of a town.

The road went north over bleached hardpan crazed with fissures. It seemed to be leading them towards a solitary mountain far away that looked to Mark like a colossal sinking ship. Phantom water glistened in the desert. Rabbits darted back and forth across the road. Finally they came to the gas station, an unpainted cement-block building with some pickup trucks parked in front. Mark pulled in.

There were four men sitting on a bench in the shade of the building. They watched the car come towards them.

'Cowboys,' Krystal said. 'Look, Hans, cowboys!'

Hans stood on Krystal's legs and looked out the window.

Krystal still thought that everyone who wore a cowboy hat was a cowboy. Mark had tried to explain that it was a style, but she refused to understand. He drove up to a pump and turned off the engine.

The four men stared at them. Their faces were dark under the wide brims of their hats. They looked as if they had been there forever. One of the men got up from the bench and walked over. He was tall and carried a paunch that seemed out of place on his bony frame. He bent down and looked inside the car. He had little black eyes with no eyebrows. His face was red, as if he were angry about something.

'Regular, please,' Mark said. 'All she'll take.'

The man stared openly at Krystal's belly. He straightened up and walked away, past the men on the bench, up to the open door of the building. He stuck his head inside and yelled. Then he sat on the bench again. The man next to him looked down and mumbled something. The others laughed.

Somebody else in a cowboy hat came out of the building and went around to the back of the car. 'Mark,' Krystal said.

'I know,' Mark said. 'The bathroom.' He got out of the car. The heat took him by surprise; he could feel it coming down like rain. The person pumping gas said, 'You need oil or anything?' and that was when Mark realized it was a woman. She was looking down at the nozzle, so he couldn't see her face, only the top of her hat. Her hands were black with grease. 'My wife would like to use your bathroom,' he said.

She nodded. When the tank was full she thumped on the roof of the car. 'Okay,' she said, and walked towards the building.

Krystal opened the door. She swung her legs out, then rocked forward and pushed herself up into the light. She stood for a moment, blinking. The four men looked at her. So did Mark. He made allowances for the fact that Krystal was pregnant, but she was still too heavy. Her bare arms were flushed from the heat. So was her face. She looked like one of those stein-slinging waitresses in the *Biergarten* where she and Mark used to drink. He wished that these fellows could have seen the way Krystal looked wearing that black dress of hers, with her hair long, when they'd first started going out together.

Krystal shaded her eyes with one hand. With the other hand she pulled her blouse away from where it stuck to her skin. 'More desert,' she said. She lifted Hans out of the car and began to carry him towards the building, but he kicked free and ran over to the bench. He stood there in front of the men, naked except for his diaper.

'Come here,' Krystal said. When he didn't obey she started towards him, then looked at the men and stopped. Mark went over. 'Let's go, Hansy,' he said. He picked Hans up, and felt a sudden tenderness that vanished when Hans began to struggle.

The woman took Krystal and Hans inside the building, then came out and sat on the pile of scrap lumber beside the door. 'Hans,' she said. 'That's a funny name for a little boy.'

'It was her father's name,' Mark said, and so it was. The original Hans had died shortly before the baby was born. Otherwise Mark never would have agreed. Even Germans didn't name their kids Hans anymore.

One of the men flicked a cigarette butt towards Mark's car. It fell just short and lay there, smouldering. Mark took it as a judgment on the car. It was a good car, a 1958 Bonneville he'd bought two weeks ago when the Ford started to smoke, but a previous owner had put a lot of extra chrome on it and right now it was gleaming every which way. It looked foolish next to these dented pickups with their gun racks and dull, blistering paint. Mark wished he'd tanked up in Blythe.

Krystal came outside again, carrying Hans. She had brushed her hair and looked better.

Mark smiled at her. 'All set?'

She nodded. 'Thank you,' she said to the woman.

Mark would have liked to use the bathroom too, but he wanted to get out of there. He started towards the car, Krystal behind him. She laughed deep in her throat. 'You should have seen,' she said. 'They have a motorcycle in their bedroom.' Krystal probably thought she was whispering but to Mark every word was like a shout.

He didn't say anything. He adjusted the visor while Krystal settled Hans on the back seat. 'Wait,' she told Mark, and got out of the car again. She had the camera.

'Krystal,' Mark said.

She aimed the camera at the four men. When she snapped the

shutter their heads jerked up. Krystal advanced the film, then aimed the camera again.

Mark said, 'Krystal, get in!'

'Yes,' Krystal said, but she was still aiming, braced on the open door of the car, her knees bent slightly. She snapped another picture and slid onto the seat. 'Good,' she said. 'Cowboys for Reiner.'

Reiner was Krystal's brother. He had seen *Shane* more than a hundred times.

Mark didn't dare look towards the bench. He put the key in the ignition and glanced up and down the road. He turned the key. Nothing happened.

Mark took a deep breath and waited for a moment. Then he tried again. Still nothing happened. The ignition went *tick tick tick tick*, and that was all. Mark turned it off and the three of them sat there. Even Hans was quiet. Mark felt the men watching him. That was why he did not lower his head to the wheel and give way to tears. But they were in his eyes, blurring the line of the horizon, the shape of the building, the dark forms of the trucks and the figure coming towards them over the white earth.

It was the woman. She bent down. 'Okay,' she said. 'What's the trouble?' The smell of whiskey filled the car.

For almost half an hour the woman messed with the engine. She had Mark turn the key while she watched, then turn it some more while she did various things under the hood. At last she decided that the trouble was in the alternator. She couldn't fix it, and she had no parts on hand. Mark would have to get one in Indio or Blythe or maybe as far away as Palm Springs. It wasn't going to be easy, finding an alternator for a ten-year-old car. But she said she'd call around for him.

Mark waited in the car. He tried to act as if everything were all right, but when Krystal looked at him she made a sympathetic noise and squeezed his arm. Hans was asleep in her lap. 'Everything will be fine,' Krystal said.

Mark nodded.

The woman came back towards the car, and Mark got out to meet her.

'Aren't you the lucky one,' she said. She gave Mark a piece of paper with an address written on it. 'There wasn't anything in Indio,' she said, 'but this fellow in Blythe can fix you up. I'll need two dollars for the calls.'

Mark opened his wallet and gave her the two dollars. He had sixty-five dollars left, all that remained of his army severance pay. 'How much will the alternator cost?' he asked.

She closed the hood of the car. 'Fifty-eight dollars, I think it was.'

'Jesus,' Mark said.

The woman shrugged. 'You're lucky they had one.'

'I suppose so,' Mark said. 'It just seems like a lot of money. Can you jump-start me?'

'If you've got cables. Mine are lent out.'

'I don't have any,' Mark said. He squinted against the sun. Though he had not looked directly at the men on the bench, he knew that they had been watching him. He was sure that they had heard everything. He was also sure that they had jumper cables. People who drove trucks always carried stuff like that.

But if they didn't want to help, he wasn't going to ask.

'I guess I could walk up to the highway and hitch a ride,' Mark said, more loudly than he meant to.

'I guess you could,' the woman said.

Mark looked back at Krystal. 'Is it okay if my wife stays here?'

'I guess she'll have to,' the woman said. She took off her hat and wiped her brow with the back of her sleeve. Her hair was pure yellow, gathered in a loose bun that glowed in the light. Her eyes were black. She put her hat back on and told Mark how to get to the parts store. She made him repeat the directions. Then he went back to the car.

Krystal looked straight ahead and bit her lip while Mark explained the situation. 'Here?' she said. 'You are going to leave us here?'

Hans was awake again. He had pulled the volume knob off the radio and was banging it on the dashboard.

'Just for a couple of hours,' Mark said, though he knew it would take twice as long, maybe longer.

Krystal wouldn't look at him.

'There's no choice,' he said.

The woman had been standing next to Mark. She moved him aside and opened the door. 'You come with me,' she said. 'You and the little one.' She held out her arms. Hans went to her immediately and peered over her shoulder at the men on the bench. Krystal hesitated, then got out of the car, ignoring Mark's hand when he reached down to help her.

'It won't take long,' he said. He smiled at Hans. 'Pretty soon, Hansy,' he said, and turned and began to walk towards the road.

The woman went inside with Hans. Krystal stood beside the car and watched Mark move farther and farther away, until the line of his body started to waver in the heat and then vanished altogether. This happened slowly. It was like seeing someone slip below the surface of a lake.

The men stared at Krystal as she walked towards the building. She felt heavy, and vaguely ashamed.

The woman had all the shades pulled down. It was like evening inside: dim, peaceful, cool. Krystal could make out the shapes of things but not their colours. There were two rooms. One had a bed and a motorcycle. The second, a big room, had a sofa and chairs on one side and on the other a refrigerator and stove and table.

Krystal sat at the table with Hans in her lap while the woman poured Pepsi from a big bottle into three tumblers full of ice. She had taken her hat off, and the weak light shining from the open door of the refrigerator made a halo around her face and hair. Usually Krystal measured herself against other women, but this one she watched with innocent, almost animal curiosity.

The woman took another, smaller bottle down from the top of the refrigerator. She wiggled it by the neck. 'You wouldn't want any of this,' she said. Krystal shook her head. The woman poured some of the liquor into her glass and pushed the other two glasses across the table. Hans took a drink, then began to make motorboat noises.

'That boy,' the woman said.

'His name is Hans.'

'Not this one,' the woman said. 'The other one.'

'Oh,' Krystal said. 'Mark. Mark is my husband.'

The woman nodded and took a drink. She leaned back in her chair. 'Where are you people headed?'

Krystal told her about Los Angeles, about Mark finding work in the entertainment field. The woman smiled, and Krystal wondered if she had expressed herself correctly. In school she had done well in English, and the American boys she talked to always complimented her, but during those weeks with Mark's parents in Phoenix she had lost her confidence. Dutch and Dottie always looked bewildered when she spoke, and she herself understood almost nothing of what was said around her though she pretended that she did.

The woman kept smiling, but there was a tightness to her mouth that made the smile look painful somehow. She took another drink.

'What does he do?' she asked.

Krystal tried to think of a way to explain what Mark did. When she first saw him, he had been sitting on the floor at a party and everyone around him was laughing. She had laughed too, though she didn't know why. It was a gift he had. But it was difficult to put into words. 'Mark is a singer,' she said.

'A singer,' the woman said. She closed her eyes and leaned her head back and began to sing. Hans stopped fidgeting and watched her.

When the woman was through, Krystal said, 'Good, good,' and nodded, though she hadn't been able to follow the song and hated the style, which sounded to her like yodelling.

'My husband always liked to hear me sing,' the woman said. 'I suppose I could have been a singer if I'd wanted.' She finished her drink and looked at the empty glass.

From outside Krystal heard the voices of the men on the bench, low and steady. One of them laughed.

'We had Del Ray to sing at our prom,' the woman said.

The door banged. The man who'd stared at Krystal's belly stomped into the kitchen and stared at her again. He turned and started pulling bottles of Pepsi out of the refrigerator. 'Webb, what do you think?' the woman said. 'This girl's husband's a singer.' She reached out and ran one hand up and down his back. 'We'll need something for supper,' she said, 'unless you want rabbit again.'

He kicked the refrigerator door shut with his foot and started out of the kitchen, bottles clinking against each other. Hans slid to the floor and ran after him.

'Hans,' Krystal said.

The man stopped and looked down at him. 'That's right,' he said. 'You come with me.'

It was the first time Krystal had heard him speak. His voice was thin and dry. He went back outside with Hans behind him.

The shoes Mark had on were old and loose, comfortable in the car, but his feet started to burn after a few minutes of walking in them. His eyes burned too, from sweat and the bright sun shining into his face.

For a while he sang songs, but after a couple of numbers his throat cracked with dryness so he gave it up. Anyway it made him feel stupid singing about Camelot in this desert, stupid and a little afraid because his voice sounded so small. He walked on.

The road was sticky underfoot. Mark's shoes made little sucking noises at every step. He considered walking beside the road instead of on it but he was afraid that a snake would bite him.

He wanted to stay cheerful, but he kept thinking that now they would never get to Los Angeles in time for dinner. They'd pull in late like they always did, stuff spilling out of the car, Mark humping the whole mess inside while Krystal stood by looking dazed in the glare of the headlights, Hans draped over her shoulder. Mark's buddy would be in his bathrobe. They'd try to joke but Mark would be too preoccupied. After they made up a bed for Krystal and put the crib together for Hans, which would take forever because half the screws were missing, Mark and his buddy would go down to the kitchen and drink a beer. They'd try to talk but they would end up yawning in each other's faces. Then they would go to bed.

Mark could see the whole thing. Whatever they did, it always turned out like this. Nothing ever worked.

A truck went past going the other way. There were two men inside wearing cowboy hats. They glanced at Mark, then looked straight ahead again. He stopped and watched the truck disappear into the heat.

He turned and kept walking. Broken glass glittered along the roadside.

If Mark lived here and happened to be driving down this road and saw some person walking all by himself, he would stop and ask if there was anything wrong. He believed in helping people.

But he didn't need them. He would manage without them, just as he'd manage without Dutch and Dottie. He would do it alone, and someday they would wish they'd helped. He would be in some place like Las Vegas, performing at one of the big clubs. Then, at the end of his booking, he would fly Dutch and Dottie out for his last big show – the finale. He'd fly them first class and put them up in the best hotel, the Sands or whatever, and he'd get them front-row seats. And when the show was over, when the people were going crazy, whistling and stamping on the floor and everything, he would call Dutch and Dottie up to the stage. He would stand between them, holding their hands, and then, when all the clapping and yelling trailed off and everybody was quiet, smiling at him from the tables, he would raise Dutch and Dottie's hands above his head and say, Folks, I just wanted you to meet my parents and tell you what they did for me. He would stop for a second and get this really serious look on his face. It's impossible to tell you what they did for me, he would say, pausing for effect – because they didn't do *anything* for me! They didn't do *squat* for me!

Then he would drop their hands and jump off the stage and leave them there.

Mark walked faster, leaning forward, eyes narrowed against the light. His hands flicked back and forth as he walked.

No, he wouldn't do that. People might take it wrong. A stunt like that could ruin his career. He would do something even better. He would stand up there and tell the whole world that without the encouragement and support the two of them had given him, the faith and love, et cetera, he would have thrown in the towel a long time ago.

And the great part was, *it wouldn't be true!* Because Dutch and Dottie wouldn't do a thing for him unless he stayed in Phoenix and got a 'real' job – like selling houses. But nobody would know that except Dutch and Dottie. They would stand up on the stage listening to all those lies, and the more he complimented them the more they would see the kind of parents they could have been and weren't, and the more ashamed they would feel, and the more grateful to Mark for not exposing them.

He could hear a faint rushing sound in the hot air, a sound like applause. He walked faster still. He hardly felt the burning of his feet. The rushing sound grew louder, and Mark looked up. Ahead of him, no more than a hundred yards off, he saw the highway – not the road itself, but a long convoy of trucks moving across the desert, floating westward through a blue haze of exhaust.

The woman told Krystal that her name was Hope.

'Hope,' Krystal said. 'How lovely.'

They were in the bedroom. Hope was working on the motorcycle. Krystal lay on the bed, propped up with pillows, watching Hope's long fingers move here and there over the machine and through the parts on the floor, back to the sweating glass at her side. Hans was outside with the men.

Hope took a drink. She swirled the ice around and said, 'I don't know, Krystal.'

Krystal felt the baby move in her. She folded her hands across her belly and waited for the bump to come again.

All the lights were off except for a lamp on the floor beside Hope. There were engine parts scattered around her, and the air smelled of oil. She picked up a part and looked at it, then began to wipe it down with a cloth. 'I told you we had Del Ray to our prom,' she said. 'I don't know if you ever heard of Del Ray where you came from, but us girls were flat crazy about him. I had a Del Ray pillow I slept on.

Then he showed up and it turned out he was only about yay high.' Hope held her hand a few inches above the floor. 'Personally,' she said, 'I wouldn't look twice at a man that couldn't stand up for me if it came to the point. No offence,' she added.

Krystal didn't understand what Hope had said, so she smiled.

'You take Webb,' Hope said. 'Webb would kill for me. He almost did, once. He beat a man to an inch of his life.'

Krystal understood this. She felt sure it was true. She ran her tongue over her dry lips. 'Who?' she asked. 'Who did he beat?'

Hope looked up from the part she was cleaning. She smiled at Krystal in such a way that Krystal had to smile back.

'My husband,' Hope said. She looked down again, still smiling.

Krystal waited, uncertain whether she had heard Hope right.

'Webb and me were hot,' Hope said. 'We were an item. When we weren't together, which was most of the time, we were checking up on each other. Webb used to drive past my house at all hours and follow me everywhere. Sometimes he'd follow me places with his wife in the car next to him.' She laughed. 'It was a situation.'

The baby was pressing against Krystal's spine. She shifted slightly.

Hope looked up at her. 'It's a long story.'

'Tell me.'

'I need some mouthwash,' Hope said. She got up and went out to the kitchen. Krystal heard the crack of an ice tray. It was pleasant to lie here in this dark, cool room.

Hope came back and settled on the floor. 'Don't get me going,' she said. She took a drink. 'The long and the short is, Webb lost his senses. It happened at the movie theatre in front of half the town. Webb was sitting behind us and saw my husband put his arm around me. He came right over the chairs.' She shook her head. 'I can tell you we did some fancy footwork after that. Had to. My husband had six brothers and two of them in the police. We got out of there and I mean we *got.* Nothing but the clothes we had on. Never gone back since. Never will, either.'

'Never,' Krystal said. She admired the sound of the word. It was like Beethoven shaking his fist at the heavens.

Hope picked up the rag again. But she didn't do anything with it. She leaned against the wall, out of the little circle of light the lamp made.

'Did you have children?' Krystal asked.

Hope nodded. She held up two fingers.

'It must have been hard, not to see them.'

'They'll do all right,' Hope said. 'They're both boys.' She ran her fingers over the floor, found the part she'd been cleaning, and without looking at it began to wipe it down again.

'I couldn't leave Hans,' Krystal said.

'Sure you could,' Hope said. The motion of her arms slowed. She grew still. 'I remember when I fell for Webb. We'd known him for years, but this one day he came into our station on his Harley. It was cold. His cheeks were red and his hair was all blown back. I remember it like it was yesterday.'

Hope sat there with her hands in her lap. Her breathing got deep and slow, and Krystal, peering through the gloom, saw that her eyes were closed. She was asleep, or just dreaming – maybe of that man out there riding over the desert on his machine, his hair pushed back in the way that was special to her.

Krystal settled herself on her side. The baby was quiet now.

The air conditioner went off abruptly. Krystal lay in the dark and listened to the sounds it had covered, the dry whirr of insects, the low voices of the men, Hope's soft snoring. Krystal closed her eyes. She felt herself drifting, and as she drifted she remembered Hans. *Hans*, she thought. Then she slept.

Mark had assumed that when he reached the highway someone would immediately pick him up. But car after car went by, and the few drivers who looked at him scowled as if they were angry with him for needing a ride and putting them on the spot.

Mark's face burned, and his throat was so dry it hurt to swallow. Twice he had to leave the road to stand in the shade of a billboard. Cars passed him by for more than an hour, cars from Wisconsin and Utah and Georgia and just about everywhere. Mark felt like the whole country had turned its back on him. The thought came to him that he could die out here.

Finally a car stopped. It was a hearse. Mark hesitated, then ran towards it.

There were three people in the front seat, a man between two women. The space in the back was full of electrical equipment. Mark pushed some wires out of his way and sat cross-legged on the floor. He felt the breeze from the air conditioner; it was like a stream of cold water running over him.

The driver pulled back onto the road.

'Welcome to the stiffmobile,' said the man beside her. He turned around. His head was shaved except for one bristling stripe of hair down the centre. It was the first Mohawk haircut Mark had ever seen. The man's eyebrows were the same carroty colour as his hair. He had freckles. The freckles covered his entire face and even the shaved parts of his skull.

'Stiffmobile, cliffmobile,' said the woman driving. 'Riffmobile.'

'Bet you thought you'd be riding with a cold one,' the man said.

Mark shrugged. 'I'd rather ride with a cold one than a hot one.'

The man laughed and pounded on the back of the seat.

The two women also laughed. The one not driving turned around and smiled at Mark. She had a round, soft-looking face. Her lips were full. She wore a small gold earring in one side of her nose. 'Hi,' she said.

'Speaking of cold ones,' the man said, 'there's a case of them right behind you.'

Mark fished four cans of beer out of the cooler and passed three of them up front. He took a long swallow, head back, eyes closed. When he opened his eyes again the man with the Mohawk was watching him. They introduced themselves, all but the woman driving. She never looked at Mark or spoke, except to herself. The man with the Mohawk was Barney. The girl with the earring was Nance. They joked back and forth, and Mark discovered that Nance had a terrific sense of humour. She picked up on almost everything he said. After a while the earring in her nose ceased to bother him.

When Barney heard that Mark had been in the army he shook his head. 'Pass on that,' he said. 'No bang-bang for Barney. I can't stand the sight of my own brains.'

'Trains,' the driver said. 'Cranes, lanes, stains.'

'Smooth out,' Barney told her. He turned back to Mark. 'So what was it like over there?'

Mark realized that Barney meant Vietnam. Mark had not been to Vietnam. He'd had orders to go, but the orders were killed just before he left and never reissued. He didn't know why. It was too complicated to explain, so he just said, 'Pretty bad,' and left it at that.

'Wrong question,' Barney said. 'That subject is strictly underwater. Scout's honour.' He held up three fingers.

The mention of Vietnam broke the good feeling between them. They drank their beers and looked at the desert passing by. Then Barney crumpled his can and threw it out the window. Hot air blew into Mark's face. He remembered what it was like out there, and felt glad to be right where he was.

'I could get behind another beer,' Nance said.

'Right,' Barney said. He turned around and told Mark to pop some more frosties. While Mark was getting the cans out of the cooler Barney watched him, playing his fingers over the top of the seat as if it were a keyboard. 'So what's in Blythe?' he said.

'Smythe,' the driver said. 'Smythe's in Blythe.'

'Be cool,' Nance said to her.

'I need a part,' Mark said. He handed out the beers. 'An alternator. My car's on the fritz.'

'Where's your car?' Barney said.

Mark jerked his thumb over his shoulder. 'Back there. I don't know the name of the place. It's just this gas station off the highway.' Nance was looking at him. He smiled. She kept watching him.

'Hey,' she said. 'What if you didn't stop smiling? What if you just kept smiling and never stopped?'

Barney looked at her. Then he looked back at Mark. 'To me,' he said, 'there are places you go and places you don't go. You don't go to Rochester. You don't go to Blythe.'

'You definitely don't go to Blythe,' Nance said.

'Right,' Barney said. Then he listed some of the places where, in his opinion, you do go. They were going to one of them now, San Lucas, up in the mountains above Santa Fe. They were part of a film crew shooting a Western there. They had shot another movie in the same place a year ago and this was the sequel. Barney was a sound man. Nance did make-up. They didn't say anything about the driver.

'The place is unbelievable,' Barney said. He paused and shook his head. Mark was waiting for him to describe San Lucas, but Barney just shook his head again and said, 'The place is completely unbelievable.'

'Really,' Nance said.

It turned out that the star of the picture was Nita Damon. This was a real coincidence, because Mark had seen Nita Damon about six months ago in a show in Germany, a Bob Hope Christmas Special.

'That's amazing,' Nance said. She and Barney looked at each other. 'You should scratch Blythe,' Barney said.

Mark grinned.

Nance was staring at him. 'Marco,' she said. 'You're not a Mark, you're a Marco.'

'You should sign on with us,' Barney said. 'Ride the stiffmobile express.'

'You should,' Nance said. 'San Lucas is just incredible.'

'Partyville,' Barney said.

'Jesus,' Mark said. 'No. I couldn't.'

'Sure you could,' Barney said. 'Lincoln freed the slaves, didn't he? Get your car later.'

Mark was laughing. 'Come on,' he said. 'What would I do up there?'

Barney said, 'You mean like work?'

Mark nodded.

'No problem,' Barney said. He told Mark that there was always something to do. People didn't show up, people quit, people got sick – there was always a call out for warm bodies. Once you found a tasty spot, you just settled in.

'You mean I'd be working on the movie? On the film crew?'

'Absitively,' Barney said. 'I guarantee.'

'Jesus,' Mark said. He took a breath. He looked at Barney and Nance. 'I don't know,' he said.

'That's all right,' Barney said. 'I know.'

'Barney knows,' Nance said.

'What have you got to lose?' Barney said.

Mark didn't say anything. He took another breath. Barney watched him. 'Marco,' he said. 'Don't tell me – you've got a little something else back there besides the car, right?' When Mark didn't answer, Barney laughed. 'That's mellow,' he said. 'You're among friends. Anything goes.'

'I have to think,' Mark said.

'Okay,' Barney said. 'Think. You've got till Blythe.' He turned around. 'Don't disappoint me,' he said.

Nance smiled. Then she turned around too. The top of her head was just visible over the high seat-back.

The desert went past the window, always the same. The road had an oily look. Mark felt rushed, a little wild.

His first idea was to get the directions to San Lucas, then drive up with Krystal and Hans after the car was fixed. But that wouldn't work. He wouldn't have enough money left for the gas, let alone food and motels and a place to live once they got there. He'd miss his chance. Because that's what this was – a chance.

There was no point in fooling himself. He could go to Los Angeles and walk the streets for months, years maybe, without ever getting anywhere. He could stand outside closed doors and suck up to nobodies and sit in plastic chairs half his life without ever coming close to where he was right now, on his way to a guaranteed job in Partyville.

Los Angeles wasn't going to work. Mark could see that. He'd borrow money from his friend and start hustling and he wouldn't get the time of day from anyone, because he was hungry, and nobody ever had time for hungry people. Hungry people got written off. It was like Dutch said – them as has, gets.

He would run himself ragged and the money would disappear, the way all his other money had disappeared. Krystal would get worried and sad. After a couple of weeks Mark and his buddy wouldn't have anything to say to each other, and his buddy would get tired of living with a guy he didn't really know that well and a yelling kid and a sad, pregnant woman. He would tell Mark some lie to get rid of them – his girl was moving in, his parents had decided to stay together after all. By then Mark would be broke again. Krystal would have a fit and probably go into labour.

What if that happened? What then?

Mark knew what. Crawl home to Dutch and Dottie.

No. No sir. The only way he was going back to Phoenix was in a coffin.

The driver started talking to herself. Barney rapped her on top of the head with his knuckles. 'Do you want me to drive?' he said. It sounded like a threat. She quieted down. 'All right,' he said. Without looking back he said, 'Five miles to Blythe.'

Mark looked out the window. He couldn't get it out of his mind that here he had exactly what he needed. A chance to show what he was made of. He'd have fun, sure, but he'd also be at work on time in the morning. He would do what he was told and do it right. He would keep his eyes open and his mouth shut and after a while people would start to notice him. He wouldn't push too hard, but now and then he might do a song at one of the parties, or impersonate some of the actors. He could just hear Nita Damon laughing and saying, 'Stop it, Mark! Stop it!'

What he could do, Mark thought, was to call Krystal and arrange to meet up with her at his buddy's house in a month or two, after they'd shot the film. Mark would have something going then. He'd be on his way. But that wouldn't work, either. He didn't know how to call her. She had no money. And she wouldn't agree.

Mark wasn't going to fool himself. If he left Krystal and Hans back there, she would never forgive him. If he left them, he left them for good.

I can't do that, Mark thought. But he knew this wasn't true. He had decided not to fool himself, and that meant being honest about everything. He could leave them. People left one another, and got left, every day. It was a terrible thing. But it happened and people survived, as they survived worse things. Krystal and Hans would survive, too. When she understood what had happened she would call Dutch. Dutch would hit the roof, but in the end he would come through for them. He didn't have any choice. And in four or five years what happened today would be nothing but a bad memory.

Krystal would do well for herself. Men liked her. Even Dutch liked her, though he'd been dead set against the marriage. She would meet a good man someday, a man who could take care of her. She and Hans and the new baby would be able to go to sleep at night without wondering what would happen to them when they woke up. They didn't need Mark. Without him they would have a better life than if he and Krystal stayed together.

This was a new thought for Mark, and when he had it he felt aggrieved. It hurt him to see how unimportant he really was to Krystal. Before now he had always assumed that their coming together had somehow been ordained, and that in marrying Krystal he had filled some need of the universe. But if they could live without each other, and do better without each other, then this could not be true and must never have been true.

They did not need each other. There was no particular reason for them to be together. Then what was it all about? If he couldn't make her happy, then what was the point? They were dragging each other down like two people who couldn't swim. If they were lucky, they might keep at it long enough to grow old in the same house.

It wasn't right. She deserved better, and so did he.

Mark felt that he had been deceived, played with. Not by Krystal, she would never do that, but by everyone who had ever been married and knew the truth about it and went on acting as if it were something good. The truth was different. The truth was that when you got married you had to give up one thing after another. It never ended. You had to give up your life – the special one that you were meant to have – and lead some middle kind of life that went where neither of you had ever thought of going, or wanted to go. And you never knew what was happening. You gave up your life and didn't even know it.

'Blythe,' Barney said.

Mark looked at the town, what he could see of it from the road. Lines of heat quivered above the rooftops.

'Blythe,' Barney said again. 'Going, going, gone.'

When Krystal came up from sleep she expected to open her eyes on the sight of water. She blinked in the gloom. In a moment she knew where she was.

'Hans,' she whispered.

'He's outside,' Hope said. Hope was standing over the lamp, feeding shells into a shotgun. Her shadow swayed back and forth against the wall. 'I'm going to get us some dinner,' she said. 'You just lie here and rest up. The boy will be fine.' She finished loading the gun and pushed a few more shells into the pockets of her jeans. 'Be right back,' she said.

Krystal lay on the bed, restless and thirsty, but feeling too heavy to rise. Outside the men had a radio on. One of those whiny songs was playing, like Hope had sung in the kitchen. Krystal had heard no good music for two months now, since the day she left home. A warm day in late spring – lieder playing on the radio, sunlight flickering through the trees along the road.

'Ah, God,' Krystal said.

She pushed herself up. She lifted the shade of the window and looked out. There was the desert, and the mountains. And there was Hope, walking into the desert with her shotgun. The light was softer than before, still white but not so sharp. The tops of the mountains were touched with pink.

Krystal stared out the window. How could anyone live in such a place? There was nothing, nothing at all. Through all those days in Phoenix, Krystal had felt a great emptiness around her where she would count for no more than a rock or a spiny tree; now she was there.

Krystal thought she might cry, but she gave the idea up. It didn't interest her.

She closed her eyes and leaned her forehead against the glass.

I will say a poem, Krystal thought, and when I am finished he will be here. At first silently, because she had promised to speak only English now, then in a whisper, and at last plainly, Krystal recited a poem the nuns had made her learn at school long ago, the only poem she remembered. She repeated it twice, then opened her eyes. Mark was not there. As if she had really believed he would be there, Krystal kicked the wall with her bare foot. The pain gave an edge of absolute clarity to what she'd been pretending not to know: that he had never really been there and was never going to be there in any way that mattered.

The window was hot under Krystal's forehead. She watched Hope move farther and farther away. Then Hope stopped. She raised her gun. A moment later Krystal heard the boom, and felt the glass shudder against her skin.

A few miles past Blythe the driver began to talk to herself again. Her voice was flat. Mark looked out of the window and tried to ignore it but after a time he found himself listening, trying to make sense of the things she said. There wasn't any reason to her words. Every possibility of meaning ended in the beginning of another possibility. It was frustrating to Mark. He became uncomfortable.

Then he noticed that the hearse was moving at great speed, really racing. The driver passed every car they came upon. She changed lanes without any purpose.

Mark tried to find a break between her words to say something, just a note of caution, something about how tough the police were around here, but no break came. The car was going faster and faster. He hoped that Barney would tell her to shut up and slow down, maybe even take over himself for a while, but Barney wasn't saying anything and neither was Nance. She had disappeared completely and all Mark could see of Barney were the bristles of his hair.

'Hey,' Mark said. 'What's the hurry?'

The driver seemed not to hear him. She passed three more cars and went on talking to herself. Then Mark saw that she had only one hand on the steering wheel, her left hand. She was gripping the wheel so tightly that her hand had turned white. He could see the bones of her fingers.

'Better slow down,' Mark said.

'Blue horse sells kisses,' she said, then repeated the words.

'Jesus,' Mark said. He bent forward and leaned over the top of the seat to get a look at the speedometer. He had never seen anything like that before. It took the wind out of him. The driver was making what sounded like animal noises in the jungle. Nance giggled.

'Stop the car,' Mark said.

'Stop the war,' the driver said.

'Stop the car,' Mark said again.

'Hey,' Barney said. 'What's the problem?' His voice was soft, remote.

'I want out,' Mark said.

Nance giggled again. The tyres began to whine. 'Everything's sweet,' Barney said. 'Just settle into it, Marco. You decided, remember?'

Mark didn't know what to say. It was hard to talk to someone he couldn't see.

He heard Nance whispering. Then Barney said, 'Hey – Marco. Come on up here.'

'Midnight phone book,' the driver said.

'Come on,' Barney said. 'You're with us now.'

'Stop the car,' Mark said. He reached over the seat and began to rap on the driver's head, softly at first, then hard. He could hear the knocking of his knuckles against her skull. She stopped the hearse in the middle of the road. Mark looked back. There was a car bearing down on them. It swerved into the other lane and went past with its horn wailing.

'Okay, Marco,' Barney said. 'Ciao. You blew it.'

Mark scrambled over equipment and cords and let himself out the back. When he closed the gate the driver pulled away, fast. Mark crossed the road and watched the hearse until it disappeared. The road was empty. He turned and walked back towards Blythe.

A few minutes later an old man stopped for him. He took a liking to Mark and drove him all the way to the parts store. They were closing up when he arrived, but after Mark explained his situation the boss let him inside and found the alternator for him. With tax, the price came to seventy-one dollars.

'I thought it was fifty-eight,' Mark said.

'Seventy-one,' the boss said.

Mark showed him the figures that the woman had written down, but it did no good. Mark stared at the alternator. 'I've only got sixty-five.'

'I'm sorry,' the boss said. He put his hands on the counter and waited.

'Look,' Mark said. 'I just got back from Vietnam. Me and my wife are on our way to Los Angeles. Once we get there I can send you the other six. I'll put it in the mail tomorrow morning. I swear.'

The boss looked at him. Mark could see that he was hesitating.

'I've got a job waiting,' Mark said.

'What kind of job?'

'I'm a sound man,' Mark said.

'Sound man.' The boss nodded. 'I'm sorry,' he said. 'You think you'll send the money but you won't.'

Mark argued for a while but without heat, because he knew that the man was right – he would never send the money. He gave up and went outside again. The parts store adjoined a salvage yard filled with crumpled cars. Across the street there was a U-Haul depot and a gas station. Mark began to walk towards the gas station. A black dog appeared on the other side of the salvage yard fence and kept pace with Mark. When Mark looked at him, the dog silently bared his fangs and gave Mark such a fright that he crossed the street.

He was hot and tired. He could smell himself. He remembered the coolness of the hearse and thought, *I blew it.*

There was a pay phone outside the gas station. Mark got a handful of change and shut himself in. He wanted to call his buddy in Los Angeles and figure something out, but he had left the address book in the car and it turned out that the number was unlisted. He tried to explain things to the operator but she refused to listen. She hung up on him.

Mark looked out at the street. The dog was still at the fence, watching him. The only thing he could do, Mark decided, was to keep calling Los Angeles information until he got a human being on the other end. There had to be somebody sympathetic out there.

But first he was going to call Phoenix and give Dutch and Dottie a little something to sleep on. He would put on his official voice and tell them that he was Sergeant Smith – no, *Smythe* – Sergeant Smythe of the highway patrol, calling to report an accident. A head-on collision just outside of Palm Springs. It was his duty, he was sorry to say – his voice would crack – there were no survivors. No, ma'am, not one. Yes, ma'am, he was sure. He'd been at the scene. The one good thing he could tell her was that nobody had suffered. It was over just like *that*, and here Mark would snap his fingers into the receiver.

He closed his eyes and listened to the phone ring through the cool, quiet house. He saw Dottie where she sat in her avocado kitchen, drinking coffee and making a list, saw her rise and gather her cigarettes and lighter and ashtray. He heard her shoes tapping on the tile floor as she came towards the phone.

But it was Dutch who answered. 'Strick here,' he said.

Mark took a breath.

'Hello,' Dutch said.

'It's me,' Mark said. 'Dad, it's me – Mark.'

Krystal was washing her face when she heard the gun go off again. She paused, water running through her fingers, then finished up and left the bedroom. She wanted to find Hans. He should have been changed long before now, and it was almost time for him to eat. She missed him.

Picking her way through the parts on the floor, she went into the main room. It was almost completely dark. Krystal felt her way along the wall to the light switch. She turned the light on and stood there with her hand against the wall.

Everything was red. The carpet was red. The lamp shades were red, and had little red tassels hanging down from them. The chairs and the couch were red. The pillows on the couch were shaped like hearts and covered in a satiny material that looked wet under the light, so that for a moment they had the appearance of real organs.

Krystal stared at the room. In a novel she'd once read she had come upon the expression 'love nest', and after considering it for a moment imagined light-washed walls, tall pines reaching to the balcony outside. But this, she thought, looking at the room, this was a love nest. It was horrible, horrible.

Krystal moved over to the door and opened it a crack. Someone was lying on the front seat of the car, his bare feet sticking out the window, his boots on the ground below with yellow socks hanging from the tops. She could not see the men on the bench but one of them was saying something, the same word again and again. Krystal couldn't make it out. Then she heard Hans repeat the word, and the men laughed.

She opened the door wider. Still standing inside, she said, 'Hans, come here.'

She waited. She heard someone whisper.

'Hans,' she said.

He came to the door. There was dirt all over his face but he looked happy. 'Come in,' she said.

Hans looked over his shoulder and smiled, then turned back to Krystal.

'Come, Hans,' she said.

He stood there. 'Bitch,' he said.

Krystal stepped backwards. She shook her head. 'No,' she said. 'No no no. Don't say that. Come, sweet boy.' She held out her arms.

'Bitch,' he said again.

'Oh!' Krystal said. Her hand went to her mouth. Then she pushed open the door and walked up to Hans and slapped him across the face, something she had never done before. She slapped him hard. He sat down and looked up at her. Krystal took a flat board from the pile of scrap and turned towards the three men on the bench. They were watching her from under their big hats. 'Who did that?' she said. 'Who taught him that word?' When they didn't answer she started towards the bench, reviling them in German, using words she had never used before. They stood and backed away from her. Hans began to cry. Krystal turned on him. 'Be quiet!' she said. He whimpered once and was still.

Krystal turned back to the men. 'Who taught him that word?'

'It wasn't me,' one of them said.

The other two just stood there.

'Shame,' Krystal said. She looked at them, then walked over to the car. She kicked the boots aside. Holding the board with both hands, she swung it as hard as she could across the bare feet sticking out of the window. The man inside screamed. Krystal hit his feet again and he pulled them back.

'Get out,' she said. 'Out, out, out!'

The man who'd been sleeping inside, the one called Webb, scrambled out the other door and hopped from foot to foot towards the building. He had left his hat in the car. As he danced over the hot sand his hair flapped up and down like a wing. He stopped in the shade and looked back, still shifting from foot to foot. He kept his eyes on Krystal. So did Hans, sitting by the door. So did the men near the bench. They were all watching to see what she would do next.

So, Krystal thought. She flung the board away, and one of the men flinched. Krystal almost smiled. She thought, how angry I must look, how angry I am, and then her anger left her. She tried to keep it, but it was gone the moment she knew it was there.

She shaded her eyes and looked around her. The distant mountains cast long shadows into the desert. The desert was empty and still. Nothing moved but Hope, walking towards them with the gun over her shoulder. As she drew near Krystal waved, and Hope raised her arms. A rabbit hung from each hand, swinging by its ears.

Our Story Begins

The fog blew in early again. This was the tenth straight day of it. The waiters and waitresses gathered along the window to watch, and Charlie pushed his cart across the dining room so that he could watch with them as he filled the water glasses. Boats were beating in ahead of the fog, which loomed behind them like a tall, rolling breaker. Gulls glided from the sky to the pylons along the wharf, where they shook out their feathers and rocked from side to side and glared at the tourists passing by.

The fog covered the stanchions of the bridge. The bridge appeared to be floating free as the fog billowed into the harbour and began to overtake the boats. One by one they were swallowed up in it.

'Now that's what I call hairy,' one of the waiters said. 'You couldn't get me out there for love or money.'

A waitress said something and the rest of them laughed.

'Nice talk,' the waiter said.

The maitre d' came out of the kitchen and snapped his fingers. 'Busboy!' he called. One of the waitresses turned and looked at Charlie, who put down the pitcher he was pouring from and pushed his cart back across the dining room to its assigned place. For the next half hour, until the first customer came in, Charlie folded napkins and laid out squares of butter in little bowls filled with crushed ice, and thought of the things he would do to the maitre d' if he ever got the maitre d' in his power.

But this was a diversion; he didn't really hate the maitre d'. He hated his meaningless work and his fear of being fired from it, and most of all he hated being called a busboy because being called a busboy made it harder for him to think of himself as a man, which he was just learning to do.

Only a few tourists came into the restaurant that night. All of them were alone, and plainly disappointed. They sat by themselves, across from their shopping bags, and stared morosely in the direction of the Golden Gate though there was nothing to see but the fog pressing up against the windows and greasy drops of water running down the glass. Like most people who ate alone they ordered the bargain items, scampi or cod or the Cap'n's Plate, and maybe a small carafe of the house wine. The waiters neglected them. The tourists dawdled over their food, overtipped the waiters, and left more deeply sunk in disappointment than before.

At nine o'clock the maitre d' sent all but three of the waiters home, then went home himself. Charlie hoped he'd be given the nod too, but he was left standing by his cart, where he folded more napkins and replaced the ice as it melted in the water glasses and under the squares of butter. The three waiters kept going back to the storeroom to smoke dope. By the time the restaurant closed they were so wrecked they could hardly stand.

Charlie started home the long way, up Columbus Avenue, because Columbus Avenue had the brightest streetlights. But in this fog the lights were only a presence, a milky blotch here and there in the vapour above. Charlie walked slowly and kept to the walls. He met no one on his way; but once, as he paused to wipe the dampness from his face, he heard strange ticking steps behind him and turned to see a three-legged dog appear out of the mist. It moved past in a series of lurches and was gone. 'Christ,' Charlie said. Then he laughed to himself, but the sound was unconvincing and he decided to get off the street for a while.

Just around the corner on Vallejo there was a coffeehouse where Charlie sometimes went on his nights off. Jack Kerouac had mentioned this particular coffeehouse in *The Subterraneans*. These days the patrons were mostly Italian people who came to listen to the jukebox, which was filled with music from Italian operas, but Charlie always looked up when someone came in the door; it might be Ginsberg or Corso, stopping by for old times' sake. He liked sitting there with an open book on the table, listening to music that he thought of as being classical. He liked to imagine that the rude, sluggish woman who brought him his cappuccino had once been Neil Cassady's lover. It was possible.

When Charlie came into the coffeehouse the only other customers were four old men sitting by the door. He took a table across the room. Someone had left an Italian movie magazine on the chair next to his. Charlie looked through the photographs, keeping time with his fingers to 'The Anvil Chorus' while the waitress made up his cappuccino. The coffee machine hissed as she worked the handle. The room filled with the sweet smell of coffee. Charlie also caught the smell of fish and realized that it came from him, that he was reeking of it. His fingers fell still on the table.

Charlie paid the waitress when she served him. He intended to drink up and get out. While he was waiting for the coffee to cool, a woman came in the door with two men. They looked around, held a conference, and finally sat down at the table next to Charlie's. As soon as they were seated they began to talk without regard for whether Charlie could hear them. He listened, and after a time he began to glance over at them. Either they didn't notice or they didn't care. They were indifferent to his presence.

Charlie gathered from their conversation that they were members of a church choir, making the rounds after choir practice. The woman's name was Audrey. Her lipstick was smeared, making her mouth look a little crooked. She had a sharp face with thick black brows that she raised sceptically whenever her husband spoke. Audrey's husband was tall and heavy. He shifted constantly, scraping his chair as he did so, and moved his hat back and forth from one knee to the other. Big as he was, the green suit he wore fitted him perfectly. His name was Truman, and the other man's name was George. George had a calm, reedy voice that he enjoyed using; Charlie could see him listening to it as he talked. He was a teacher of some kind, which did not surprise Charlie. George looked to him like the young professors he'd had during his three years of college: rimless spectacles, turtleneck sweater, the ghost of a smile always on his lips. But George wasn't really young. His thick hair, parted in the middle, had begun to turn grey.

No – it seemed that only Audrey and George sang in the choir. They were telling Truman about a trip the choir had just made to Los Angeles, to a festival of choirs. Truman looked from his wife to George as each of them spoke, and shook his head as they described the sorry characters of the other members of the choir and the eccentricities of the choir director.

'Of course Father Wes is nothing compared to Monsignor Strauss,' George said. 'Monsignor Strauss was positively certifiable.'

'Strauss?' Truman said. 'Which one is Strauss? The only Strauss I know is Johann.' Truman looked at his wife and laughed.

'Forgive me,' George said. 'I was being cryptic. George sometimes forgets the basics. When you've met someone like Monsignor Strauss, you naturally assume that everyone else has heard of him. The monsignor was our director for five years, prior to Father Wes's tenure. He got religion and left for the subcontinent just before Audrey joined us, so of course you wouldn't recognize the name.'

'The subcontinent,' Truman said. 'What's that? Atlantis?'

'For God's sake, Truman,' Audrey said. 'Sometimes you embarrass me.'

'India,' George said. 'Calcutta. Mother Teresa and all that.'

Audrey put her hand on George's arm. 'George,' she said, 'tell Truman that marvellous story you told me about Monsignor Strauss and the Filipino.'

George smiled to himself. 'Ah yes,' he said. 'Miguel. That's a long story, Audrey. Perhaps another night would be better.'

'Oh no,' Audrey said. 'Tonight would be perfect.'

Truman said, 'If it's that long . . .'

'It's not,' Audrey said. She knocked on the table with her knuckles. 'Tell the story, George.'

George looked over at Truman and shrugged. 'Don't blame George,' he said. He drank off the last of his brandy. 'All right then. Our story begins. Monsignor Strauss had some money from somewhere, and every year he made a journey to points exotic. When he came home he always had some unusual souvenir that he'd picked up on his travels. From Argentina he brought everyone seeds which grew into plants whose flowers smelled like, excuse me, *merde*. He got them in an Argentine joke shop, if you can imagine such a thing. When he came back from Kenya he smuggled in a lizard that could pick off flies with its tongue from a distance of six feet. The monsignor carried this lizard around on his finger and whenever a fly came within range he would say, "Watch this!" and aim the lizard like a pistol, and *poof* – no more fly.'

Audrey pointed her finger at Truman and said, 'Poof.' Truman just looked at her. 'I need another drink,' Audrey said, and signalled the waitress.

George ran his finger around the rim of his snifter. 'After the lizard,' he said, 'there was a large Australian rodent that ended up in the zoo, and after the rodent came a nineteen-year-old human being from the Philippines. His name was Miguel Lopez de Constanza, and he was a cab driver from Manila the monsignor had hired as a chauffeur during his stay there and taken a liking to. When the monsignor got back he pulled some strings at Immigration, and a few weeks later Miguel showed up. He spoke no English, really – only a few buzz words for tourists in Manila. The first month or so he stayed with Monsignor Strauss in the rectory, then he found a room in the Hotel Overland and moved in there.'

'The Hotel Overland,' Truman said. 'That's that druggy hangout on upper Grant.'

'The Hotel Overdose,' Audrey said. When Truman looked at her she said, 'That's what they call it.'

'You seem to be up on all the nomenclature,' Truman said.

The waitress came with their drinks. When her tray was empty she stood behind Truman and began to write in a notebook she carried. Charlie hoped she wouldn't come over to his table. He did not want the others to notice him. They would guess that he'd been listening to them, and they might not like it. They might stop talking. But the waitress finished making her entries and moved back to the bar without a glance at Charlie.

The old men by the door were arguing in Italian. The window above them was all steamed up, and Charlie could feel the closeness of the fog outside. The jukebox glowed in the corner. The song that was playing ended abruptly, the machinery whirred, and 'The Anvil Chorus' came on again.

'So why the Hotel Overland?' Truman asked.

'Truman prefers the Fairmont,' Audrey said. 'Truman thinks everyone should stay at the Fairmont.'

'Miguel had no money,' George said. 'Only what the monsignor gave him. The idea was that he would stay there just long enough to learn English and pick up a trade. Then he could get a job. Take care of himself.'

'Sounds reasonable,' Truman said.

Audrey laughed. 'Truman, you slay me. That is *exactly* what I thought you would say. Now let's just turn things around for a minute. Let's say that for some reason you, Truman, find yourself in Manila dead broke. You don't know anybody, you don't understand anything anyone says, and you wind up in a hotel where people are sticking needles into themselves and nodding out on the stairs and setting their rooms on fire all the time. How much Spanish are you going to learn living like that? What kind of trade are you going to pick up? Get real,' Audrey said. 'That's not a reasonable existence.'

'San Francisco isn't Manila,' Truman said. 'Believe me – I've been there. At least here you've got a chance. And it isn't true that he didn't know anybody. What about the monsignor?'

'Terrific,' Audrey said. 'A priest who walks around with a lizard on his finger. Great friend. Or, as you would say, great connection.'

'I have never, to my knowledge, used the word *connection* in that way,' Truman said.

George had been staring into his brandy snifter, which he held cupped in both hands. He looked up at Audrey. 'Actually,' he said, 'Miguel was not entirely at a loss. In fact he managed pretty well for a time. Monsignor Strauss got him into a training course for mechanics at the Porsche-Audi place on Van Ness, and he picked up English at a terrific rate. It's amazing, isn't it, what one can do if one has no choice.' George rolled the snifter back and forth between his palms. 'The druggies left him completely alone, incredible as that may seem. No hassles in the hallways, nothing. It was as if Miguel lived in a different dimension from them, and in a way he did. He went to Mass every day, and sang in the choir. That's where I made his acquaintance. Miguel had a gorgeous baritone, truly gorgeous. He was extremely proud of his voice. He was proud of his body, too. Ate precisely so much of this, so much of that. Did elaborate exercises every day. He even gave himself facial massages to keep from getting a double chin.'

'There you are,' Truman said to Audrey. 'There is such a thing as character.' When she didn't answer he added, 'What I'm getting at is that people are not necessarily limited by their circumstances.'

'I know what you're getting at,' Audrey said. 'The story isn't over yet.'

Truman moved his hat from his knee to the table. He folded his arms across his chest. 'I've got a full day ahead of me,' he said to Audrey. She nodded but did not look at him.

George took a sip of his brandy. He closed his eyes afterwards and ran the tip of his tongue around his lips. Then he lowered his head again and stared back into the snifter. 'Miguel met a woman,' he said, 'as do we all. Her name was Senga. My guess is that she had originally been called Agnes, and that she turned her name around in hopes of making herself more interesting to people of the male persuasion. Senga was older than Miguel by at least ten years, maybe more. She had a daughter in, I believe, fifth grade. Senga was a finance officer at B of A. I don't remember how they met. They went out for a while, then Senga broke it off. I suppose it was a casual thing for her, but for Miguel it was serious. He worshipped Senga, and I use that word advisedly. He set up a little shrine to her in his room. A high school graduation picture of Senga surrounded by different objects that she had worn or used. Combs. Handkerchiefs. Empty perfume bottles. A whole pile of things. How he got them I have no idea – whether she gave them to him or whether he just took them. The odd thing is, he only went out with her a few times. I very much doubt that they ever reached the point of sleeping together.'

'They didn't,' Truman said.

George looked up at him.

'If he'd slept with her,' Truman said, 'he wouldn't have built a shrine to her.'

'Pure Truman,' Audrey said. 'Vintage Truman.'

He patted her arm. 'No offence,' he told her.

'Be that as it may,' George said, 'Miguel wouldn't give up, and that's what caused all the trouble. First he wrote her letters, long mushy letters in broken English. He gave me one to read through for spelling and so on, but it was utterly hopeless. All fragments and run-ons. No paragraphs. I just gave it back after a few days and said it was fine. Miguel thought that the letters would bring Senga around, but she never answered and after a while he began calling her at all hours. She wouldn't talk to him. As soon as she heard his voice she hung up. Eventually she got an unlisted number. She wouldn't talk to Miguel, but Miguel thought that she would listen to yours truly. He wanted me to go down to B of A and plead his cause. Act as a kind of character witness. Which, after some reflection, I agreed to do.'

'Oho,' Truman said. 'The plot thickens. Enter Miles Standish.'

'I *knew* you would say that,' Audrey said. She finished her drink and looked around, but the waitress was sitting at the bar with her back to the room, smoking a cigarette.

George took his glasses off, held them up to the light, and put them on again. 'So,' he said, 'George sallies forth to meet Senga. Senga – doesn't it make you think of a jungle queen, that name? Flashing eyes, dagger at the hip, breasts bulging over a leopard-skin halter? Such was not the case. This Senga was still an Agnes. Thin. Businesslike. And *very* grouchy. No sooner did I mention Miguel's name than I was shown the door, with a message for Miguel: if he bothered her again she would set the police on him.

'"Set the police on him." Those were her words, and she meant them. A week or so later Miguel followed her home from work and she forthwith got a lawyer on the case. The upshot of it was that Miguel had to sign a paper saying that he understood he would be arrested if he wrote, called, or followed Senga again. He signed, but with his fingers crossed, as it were. He told me, "Horhay, I sign – but I do not accept." "Nobly spoken," I told him, "but you'd damn well better accept or that woman will have you locked up." Miguel said that prison did not frighten him, that in his country all the best people were in prison. Sure enough, a few days later he followed Senga home again and she did it – she had him locked up.'

'Poor kid,' Audrey said.

Truman had been trying to get the attention of the waitress, who wouldn't look at him. He turned to Audrey. 'What do you mean, "Poor kid"? What about the girl? Senga? She's trying to hold down a job and feed her daughter and meanwhile she has this Filipino stalking her all over the city. If you want to feel sorry for someone, feel sorry for her.'

'I do,' Audrey said.

'All right then.' Truman looked back towards the waitress again, and as he did so Audrey picked up George's snifter and took a drink from it. George smiled at her. 'What's wrong with that woman?' Truman said. He shook his head. 'I give up.'

'George, go on,' Audrey said.

George nodded. 'In brief,' he said 'it was a serious mess. *Très sérieux*. They set bail at twenty thousand dollars, which Monsignor Strauss could not raise. Nor, it goes without saying, could yours truly. So Miguel remained in jail. Senga's lawyer was out for blood, and he got Immigration into the act. They were threatening to revoke Miguel's visa and throw him out of the country. Monsignor Strauss finally got him off, but it was a damn close-run thing. It turned out that Senga was going to be transferred to Portland in a month or so, and the monsignor persuaded her to drop charges with the understanding that Miguel would not come within ten miles of the city limits as long as she lived there. Until she left, Miguel would stay with Monsignor Strauss at the rectory, under his personal supervision. The monsignor also agreed to pay Senga for her lawyer's fees, which were outrageous. Absolutely outrageous.'

'So what was the bottom line?' Truman asked.

'Simplicity itself,' George said. 'If Miguel messed up, they'd throw him on the first plane to Manila.'

'Sounds illegal,' Truman said.

'Perhaps. But that was the arrangement.'

A new song began on the jukebox. The men by the door stopped arguing, and each of them seemed all at once to draw into himself.

'Listen,' Audrey said. 'It's him. Caruso.'

The record was worn and gave the effect of static behind Caruso's voice. The music coming through the static made Charlie think of the cultural broadcasts from Europe his parents had listened to so gravely when he was a boy. At times Caruso's voice was almost lost, and then it would swell again. The old men were still. One of them began to weep. The tears fell freely from his open eyes, down his shining cheeks.

'So that was Caruso,' Truman said when it ended. 'I always wondered what all the fuss was about. Now I know. That's what I call singing.' Truman took out his wallet and put some money on the table. He examined the money left in the wallet before putting it away. 'Ready?' he said to Audrey.

'No,' Audrey said. 'Finish the story, George.'

George took his glasses off and laid them next to his snifter. He rubbed his eyes. 'All right,' he said. 'Back to Miguel. As per the agreement, he lived in the rectory until Senga moved to Portland. Behaved himself, too. No letters, no calls, no following her around. In his pyjamas every night by ten. Then Senga left town and Miguel went back to his room at the Overland. For a while there he looked pretty desperate, but after a few weeks he seemed to come out of it.

'I say "seemed". There was in fact more going on than met the eye. My eye, anyway. One night I am sitting at home and listening, believe it or not, to *Tristan*, when the telephone rings. At first no one says anything; then this voice comes on the line whispering, "Help me, Horhay, help me," and of course I know who it is. He says he needs to see me right away. No explanation. He doesn't even tell me where he is. I just have to assume he's at the Overland, and that's where I find him, in the lobby.'

George gave a little laugh. 'Actually,' he said, 'I almost missed him. His face was all bandaged up, from his nose to the top of his forehead. If I hadn't been looking for him I never would have recognized him. Never. He was sitting there with his suitcases all around him and a white cane across his knees. When I made my presence known to him he said, "Horhay, I am blind." How, I asked him, had this come to pass? He would not say. Instead he gave me a piece of paper with a telephone number on it and asked me to call Senga and tell her that he had gone blind, and that he would be arriving in Portland by Trailways at eleven o'clock the next morning.'

'Great Scott,' Truman said. 'He was faking it, wasn't he? I mean he wasn't really blind, was he?'

'Now that is an interesting question,' George said. 'Because, while I would have to say that Miguel was not really blind, I would also have to say that he was not really faking it, either. But to go on. Senga was unmoved. She instructed me to tell Miguel that not she but the police would be waiting to meet his bus. Miguel didn't believe her. "Horhay," he said, "she will be there," and that was that. End of discussion.'

'Did he go?' Truman asked.

'Of course he went,' Audrey said. 'He loved her.'

George nodded. 'I put him on the bus myself. Led him to his seat, in fact.'

'So he still had the bandages on,' Truman said.

'Oh yes. Yes, he still had them on.'

'But that's a twelve-, thirteen-hour ride. If there wasn't anything wrong with his eyes, why didn't he just take the bandages off and put them on again when the bus reached Portland?'

Audrey put her hand on Truman's. 'Truman,' she said. 'We have to talk about something.'

'I don't get it,' Truman went on. 'Why would he travel blind like that? Why would he go all that way in the dark?'

'Truman, listen,' Audrey said. But when Truman turned to her she took her hand away from his and looked across the table at George.

George's eyes were closed. His fingers were folded together as if in prayer.

'George,' Audrey said. 'Please. I can't.'

George opened his eyes.

'Tell him,' Audrey said.

Truman looked back and forth between them. 'Now just wait a minute,' he said.

'I'm sorry,' George said. 'This is not easy for me.'

Truman was staring at Audrey. 'Hey,' he said.

She pushed her empty glass back and forth. 'We have to talk,' she said.

He brought his face close to hers. 'Do you think that just because I make a lot of money I don't have feelings?'

'We have to talk,' she repeated.

'Indeed,' George said.

The three of them sat there for a while. Then Truman said, 'This takes the cake,' and put his hat on. A few minutes later they all got up and left the coffeehouse.

The waitress sat by herself at the bar, motionless except when she raised her head to blow smoke at the ceiling. Over by the door the Italians were throwing dice for toothpicks. 'The Anvil Chorus' was playing on the jukebox. It was the first piece of classical music Charlie had heard often enough to get sick of, and he was sick of it now. He closed the magazine he'd been pretending to read, dropped it on the table, and went outside.

It was still foggy, and colder than before. Charlie's father had warned him about moving here in the middle of the summer. He had even quoted Mark Twain at Charlie, to the effect that the coldest winter Mark Twain ever endured was the summer he spent in San Francisco. This had been a particularly bad one; even the natives said so. In truth it was beginning to get to Charlie. But he had not admitted this to his father, any more than he had admitted that his job was wearing him out and paying him barely enough to keep alive on, or that the friends he wrote home about did not exist, or that the editors to whom he'd submitted his novel had sent it back without comment – all but one, who had scrawled in pencil across the title page, 'Are you kidding?'

Charlie's room was on Broadway, at the crest of the hill. The hill was so steep they'd had to carve steps into the sidewalk and block the street with a cement wall because of the cars that had lost their brakes going down. Sometimes, at night, Charlie would sit on that wall and look out over the lights of North Beach and think of all the writers out there, bent over their desks, steadily filling pages with well-chosen words. He thought of these writers gathering together in the small hours to drink wine, and read each other's work, and talk about the things that weighed on their hearts. These were the brilliant men and women, the deep conversations Charlie wrote home about.

He was close to giving up. He didn't even know how close to giving up he was until he walked out of the coffeehouse that night and felt himself deciding that he would go on after all. He stood there and listened to the foghorn blowing out upon the Bay. The sadness of that sound, the idea of himself stopping to hear it, the thickness of the fog all gave him pleasure.

Charlie heard violins behind him as the coffeehouse door opened; then it banged shut and the violins were gone. A deep voice said something in Italian. A higher voice answered, and the two voices floated away together down the street.

Charlie turned and started up the hill, picking his way past lampposts that glistened with running beads of water, past sweating walls and dim windows. A Chinese woman appeared beside him. She held before her a lobster that was waving its pincers back and forth as if conducting music. The woman hurried past and vanished. The hill had begun to steepen under Charlie's feet. He stopped to catch his breath, and listened again to the foghorn. He knew that somewhere out there a boat was making its way home in spite of the solemn warning, and as he walked on Charlie imagined himself kneeling in the prow of that boat, lamp in hand, intent on the light shining just before him. All distraction gone. Too watchful to be afraid. Tongue wetting the lips and eyes wide open, ready to call out in this shifting fog where at any moment anything might be revealed.

Leviathan

On her thirtieth birthday Ted threw a surprise party for Helen. It was a small party – Mitch and Bliss were the only guests. They'd chipped in with Ted and bought Helen three grams of white-out blizzard that lasted the whole night and on into the next morning. When it got light enough everyone went for a swim in the courtyard pool. Then Ted took Mitch up to the sauna on the fifth floor while Helen and Bliss put together a monster omelette.

'So how does it feel,' Bliss said, 'being thirty?' The ash fell off her cigarette into the eggs. She stared at the ash for a moment, then stirred it in. 'Mitch had his fortieth last month and totally freaked. He did so much Maalox he started to taste like chalk. I thought he was going to start freebasing or something.'

'Mitch is *forty*?' Helen said.

Bliss looked over at her. 'That's classified information, okay?'

Helen shook her head. 'Incredible. He looks about twenty-five, maybe twenty-seven at the absolute most.' She watched Bliss crumble bacon into the bowl. 'Oh God,' she said, 'I don't believe it. He had a face lift.'

Bliss closed her eyes and leaned against the counter. 'I shouldn't have told you. Please don't say anything,' she murmured hopelessly.

When Mitch and Ted came back from the sauna they all had another toot, and Ted gave Helen the mirror to lick. He said he'd never seen three grams disappear so fast. Afterwards Helen served up the omelette while Ted tried to find something on the TV. He kept flipping the dial until it drove everyone crazy, looking for Roadrunner cartoons, then he gave up and tuned in on the last part of a movie about the Bataan Death March. They didn't watch it for very long though because Bliss started to cry. Ted switched over to an inspirational programme but Bliss kept crying and began to hyperventilate. 'Come on, everyone,' said Mitch. 'Love circle.' Ted and Mitch went over to Bliss and put their arms around her while Helen watched them from the sofa, sipping espresso from a cup as blue and dainty as a robin's egg – the last of a set her grandmother had brought from the old country. Helen would have hugged Bliss too but there wasn't really any point; Bliss pulled this stunt almost every time she got herself a noseful, and it just had to run its course.

When Helen finished her espresso she gathered the plates and carried them out to the kitchen. She scattered leftover toast into the courtyard below, and watched the squirrels carry it away as she scoured the dishes and listened to the proceedings in the next room. This time it was Ted who talked Bliss down. 'You're beautiful,' he kept telling her. It was the same thing he always said to Helen when she felt depressed, and she was beginning to feel depressed right now.

She needed more fuel, she decided. She ducked into the bedroom and did a couple of lines from Ted's private stash, which she had discovered while searching for matches in the closet. Afterwards she looked at herself in the mirror. Her eyes were bright. They seemed lit from within and that was how Helen felt, as if there were a column of cool white light pouring from her head to her feet. She put on a pair of sunglasses so nobody would notice and went back to the kitchen.

Mitch was standing at the counter, rolling a bone. 'How's the birthday girl?' he asked without looking up.

'Ready for the next one,' Helen said. 'How about you?'

'Hey, bring it on,' Mitch answered.

At that moment Helen came close to letting him know she knew, but she held back. Mitch was good people and so was Bliss. Helen didn't want to make trouble between them. All the same, Helen knew that someday she wasn't going to be able to stop herself from giving Mitch the business. It just had to happen. And Helen knew that Bliss knew. But she hadn't done it this morning and she felt good about that.

Mitch held up the joint. 'Taste?'

Helen shook her head. She glanced over her shoulder towards the living room. 'What's the story on Bliss?' she asked. 'All bummed out over World War Two? Ted should have known that movie would set her off.'

Mitch picked a sliver of weed from his lower lip. 'Her ex is threatening to move back to Boston. Which means she won't get to see her kids except during the summer, and that's only if we can put together the scratch to fly them here and back. It's tough. Really tough.'

'I guess,' Helen said. She dried her hands and hung the towel on the refrigerator door. 'Still, Bliss should have thought about that when she took a walk on them, right?'

Mitch turned and started out of the kitchen.

'Sorry,' Helen called after him. 'I wasn't thinking.'

'Yes you were,' Mitch said, and left her there.

Oh, hell, she thought. She decided she needed another line but made no move to get it. Helen stood where she was, looking down at the pool through the window above the sink. The manager's Afghan dog was lapping water from the shallow end, legs braced in the trough that ran around the pool. The two British Airways stewardesses from down the hall were bathing their white bodies in the morning sunshine, both wearing blue swimsuits. The redheaded girl from upstairs was floating on an air mattress. Helen could see the long shadow of the air mattress glide along the bottom of the pool like something stalking her.

Helen heard Ted say, 'Jesus, Bliss, I can understand that. Everyone has those feelings. You can't always beat them down.' Bliss answered him in a voice so soft that Helen gave up trying to hear; it was hardly more than a sigh. She poured herself a glass of Chablis and joined the others in the living room. They were all sitting cross-legged on the floor. Helen caught Mitch's eye and mouthed the word *sorry*. He stared at her, then nodded.

'I've done worse things than that,' Ted was saying. 'I'll bet Mitch has, too.'

'Plenty worse,' Mitch said.

'Worse than what?' Helen asked.

'It's awful.' Bliss looked down at her hands. 'I'd be embarrassed to tell you.' She was all cried out now, Helen could see that. Her eyes were heavy-lidded and serene, her cheeks flushed, and a little smile played over her swollen lips.

'It couldn't be that bad,' Helen said.

Ted leaned forward. He still had on the bathrobe he'd worn to the sauna and it fell open almost to his waist, as Helen knew he intended it to do. His chest was hard-looking from the Nautilus machine in the basement, and dark from their trip to Mazatlán. Helen had to admit it, he looked great. She didn't understand why he had to be so obvious and crass, but he got what he wanted: she stared at him and so did Bliss.

'Bliss, it *isn't* that bad,' Ted went on. 'It's just one of those things.' He turned to Helen. 'Bliss's little girl came down with tonsillitis last month and Bliss never got it together to go see her in the hospital.'

'I can't deal with hospitals,' Bliss said. 'The minute I set foot inside of one my stomach starts doing flips. But still. When I think of her all alone in there.'

Mitch took Bliss's hands in his and looked right at her until she met his gaze. 'It's over,' he said. 'The operation's over and Lisa's out of the hospital and she's all right. Say it, Bliss. *She's all right.*'

'She's all right,' Bliss said.

'Again.'

'She's all right,' Bliss repeated.

'Okay. Now believe it.' Mitch put her hands together and rubbed them gently between his palms. 'We've built up this big myth about kids being helpless and vulnerable and so on because it makes us feel important. We think we're playing some heavy role just because we're parents. We don't give kids any credit at all. Kids are tough little monkeys. Kids are survivors.'

Bliss smiled.

'But I don't know,' Mitch said. He let go of Bliss's hands and leaned back. 'What I said just then is probably complete bullshit. Everything I say these days sounds like bullshit.'

'We've all done worse things,' Ted told Bliss. He looked over at Helen. When Helen saw that he was waiting for her to agree with him she tried to think of something to say. Ted kept looking at her. 'What have you got those things on for?' he asked.

'The light hurts my eyes.'

'Then close the curtains.' He reached across to Helen and lifted the sunglasses away from her face. 'There,' he said. He cupped her chin in one hand and with the other brushed her hair back from her forehead. 'Isn't she something?'

'She'll do,' Mitch said.

Ted stroked Helen's cheek with the back of his hand. 'I'd kill for that face.'

Bliss was studying Helen. 'So lovely,' she said in a solemn, wistful voice.

Helen laughed. She got up and drew the curtains shut. Spangles of light glittered in the fabric. She moved across the dim room to the dining nook and brought back a candle from the table there. Ted lit the candle and for a few moments they silently watched the flame. Then, in a thoughtful tone that seemed part of the silence, Mitch began to speak.

'It's true that we've all done things we're ashamed of. I just wish I'd done more of them. I'm serious,' he said when Ted laughed. 'I wish I'd raised more hell and made more mistakes, real mistakes, where you actually do something wrong instead of just let yourself drift into things you don't like. Sometimes I look around and I think, *Hey – what happened?* No reflection on you,' he said to Bliss.

She seemed puzzled.

'Forget it,' Mitch told her. 'All I'm saying is that looking out for the other fellow and being nice all the time is a bunch of crap.'

'But you *are* nice,' Bliss said.

Mitch nodded. 'I know,' he said bitterly. 'I'm working on it. It get you exactly nowhere.'

'Amen,' said Ted.

'Case in point,' Mitch went on. 'I used to paralegal with this gu in the city and he decided that he couldn't live without some gi he was seeing. So he told his wife and of course she threw him out Then the girl changed her mind. She didn't even tell him why. W used to eat lunch together and he would give me the latest instalmen and I swear to God it was enough to break your heart. He wante to get back together with his family but his wife couldn't make u her mind whether to take him. One minute she'd say yes, the nex minute she'd say no. Meanwhile he was living in this ratbag on Pos Street. All he had in there was lawn furniture. I don't know, I just fel sorry for him. So I told him he could move in with us until things go straightened out.'

'I can feel this one coming,' Helen said.

Mitch stared at the candle. 'His name was Raphael. Like the angel He was creative and good-looking and there was a nice aura aroun him. I guess I wanted to be his friend. But he turned out to be complete bad news. In the nine months he stayed with us he never once washe a glass or emptied an ashtray. He ran up hundreds of dollars worth o calls on our phone bill and didn't pay for them. He wrecked my car He stole things from me. He even put the moves on my wife.'

'Classic,' Helen said.

'You know what I did about it?' Mitch asked. 'I'll tell you. Nothing I never said a word to him about any of it. By the time he left, my wif couldn't stand the sight of me. Beginning of the end.'

'What a depressing story,' Helen said.

'I should have killed him,' Mitch said. 'I might have regretted i later on but at least I could say I *did* something.'

'You're too sweet,' Bliss told him.

'I know,' Mitch said. 'But I wish I had, anyway. Sometimes it' better to do something really horrendous than to let things slide.'

Ted clapped his hands. 'Hear, hear. You're on the right track, Mitch All you need is a few pointers, and old Ted is just the man to give the o you. Because where horrendous is concerned I'm the expert. You ight say that I'm the king of horrendous.'

Helen held up her empty glass. 'Anybody want anything?'

'Put on your crash helmets,' Ted went on. 'You are about to hear ny absolute bottom-line confession. The Worst Story Ever Told.'

'No thanks,' said Helen.

He peered at her. 'What do you mean, "No thanks." Who's asking ermission?'

'I wouldn't mind hearing it,' Mitch said.

'Well I would.' Helen stood and looked down at Ted. 'It's my irthday party, remember? I just don't feel like sitting around and stening to you talk about what a crud you are. It's a downer.'

'That's right,' Bliss said. 'Helen's the birthday girl. She gets to choose. ight, Ted?'

'I know what,' Helen said. 'Why don't you tell us something good ou did? The thing you're most proud of.'

Mitch burst out laughing. Ted grinned and punched him in e arm.

'I mean it,' Helen said.

'Helen gets to choose,' Bliss repeated. She patted the floor beside her nd Helen sat down again. 'All right,' Bliss said. 'We're listening.'

Ted looked from Bliss to Helen. 'I'll do it if you will,' he said. 'But ou have to go first.'

'That's not fair,' Helen said.

'Sounds fair to me,' said Mitch. 'It was your idea.'

Bliss smiled at Helen. 'This is fun.'

efore Helen began, she sent Ted out to the kitchen for more wine. litch did some sit-ups to get his blood moving again. Bliss sat behind lelen and let down Helen's hair. 'I could show you something for his dryness,' she said. She combed Helen's hair with her fingers, then tarted to brush it, counting off the strokes in a breathy whisper until 'ed came back with the jug.

They all had a drink.

'Ready and waiting,' Ted told Helen. He lay back on the sofa and clasped his hands behind his head. 'One of my mother's friends had a boy with Down's syndrome,' Helen began. 'Actually, three or four of her friends had kids with problems like that. One of my aunts, too. They were all good Catholics and they didn't think anything about having babies right into their forties. This was before Vatican Two and the pill and all that – before everything got watered down.

'Anyway, Tom wasn't really a boy. He was older than me by a couple of years, and a lot bigger. But he seemed like a boy – very sweet, very gentle, very happy.'

Bliss stopped the brush in midstroke and said, 'You're going to make me cry again.'

'I used to take care of Tom sometimes when I was in high school. I was into a serious good-works routine back then. I wanted to be a saint. Honestly, I really did. At night, before I went to sleep, I used to put my fingers under my chin like I was praying and smile in this really holy way that I practised all the time in front of the mirror. Then if they found me dead in the morning they would think that I'd gone straight to heaven – that I was smiling at the angels coming to get me. At one point I even thought of becoming a nun.'

Bliss laughed. 'I can just see you in a habit – Sister Morphine. You'd have lasted about two hours.'

Helen turned and looked at Bliss in a speculative way. 'It's not something I expect you to understand,' she said, 'but if I had gone in I would have stayed in. To me, a vow is a vow.' She turned away again. 'Like I said, I started out taking care of Tom as a kind of beatitude number, but after a while I got to look forward to it. Tom was fun to be with. And he really loved me. He even named one of his hamsters after me. We were both crazy about animals, so we would usually go to the zoo or I would take him to this stable out in Marin that had free riding lessons for special kids. That was what they called them, instead of handicapped or retarded – special.'

'Beautiful,' Mitch said.

'Don't get too choked up,' Helen told him. 'The story isn't over yet.' She took a sip of her wine. 'So. After I started college I didn't get home all that much, but whenever I did I'd stop by and get Tom

nd we'd go somewhere. Over to the Cliff House to look at the sea
ions, something like that. Then this one day I got a real brainstorm. I
hought, Hey, why not go whale-watching? Tom had whale posters
ll over his bedroom but he'd never seen a real one, and neither had
. So I called up this outfit in Half Moon Bay and they said that it was
etting towards the end of the season, but still worth a try. They were
retty sure we'd see something.

'Tom's mother wasn't too hot about the idea. She kept going on
bout the fact that he couldn't swim. But I brought her around, and
he next morning Tom and I drove down and got on board the boat.
t wasn't all that big. In fact it was a lot smaller than I thought it would
e, and that made me a little nervous at first, but after we got under
vay I figured hell with it – they must know what they're doing. The
oat rocked a little, but not dangerously. Tom loved it.

'We cruised around all morning and didn't see a thing. They would
ake us to different places and cut the engine and we would sit there,
vaiting for a whale to come along. I stopped caring. It was nice out on
he water. We were with a good bunch of people and one of them fixed
p a sort of fishing line for Tom to hang over the side while we waited.
just leaned back and got some sun. Smelled the good smells. Watched
he seagulls. After an hour or so they would start the engine up again
nd go somewhere else and do the same thing. This happened three
r four times. Everybody was kidding the guide about it, threatening
o make him walk the plank and so on. Then, right out of nowhere,
his whale came up beside us.

'He was just suddenly *there*. All this water running off his back. This
nbelievably rancid smell all around him. Covered with barnacles and
hells and long strings of seaweed trailing off him. Big. Maybe half
gain as long as the boat we were in.' Helen shook her head. 'You
ust can't imagine how big he was. He started making passes at the
oat, and every time he did it we'd pitch and roll and take on about
ive hundred gallons of water. We were falling all over each other. At
irst everyone laughed and whooped it up, but after a while it started
o get heavy.'

'He was probably playing with you,' Mitch said.

'That's what the guide told us the first couple of times it happened. Then he got scared too. I mean he went white as a sheet. You could tell he didn't know what was happening any better than the rest of us did. We have this idea that whales are supposed to be more civilized than people, smarter and friendlier and more together. Cute, even. But it wasn't like that. It was hostile.'

'You probably got a bad one,' Mitch said. 'It sounds like he was bent out of shape about something. Maybe the Russians harpooned his mate.'

'He was a monster,' Helen said. 'I mean that. He was hostile and huge and he stank. He was hideous, too. There were so many shells and barnacles on him that you could hardly see his skin. It looked as if he had armour on. He scraped the boat a couple of times and it made the most terrible sound, like people moaning under water. He'd swim ahead a ways and go under and you'd think Please God don't let him come back, and then the water would start to churn alongside the boat and there he'd be again. It was just terrifying. I've never been so afraid in my life. And then Tom started to lose it.'

Bliss put the brush on the floor. Helen could feel her stillness and hear the sound of her breathing.

'He started to make these little noises,' Helen said. 'I'd never heard him do that before. Little mewing noises. The strange thing was, I hadn't even thought of Tom up to then. I'd completely forgotten about him. So it gave me a shock when I realized that he was sitting right next to me, scared half to death. At first I thought, Oh no, what if he goes berserk! He was so much bigger than me I wouldn't have been able to control him. Neither would anyone else. He was incredibly strong. If anyone had tried to hold him down he'd have thrown them off like a dog shakes off water. And then what?

'But the thing that worried me most was that Tom would get so confused and panicky that he'd jump overboard. In my mind I had a completely clear picture of him doing it.'

'Me too,' Mitch said. 'I have the same picture. He did it, didn't he? He jumped in and you went after him and pulled him out.'

Bliss said, 'Ssshhh. Just listen, okay?'

'He didn't jump,' Helen said. 'He didn't go berserk either. Here we come to the point of the story – Helen's Finest Hour. How did I get started on this, anyway? It's disgusting.'

The candle hissed and flared. The flame was burning in a pool of wax. Helen watched it flare up twice more, and then it died. The room went grey.

Bliss began to rub Helen's back. 'Go on,' she said.

'I just talked him down,' Helen said. 'You know, I put my arm around his shoulder and said, Hey, Tom, isn't this something! Look at that big old whale! Wow! Here he comes again, Tom, hold on! And then I'd laugh like crazy. I made like I was having the time of my life, and Tom fell for it. He calmed right down. Pretty soon after that the whale took off and we went back to shore. I don't know why I brought it up. It was just that even though I felt really afraid, I went ahead and acted as if I was flying high. I guess that's the thing I'm most proud of.'

'Thank you, Helen,' Mitch said. 'Thank you for sharing that with us. I know I sound phony but I mean it.'

'You don't talk about yourself enough,' Bliss said. Then she called, 'Okay, Ted – it's your turn.'

Ted did not answer.

Bliss called his name again.

'I think he's asleep,' Mitch said. He moved closer to the sofa and looked at Ted. He nodded. 'Dead to the world.'

'Asleep,' Helen said. 'Oh, God.'

Bliss hugged Helen from behind. 'Mitch, come here,' she said. 'Love circle.'

Helen pulled away. 'No,' she said.

'Why don't we wake him up?' Mitch suggested.

'Forget it,' Helen told him. 'Once Ted goes under he stays under. Nothing can bring him up. Watch.' She went to the sofa, raised her hand, and slapped Ted across the face.

He groaned softly and turned over.

'See?' Helen said.

'What a slug,' Bliss said.

'Don't you dare call him names,' Helen told her. 'Not in front of me, anyway. Ted is my husband. Forever and ever. I only did that to make a point.'

Mitch said, 'Helen, do you want to talk about this?'

'There's nothing to talk about,' Helen answered. 'I made my own bed.' She hefted the jug of wine. 'Who needs a refill?'

Mitch and Bliss looked at each other. 'My energy level isn't too high,' Bliss said. Mitch nodded. 'Mine's pretty low, too.'

'Then we'll just have to bring it up,' Helen said. She left the room and came back with three candles and a mirror. She screwed one of the candles into the holder and held a match to the wick. It sputtered, then caught. Helen felt the heat of the flame on her cheek. 'There,' she said, 'that's more like it.' Mitch and Bliss drew closer as Helen took a glass vial from her pocket and spilled the contents onto the mirror. She looked up at them and grinned.

'I don't believe this,' Bliss said. 'Where did you get it?'

Helen shrugged.

'That's a lot of toot,' Mitch said.

'We'll just have to do our best,' Helen said. 'We've got all day.'

Bliss looked at the mirror. 'I really should go to work.'

'Me too,' Mitch said. He laughed, and Bliss laughed with him. They watched over Helen's shoulders as Helen bent down to sift the gleaming crystal. First she chopped it with a razor. Then she began to spread it out. Mitch and Bliss smiled up at her from the mirror, and Helen smiled back between them. Their faces were rosy with candlelight. They were the faces of three well-wishers, carollers, looking in at Helen through a window filling up with snow.

The Rich Brother

There were two brothers, Pete and Donald.

Pete, the older brother, was in real estate. He and his wife had a Century 21 franchise in Santa Cruz. Pete worked hard and made a lot of money, but not any more than he thought he deserved. He had two daughters, a sailboat, a house from which he could see a thin slice of the ocean, and friends doing well enough in their own lives not to wish bad luck on him. Donald, the younger brother, was still single. He lived alone, painted houses when he found the work, and got deeper in debt to Pete when he didn't.

No one would have taken them for brothers. Where Pete was stout and hearty and at home in the world, Donald was bony, grave, and obsessed with the fate of his soul. Over the years Donald had worn the images of two different Perfect Masters around his neck. Out of devotion to the second of these he entered an ashram in Berkeley, where he nearly died of undiagnosed hepatitis. By the time Pete finished paying the medical bills Donald had become a Christian. He drifted from church to church, then joined a pentecostal community that met somewhere in the Mission District to sing in tongues and swap prophecies.

Pete couldn't make sense of it. Their parents were both dead, but while they were alive neither of them had found it necessary to believe in anything. They managed to be decent people without making fools of themselves, and Pete had the same ambition. He thought that the whole thing was an excuse for Donald to take himself seriously.

The trouble was that Donald couldn't content himself with worrying about his own soul. He had to worry about everyone else's, and especially Pete's. He handed down his judgments in ways that he seemed to consider subtle: through significant silence, innuendo, looks of mild despair that said, *Brother, what have you come to*. What Pete had come to, as far as he could tell, was prosperity. That was the real issue between them. Pete prospered and Donald did not prosper.

At the age of forty Pete took up sky diving. He made his first jump with two friends who'd started only a few months earlier and were already doing stunts. He would never have used the word *mystical*, but that was how Pete felt about the experience. Later he made the mistake of trying to describe it to Donald, who kept asking how much it cost and then acted appalled when Pete told him.

'At least I'm trying something new,' Pete said. 'At least I'm breaking the pattern.'

Not long after that conversation Donald also broke the pattern, by going to live on a farm outside Paso Robles. The farm was owned by several members of Donald's community, who had bought it and moved there with the idea of forming a family of faith. That was how Donald explained it in the first letter he sent. Every week Pete heard how happy Donald was, how 'in the Lord'. He told Pete that he was praying for him, he and the rest of Pete's brothers and sisters on the farm.

'I only have one brother,' Pete wanted to answer, 'and that's enough.' But he kept this thought to himself.

In November the letters stopped. Pete didn't worry about this at first, but when he called Donald at Thanksgiving Donald was grim. He tried to sound upbeat but he didn't try hard enough to make it convincing. 'Now listen,' Pete said, 'you don't have to stay in that place if you don't want to.'

'I'll be all right,' Donald answered.

'That's not the point. Being all right is not the point. If you don't like what's going on up there, then get out.'

'I'm all right,' Donald said again, more firmly. 'I'm doing fine.'

But he called Pete a week later and said that he was quitting the farm. When Pete asked him where he intended to go, Donald admitted that he had no plan. His car had been repossessed just before he left the city, and he was flat broke.

'I guess you'll have to stay with us,' Pete said.

Donald put up a show of resistance. Then he gave in. 'Just until I get my feet on the ground,' he said.

'Right,' Pete said. 'Check out your options.' He told Donald he'd send him money for a bus ticket, but as they were about to hang up Pete changed his mind. He knew that Donald would try hitchhiking to save the fare. Pete didn't want him out on the road all alone where some head case could pick him up, where anything could happen to him.

'Better yet,' he said, 'I'll come and get you.'

'You don't have to do that. I didn't expect you to do that,' Donald said. He added, 'It's a pretty long drive.'

'Just tell me how to get there.'

But Donald wouldn't give him directions. He said that the farm was too depressing, that Pete wouldn't like it. Instead, he insisted on meeting Pete at a service station called Jonathan's Mechanical Emporium.

'You must be kidding,' Pete said.

'It's close to the highway,' Donald said. 'I didn't name it.'

'That's one for the collection,' Pete said.

The day before he left to bring Donald home, Pete received a letter from a man who described himself as 'head of household' at the farm where Donald had been living. From this letter Pete learned that Donald had not quit the farm, but had been asked to leave. The letter was written on the back of a mimeographed survey form asking people to record their response to a ceremony of some kind. The last question said:

What did you feel during the liturgy?
a) Being
b) Becoming
c) Being and Becoming
d) None of the Above
e) All of the Above

Pete tried to forget the letter. But of course he couldn't. Each time he thought of it he felt crowded and breathless, a feeling that came over him again when he drove into the service station and saw Donald sitting against a wall with his head on his knees. It was late afternoon. A paper cup tumbled slowly past Donald's feet, pushed by the damp wind.

Pete honked and Donald raised his head. He smiled at Pete, then stood and stretched. His arms were long and thin and white. He wore a red bandanna across his forehead, a T-shirt with a couple of words on the front. Pete couldn't read them because the letters were inverted.

'Grow up,' Pete yelled. 'Get a Mercedes.'

Donald came up to the window. He bent down and said, 'Thanks for coming. You must be totally whipped.'

'I'll make it.' Pete pointed at Donald's T-shirt. 'What's that supposed to say?'

Donald looked down at his shirt front. 'Try God. I guess I put it on backwards. Pete, could I borrow a couple of dollars? I owe these people for coffee and sandwiches.'

Pete took five twenties from his wallet and held them out the window.

Donald stepped back as if horrified. 'I don't need that much.'

'I can't keep track of all these nickels and dimes,' Pete said. 'Just pay me back when your ship comes in.' He waved the bills impatiently. 'Go on – take it.'

'Only for now.' Donald took the money and went into the service station office. He came out carrying two orange sodas, one of which he gave to Pete as he got into the car. 'My treat,' he said.

'No bags?'

'Wow, thanks for reminding me.' Donald balanced his drink on the dashboard, but the slight rocking of the car as he got out tipped it onto the passenger's seat, where half its contents foamed over before Pete could snatch it up again. Donald looked on while Pete held the bottle out the window, soda running down his fingers.

'Wipe it up,' Pete told him. 'Quick!'

'With what?'

Pete stared at Donald. 'That shirt. Use the shirt.'

Donald pulled a long face but did as he was told, his pale skin puckering against the wind.

'Great, just great,' Pete said. 'We haven't even left the gas station yet.'

Afterwards, on the highway, Donald said, 'This is a new car, isn't it?'

'Yes. This is a new car.'

'Is that why you're so upset about the seat?'

'Forget it, okay? Let's just forget about it.'

'I said I was sorry.'

Pete said, 'I just wish you'd be more careful. These seats are made of leather. That stain won't come out, not to mention the smell. I don't see why I can't have leather seats that smell like leather instead of orange pop.'

'What was wrong with the other car?'

Pete glanced over at Donald. Donald had raised the hood of the blue sweatshirt he'd put on. The peaked hood above his gaunt, watchful face gave him the look of an inquisitor.

'There wasn't anything wrong with it,' Pete said. 'I just happened to like this one better.'

Donald nodded.

There was a long silence between them as Pete drove on and the day darkened towards evening. On either side of the road lay stubble-covered fields. A line of low hills ran along the horizon, topped here and there with trees black against the grey sky. In the approaching line of cars a driver turned on his headlights. Pete did the same.

'So what happened?' he asked. 'Farm life not your bag?'

Donald took some time to answer, and at last he said, simply, 'I was my fault.'

'What was your fault?'

'The whole thing. Don't play dumb, Pete. I know they wrote to you.' Donald looked at Pete, then stared out the windshield again.

'I'm not playing dumb.'

Donald shrugged.

'All I really know is they asked you to leave,' Pete went on. 'I don't know any of the particulars.'

'I blew it,' Donald said. 'Believe me, you don't want to hear the gory details.'

'Sure I do,' Pete said. He added, 'Everybody likes the gory details.'

'You mean everybody likes to hear how someone else messed up.'

'Right,' Pete said. 'That's the way it is here on Spaceship Earth.'

Donald bent one knee onto the front seat and leaned against the door so that he was facing Pete instead of the windshield. Pete was aware of Donald's scrutiny. He waited. Night was coming on in a rush now, filling the hollows of the land. Donald's long cheeks and deep-set eyes were dark with shadow. His brow was white. 'Do you ever dream about me?' Donald asked.

'Do I ever dream about you? What kind of a question is that? Of course I don't dream about you,' Pete said, untruthfully.

'What do you dream about?'

'Sex and money. Mostly money. A nightmare is when I dream I don't have any.'

'You're just making that up,' Donald said.

Pete smiled.

'Sometimes I wake up at night,' Donald went on, 'and I can tell you're dreaming about me.'

'We were talking about the farm,' Pete said. 'Let's finish that conversation and then we can talk about our various out-of-body experiences and the interesting things we did during previous incarnations.'

For a moment Donald looked like a grinning skull; then he turned serious again. 'There's not that much to tell,' he said. 'I just didn't do anything right.'

'That's a little vague,' Pete said.

'Well, like the groceries. Whenever it was my turn to get the groceries I'd blow it somehow. I'd bring the groceries home and half of them would be missing, or I'd have all the wrong things, the wrong kind of flour or the wrong kind of chocolate or whatever. One time I gave them away. It's not funny, Pete.'

Pete said, 'Who did you give the groceries to?'

'Just some people I picked up on the way home. Some fieldworkers. They had about eight kids with them and they didn't even speak English – just nodded their heads. Still, I shouldn't have given away the groceries. Not all of them, anyway. I really learned my lesson about that. You have to be practical. You have to be fair to yourself.' Donald leaned forward, and Pete could sense his excitement. 'There's nothing actually wrong with being in business,' he said. 'As long as you're fair to other people you can still be fair to yourself. I'm thinking of going into business, Pete.'

'We'll talk about it,' Pete said. 'So, that's the story? There isn't any more to it than that?'

'What did they tell you?' Donald asked.

'Nothing.'

'They must have told you something.'

Pete shook his head.

'They didn't tell you about the fire?' When Pete shook his head again Donald regarded him for a time, then folded his arms across his chest and slumped back into the corner. 'Everybody had to take turns cooking dinner. I usually did tuna casserole or spaghetti with garlic bread. But this one night I thought I'd do something different, something really interesting.' Donald looked sharply at Pete. 'It's all a big laugh to you, isn't it?'

'I'm sorry,' Pete said.

'You don't know when to quit. You just keep hitting away.'

'Tell me about the fire, Donald.'

Donald kept watching him. 'You have this compulsion to make me look foolish.'

'Come off it, Donald. Don't make a big thing out of this.'

'I know why you do it. It's because you don't have any purpos in life. You're afraid to relate to people who do, so you make fu of them.'

'Relate,' Pete said softly.

'You're basically a very frightened individual,' Donald said. 'Ver threatened. You've always been like that. Do you remember whe you used to try to kill me?'

'I don't have any compulsion to make you look foolish, Donald – you do it yourself. You're doing it right now.'

'You can't tell me you don't remember,' Donald said. 'It was afte my operation. You remember that.'

'Sort of.' Pete shrugged. 'Not really.'

'Oh yes,' Donald said. 'Do you want to see the scar?'

'I remember you had an operation. I don't remember the specifics that's all. And I sure as hell don't remember trying to kill you.'

'Oh yes,' Donald repeated, maddeningly. 'You bet your life yo did. All the time. The thing was, I couldn't have anything happe to me where they sewed me up because then my intestines woul come apart again and poison me. That was a big issue, Pete. Mon was always in a state about me climbing trees and so on. And yo used to hit me there every chance you got.'

'Mom was in a state every time you burped,' Pete said. 'I don' know. Maybe I bumped into you accidentally once or twice. I neve did it deliberately.'

'Every chance you got,' Donald said. 'Like when the folks went ou at night and left you to babysit. I'd hear them say good night, and the I'd hear the car start up, and when they were gone I'd lie there and listen After a while I would hear you coming down the hall, and I would clos my eyes and pretend to be asleep. There were nights when you woul stand outside the door, just stand there, and then go away again. Bu most nights you'd open the door and I would hear you in the roon with me, breathing. You'd come over and sit next to me on the be – you remember, Pete, you have to – you'd sit next to me on the be and pull the sheets back. If I was on my stomach you'd roll me over

Then you would lift up my pyjama shirt and start hitting me on my stitches. You'd hit me as hard as you could, over and over. I was afraid that you'd get mad if you knew I was awake. Is that strange or what? I was afraid that you'd get mad if you found out that I knew you were trying to kill me.' Donald laughed. 'Come on, you can't tell me you don't remember that.'

'It might have happened once or twice. Kids do those things. I can't get all excited about something I maybe did twenty-five years ago.'

'No maybe about it. You did it.'

Pete said, 'You're wearing me out with this stuff. We've got a long drive ahead of us and if you don't back off pretty soon we aren't going to make it. You aren't, anyway.'

Donald turned away.

'I'm doing my best,' Pete said. The self-pity in his own voice made the words sound like a lie. But they weren't a lie! He was doing his best.

The car topped a rise. In the distance Pete saw a cluster of lights that blinked out when he started downhill. There was no moon. The sky was low and black.

'Come to think of it,' Pete said, 'I did have a dream about you the other night.' Then he added, impatiently, as if Donald were badgering him, 'A couple of other nights too. I'm getting hungry,' he said.

'The same dream?'

'Different dreams. I only remember one of them well. There was something wrong with me, and you were helping out. Taking care of me. Just the two of us. I don't know where everyone else was supposed to be.'

Pete left it at that. He didn't tell Donald that in this dream he was blind.

'I wonder if that was when I woke up,' Donald said. He added, 'I'm sorry I got into that thing about my scar. I keep trying to forget it but I guess I never will. Not really. It was pretty strange, having someone around all the time who wanted to get rid of me.'

'Kid stuff,' Pete said. 'Ancient history.'

They ate dinner at a Denny's on the other side of King City. As

Pete was paying the check he heard a man behind him say, 'Excuse me, but I wonder if I might ask which way you're going?' and Donald answer, 'Santa Cruz.'

'Perfect,' the man said.

Pete could see him in the fish-eye mirror above the cash register: a red blazer with some kind of crest on the pocket, little black moustache, glossy black hair combed down on his forehead like a Roman emperor's. A rug, Pete thought. Definitely a rug.

Pete got his change and turned. 'Why is that perfect?' he asked.

The man looked at Pete. He had a soft ruddy face that was doing its best to express pleasant surprise, as if this new wrinkle were all he could have wished for, but the eyes behind the aviator glasses showed signs of regret. His lips were moist and shiny. 'I take it you're together,' he said.

'You got it,' Pete told him.

'All the better, then,' the man went on. 'It so happens I'm going to Santa Cruz myself. Had a spot of car trouble down the road. The old Caddy let me down.'

'What kind of trouble?' Pete asked.

'Engine trouble,' the man said. 'I'm afraid it's a bit urgent. My daughter is sick. Urgently sick. I've got a telegram here.' He patted the breast pocket of his blazer.

Pete grinned. Amazing, he thought, the old sick daughter ploy, but before he could say anything Donald got into the act again. 'No problem,' Donald said. 'We've got tons of room.'

'Not that much room,' Pete said.

Donald nodded. 'I'll put my things in the trunk.'

'The trunk's full,' Pete told him.

'It so happens I'm travelling light,' the man said. 'This leg of the trip anyway. In fact I don't have any luggage at this particular time.'

Pete said, 'Left it in the old Caddy, did you?'

'Exactly,' the man said.

'No problem,' Donald repeated. He walked outside and the man went with him. Together they strolled across the parking lot, Pete following at a distance. When they reached Pete's car Donald raised his face to the sky, and the man did the same. They stood there looking up. 'Dark night,' Donald said.

'Stygian,' the man said.

Pete still had it in mind to brush him off, but he didn't do that. Instead he unlocked the door for him. He wanted to see what would happen. It was an adventure, but not a dangerous adventure. The man might steal Pete's ashtrays but he wouldn't kill him. If Pete got killed on the road it would be by some spiritual person in a sweatsuit, someone with his eyes on the far horizon and a wet Try God T-shirt in his duffel bag.

As soon as they left the parking lot the man lit a cigar. He blew a cloud of smoke over Pete's shoulder and sighed with pleasure. 'Put it out,' Pete told him.

'Of course,' the man said. Pete looked into the rearview mirror and saw the man take another long puff before dropping the cigar out the window. 'Forgive me,' he said. 'I should have asked. Name's Webster, by the way.'

Donald turned and looked back at him. 'First name or last?'

The man hesitated. 'Last,' he said finally.

'I know a Webster,' Donald said. 'Mick Webster.'

'There are many of us,' Webster said.

'Big fellow, wooden leg,' Pete said.

Donald gave Pete a look.

Webster shook his head. 'Doesn't ring a bell. Still, I wouldn't deny the connection. Might be one of the cousinry.'

'What's your daughter got?' Pete asked.

'That isn't clear,' Webster answered. 'It appears to be a female complaint of some nature. Then again it may be tropical.' He was quiet for a moment, and added: 'If indeed it *is* tropical, I will have to assume some of the blame myself. It was my own vaulting ambition that first led us to the tropics and kept us in the tropics all those many years, exposed to every evil. Truly I have much to answer for. I left my wife there.'

Donald said quietly, 'You mean she died?'

'I buried her with these hands. The earth will be repaid, gold for gold.'

'Which tropics?' Pete asked.

'The tropics of Peru.'

'What part of Peru are they in?'

'The lowlands,' Webster said.

Pete nodded. 'What's it like down there?'

'Another world,' Webster said. His tone was sepulchral. 'A world better imagined than described.'

'Far out,' Pete said.

The three men rode in silence for a time. A line of trucks went past in the other direction, trailers festooned with running lights, engines roaring.

'Yes,' Webster said at last, 'I have much to answer for.'

Pete smiled at Donald, but Donald had turned in his seat again and was gazing at Webster. 'I'm sorry about your wife,' Donald said.

'What did she die of?' Pete asked.

'A wasting illness,' Webster said. 'The doctors have no name for it, but I do.' He leaned forward and said, fiercely, '*Greed*. My greed, not hers. She wanted no part of it.'

Pete bit his lip. Webster was a find and Pete didn't want to scare him off by hooting at him. In a voice low and innocent of knowingness, he asked, 'What took you there?'

'It's difficult for me to talk about.'

'Try,' Pete told him.

'A cigar would make it easier.'

Donald turned to Pete and said, 'It's okay with me.'

'All right,' Pete said. 'Go ahead. Just keep the window rolled down.'

'Much obliged.' A match flared. There were eager sucking sounds.

'Let's hear it,' Pete said.

'I am by training an engineer,' Webster began. 'My work has exposed me to all but one of the continents, to desert and alp and forest, to every terrain and season of the earth. Some years ago I was hired by the Peruvian government to search for tungsten in the tropics. My wife and daughter accompanied me. We were the only white people for a thousand miles in any direction, and we had no choice but to live as the Indians lived – to share their food and drink and even their culture.'

Pete said, 'You knew the lingo, did you?'

'We picked it up.' The ember of the cigar bobbed up and down. 'We were used to learning as necessity decreed. At any rate, it became evident after a couple of years that there was no tungsten to be found. My wife had fallen ill and was pleading to be taken home. But I was deaf to her pleas, because by then I was on the trail of another metal – a metal far more valuable than tungsten.'

'Let me guess,' Pete said. 'Gold?'

Donald looked at Pete, then back at Webster.

'Gold,' Webster said. 'A vein of gold greater than the Mother Lode itself. After I found the first traces of it nothing could tear me away from my search – not the sickness of my wife nor anything else. I was determined to uncover the vein, and so I did – but not before I laid my wife to rest. As I say, the earth will be repaid.'

Webster was quiet. Then he said, 'But life must go on. In the years since my wife's death I have been making the arrangements necessary to open the mine. I could have done it immediately, of course, enriching myself beyond measure, but I knew what that would mean – the exploitation of our beloved Indians, the brutal destruction of their environment. I felt I had too much to atone for already.' Webster paused, and when he spoke again his voice was dull and rushed, as if he had used up all the interest he had in his own words. 'Instead I drew up a programme for returning the bulk of the wealth to the Indians themselves. A kind of trust fund. The interest alone will allow them to secure their ancient lands and rights in perpetuity. At the same time, our investors will be rewarded a thousandfold. Two-thousandfold. Everyone will prosper together.'

'That's great,' Donald said. 'That's the way it ought to be.'

Pete said, 'I'm willing to bet that you just happen to have a few shares left. Am I right?'

Webster made no reply.

'Well?' Pete knew that Webster was on to him now, but he didn't care. The story had bored him. He'd expected something different, something original, and Webster had let him down. He hadn't even tried. Pete felt sour and stale. His eyes burned from cigar smoke and the high beams of road-hogging truckers. 'Douse the stogie,' he said to Webster. 'I told you to keep the window down.'

'Got a little nippy back here.'

Donald said, 'Hey, Pete. Lighten up.'

'Douse it!'

Webster sighed. He got rid of the cigar.

'I'm a wreck,' Pete said to Donald. 'You want to drive for a while?'

Donald nodded.

Pete pulled over and they changed places.

Webster kept his counsel in the back seat. Donald hummed while he drove, until Pete told him to stop. Then everything was quiet.

Donald was humming again when Pete woke up. Pete stared sullenly at the road, at the white lines sliding past the car. After a few moments of this he turned and said, 'How long have I been out?'

Donald glanced at him. 'Twenty, twenty-five minutes.'

Pete looked behind him and saw that Webster was gone. 'Where's our friend?'

'You just missed him. He got out in Soledad. He told me to say thanks and good-bye.'

'Soledad? What about his sick daughter? How did he explain her away?'

'He has a brother living there. He's going to borrow a car from him and drive the rest of the way in the morning.'

'I'll bet his brother's living there,' Pete said. 'Doing fifty concurrent life sentences. His brother and his sister and his mom and his dad.'

'I kind of liked him,' Donald said.

'I'm sure you did,' Pete said wearily.

'He was interesting. He'd been places.'

'His cigars had been places, I'll give you that.'

'Come on, Pete.'

'Come on yourself. What a phony.'

'You don't know that.'

'Sure I do.'

'How? How do you know?'

Pete stretched. 'Brother, there are some things you're just born knowing. What's the gas situation?'

'We're a little low.'

'Then why didn't you get some more?'

'I wish you wouldn't snap at me like that,' Donald said.

'Then why don't you use your head? What if we run out?'

'We'll make it,' Donald said. 'I'm pretty sure we've got enough to make it. You didn't have to be so rude to him,' Donald added.

Pete took a deep breath. 'I don't feel like running out of gas tonight, okay?'

Donald pulled in at the next station they came to and filled the tank while Pete went to the men's room. When Pete came back, Donald was sitting in the passenger's seat. The attendant came up to the driver's window as Pete got in behind the wheel. He bent down and said, 'Twelve fifty-five.'

'You heard the man,' Pete said to Donald.

Donald looked straight ahead. He didn't move.

'Cough up,' Pete said. 'This trip's on you.'

'I can't.'

'Sure you can. Break out that wad.'

Donald glanced up at the attendant, then at Pete. 'Please,' he said. 'Pete, I don't have it anymore.'

Pete took this in. He nodded, and paid the attendant.

Donald began to speak when they left the station but Pete cut him off. He said, 'I don't want to hear from you right now. You just keep quiet or I swear to God I won't be responsible.'

They left the fields and entered a tunnel of tall trees. The trees went on and on. 'Let me get this straight,' Pete said at last. 'You don't have the money I gave you.'

'You treated him like a bug or something,' Donald said.

'You don't have the money,' Pete said again.

Donald shook his head.

'Since I bought dinner, and since we didn't stop anywhere in between, I assume you gave it to Webster. Is that right? Is that what you did with it?'

'Yes.'

Pete looked at Donald. His face was dark under the hood but he still managed to convey a sense of remove, as if none of this had anything to do with him.

'Why?' Pete asked. 'Why did you give it to him?' When Donald didn't answer, Pete said, 'A hundred dollars. Gone. Just like that. I *worked* for that money, Donald.'

'I know, I know,' Donald said.

'You don't know! How could you? You get money by holding out your hand.'

'I work too,' Donald said.

'You work too. Don't kid yourself, brother.'

Donald leaned towards Pete, about to say something, but Pete cut him off again.

'You're not the only one on the payroll, Donald. I don't think you understand that. I have a family.'

'Pete, I'll pay you back.'

'Like hell you will. A hundred dollars!' Pete hit the steering wheel with the palm of his hand. 'Just because you think I hurt some goofball's feelings. Jesus, Donald.'

'That's not the reason,' Donald said. 'And I didn't just *give* him the money.'

'What do you call it, then? What do you call what you did?'

'I *invested* it. I wanted a share, Pete.' When Pete looked over at him Donald nodded and said again, 'I wanted a share.'

Pete said, 'I take it you're referring to the gold mine in Peru.'

'Yes,' Donald said.

'You believe that such a gold mine exists?'

Donald looked at Pete, and Pete could see him just beginning to catch on. 'You'll believe anything,' Pete said. 'Won't you? You really will believe anything at all.'

'I'm sorry,' Donald said, and turned away.

Pete drove on between the trees and considered the truth of what he had just said – that Donald would believe anything at all. And it came to him that it would be just like this unfair life for Donald to come out ahead in the end, by believing in some outrageous promise that would turn out to be true and that he, Pete, would reject out of hand because he was too wised up to listen to anybody's pitch anymore except for laughs. What a joke. What a joke if there really was a blessing to be had, and the blessing didn't come to the one who deserved it, the one who did all the work, but to the other.

And as if this had already happened Pete felt a shadow move upon him, darkening his thoughts. After a time he said, 'I can see where all this is going, Donald.'

'I'll pay you back,' Donald said.

'No,' Pete said. 'You won't pay me back. You can't. You don't know how. All you've ever done is take. All your life.'

Donald shook his head.

'I see exactly where this is going,' Pete went on. 'You can't work, you can't take care of yourself, you believe anything anyone tells you. I'm stuck with you, aren't I?' He looked over at Donald. 'I've got you on my hands for good.'

Donald pressed his fingers against the dashboard as if to brace himself. 'I'll get out,' he said.

Pete kept driving.

'Let me out,' Donald said. 'I mean it, Pete.'

'Do you?'

Donald hesitated. 'Yes,' he said.

'Be sure,' Pete told him. 'This is it. This is for keeps.'

'I mean it.'

'All right. You made the choice.' Pete braked the car sharply and swung it to the shoulder of the road. He turned off the engine and got out. Trees loomed on both sides, shutting out the sky. The air was cold and musty. Pete took Donald's duffel bag from the back seat and set it down behind the car. He stood there, facing Donald in the red glow of the taillights. 'It's better this way,' Pete said.

Donald just looked at him.

'Better for you,' Pete said.

Donald hugged himself. He was shaking. 'You don't have to say all that,' he told Pete. 'I don't blame you.'

'Blame me? What the hell are you talking about? Blame me for what?'

'For anything,' Donald said.

'I want to know what you mean by blame me.'

'Nothing. Nothing, Pete. You'd better get going. God bless you.'

'That's it,' Pete said. He dropped to one knee, searching the packed dirt with his hands. He didn't know what he was looking for, his hands would know when they found it.

Donald touched Pete's shoulder. 'You'd better go,' he said.

Somewhere in the trees Pete heard a branch snap. He stood up. He looked at Donald, then went back to the car and drove away. He drove fast, hunched over the wheel, conscious of the way he was hunched and the shallowness of his breathing, refusing to look at the mirror above his head until there was nothing behind him but darkness.

Then he said, 'A hundred dollars', as if there were someone to hear.

The trees gave way to fields. Metal fences ran beside the road, plastered with windblown scraps of paper. Tule fog hung above the ditches, spilling into the road, dimming the ghostly halogen lights that burned in the yards of the farms Pete passed. The fog left beads of water rolling up the windshield.

Pete rummaged among his cassettes. He found Pachelbel's Canon and pushed it into the tape deck. When the violins began to play he leaned back and assumed an attentive expression as if he were really listening to them. He smiled to himself like a man at liberty to enjoy music, a man who has finished his work and settled his debts, done all things meet and due.

And in this way, smiling, nodding to the music, he went another mile or so and pretended that he was not already slowing down, that he was not going to turn back, that he would be able to drive on like this, alone, and have the right answer when his wife stood before him in the doorway of his home and asked, Where is he? Where is your brother?

The Barracks Thief

1

When his boys were young, Guy Bishop formed the habit of stopping in their room each night on his way to bed. He would look down at them where they slept, and then he would sit in the rocking chair and listen to them breathe. He was a man who had always gone from one thing to another, place to place, job to job, and, even since his marriage, woman to woman. But when he sat in the dark between his two sleeping sons he felt no wish to move.

Sometimes, because it seemed unnatural, this peace he felt gave him fears. The worst fear he had was that by loving his children so much he was somehow endangering them, putting them in harm's way. At times he knew for a certainty that some evil was about to overtake them. As the boys grew older he had this fear less often, but it still came upon him from time to time. Then he tried to imagine what form the evil might take, from which direction it might come. When he had these thoughts Guy Bishop would close his eyes, give his head a little shake, and turn his mind to some more pleasant subject.

He was seeing a woman off and on. They had good times together and that was all either of them wanted, at least in the beginning. Then they began to feel miserable when they were away from each other. They agreed to break it off, but couldn't. There were nights when Guy

Bishop woke up weeping. At one point he considered killing himself, but the woman made him promise not to. When he couldn't hold out any longer he left his family and went to live with her.

This was in October. Keith, the younger of the boys, had just begun his freshman year in high school. Philip was a junior. Guy Bishop thought that they were old enough to accept this change and even to grow stronger from it, more realistic and adaptable. Most of the worry he felt was for his wife. He knew that the break-up of their marriage was going to cause her terrible suffering, and he did what he could to arrange things so that, except for his leaving, her life would not be disrupted. He signed the house over to her and each month he sent her most of his salary, holding back only what he needed to live on.

Philip did learn to get along without his father, mainly by despising him. His mother held up, too, better than Guy Bishop had expected. She caved in every couple of weeks or so, but most of the time she was cheerful in a determined way. Only Keith lost heart. He could not stop grieving. He cried easily, sometimes for no apparent reason. The two boys had been close; now, even in the act of comforting Keith, Philip looked at him from a distance. There was only a year and a half between them but it began to seem like five or six. One night, coming in from a party, he shook Keith awake with the idea of having a good talk, but after Keith woke up Philip went on shaking him and didn't say a word. One of the cats had been sleeping with Keith. She arched her back, stared wide-eyed at Philip, and jumped to the floor.

'You've got to do your part,' Philip said.

Keith just looked at him.

'Damn you,' Philip said. He pushed Keith back against the pillow. 'Cry,' he said. 'Go ahead, cry.' He really did hope that Keith would cry, because he wanted to hold him. But Keith shook his head. He turned his face to the wall. After that Keith kept his feelings to himself.

In February Guy Bishop lost his job at Boeing. He told everyone that the company was laying people off, but the opposite was true. This was 1965. President Johnson had turned the bombers loose on North

Vietnam and Boeing had orders for more planes than they could build. They were bringing people in from all over, men from Lockheed and Convair, boys fresh out of college. It seemed that anyone could work at Boeing but Guy Bishop. Philip's mother called the wives of men who might know what the trouble was, but either they hadn't heard or they weren't saying.

Guy Bishop found another job but he didn't stay with it, and just before school let out, Philip's mother put the house up for sale. She gave away all but one of her five cats and took a job as cashier in a movie theatre downtown. It was the same work she'd been doing when Guy Bishop met her in 1945. The house sold within a month. A retired Coast Guard captain bought it. He drove by the house nearly every day with his wife and sometimes they parked in front with the engine running.

Philip's mother took an apartment in West Seattle. Philip worked as a camp counsellor that summer, and while he was away she and Keith moved again, to Ballard. In the fall both boys enrolled at Ballard High. It was a big school, much bigger than the one where they'd gone before, and it was hard to meet people. Philip kept in touch with his old friends, but now that they weren't in school together they found little to talk about. When he went to parties with them he usually ended up sitting by himself in the living room, watching television or talking to some kid's parents while everyone else slow-danced in the rec room downstairs.

After one of these parties Philip and the boy who'd brought him sat in the boy's car and passed a paper cup full of vodka back and forth and talked about things they used to do. At some point in their conversation Philip realized that they weren't friends anymore. He felt restless and got out of the car. He stood there, looking at the darkened house across the street. He wanted to do something. He wished he was drunk.

'I've got to go,' the other boy said. 'My dad wants me in early tonight.'

'Just a minute,' Philip said. He picked up a rock, hefted it, then threw it at the house. A window broke. 'One down,' Philip said. He picked up another rock.

'Jesus,' the other boy said. 'What are you doing?

'Breaking windows,' Philip said. At that moment a light came on upstairs. He threw the rock and hit the side of the house. 'I'm getting out of here,' the other boy said. He started the car and Philip got back inside. He began to laugh as they drove away, though he knew there was nothing funny about what he'd done. The other boy stared straight ahead and said nothing. Philip could see that he was disgusted. 'Wait a minute,' Philip said, grabbing the sleeve of the Nehru jacket the other boy had on. 'I don't believe it. Where did you get the Nehru jacket?' When the other boy didn't answer Philip said, 'Don't tell me – it's your dad's. That's why your dad wants you home early. He likes to know where his Nehru jacket is.'

When they got to Philip's apartment building they sat for a moment without talking. Finally Philip said, 'I'm sorry,' and put out his hand. But the other boy looked away.

Philip got out of the car. 'I'll give you a call,' he said, and when he got no response he added: 'I was just kidding about the Nehru jacket. It must have looked really great about twenty years ago.'

Philip had always wanted to go to Reed College, but by the time he finished high school that year his grades were so bad he was lucky to graduate at all. Reed sent him a form rejection letter and so did the University of Washington, his second choice. He went to work as a busboy in a motel restaurant and tried to stay out of the apartment. Keith was always there, playing records or just lying around, his sadness plain to see though he had begun to affect a breezy manner. Philip suspected that he was stoned a lot of the time, but he didn't know what to do about it, or if he should do anything at all. Though he felt sorry for Keith, Philip was beginning to dislike him. He wanted to avoid anything that might cause trouble between them and add to the dislike he felt. Besides, he had a smoke now and then himself. It made him feel interesting – witty, sensitive, perceptive.

Sometimes the owner of the theatre where she worked gave Philip's mother a ride home. One night, coming home late himself, he saw them kissing in the owner's car. Philip turned around and went back up the street. The next day he refused to speak to her, and refused to tell her why, though he knew he was being theatrical and unfair. Finally it drove her to tears. As he sat reading, Philip heard her cry out in the kitchen. He jumped up, thinking she must have burned herself. He found her leaning on the sink, her face in her hands. What had happened to them? Where were they? Where was her home, her cats, her garden? Where was the regard of her neighbours, the love of her family? Everything was gone.

Philip did his best to calm her. It wasn't easy, but after a time she agreed to go for a walk with him, and managed to collect herself. Philip knew he had been in the wrong. He told his mother that he was sorry, and that his moodiness had had nothing to do with her – he was just a little on edge. She squeezed his arm. This won't go on forever, Philip thought. In silence, they continued to walk the circular path round the small park. It was August and still warm, but the benches were empty. Now and then a pigeon landed with a rush of wings, looked around, and flew away again.

Their parish priest from the old neighbourhood had friends among the local Jesuits. He succeeded in getting Philip a probationary acceptance to Seattle University. It was a good school, but Philip wanted to get away from home. In September he moved to Bremerton and enrolled at the junior college there. During the day he tried to keep awake in his classes and at night he worked at the Navy Yard, doing inventory in warehouses and dodging forklifts driven by incompetents.

Philip didn't get to know many people in Bremerton, but sometimes when he got off work at midnight he went drinking with a few of the Marine guards. Bremerton was a soft berth for them after a year in Vietnam. They'd been in the fighting, and some of them had been wounded. They were all a little crazy. Philip didn't understand their jokes, and if he laughed anyway they gave him mean looks. They talked about 'asshole civilians' as if he weren't there.

The Marines tolerated Philip because he had a car, an old Pontiac he'd bought for fifty dollars at a police auction. He ferried them to different bars and sometimes to parties, then back to the Yard through misty wet streets, trying to keep his eyes open while they laughed and yelled out the window and threw beer on each other. If one of them got into a fight all the others piled in immediately, no questions asked. Philip was often amazed at their brutishness, but there were times, after he'd let them off and watched them go through the gate together, when he envied them.

At Christmas Philip's mother asked him to talk to Keith. Keith was doing badly in school, and just before vacation one of his teachers had caught him smoking a joint in a broom closet. He'd been alone, which seemed grotesque to Philip. When he thought of Keith standing in the dark surrounded by brooms and cleanser and rolls of toilet paper, puffing away all by himself, he felt sick. Only by going down to the school and pleading with the principal, 'grovelling' as she put it, had Philip's mother been able to dissuade him from reporting Keith to the police. As it was, he'd been suspended for two weeks.

'I'll talk to him,' Philip said, 'but it won't do any good.'

'It might,' she said. 'He looks up to you. Remember the way he used to follow you around?'

They were sitting in the living room. Philip's mother was smoking and had her feet on the coffee table. Her toenails were painted red. She caught Philip staring at them and looked down at her drink.

Philip got up and walked over to the window. 'I'm going to enlist,' he said. This was an idea he'd had for some time now, but hearing himself put it into words surprised him and gave him a faint sensation of fear.

His mother sat forward. 'Enlist? Why would you want to enlist?'

'In case you haven't heard,' Philip said, 'there's a war on.' That sounded false to him and he could see it sounded false to his mother as well. 'It's just something I want to do,' he said. He shrugged.

His mother put her glass down. 'When?'

'Pretty soon.'

'Give me a year,' she said. She stood and came over to Philip. 'Give me six months, anyway. Try to understand. This thing with Keith has got me coming and going.'

'Keith,' Philip said. He shook his head. Finally he agreed to wait the six months.

They spent Christmas Day in the apartment. Philip gave Keith a puzzle that he worked on all afternoon and never came close to solving, though it looked simple enough to Philip. They had dinner in a restaurant and after they got back Keith went at the puzzle again, still with no success. Philip wanted to help, but whenever he offered a suggestion Keith went on as if he hadn't heard. Philip watched him, impatiently at first, then thoughtfully; he wondered what it was in Keith that found satisfaction in losing. If he went on the way he was, losing would become a habit, and he would never be able to pull his weight.

They had their talk but it went badly, as Philip knew it would. Though he tried to be gentle, he ended up calling Keith a coward. Keith laughed and made sarcastic remarks about Philip going into the service. He had suddenly decided that he was against the war. Philip pointed out that it had taken Keith seven tries to pass his driver's licence examination, and said that anyone who had that much trouble driving a car, or solving a simple puzzle, had no right to an opinion on any subject.

'That's it,' Philip told his mother afterwards. 'Never again.'

A few nights later Philip came back from a movie and found his mother in tears and Keith trying to soothe her, though it was obvious that he was close to the breaking point himself. Oh, hell, Philip thought, but it wasn't what he had assumed. They weren't just feeling sorry for themselves. Philip's father had come by and when they refused to open the door for him he had tried to break in. He'd made a scene, yelling at them and ramming the door with his shoulder.

Philip left Keith with his mother and drove out to his father's place in Bellevue, an efficiency apartment near the lake. Guy Bishop had moved to Bellevue a few months earlier when the woman he'd been living with went to Sarasota to visit her family, and decided to stay there.

He still had his windbreaker on when he opened the door. 'Philip,' he said. 'Come in.' Philip shook his head. 'Please, son,' his father said, 'come in.'

They sat at a counter that divided the kitchen from the rest of the room. There were several pairs of gleaming shoes lined up along the wall, and the air smelled of shoe polish. On the coffee table there was a family portrait taken at Mount Rushmore in 1963. Keith and Philip were in the middle, grinning because the photographer, a Canadian, had just said 'aboot' for 'about'. The four presidents, eyes blank, seemed to be looking down at them. Next to the picture a stack of magazines had been arranged in a fan, so that a strip of each cover was visible.

Philip told his father to stay away from the apartment. That was where the family lived, Philip said, and Guy Bishop wasn't part of the family.

Suddenly his father reached out and put his hand on Philip's cheek. Philip stared down at the counter. A moment later his father took his hand away. Of course, he said. He would call first thing in the morning and apologize.

'Forget the apology,' Philip said. 'Just leave her alone, period.'

'It's not that simple,' his father said. 'She called me first.'

'What do you mean, she called you first?'

'She asked me to come over,' he said. 'When I got there she wouldn't let me in. Which is no excuse for acting the way I did.' He folded his hands and looked down at them.

'I don't believe you,' Philip said.

His father shrugged. A moment later he looked over at Philip and smiled. 'I've got something for you. It was meant to be a graduation present, but I didn't have a chance to give it to you then.' He went over to the closet and pulled out a suitcase. 'Come on,' he said.

Philip followed him out of the room and down the steps into the parking lot. It had rained. The pavement shone under the lights, and the cars gleamed. Philip's father bent down and unzipped the suitcase. It was full of what looked like silver pipes. He lifted them out all at once, and Philip saw that they were connected. His father arranged them, tightening wingnuts here and there, until finally a frame took shape with prongs at each end. He got two wheels from the suitcase and fastened them between the prongs. Then he bolted a leather seat to the top of the frame. It was a bicycle, a folding bicycle. He put down the kickstand and stepped back.

'*Voilà*,' he said.

They looked at it.

'It works,' he said. He put up the kickstand and straddled it, searching with his feet for the pedals. He pushed himself around the parking lot, bumping into cars, wobbling badly. With its little wheels and elevated seat the bicycle looked like the kind bears ride in circuses. The chrome frame glittered. The spokes caught the light as they went around and around.

'You'll never be without transportation,' Philip's father said. 'You can keep it in the trunk of your car. Then, if something breaks down or you run out of gas, you won't be forced to hitchhike.' He almost fell taking a turn but managed to right himself. 'Or say you go to Europe. What better way,' he said, and then the bicycle caught the fender of a car and he pitched over the handlebars. He fell heavily. The bicycle came down with him and he lay there, all tangled up in it.

'My God,' he said. 'Give me a hand, son.' When Philip didn't come to him he said, 'I can't move. Give me a hand.'

Philip turned and walked towards his car.

The next morning Philip got up early and took a bus downtown. The Marine recruiting office was closed. He wandered around, and when it still hadn't opened two hours later he walked up the street and enlisted in the Army. That night, when he knew his mother would be at work, he called home from Fort Lewis. At first Keith thought he was joking. Then the idea took hold. 'You're really in the Army,' he said. 'What a trip. Jesus. Well, good luck. I mean that.'

Philip could tell he was serious. It touched him, and he did something he came to regret. He gave Keith his car.

2

Five months later Keith disappeared. I was in jump school at Fort Benning when it happened, at the tail end of a training course that proved harder than anything I had ever done.

When I got the message to call home we had just come back from our third of five parachute jumps. We'd been dropped after a heavy rain and landed in mud to our ankles, struggling against a wind that pulled us down and dragged us through a mess of other men, scrub pine, tangled silk and rope. I was still spitting out mud when we got back to camp.

My mother told me that Keith had been gone for three days. He had left no message, not even a goodbye. The police had a description of the car and they'd talked to his friends, but so far they seemed no closer to finding him. We agreed that he had probably gone to San Francisco.

'No doubt about it,' I said. 'That's where all the losers are going now.'

'Don't take that tone,' she said. 'It breaks my heart to hear you talk like that. Is that what you're learning in the Army?'

It had started to rain again. I was using an unsheltered pay phone near the orderly room, and the rain began to melt the caked mud on my uniform. Brown streams of it ran off my boots. 'What do you want me to do?' I asked.

'I want you to go to San Francisco and look for Keith.'

I couldn't help laughing. 'Now how am I supposed to do that? This is Georgia, remember?'

'I've talked to a man at the Red Cross,' she said. 'You could get an emergency leave. They'll even lend you money.'

'That's ridiculous,' I said, though I realized what she was saying was true. I could go on leave. But I didn't want to. It would mean missing the last two jumps, dropping out of the course. If I came back I would have to start all over again. I doubted I had the courage to do that; jump school was no day at the beach and I'd only made it this far out of ignorance of what lay ahead. I wanted those wings. I wanted them more than anything.

And if I did go, where would I look? Who would help me in San Francisco, me with my head shaved to the bone in a city full of freaks?

'You have to,' she said. 'He's your brother.'

'I'm sorry,' I told her. 'It's just not possible.'

'But he's so young. What is happening to us? Will somebody please tell me what is happening to us?'

I said that the police would find Keith, that he'd be glad to get home, that a taste of the real world would give him a new angle on things. I didn't believe what I was saying, but it calmed her down. Finally she let me go.

On our last jump, a night jump in full field equipment, a man was killed. His main chute didn't open. I heard him yell going down but it only lasted a moment and I paid no attention. Some clown was always yelling. It ended and there was no sound save the rhythmic creaking of my shoulder straps. I felt the air move past my face. The full moon lit up the silk above me, above the hundred other men falling in silence overhead and below and all around me. It seemed that every one of us fell under his own moon. Then a tree stabbed up to my right and I braced and hit the ground rolling.

The dead man was carried to the side of the road and left there for the ambulance. They didn't bother to cover him up. They wanted us to take a good look, and remember him, because he had screwed up. He had forgotten to pull his reserve parachute. As our truck went past him a sergeant said, 'There's just two kinds of men in this business – the quick and the dead.'

The fellow across from me laughed. So did several others. I didn't laugh, but I felt the impulse. The man lying by the road had been alive an hour ago, and now he was dead. Why did that make me want to smile? It seemed wrong. Someone was passing around a number. I took a hit and gave it to the man next to me. 'All right!' he said. 'Airborne!'

Two black guys started a jump song. I leaned back and looked up at the stars and after a while I joined in the song the others were singing.

3

After jump school I was sent to the 82nd Airborne Division at Fort Bragg. Most of the men in my company had served together in Vietnam. Like the Marines I'd known in Bremerton, they had no use for outsiders. I was an outsider to them. So were the other new men, Lewis and Hubbard. The three of us didn't exist for the rest of the company. For days at a time nobody spoke to me except to give me orders. Because we were the newest and lowest in rank we got picked to pull guard duty on the Fourth of July while everyone else scattered to Myrtle Beach and the air-conditioned bars in Fayetteville.

That's where I'd wanted to spend the Fourth, in a bar. There was one place in particular I liked. Smitty's. They had a go-go dancer at Smitty's who chewed gum while she danced. Prostitutes, Fayettecong we called them, gathered in the booths with pitchers of beer between them. Car salesmen from the lots down the street sat around figuring out ways to unload monster Bonnevilles on buck privates who made seventy-eight dollars a month before taxes. The bartender knew my name.

The last way I wanted to spend my Fourth was pulling guard with Lewis and Hubbard. We had arrived on the same day and avoided each other ever since. I could see that they were as lonely as I was, but we kept our distance; if we banded together we would always be new.

So when I saw the duty roster and found myself lumped together with them it made me bitter. Lewis and Hubbard were bitter, too. I could feel it in the way they looked at me when I joined them outside the orderly room. They didn't greet me, and while we waited for the duty officer they stared off in different directions. It was late afternoon but still steaming. The straight lines of the camp – files of barracks, flagpoles, even the white-washed rocks arranged in rows – wavered in the heat. Locusts sawed away in frantic bursts.

Lewis, gaunt and red-faced, began to whistle. Then he stopped. Our uniforms darkened with sweat. The oil on our rifles stank. Our faces glistened. The silence between us grew intense and I was glad when the first sergeant came up and began to shout at us.

He told us that we were little girls, piglets, warts. We were toads. We didn't belong in his army. He lined us up and inspected us. He said that we should be court-martialled for our ugliness and stupidity. Then he drove us to an ammunition dump in the middle of a pine forest thirty miles from the post and made us stand with our rifles over our heads while he gave us our orders and filled our clips with live rounds. We were to patrol the perimeter of the ammunition dump until he relieved us. He didn't say when that would be. If anyone so much as touched the fence we should shoot to kill. *Shoot to kill*, he repeated. No yakking. No grabass. If we screwed up he would personally bring grief upon us. 'I know everything,' he said, and he ordered us to run around the compound with our rifles still over our heads. When we got back he was gone, along with the three men whose places we had taken.

Lewis had the first shift. Hubbard and I sat in the shade of an old warehouse weathered down to bare grey boards with patches of green paint curling off. It had no windows. On the loading ramp where we sat two sliding doors were padlocked together and plastered with prohibitions, No Smoking and so on, with a few strange ones thrown in, like No Hobnailed Boots.

There were five other buildings, all in bad repair. Weeds grew between the buildings and alongside the chain-link fence. In places the weeds were waist-high. I don't know what kind of ammunition was inside the buildings.

Hubbard and I put our ponchos under our heads and tried to sleep. But we couldn't lie still. Gnats crawled up our noses. Mosquitoes hung in clouds around our heads. The air smelled like turpentine from the resin oozing out of the trees.

'I wish I was home,' Hubbard said.

'Me too,' I said. There didn't seem to be much point in ignoring Hubbard out here, where nobody could see me do it. But the word 'home' meant nothing anymore. My father was in Southern California, looking for work. Keith was still missing. The last time I'd spoken to her my mother's voice had been cold, as if I were somehow to blame.

'If I was home,' Hubbard said, 'I'd be out at the drags with Vogel and Kirk. Don't ask me what I'm doing here because I sure don't know.' He took off his helmet and wiped his face with his sleeve. He had a soft, square face with a little roll of flesh under his chin. It was the face he'd have for the rest of his life. 'Look,' he said. He took out his wallet and showed me a picture of a '49 Mercury.

'Nice,' I said.

'It isn't mine.' Hubbard looked at the picture and then put it away. 'I was going to buy it before Uncle got me. I wouldn't race it, though. I'd take it out to the track and sit on the hood with Vogel and Kirk and drink beer.'

Hubbard went on talking about Vogel and Kirk. Then he stopped and shook his head. 'How about you?' he asked. 'What would you be doing if you were home?'

'If I were home,' I said, remembering us all together, 'we would drive up to the fair at Mount Vernon. Then we'd have dinner at my grandfather's place – he has this big barbecue every year – and afterward we'd stay in a motel with a swimming pool. My brother and I would swim all night and watch the fireworks from the water.'

We had not been to Mount Vernon since my grandfather died when I was fourteen, so the memory was an old one. But it didn't feel old. It felt fresh and true, the starry night, the soft voices from the open doorways around the pool, the water so warm you forgot about it, forgot your own skin. Shaking hands with Keith underwater and looking up from the bottom of the pool at the rockets flaring overhead, the wrinkled surface of the water all a-shimmer with their light. My father on the balcony above, leaning over the rail, calling down to us. That's enough, boys. Come in. It's late.

'You like it, don't you?' Hubbard asked.

'Like what?'

'All this stuff. Marching everywhere. Carrying a rifle. The Army.'

'Come off it,' I said. I shook my head.

'It's true,' he said. 'I can tell.'

I shook my head again but made no further denials. Hubbard's admission that the car in the picture wasn't his had put me in an honest mood. And I was flattered that he had taken the trouble to come to a conclusion about me. Even this one. 'The Army has its good points,' I said.

'Name me one.' Hubbard leaned against the ramp. He closed his eyes. I could hear Lewis whistling as he walked along the fence.

I couldn't explain why I liked the Army because I didn't

understand the reason myself. 'Travel,' I said. 'You can go all over the world.'

Hubbard opened his eyes. 'You know where I've been to? South Carolina, Georgia, and North Carolina. All I've seen is a lot of hicks. And when they do send us overseas it will just be to kill slopes. You know the first sergeant? They say he killed over twenty of them. I could never do that. I shot a squirrel once and cried all night.'

We talked some more and Hubbard told me that he hadn't been drafted, as I'd assumed. Like me, he had enlisted. He said that the Army had tricked him. They'd sent a recruiter to his high school just before graduation to talk to the boys in Hubbard's class. The recruiter got them together in the gym and ran movies of soldiers being massaged by girls in Korea, and drinking beer in Germany out of steins. Then he visited the boys in their homes and showed each of them why the Army was the right choice. He told Hubbard that anyone who could drive a tractor automatically got to drive a tank, which turned out not to be true. Hubbard hadn't even set foot in a tank, not once. 'Of course he didn't mention Vietnam,' Hubbard said.

When I asked Hubbard what he was doing in the Airborne he shrugged. 'I thought it might be interesting,' he said. 'I should have known better. Just more of the same. People running around yelling their heads off.'

He waved his hand through a swarm of mosquitoes overhead. 'We'll be getting orders pretty soon,' he said. 'Are you scared?'

'A little. I don't think about it much.'

'I think about it all the time. I just hope I don't get killed. They can shoot my dick off as long as they don't kill me.'

I didn't know what to say. The sound of Lewis's whistling grew louder.

'Nuts,' Hubbard said. 'I don't know what he's so cheerful about.'

Lewis came around the corner and climbed the ramp. 'Shift's up,' he said. 'Best watch how you go along that fence. There's nettles poking through everyplace.' He held out his hand for us to see. It was swollen and red. He leaned his rifle against the warehouse and began to unlace his boots.

'I'm allergic to nettles,' Hubbard said. 'I could die out there.' He stood and put on his helmet. 'Wish me luck. If I don't make it back tell Laura I love her.'

Lewis watched Hubbard go, then turned to me. 'I never saw so many bugs in my life,' he said. 'Wish I was at the beach. You ever been to Nags Head? Those girls up there just go and go.'

'Never been there,' I said.

'I had one of those girls almost tore my back off,' Lewis said. 'Still got the marks.' He leaned towards me and for a moment there I thought he was going to take his shirt off and show me his back as he'd shown me his hand.

'Ever been to Kentucky?' he asked.

I shook my head.

'That's where I'm from. Lawton. It's a dry town but I've been drinking since I was thirteen. Year after that I started on intercourse. Now it's got to where I can't go to sleep anymore unless I ate pussy.'

'I'm from Washington,' I said. 'The state.'

Lewis took off his helmet. He had close-cropped hair, red like his face. He could have worn it longer if he'd wanted, now that we were out of training. But he chose to wear it that way. It was his style.

He studied me. 'You never been to Lawton,' he said. 'You ought to go. You won't want to leave and that's a guarantee.' He took off one of his socks and started doing something to his foot. It seemed to require all his concentration. He sucked in his long cheeks and stuck the tip of his tongue out of the side of his mouth. 'There,' he said and wiggled his toes. 'I guess you know about what happened the other day,' he said. 'It wasn't the way you probably heard.'

I didn't know what Lewis was talking about, but he gave me no chance to say so.

'I just didn't have the rope fixed right,' he said. 'I wasn't afraid. You ought to see me go off the high dive back home. I wanted to straighten out the rope was all.'

Now I understood. Our company had practised rappelling the week before off a fifty-foot cliff and someone had refused the descent. I'd heard the first sergeant raising hell but I was at the base of the cliff nd couldn't make out what he was saying or see who he was yelling at.

'He called me Tinkerbell,' Lewis said.

'He calls everybody that,' I said. He did, too. Tinkerbell and Sweety Pie.

'You go ask around home,' Lewis told me. 'Just talk to those girls ack there. They'll tell you if I'm a Tinkerbell.'

'He didn't mean anything.'

'I know what he meant,' Lewis said, and gave me a fierce look. Then e put his sock back on and stared at it. 'What's the matter with these ellows here, anyway? Pretty stuck on themselves if you ask me.'

'I guess so,' I said. 'Look, don't mind me. I'm going to get some leep before my shift.' I closed my eyes. I hoped that Lewis would e quiet. He was starting to get on my nerves. It wasn't just his loud oice or the things he said. He seemed to want something from me.

'There's not one of these fellows would last a day in Lawton,' he aid. 'We've got a guard in the bank that bit a man's tongue out of is head.'

I opened my eyes. Lewis was watching me. 'It's just because we're ew,' I said. 'They'll be friendlier when we've been around for a while. Now if you don't mind I'm going to catch some sleep.'

'What burns me,' Lewis said, 'is how you meet one of them in the X or downtown somewhere and they look past you like they never aw you.'

Off in the distance a siren wailed. The sound was weak, only a pulse n the air, but Lewis cocked his head at it. He squinted. When the siren topped Lewis held his listening attitude for a moment, then gave a ittle shake. 'I'm just as good as them,' he said. 'Look here. You got amily?'

I nodded.

'I'm the only one left,' Lewis said. 'It was me and my dad, but now e's gone too. Heart attack.' He shrugged. 'That's all right. I get along ust fine.'

Another siren went off, right in my ear it seemed. The sound made ne wince. Then everything went quiet. Lewis's eyes were pink.

Hubbard came around the side of the building and started up the ramp. I was glad to see him. He waved and I waved back. He gave me an odd stare then and I realized he'd only been flapping mosquitoes out of his face.

'There's a man out by the gate who wants to talk to us,' he said.

Lewis started lacing up his boots. 'Officer?'

Hubbard shook his head. 'Civilian.'

'What does he want?' I asked, but Hubbard had already turned away. I followed him and Lewis came after me, muttering to himself and trying to tie his boots.

There was a car parked in the turn-around outside the gate. It had a decal on the door and a red blinker flashing on top, dim in the grey light of early evening. A man was sitting in the front seat. Another man leaned against the fence. He was tall and stooped. He wiped at his face with a red bandanna which he put in his back pocket when he saw us coming.

'Okay, mister,' Hubbard said, 'we're all here.'

'Bet you'd rather be someplace else, too.' He smiled at us. 'Terrible way to spend the holiday.'

None of us said anything.

The man stopped smiling. 'We have a fire,' he said. He pointed to the east, at a black cloud above the trees. 'It's an annual event,' the man said. 'A couple of kids blew up a pipe full of matches. Almost took their hands off.' He turned his head and barked twice. He might have been laughing or he might have been coughing.

'So what?' Lewis said.

The man looked at him, then at me. I noticed for the first time that his eyes were blinking steadily. 'This isn't the best place to be,' he said.

I knew what he meant – the dry weeds, the warped ramshackle buildings, the ammunition inside. 'That fire's a mile off at least,' I said. 'Can't you put it out?'

'I think we can,' he said. He tugged at his pants. It must have been a habit. They were already high on his waist, held there by leather suspenders. 'The problem is,' he said, 'if you catch one spark in there that's all she wrote.'

Hubbard and I looked at each other.

The man leaned against the fence. 'You boys just come with us and I'll see that someone takes you back to Bragg.'

'That's a good way to get dead,' said Lewis. He cocked his rifle. The bolt slid forward with a sharp, heavy smack, a sound I'd heard thousands of times since joining the Army but never so distinctly. It changed everything. Everything became vivid, interesting.

The man froze. His eyes stopped their endless blinking.

'You heard me,' Lewis said. 'Let loose of that fence or you're dog meat.'

The man stepped back. He stood with his arms at his sides and watched Lewis. I could hear the breath pass in and out of his mouth. A few minutes earlier I had been glad to see him. He was worried about me. He didn't want me to get blown up and that spoke well of him. But when I looked at him now, without weapon, without uniform, without anyone to back him up, I felt hard and cold. Nobody had the right to be that helpless.

None of us spoke. Finally the man turned and went back to the car.

'Godalmighty,' Hubbard said. He turned to Lewis. 'Why did you do that?'

'He touched the fence,' Lewis said.

'You're crazy,' Hubbard said. 'You're really crazy.'

'Maybe I am and maybe I'm not.'

'You are,' Hubbard said. 'Take my word for it. Crazy hick.'

'You calling me a hick?' Lewis said.

Out in the car I could see the two men talking. The one Lewis had scared off kept shaking his head.

'Tell me something, hick,' Hubbard said. 'Tell me what we're supposed to do if this place goes up.'

'That's no concern of mine,' Lewis said.

'Jesus,' Hubbard said. He looked at me, appealing for help. I disappointed him. 'What are you grinning at?' he said.

'Nothing,' I said. But I might just as well have said 'Everything'. I liked this situation. It was interesting. It had a last-stand quality about

it. But I didn't really believe that anything would happen, not to m
Getting hurt was just a choice some people made, like bad luck, c
growing old.

'I don't believe this,' Hubbard said.

'If you don't like it here,' Lewis said, 'you can go somewhere els
Won't nobody stop you.'

Hubbard stared at the hand Lewis was shaking at him. It was beet-re
and so bloated that you couldn't see his knuckles anymore. It looke
like an enormous baby's hand, even to the crease around the wris
'Godalmighty,' Hubbard said. 'Those must have been some kille
nettles you ran into. With plants like that I don't know what the
need us for.'

'Look,' I said. 'We've got a visitor.'

The other man had gotten out of the car and was walking up t
the fence. He smiled as he came towards us. 'Hello there,' he said. H
took off his sunglasses as if to show us he had nothing to hide. His fac
was dark with soot. 'I'm Deputy Chief Ellingboe,' he said. He held u
a card. When we didn't look at it he put it back in his shirt pocke
He glanced over at the man sitting in the car. 'You certainly gave ol
Charlie there something to talk about,' he said.

'Old Charlie about got his ears peeled,' Lewis said.

'There's no call for that talk,' the man said. He came up to th
fence and looked at Lewis. Then he looked at me. Finally he turne
to Hubbard and started talking to him as if they were alone. 'I kno
you think you're doing your duty, following orders. I appreciate that
I was a soldier myself once.' He leaned towards us, fingers woun
through the iron mesh. 'I was in Korea. Men dropped like flies a
around me but at least they died in a good cause.'

'Back off,' Lewis said.

The man went on talking to Hubbard. 'Nobody would expect yo
to stay in there,' he said. 'All you have to do is walk out and no on
will say a thing. If they do I will personally take it up with Genera
Paterson. Word of honour. I'll shake on it.' He wiggled the finger
of his right hand.

'Back off,' Lewis said again.

The man kept his eyes on Hubbard. He said, 'You don't want to tay in there, do you?'

Hubbard looked over at Lewis. A fat bug flew between them with whine. They both flinched. Then they smiled at each other. I was miling too.

'You're a smart boy,' the man said. 'I can see that. Use the brains God gave you. Just put one foot in front of the other.'

'You've been told to back off,' Hubbard said. 'You won't be old again.'

'Boys, be reasonable.'

Hubbard swung his rifle up and aimed it at the man's head. The notion was natural. The other man leaned out the car window and houted, 'Come on! Hell with 'em!' The deputy chief looked at him nd back at us. He took his hands away from the fence. He was shaking ll over. A grasshopper flew smack into his cheek and he threw up his rms as if he'd been shot. The car horn honked twice. He turned and valked to the car, got inside, and the two men drove away.

We stood at the fence and watched the car until it disappeared round a curve.

'It's no big deal,' I said. 'They'll put the fire out.'

And so they did. But before that happened there was one bad noment when the wind shifted in our direction. We had our first aste of smoke then. The air was full of insects flying away from the ire, all kinds of insects, so many it looked like rain falling sideways. They rattled against the buildings and pinged into the fence.

Hubbard had a coughing fit. He sat on his helmet and put his head between his knees. Lewis went over to him and started pounding him on the back. Hubbard tried to wave Lewis off, but he kept at it. 'A little moke won't hurt you,' Lewis said. Then Lewis began to cough. A few ninutes later so did I. We couldn't stop. Whenever I took another breath it got worse. I ached from it, and began to feel dizzy. For the first time that day I was afraid. Then the wind changed again, and the moke and the bugs went off in another direction. A few minutes later we were laughing.

The black smudge above the trees gradually disappeared. It was gone by the time the first sergeant pulled up to the gate. He only spoke once on the drive home, to ask if we had anything to report. We shook our heads. He gave us a look, but didn't ask again. Night came on as we drove through the woods, headlights jumping ahead of us on the rough road. Tall pines crowded us on both sides. Overhead was a ribbon of dark blue. As we bounced through the potholes I steadied myself with my rifle, feeling like a commando returning from a suicide mission.

The first sergeant let us out at company headquarters. He said, 'Sweet dreams, toads,' and went off down the street, gunning the engine and doing racing-shifts on the gears.

We turned in our rifles and lingered outside the orderly room. We didn't want to go away from each other. Without saying so, we believed that we had done something that day, that we were proven men. We weren't, of course, but we thought we were and that was a sweet thing to believe for an hour or two. We had stood our ground together. We knew what we were made of now, and the stuff was good.

We sat on the steps of the orderly room, sometimes talking, mostly just sitting there. Hubbard suddenly threw his hands in the air. In a high voice he said 'Boys, be reasonable,' and we all started laughing. I was in the middle. I didn't think about it, I just reached out and put my arms on their shoulders. We were in a state. Every time we stopped laughing one of us would giggle and set it off again. The yellow moon rose above the mess hall. Behind us the poker-wise desk clerk, 'Chairborne' we called him, typed steadily away at some roster or report or maybe a letter to the girl he dreamed of – who, if he was lucky, kept a picture of him on her dresser, and looked at it sometimes.

4

The three of us fooled around together for the next couple of days. One night we went to a movie in town, but Lewis spoiled it by talking all the time You'd think he had never seen a movie before. If an aeroplane came on the screen he said 'Aeroplane'. If someone got hit he said 'Ouch!'. The next night we went bowling and he spoiled ıat, too. He had to use his left hand because his right hand was still vollen up, and his ball kept bouncing into the gutter. The people in ıe next lane thought it was funny, but it got on my nerves.

I was in a bad mood anyway. My mother had called the day after the ourth to tell me that my car had been located in Bolinas, California. 'wo hippies were living in it. They said that Keith had sold it to them ut they had no idea where he was now. They'd met him by chance ı a crash pad in Berkeley. When my mother said 'crash pad' I thought, ;ood God. I could see the whole thing.

She was beside herself. She said that she was going to quit her job ıd take a bus to San Francisco. Keith could be in trouble. He could e hungry. He could be sick. For a moment she didn't say anything, ıd I thought, He could be dead. I'm sure that's what she was thinking, ›o. I told her to stay home. When Keith got hungry he'd be in touch. 'here was no point in her wandering around a strange city, she'd never nd him that way.

'Someone has to look for him,' she said.

'Someone like me, you mean.' I hadn't wanted to sound so rough. ›efore I had a chance to soften my words, though, my mother said, Iow far away you are. Nothing reaches you.'

We patched it up as well as we could. I told her I'd be getting ıy orders for Vietnam any day now, and promised to look around ›r Keith while I was in Oakland waiting to ship out.

On Monday the rest of the company returned to duty. Almost veryone had been drinking all weekend, and looked it. Some of ıe men had been in fights. The ones who'd gone to the beach had :rrible sunburns and were forced to walk stiff-legged because they ouldn't bend their knees. As they marched they swayed from side to .de like penguins. There were over thirty of them in this condition nd when we moved out together it was something to see.

Two days later our company was detailed for crowd control. A group f protesters had camped out on the main entrance to the post, on either .de of the road. We were supposed to keep them from moving past ıe gate.

At first it was friendly enough. The protesters waved and threw us sandwiches which we were forbidden to touch. Some of the wome were good looking in a soulful way and that didn't hurt their caus The men were something else. They were all decked out in differe costumes and seemed pleased with themselves in a way that I fou disagreeable. There was one in particular I had my eye on. He w always chanting something, and he was the one who finally round everybody up and got them on the road.

They stood there for a while. With their arms joined they sang song Then they moved towards us. They stopped just short of the gate a began to talk to us. There was a tired-looking blonde girl across fro me and next to her was the fellow I'd been watching. I didn't ca for him. He was prettier than the girl, and his long black hair curle up at the ends. He looked like Prince Valiant.

The girl said hello, and told me her first name. 'What's yours she said.

I didn't answer. We'd been told not to, but I wouldn't ha anyway.

Prince Valiant shook his head. 'You're not allowed to talk,' he sai 'Doesn't that strike you as paradoxical? Here you are supposed to b defending freedom and you can't talk.'

'Why do you want to kill your brothers?' the girl said.

The man next to me began swearing under his breath.

Prince Valiant smiled at him. 'Speak up,' he said loudly. 'Haven you ever heard of the First Amendment?'

The girl kept talking to me. 'Your brothers and sisters in Vietna don't want a war,' she said. 'If you didn't go, there wouldn't b any war.'

'Don't be a CIA robot,' Prince Valiant said.

'Cocksucker,' said the man next to me.

Prince Valiant smiled at him. He looked at me. 'I think your friend got a problem,' he said.

I was trembling. I wanted to take my rifle to that smile of his an put it down his gullet. The sun was overhead, baking our helmet Sweat ran down our faces. Everything got quiet. All along the line could feel the tautness of something about to break. At that momen ıe highway patrol pulled up, four cars with lights flashing. The atrolmen got out and started clearing the protesters off the road. 'here was no resistance. Prince Valiant backed away. 'You should et some help with that problem of yours,' he said to the man beside ıe, who stepped forward out of line. The blonde girl looked at us. 'lease,' she said, 'please don't.' She was pulling on Prince Valiant's rm. The first sergeant yelled at the man beside me to get back in line. Ie hesitated. Then he stepped back. Prince Valiant laughed and gave s the finger.

The protesters sang more songs, then broke up. After they left we 'ere relieved by another company. I was still trembling. The other ıen were upset, too. We got back in time for dinner, but hardly any f us went to the mess hall. Instead we sat around and talked about 'hat had happened, and what would have happened if they'd turned s loose. It was the first time I'd joined in a general conversation. Vhile we were talking, Lewis came in. He'd been on KP that day) he'd missed the excitement. He listened for a while, then asked ıe in a loud voice if I wanted to go see the Bob Hope movie that 'as playing in town.

Everyone stopped talking.

I told Lewis no, I wasn't in the mood.

He looked at the other men. He stood there for a moment. Then e shrugged and walked outside again.

'he stealing began a few days after the protest. A corporal had his 'allet taken from under his pillow. It was found beneath the barracks eps, empty. The corporal swore that he'd had over a hundred dollars ı it, which was probably a lie. Nobody in the company owned that ıuch money except the clerk-typist, who regularly cleaned everyone ut at marathon poker games in the mess hall.

Nothing like this had ever happened before in our company, not in ıyone's memory, and everybody assumed that the thief must be from ıother unit – maybe even a civilian. Our platoon sergeants told us to eep our eyes open. That was all that was said about it.

The next night a man had his fatigue pants stolen while he slept.

The thief balled them up and stuffed them into a trash can in th
latrine along with his empty wallet. There was something intimat
about this theft. Now we all knew, as these things are known, th
the thief was one of us.

After the second theft our first sergeant went through all the barrack
and made a speech. He had a vivid red scar that ran from the corner c
one eye across his cheek and down under his collar. He had been badl
wounded in Vietnam, so badly wounded that the Army was forcin
him to take early retirement. He had just a few weeks left to go.

The scar gave weight to everything the first sergeant said. He spok
with painful slowness and agitation, as if each word was a fish he ha
to catch with his hands. He said that to his mind an infantry compan
was like a family, a family without any women in it, but a family. H
wanted the thief to think about that, and then ask himself one questior
What sort of a man would turn his back on his own kind?

'Think about it,' the first sergeant said. Then he went to the barrack
next door where through the open window we could hear him sayin
exactly the same thing.

Because the stealing was something new, and I was new, I felt accuse
by it. No one said anything, but I felt in my heart that I was suspectec
It made me furious. For the first time in my life I was spoiling for
fight, just waiting for someone to say something so I could swing a
him and prove my innocence. I noticed that Lewis carried himse
the same way – swaggering and glaring at everyone all the time. H
looked ridiculous, but I thought I understood. We were all breathin
poison in and out. It was a bad time.

Hubbard was different. He seemed to wilt. He walked around wit
his hands in his pockets and his eyes on the ground, and I could hardl
get a word out of him. Later I discovered that it wasn't the stealin
that got him down, or the suspicion, but pure grief. His friends Voge
and Kirk had been killed, along with their dates, in a car smash-up o
the Fourth.

We all had our suspicions. My suspicions lay on a man who ha
never given me any reason to think badly of him. To me he jus
looked like a thief. I suppose that someone even suspected Hubbarc

miserable as he was. If so, Hubbard got clear of suspicion four days after the second theft.

It happened like this. He had left the mess hall early to take a shower. At some point he apparently looked up and saw someone lift his pants off the hook where he'd hung them. He shouted and whoever it was hauled off and hit him dead on the nose. He hadn't seen the thief's face because of the steam in the shower stall, and the blow knocked him down so he had no chance to give chase. His nose was broken, mashed flat against one cheek.

As soon as the story got around, the barracks emptied out. Everyone wanted to get away from the company that night. So did I. But I wanted to see Hubbard even more, partly out of concern and partly for some need that was not clear to me. So I sat on the orderly room steps and waited for him. Men from another company were playing softball on the parade ground. They yelled insults at each other until it got dark and they quit. Then I heard the smaller sounds, moths rustling against the bare light bulb overhead, frogs croaking, one of the Puerto Rican cooks in the mess hall singing happily to himself in that beautiful language that set him apart from us, and made him a figure of fun.

Hubbard came back from the hospital in a white jeep. He was wearing a shiny metal cast over his nose, held by two strips of tape that went across his face. The first sergeant met him and I waited while they talked. When Hubbard finally turned and started towards the barracks, I came up to him. We walked together without speaking for a moment, then I said, 'Who was it?'

'I don't know,' he said.

I followed him inside and sat on the next bunk while he took his boots off and stretched out, hands behind his head. He stared up at the ceiling. The cast gleamed dully.

'You really didn't see him?' I asked.

He shook his head.

'Well, I didn't do it,' I said. 'I swear I didn't.'

I could feel my heart beating.

Hubbard looked at me. His lips were pressed together. He was utterly dejected. I could not imagine him pointing a rifle at someone's head. He looked back up at the ceiling. 'Who said you did?' he asked.

'Nobody. I just wanted you to know.'

'Fine,' he said. 'I never thought it was you anyway.' Suddenly he turned his head and looked at me again. It made me uncomfortable.

'Just between us,' I said, 'who do you think it was?'

'I don't know. I'd like to be alone right now if that's all right with you.'

'Whatever you want,' I said. 'If I can do anything, let me know. That's what friends are for.'

At first he didn't answer. Then he said, 'That was stupid, what we did out at the ammo dump. You probably think it was some big deal, but if you want to know the truth I almost throw up every time I think of it. We nearly got ourselves killed. Don't you ever think about that?'

'Sure I do.'

'About being dead? Do you think about being dead?'

'Not exactly.'

'Not exactly,' he said. 'Boy, you're really something. No wonder you like the Army so much.'

I waited for Hubbard to go on, and when he didn't I stood up and looked down at him. His eyes were closed. 'I'm sorry about what happened to you,' I said. 'That's why I came by.'

'Thanks,' he said, and touched the cast on his nose curiously, as if I had just reminded him of it. 'It isn't only this,' he said. Then, with his eyes still closed, he told me about his friends getting killed.

It spooked me. It was like a ghost story, the way Hubbard had talked about them so much on the day it happened. I thought I should say something. 'That's tragic,' I said, the word used in my family for all deaths, and as soon as it was out of my mouth I regretted it. I didn't know then that it is nearly impossible to talk to other people about their own suffering. Instead of giving up I tried again. 'I know how you feel,' I said. 'I'd feel the same way if I lost my best friends.'

'You don't have any,' Hubbard said, 'not like Vogel and Kirk, anyway.' He rolled onto his side so that he was facing away from me. 'Nobody that close,' he said.

'How do you know?' I said.

'I just know.'

I understood that Hubbard wanted me to leave. And I was glad to get away from him. It was too late to go anywhere so I went back to my own building. It was empty. I sat down on my bunk. I thought about what Hubbard had said, that I had nobody close. It got to me, coming from Hubbard, because we should have been close after what we'd been through together, he and Lewis and I.

Anyway, it just wasn't true.

I tried to read, but it took an effort in that big quiet room full of bunks. While I stared at the book I thought of other things. I wondered how I would hold up if I got wounded. I'd only been hurt once before, when I was eight, in a fall from a tree. My leg had been broken and I wasn't very brave about it. For several months everyone knew exactly how uncomfortable I was at any given moment. Keith was following me in those days. After I got out of the cast I walked with a limp, and Keith began to limp, too. It drove me crazy. I used to scream at him. Once I shot him with my B-B gun, trying to make him go away – but he kept limping after me, bawling his eyes out.

The door banged open and two men came in, a little drunk. Though it was still fairly early they turned off all the lights and went to bed. I had no choice but to do the same.

For a long while I lay in the dark with my eyes open. My unhappiness made me angry, and as I became more angry I began to brood about the thief. Who was he? What kind of person would do a thing like that?

5

Lewis shuffles along the road leading out of Fort Bragg, muttering to himself and trying to hitch a ride, but he is so angry that he glares at all the drivers and they pass him up. He's angry because he couldn't talk his friends into going to the pictures with him. Bob Hope is his favourite actor but it's not as much fun going alone. He thinks they owed it to him to come.

When he gets to the bottom of Smoke Bomb Hill someone in a convertible stops for him. The driver of the convertible is a teacher who works at the elementary school on post. He is nervous, shy. Lewis leans over the side of the convertible and asks him something which he can't understand because Lewis's voice is so loud and thick. The teacher just keeps looking straight ahead and gives a little nod.

Lewis gets in. He tells the teacher that a fellow in Lawton had a car like this one and drove it across someone's yard one night and got his head cut off by a metal clothesline. They never did find the head, either. Lewis says he figures one of the dogs on the street got ahold of it and buried it somewhere.

He takes out a package of gum and crams four sticks in his mouth, dropping the wrappers on the floor of the car. He has unwrapped the last stick and is about to put it in his mouth when he remembers his manners and holds the gum out to the teacher. The teacher shakes his head, but Lewis stabs it at him until he takes it. When he starts to chew on it Lewis smiles and nods.

They leave the post and head toward town. The road is lined with drive-in restaurants and used-car lots advertising special deals for servicemen. American flags hang limp above the air-conditioned trailers where terms are struck, and salesmen in white shirts stand around in groups. In the early dusk their shirts seem to glow. The air smells of burgers.

The teacher sneaks a look at Lewis. Lewis says something incomprehensible and the teacher looks away quickly and nods. Lewis turns the radio on full blast and starts punching the buttons. When he doesn't get anything he wants he spins the tuning knob back and forth. Finally he settles on a telephone call-in show. People are calling in their opinions as to whether we should drop an atomic bomb on North Vietnam.

A man says we should, right away. Then a woman gets on the line and says that she believes the average person in North Vietnam is probably a lot like the average person here at home, and that their leaders are the ones making the trouble. Lewis chews up a storm. He watches the radio as if listening with his eyes.

He reminds the teacher of one of his students. It's the unfinished ce, the way he stares, his restlessness. He asks Lewis to turn down e radio, and as Lewis reaches for the knob the teacher notices his nd puffed-up and livid. In the five days since Lewis's brush with e nettles the swelling has hardly gone down at all. The teacher asks ewis what happened to it.

Lewis holds it up in front of his face and turns it back and forth. ettles, he says. Hurts like hell, too, and that's no lie.

What did you put on it? the teacher asks.

Nothing, Lewis says.

Nothing?

I'm in the Army, Lewis says.

The teacher is going to say that Lewis should go on sick call, but decides that they've probably bullied him into thinking there's mething wrong with that. His father was an Army officer and he nows how they do things. He feels sorry for Lewis, for being helpless d in the Army and having his hand so hideously swollen. You really ould put some calamine lotion on it, he says.

Never heard of it, Lewis says.

It's what you do for nettles, the teacher says. It eases the pain and akes the swelling go down.

I don't know, Lewis says. I just as soon wait and see. Every time ou go to the doctor it ends up they stick a needle in you.

You don't have to go to a doctor, the teacher says. You can buy it a drugstore. Lewis nods and looks off. The teacher can tell that he as no intention of spending his money on calamine lotion. He can most see that hand throbbing away, getting worse and worse, and e boy doing nothing about it. Everybody uses it, he says. We've ways got a bottle around.

The teacher is not inviting Lewis to his home. He just wants him comprehend that calamine lotion is no big undertaking. But Lewis isunderstands. What the hell, he says, I'll try anything once. Long I get to the pictures by eight.

The teacher turns to explain. But there's no way to do it without ounding like he's backing out. Just before they reach town he pulls off n a side-street bordered with pines. Almost immediately the sound of

traffic dies. The nasal voice coming out of the radio seems unbearabl
loud and stupid. It embarrasses the teacher to belong to a species th
can think such things. When he stops the car in front of the house h
sits for a moment, letting the silence calm him.

They go in through a redwood gate in the back. Lewis whistles whe
he sees the pool, a piano-shaped pool designed by the teacher's fathe
who also designed the house. The house has sliding doors everywher
with ricepaper panels. All the drawers and cabinets have brass handl
with Japanese ideograms signifying 'Long Life', 'Good Luck', 'Exceller
Health'. The teacher's father was stationed in Japan after the war an
fell in love with Japanese culture. There's even a rock garden in th
front yard.

The house is empty. The teacher's mother is visiting friends i
California. His father died two years ago. The teacher leads Lewis t
the living room and tells him to sit down. The chairs are heavy an
ornately carved. The arms are dragons and the legs are bearded ol
men with their arms raised to look like they're holding the seats up
Lewis hesitates, then lowers himself into the smallest chair as if that
the polite thing to do.

The teacher goes to the medicine cabinet and takes out the calamin
lotion. He comes back to the living room, shaking the bottle. He give
the bottle to Lewis, but Lewis can't open it because of his bad hand, s
the teacher takes it back and twists off the cap. He gives the bottle t
Lewis again, then sees that Lewis doesn't know what to do with i
Here, the teacher says. Look. He sits in the chair across from Lewis
He pulls the chair close. He pours some lotion into his palm, the
takes Lewis's hand by the wrist and starts to work it in, over th
swollen, dimpled knuckles, between the thick fingers. Lewis's han
is unbelievably hot.

Hey! Lewis says. That feels fine. I wish I had some before.

The burning skin drinks up the lotion. The teacher shakes more out
directly onto the back of Lewis's wrist. Lewis leans back and closes hi
eyes. The room is cool, blue. A cardinal is singing outside, one o
three birds the teacher can identify. He rubs the lotion into Lewis'
hand, feeling the heat leave little by little, the motions of his own

hand circular and rhythmic. After a time he forgets what he is doing. He forgets his stomach which always hurts, he forgets the children he teaches who seem bent on becoming brutes and slatterns, he forgets his hatred of the house and his fear of being anywhere else. He forgets his sense of being absolutely alone.

So does Lewis.

Then the room is silent and grey. The teacher has no idea when the bird stopped singing. He looks down where his hand and Lewis's are joined, fingers interlaced. For once Lewis is still. He breathes so peacefully and deeply that the teacher thinks he is asleep. Then he sees that Lewis's eyes are open. There is a thin gleam of light upon them.

The teacher unclasps his hand from Lewis's hand.

I have to admit that stuff is all right, Lewis says. I might just go and buy me a bottle.

The teacher screws the cap on and holds the bottle out. Here, he says. Keep it. Go on.

Lewis takes it. Thanks, he says.

The teacher stands and stretches. I guess we'd better go, he says. You don't want to miss that movie.

Lewis follows him out of the house. He stops for a moment by the pool, which the teacher walks past as if it isn't there. The moon is full. It looks like a big silver dish floating on the water. Lewis puts his hand in his pocket and jingles the change.

He and the teacher don't talk on the way to town. Lewis leans into the corner, one arm hanging over the car door and the other on top of the seat. He strokes the leather with just that tenderness his dog used to feel. In town the sidewalks are crowded. Recruits with shaved heads, as many as fifteen or twenty in a group, walk from bar to bar, pushing each other and laughing too loudly, the ones in the rear almost running to keep up. They fall silent when they come up to the clusters of prostitutes, but when they are well past they call things over their shoulders. Different groups shout at each other back and forth across the street. The lights are on over the bars, in the tattoo parlours and clothing stores, in the gadget shops that sell German helmets and Vietcong flags, Mexican throwing knives, lighters that look like pistols, exotic condoms, fireworks and dirty books. The lights flash on the hood of the convertible and along the sides of the cars they pass.

The teacher stops in front of the movie theatre. He tells Lewis to be sure and use that lotion and Lewis promises he will. They wave to each other as the convertible pulls away.

The previews are just beginning. Lewis buys a jumbo popcorn and a jumbo coke and a Sugar Daddy. He sits down. A giant tarantula towers over a house. From inside a woman looks out and sees the hairy legs and screams. Lewis laughs. That's some spider, he says out loud. The previews end and the first cartoon begins, a Tom and Jerry. Every time the cat runs into a wall or sticks his tail into a light plug Lewis cracks up. Now and then he shouts advice to the mouse. The couple in front of him move across the aisle and down. The next cartoon is a Goofy. Tinkerbell does the credits, flying from one side of the screen to the other, bringing the names out of her sparkling wand.

Tinkerbell, Lewis says. When he hears the word his stomach clenches. He gets up and walks outside. He stands under the marquee for a moment, just breathing, then runs down the sidewalk in the direction the convertible went, pushing people out of his way without regard. He runs three, four, five blocks to where the downtown ends. His eyes burn from the sweat running into them and his shirt is soaked through. He takes the bottle of calamine lotion out of his pocket and throws it into the road. It shatters. I'm no Tinkerbell, he says. He watches the cars go by for a while, balling and unballing his fists, then turns and walks back into Fayetteville to find a girl.

It is too loud, too bright. One of the women on the street smiles at him but he keeps going. He has never paid for it and he's not about to start now. He's never had it free either, but he came really close once at Nags Head and has almost managed to forget that he failed. He turns off Combat Alley and heads down a side-street. The bars give out. It is quiet here. He passes the public library, a red-brick building with white pillars and high windows going dark one by one. A woman holds the door as people leave, mostly old folks. Just before she locks up two girls come out, a fat one in toreador pants and another girl in shorts, her legs white as milk. They both light cigarettes and sit on the steps. Lewis walks to the corner and turns back up the street. He stops in front of the girls. This here the library? he says.

It's closed, the fat one says.

Is that a fact, Lewis says, without looking at her. He watches the one in shorts, who is staring at her own feet and doing the French inhale with her cigarette. He can't see her face very well except for her lips, which are so red they seem to be separate from the rest of her. Shoot, Lewis says, I wanted to get this book.

What book? the fat one asks.

Just a book, Lewis says. For college.

The two girls glance at each other. The one in shorts straightens up. She walks down the steps past Lewis and looks up the street, leaning forward and lifting up one of her long legs like a flamingo.

You're from the post, the fat one says.

Here comes Bo, says the one in shorts. Give me another weed.

Both girls light fresh cigarettes. A car pulls up in front of the library, a '57 Chevvy full of boys. The girl in shorts sticks her head in the window. She backs away, holding a beer and laughing. The door opens. She gets in and the car peels off.

The fat girl says, She is so loose, and grinds out the cigarette under her shoe.

The car stops at the end of the block and comes back in reverse, gears screaming. The door opens again and the fat girl gets in and the car pulls away.

Lewis walks the side-streets. He meets no girls, but once, passing an apartment building, he looks in a window and sees a blonde woman in nothing but her panties and bra watching television. He is about to rap on the glass when a little boy comes into the room pulling a wooden train behind him and yelling his head off. The train is on its side. Without taking her eyes off the screen the woman puts the train on its wheels.

Lewis heads back to Combat Alley. There are still a couple of women on the street, but he doesn't know how to go up to them, or what they will expect him to say. And there are all these other people walking by. Finally he goes into The Drop

Zone, a bar with a picture of a paratrooper painted on the window.

Most of the prostitutes in town are reasonable women. Their reasons are their own and they aren't charitable, but they aren't crazy either. Mainly they want to do something easier than what they were doing before, so they try this for a while until they find out how hard it is. Then they go back to waitressing, or their husbands, or the bottling plant. Sometimes they get caught in the life, though, and there's a time right after they know they're caught when some of them do go crazy.

Lewis picks out the crazy one in a bar filled with reasonable girls.

She is older than the others and not the best looking, and the trouble she's in shows plainly. She hasn't brushed her hair all day and her dark eyes are ringed with circles like bruises. She is sitting by herself at the bar. The ice has melted in her ginger ale, which she pushes back and forth and never picks up. In a few years she will be talking to herself.

Lewis doesn't even look at any of the others. He is going to do something bad and she is the one to do it with. He goes straight to her and sits on the stool next to her. He avoids the bartender's gaze because he is not sure that he has enough money to pay for liquor and women both. *Liquor and women* are the words that come to his mind. He is really going to do it. Tonight, with her. He swivels on his stool and says, You come from around here?

She can't believe her ears. She stares at him and he looks down. His face is in motion, jerking and creasing and knotting. You want something? she says.

Lewis looks at her and looks away.

Well? she says.

No, he says. I mean maybe I do.

Well do you or don't you?

I don't know, he says. I never paid for it before.

Then go beat your meat, she says, and turns her shoulder to him.

The calamine lotion has dried pink on Lewis's hand and is starting to flake off. He picks at it with a fingernail. How much? he says.

She turns on him. Her eyes are raking his face. What are

you trying to pull? she says. You trying to get me jugged or something?

All I said –

I know what you said. Jesus Christ. She dips into her shiny white bag and pulls out a cigarette. She glances around, lights it, and blows smoke towards the ceiling. Drop dead, she says.

Lewis doesn't know what he's done wrong, but he will have a woman and this is the woman he will have. Hey, he says, you ever been to Kentucky?

Kentucky, she says to herself. She grabs her purse and gets off the stool and walks out of the bar. Lewis follows her. When they get outside she whips around on him. Damn you, she says. What do you want?

I want to go with you.

She looks up and down the street. People move past them and no one pays them any attention. You don't give a shit, she says. I get jugged it's all the same to you.

You asked me did I want anything, Lewis says. What are you all mad about?

She says, I had enough of you, and turns away down the sidewalk. Lewis follows her. After a while he catches up and they walk side by side. I'll show you a time, Lewis says. That's a guarantee.

She doesn't answer.

Right down the street from where Lewis threw the bottle of calamine there is a motel with separate little bungalows. She stops in front of the last one.

Ten dollars, she says.

How about eight?

Damn you, she says.

It's all I got.

She looks at him for a while, then goes up the steps and unlocks the door and backs into the bungalow. Let's have it, she says, and holds out her hand.

But there are only six ones in Lewis's wallet. He had forgotten the popcorn and the coke and the Sugar Daddy. He hands the money to her. That's six, he says. I'll give you the rest on payday.

Drop dead, she says, and starts to close the door.

Lewis says, Hey! He gets his foot in and pushes with his shoulder Hey, he says, give me my money back. She pushes from the othe side. Finally he hits the door with his whole weight and it gives. She backs away from him. He goes after her. Give me my money back he says. Then he stops. Put that knife away, he says. I just want my six dollars is all.

She doesn't move. She holds the knife as a man would, not raised by her ear but in front of her chest. Her breathing is hoarse but steady unhurried.

All right, Lewis says. Look here. You keep the six dollars and I'll bring the rest tomorrow. I'll meet you tomorrow, same place. Okay?

I don't care what you do, she says. Just get.

Tomorrow, he says. He backs out. When he's on the steps the door bangs shut and he hears the lock snap.

The next day Lewis steals the first wallet. It is not under a pillow as the owner later claims but lying on his bunk in plain sight. Lewis sees it on his way to lunch and doubles back when everyone is in the mess hall. It holds two one-dollar bills and some change. Lewis takes the money and tosses the wallet under the barracks steps. He is mad the whole time, mad at the corporal for leaving it out like that and for being so stuck on himself and never saying hello, mad at how little money there is, mad at not having any money of his own.

He doesn't think of borrowing a few dollars from his friends. He has never borrowed anything from anyone. To Lewis there is no difference between borrowing and begging. He even hates to ask questions.

Later, when he hears that the corporal is telling everyone he had a hundred dollars stolen, Lewis gets even madder. That evening at dinner he stares at the corporal openly but the corporal eats without looking up. On his way out of the mess hall Lewis deliberately bumps against the corporal's chair, hard. He stops at the door and looks back. The man is eating ice cream like nothing happened. It burns Lewis up.

It also burns him up the way everybody just automatically figures the wallet was stolen by an outsider. They are so high and mighty they think nobody in the company could ever do a thing like that.

The next day Lewis is assigned to a detail at the post laundry, humping heavy bags across the washroom. The air swirls with acrid steam. Figures appear and vanish in the mist, never speaking. It is useless to try and talk over the whining and thumping of the big machines, but now and then someone shouts an order at someone else. Lewis takes one short break in the morning but gets so far behind that he never takes another. All day he thinks about the woman in Fayetteville, how she looks, how bad she is. Doing it for money and carrying a knife. He is sure that nobody he knows has ever had a woman pull a knife on him. He thinks of different people and pictures to himself how they would act if they found out. It makes him smile.

When he gets back to the company he takes a shower and lies down for a while to catch his breath. Everyone else is getting ready for dinner, joking around, snapping each other with towels. Lewis watches them. His eyes sting from the fumes he's been working in and he closes them for a moment, just for a rest, and when he opens them again the barracks is dark and filled with sleeping men.

Lewis sits up. He hasn't eaten since breakfast and feels hollow all through. Even his legs seem empty. He remembers the woman in town, but it's too late now and anyway he doesn't have the money to pay her with. He imagines her sitting at the bar, sliding her glass back and forth.

It starts to rain. The drops rattle on the tin roof. A flash of lightning flickers on the walls and the thunder follows a while after, a rumble like shingle turning in a wave, more a feeling than a sound. Lewis gets up and walks between the bunks until he finds a pair of fatigue pants lying on a footlocker. He picks them up and goes to the latrine and takes the money out of the wallet. A five-dollar bill. Then he stuffs the wallet and pants into the trash can and goes back to bed.

He thinks about the woman again. At first he was sorry that he didn't meet her when he said he would, but now he's glad. It will teach her something. She probably thought she had him and it's best she know right off the kind of man she is dealing with. The kind that will come around when he gets good and ready. If she says anything he will just give a little smile and say, Honey, that's how it is with me. You can take it or leave it.

He wonders what she thinks happened. Maybe she thinks she scared him off with that knife. *That's a good one*, he thinks, him afraid of some old knife like you'd buy at a church sale. Kitchen knife. He remembers it pointed at him with the dim light moving up and down the blade, worn and wavy-edged from too many sharpenings, and it's true that he feels no fear. None at all.

As he dresses in the morning Lewis looks over at the man he stole from. The man is sitting on his bunk and staring at the floor.

The whole company knows about it by breakfast. And this time they know it's not an outsider but one of their own. Lewis can tell. They eat quietly instead of yelling and stealing food from one another, and nobody really looks at anybody else. Except Lewis. He looks at everyone.

That night the first sergeant comes through and makes a speech. It's a lot of crap about how an infantry company is like a family blah blah blah. Lewis makes himself deaf and leaves for town as soon as it's over.

In town Lewis looks for the woman in the same bar. But she isn't there. He tries all the bars. Finally he walks down to the bungalow. The windows are dark. He listens at the door and hears nothing. A TV on a window sill across the street makes laughing noises. He sits and waits.

He waits for two hours and more and then he sees her coming down the sidewalk with the tiniest little man he has ever seen. You could almost say he's a midget. She's walking fast, looking at the ground just in front of her, and when they get close he can hear her muttering and him huffing to keep up. Lewis comes down the steps to meet them. Hey, says the little man, what the heck's going on?

Beat it, Lewis says.

Okay, okay, the little man says, and heads back up the street.

The woman watches him go. She turns to Lewis. Who do you think you are? she says.

Lewis says, I brought you the rest of the money.

She moves up close. I remember you, she says. You get out of my way. Get!

Here's the money, Lewis says, and holds it out to her.

She takes it, looks at it, drops it on the ground and walks past him up the steps. Four dollars, she says. You think I'd go for four dollars? Get yourself a nigger.

Lewis picks it up. I already gave you six, he says. This here is the rest.

You got a receipt? she says, and sticks her key in the lock.

Lewis grabs her arm and squeezes it. She tries to jerk away but he holds on and closes her hand around the money. That makes ten, he says. He lets go of her arm.

She gives him a look and opens the door. He follows her inside. She turns on the overhead light, kicks her shoes across the room, and goes into the bathroom. He can hear her banging around in there as he sits on the bed and takes off his shoes and socks. Then he stands and strips to his underwear.

She comes out naked. She is heavy in the ankles and legs and walks flat-footed, but her breasts are small, girlish. She drops her eyes as she walks towards him and he smiles.

All right, she says, let's have a look. She yanks his underpants to his knees and grabs him between her thumb and forefinger and squints down while she rolls him back and forth. Looks okay, she says, and drops him. You won't do any harm with that little shooter. Come on. She goes to the bed and sits down. Come on, she says again, I got other fish to fry.

Lewis can't move.

Okay, softy, she says, and goes to her knees in front of Lewis.

No, Lewis says.

She ignores him.

No! Lewis says, and pushes her head back.

Christ, she says. Just my luck. A homo.

Lewis hits her. She sprawls back on the floor. They look at each other. She is breathing hard and so is Lewis, who stands with his fists in front of him like a boxer. She touches her forehead where he hit her. There's a white spot. Okay, she says. She gives a little smile and reaches her hand out.

Lewis pulls her up. She leans into him and runs her hands up and down his neck and back and legs, dragging her fingernails. She stands on his feet and pushes her hips against his. Then she rises up on her toes, Lewis nearly crying out from the pain of her weight, and she presses her teeth against his teeth and licks his mouth with her tongue. She kisses his face and whenever he goes to kiss her back she moves her mouth somewhere else, down his throat, his chest, his hips. She puts her arms around his knees and takes him in her mouth and a sound comes out of Lewis like he has never heard another human make. He puts his hands along her cheeks and closes his eyes.

When he is close to finishing he tries to think about something else. He thinks about close-order drill. They are marching in review, the whole company on parade. The files flick past like rows of corn. He looks for a familiar face but finds none. Then they are gone. He opens his eyes and pulls back.

The regular way, he says. In bed.

He wants to hold her. He wants to lie quiet with her a moment, but she straddles him. She lowers herself onto him and digs her fingers into his flanks so that he rises up into her. He tries to move his own way, but she governs him. She puts her mouth on his and bites him. His foot cramps.

Then she rolls over and wraps her legs around his back and slides her finger up inside him. He shouts and bucks to be free. She laughs and tightens around him. She holds her mouth against his ear and presses with her teeth and murmurs things. Lewis can't make out what she's saying. Then she arches and stiffens under him, holding him so tightly he can't move. Her eyes are open halfway. Only the whites show. Lewis feels himself lift and dip as she breathes. She is asleep.

She sleeps for hours. Nothing disturbs her, not the argument in the street, nor Lewis stroking her hair and saying things to her. Then he falls asleep too.

When he wakes, her eyes are open. She is watching him. Hey there, he says. He reaches out and touches her cheek. He says the same words he was saying before he dozed off. I love you, he says.

She pushes his hand away. You garbage, she says. She slides off the bed and finds her purse where she dropped it on the floor and takes out the knife. He gets up on the other side and stands there with the bed between them.

You talk to me like that, she says. You come here and mock me. You're garbage. I won't be mocked by you, not by you. You're just the same as me.

Let me stay, he says.

Get out of here, she says. Get! Get! Get!

Lewis dresses. I'll come back later, he says. He goes to the door and she follows him part way. I'll be back, he says. I'll bring you money.

She waves the knife. You'll get this, she says.

It's three o'clock in the morning. The last bus to camp left hours ago so Lewis has to make the trip on foot. The only cars on the road are filled with drunks. They yell things as they drive by. Once a bottle goes whistling past him and breaks on the shoulder. Lewis keeps going, feet sliding in his big square shoes. He doesn't even turn his head.

Just outside the base there is a tunnel with a narrow walkway along the side. The beams from the headlights of the cars glance off the white tiles and fill the tunnel with light. Lewis steadies himself on the handrail as he walks. One of the drivers notices him and leans on his horn and then the other drivers honk too, all together. The blare of the horns builds up between the tiles. It goes on in Lewis's head long after he leaves the tunnel.

He gets back to camp just after dawn and lies on his bunk, waiting for reveille. The man in the next bunk whistles as he breathes. Lewis closes his eyes, but he doesn't sleep.

At reveille the men sit up and fumble their boots on, cigarettes dangling, eyes narrowed against the smoke. Lewis thinks that he was wrong about them, that they are an okay bunch of fellows, not really conceited, just careful who they make friends with. He can understand that. You never know with people. He thinks about what good friends they are to each other and how they held the line in Vietnam against all those slopes. He wishes he had gotten to know them better. He wishes he was not this way.

For the next three days he tries to find a wallet to steal. At night, when he is sure that everyone is asleep, he prowls between the bunks and pats the clothes left on footlockers. He skips meals and checks under pillows and mattresses. As the days pass and he finds nothing he gets reckless. Once, during breakfast, he tries to break into a wall locker where he saw a man put his camera, one of those expensive kind you look through the top of, worth something as pawn, but the lock won't give and the metal door booms like thunder every time Lewis hits it with his entrenching tool. He feels dumb but he keeps at it until he can see there's no point.

During dinner on the fourth night he searches through the barracks next to his. There is nothing. On his way back out he passes the latrine and hears the hiss of a shower. He stops at the door. In one of the stalls he sees a red back through the steam, and, just outside, a uniform hanging on a nail. The bulge of the wallet is clear.

Lewis comes in along the wall. The man in the shower is making odd noises and it takes Lewis a moment to realize that he is crying. Lewis slips the pants off the hook and takes out the wallet. He is putting the pants back when the man in the shower turns around. His pink face floats in the mist. Hey! he says. Lewis hits him and the man goes down without a sound.

Outside the barracks Lewis falls in with the first group of men leaving the mess hall. He heads towards the parade ground and when he gets there he climbs to the top bench in the reviewing stands. He looks over in the direction of the company. No one has followed him, but men are drifting into small groups. They know that something has happened.

Lewis rubs his hand. It is still a little swollen and now it hurts like crazy from the punch he threw. He felt strange doing that, surprised and helpless and sad, like a bystander. What else will he watch himself do? He opens and closes his fingers.

There is a breeze. Halyards spank against the metal flagpole as the rope swings out and back.

He sees right away from the military ID that the wallet is Hubbard's. Lewis knows that he and Hubbard had a feeling once between them. He doesn't feel it now and can't recall it exactly, but he wishes he had not hit him. If there'd been any choice he'd have chosen not to. He pockets the money, three fives and some change, and looks through the pictures. Hubbard and a man who looks just like him standing in waders with four dead fish on the ground in front of them, one big one and three just legal. Hubbard in a mortarboard hat with a tassel hanging down. A car. Another car. A girl who looks exactly like Hubbard if Hubbard had a pony tail. An old man on a tractor. A white house. A piece of yellow paper folded up.

Lewis unfolds the paper and reads, *Dear Son*. He looks away, then looks back.

Dear Son, I have some very bad news. I don't think there is any way to tell you but just to write what happened. It was three days ago, on the Fourth. Norm and Bobby went down to Monroe to watch the drag races there. They were double dating with Ginny and Karen Schwartz. From what I understand they and some of the other kids did a little 'celebrating' at the track. Tom saw them and said they were not really drunk but you know how your brother is. Let's just say he isn't very observant. Norm was driving when they left for home.

They don't know for sure what happened but just the other side of Monroe the car went into a skid and hit a truck parked off the road. Norm and Bobby and Ginny were killed right away. Karen died in the hospital that night. She was unconscious the whole time.

Dear, I know I should have called you but I was afraid I wouldn't be able to talk. Tom and I and Julie and even your father have been crying like babies ever since it happened. The whole town has. Everyone you see is just miserable. It is the worst thing to ever happen here.

This is about all I can write. Call collect when you feel up to it. Dear, don't ever forget that each and every person on this earth is a beautiful gift of God. Remember that always and you will never go wrong. Your loving Mother.

Lewis sits in the stands and shakes his head because Hubbard's mother is so wrong. She doesn't know anything. He would like to know what she thinks when she hears what just happened to Hubbard. Hubbard probably won't tell her. But if she knew, and if she knew about the woman in town and all the things Lewis has done, then she would know something real and give different advice.

He throws the wallet into the shadows under the stands. He starts to drop the letter after it but it stays between his fingers and finally he folds it up again and puts it in his pocket. Then he walks out to the road and hitches a ride to town.

She is not in any of the bars. Lewis goes to the bungalow and shakes the door. You in there? he says. The window is dark and he hears nothing, but he feels her on the other side. Open up, he says. He slams his shoulder against the door and the lock gives and he stumbles inside. From the light coming in behind him he can see the dark shapes of her things on the floor. He waits, but nothing moves. He is alone.

Lewis closes the door and without turning on the light walks over to the bed. He sits down. Breathing the bad air in here makes him lightheaded. His arms ache from stacking oil drums all day in the motor pool. He's tired. After a time he takes off his shoes and stretches out on the twisted sheets. He knows that he has to keep his eyes open, that he has to be awake when she comes back. Then he knows that he won't be, and that it doesn't matter anyway.

It doesn't matter, he thinks. He starts to drift. The darkness he passes into is not sleep, but something else. No, he thinks. He pulls free of it and sits up. He thinks, *I have got to get out of here*.

Lewis can't tie his shoes, his hands are shaking so. With the laces dragging he walks outside and up the sidewalk towards town. He can hear everything, the trucks gearing down on the access road, the buzz of the streetlights, and from somewhere far away a steady, cold, tinkling noise like someone all alone breaking every plate in the house just to hear the sound. Lewis stops and closes his eyes. Dogs bark up and down the street, and as he listens he hears more and more of them. They're pitching in from every side of town. He wonders what they're so mad about, and decides that they're not really mad at all but just putting it on. It's something to do when they're all tied up. He lifts his face to the stars and howls.

The next morning Lewis wakes up feeling like a million dollars. He showers and shaves and puts on a fresh uniform with sharp creases. On his way to the mess hall he stands for a moment by the edge of the parade ground. They've got a bunch of recruits out there crawling on their bellies and lobbing dummy hand grenades at truck tyres. Sergeants are walking around screaming at them. Lewis grins.

At breakfast he eats two bowls of oatmeal and half a bowl of strawberry jam. He whistles on his way back to the barracks. Then the first sergeant calls a special formation and everything goes wrong.

Lewis falls in with the rest of the company. He knows what it's about. *Shoot*, he thinks. It doesn't seem fair. He's all ready to make a new start and he wishes that everybody else could do the same. Just wipe the slate clean and begin all over again. There's no point to it, this anger and fuss, the first sergeant walking up and down saying it gives him nerves to know there's a barracks thief in his company. Lewis wishes he could tell him not to worry, that it's all history now.

Then Hubbard goes to the front of the formation and Lewis sees the metal cast on his nose. *Oh Lord*, he thinks, *I didn't do that*. He stares at the cast. There was a man in Lawton who used to wear one just like it because his nose was gone, cut off in a fight when he was young. Underneath was nothing but two holes.

Hubbard follows the first sergeant up and down the ranks. Lewis meets his eyes for a moment and then looks at the cast again. That hurts, he thinks. He will make it up to Hubbard. He will be Hubbard's friend, the best friend Hubbard ever had. They'll go bowling together and downtown to the pictures. The next long weekend they'll hitch a ride to Nags Head and rustle up some of those girls down there. At night they will go down on the beach and have a time. Light a fire and get drunk and laugh. And when they get shipped overseas they will stick together. They'll take care of each other and bring each other back, and afterwards, when they get out of the Army, they will be friends forever.

The first sergeant is arguing with someone. Then Lewis sees that the men around him are emptying their pockets into their helmets and unblousing their pants. He does the same and straightens up. Hubbard and the first sergeant are in front of him again and Hubbard bends over the helmet and takes out the letter that Lewis could not let go of, that he's forgotten does not belong to him.

Where's my wallet? Hubbard says.

Lewis looks down.

The first sergeant says, Where is this boy's wallet?

Under the stands, Lewis says. While they wait Lewis looks at the ground. He sees the shadows of the men behind him, sees from the shadows that they are watching him. The first sergeant is saying something.

Look at him, the first sergeant says again. He puts his hand under Lewis's chin and forces it up until Lewis is face to face with Hubbard. Lewis sees that Hubbard isn't really mad after all. It is worse than that. Hubbard is looking at him as if he is something pitiful. Then Lewis knows that it will never be as it could have been with the two of them, nor with anyone else. Nothing will ever be the way it could have been. Whatever happens from now on, it will always be less.

Lewis knows this, but not as a thought. He knows it as a distracted, restless feeling like the feeling you have forgotten something when you are too far from home to go back for it.

The sun is hot on the back of his neck. A drop of sweat slides down between his shoulder blades, then another. They make him shiver. He stares over Hubbard's head, waiting for the next drop. Out on the parade ground the flag whips in a gust, but it makes no noise. Then it droops again. The metal cast glitters. Everything is still.

6

The morning after Hubbard got his nose broken the first sergeant called a special formation. He walked up and down in front of us until the silence became oppressive, and then he kept doing it. There were two spots of colour like rouge on his cheeks. The line of his scar was bright red. I couldn't look at him. Instead I kept my eyes on the man in front of me, on the back of his neck, which was pocked with tiny craters. Finally the first sergeant began to talk in a voice that was almost a whisper. It was that soft, but I could hear each word as if he were speaking just to me.

He said that a barracks thief was the lowest thing there was. A barracks thief had turned his back on his own kind. He went on like that.

Then the first sergeant called Hubbard in front of the formation. With the metal cast and the tape across his cheeks, Hubbard's face looked like a mask. The first sergeant said something to him, and the two of them began to walk up and down the ranks, staring every man full in the face. I tasted something sour at the root of my tongue. I wondered how I should look. I wanted to glance around and see the faces of the other men but I was afraid to move my head. I decided to look offended. But not too offended. I didn't want them to think that this was anything important to me.

I composed my face and waited. It seemed to me that I was weaving on my feet, in tiny circles, and I made myself go rigid. All around me I felt the stillness of the other men.

Hubbard walked by first. He barely turned his head, but the first sergeant looked at me. His eyes were dark and thoughtful. Then he moved on, and I slowly let out the breath I'd been holding in. A jet moved across the sky in perfect silence, contrails billowing like plumes. The man next to me sighed deeply.

After they had inspected the company the first sergeant ordered us to take off our helmets and put them between our feet, open end up. Then he told us to empty our pockets into our helmets and leave the pockets hanging out. My squad leader, an old corporal with a purple nose, said 'Bullshit!' and put his helmet back on.

He and the first sergeant looked at each other. 'Do it,' the first sergeant said.

The corporal shook his head. 'You don't have the right.'

The first sergeant said, 'Do it. Now.'

'I never saw this before in my whole life,' the corporal said, but he took his helmet off and emptied his pockets into it.

'Unblouse your pants,' the first sergeant said.

We took our pantlegs out of our boots and let them hang loose. Here and there I heard metal hitting the ground, knives I suppose.

The first sergeant watched us. He had gotten his wounds during an all-night battle near Kontum in which his company had almost been overrun. I think of that and then I think of what he saw when he looked at us, bareheaded, our pockets hanging down like little white flags, open helmets at our feet. A company of beggars. Nothing worth dying for. He was clearly as disappointed as a man can be.

He looked us over. Then he nodded at Hubbard and they started up the ranks again. A work detail from another company crossed the street to our left, singing the cadence, spades and rakes at shoulder arms. As they marched by they fell silent, as if they were passing a funeral. They must have guessed what was happening.

Hubbard looked into each helmet as they walked up the ranks. I had a muscle jumping in my cheek. And then it ended. Hubbard stopped in front of Lewis and bent down and took a piece of paper from his helmet. He unfolded it and looked it over. Then he said, 'Where's my wallet?'

Lewis did not answer. He was standing two ranks ahead of me and I could see from the angle of his neck that he was staring at Hubbard's boots.

'Where is this boy's wallet?' the first sergeant said.

'The parade ground,' Lewis said. 'Under the stands.'

The first sergeant sent a man for the wallet. Nobody spoke or moved except Hubbard, who folded the paper again and put it in his pocket. All my veins opened up. I felt the rush of blood behind my eyes. I was innocent.

When the runner came back with the wallet Hubbard looked through it and put it away. 'You stole from this boy,' the first sergeant said. 'You look at him.'

Lewis did not move.

'Look at him,' the first sergeant said again. He pushed Lewis's chin up until Lewis was face to face with Hubbard. They stood that way for a time. Then from behind, I could see Lewis's fatigue jacket begin to ripple. He was shaking convulsively. Everyone watched him, those in the front rank half-turned around, those behind leaning out and craning their necks. Lewis gave a soft cry and covered his face with his hands. The sound kept coming through his fingers and he bent over suddenly as if he'd been punched in the belly.

The man behind me said, 'Jesus Christ!'

Lewis staggered a little, still bent over, his feet doing a jig to stay under him. He crossed his arms over his chest and howled, leaning down until his head almost touched his knees. The howl ended and he straightened up, his arms still crossed. I could hear him wheezing.

Then he dropped his arms to his sides and arranged his feet and tried to come to attention again. He raised his head until he was looking at Hubbard, who still stood in front of him. Lewis began to make little whimpering noises. He took a step forward and a step back and then he shrieked in Hubbard's face, a haunted-house laugh that went on and on. Finally the first sergeant slapped him across the face – not hard, just a flick of the hand. Lewis went to his knees. He bent over until his forehead was on the ground. He flopped onto his side and drew his knees up almost to his chin and hugged them and rolled back and forth.

The first sergeant said, 'Dismissed!'

Nobody moved.

'Dismissed!' he said again, and this time we broke ranks and drifted away, throwing looks back to where Hubbard and the first sergeant stood over Lewis, who hugged his knees and hooted up at them from the packed red earth.

For the rest of that day we did target duty at the rifle range, raising and lowering man-sized silhouettes while a battalion of recruits blazed away. The bullets zipped and whined over the pits where we huddled. By late afternoon it was clear that the targets had won. We boarded the trucks and drove back to the company in silence, swaying together over the bumps, thinking our own thoughts. For the men who'd been in Vietnam the whole thing must have been a little close to home, and it was a discouraging business for those of us who hadn't. It was discouraging for me, anyway, to find I had no taste for the sound of bullets passing over my head. And it gave me pause to see what bad shots those recruits were. After all, they belonged to the same army I belonged to.

Hubbard ate dinner by himself that night at a table in the rear of the mess hall. Lewis never showed up at all. The rest of us talked about him. We decided that there was no excuse for what he'd done. If the clerk had busted him at poker, or if someone in his family was sick, if he'd been in true need he could have borrowed the money or gone to the company commander. There was a special kitty for things like that. When the mess sergeant's wife disappeared he'd borrowed over a hundred dollars to go home and look for her. The supply sergeant told us this. According to him, the mess sergeant never paid the money back, probably because he hadn't found his wife. Anyway, Lewis wouldn't have died from being broke, not with free clothes, a roof over his head, and three squares a day.

'I don't care what happened,' someone said, 'you don't turn on your friends.'

'Amen,' said the man across from me. Almost everyone had something to say that showed how puzzled and angry he was. I kept quiet, but I took what Lewis had done as a personal betrayal. I had myself thoroughly worked up about it.

Not everyone joined in. Several men kept to themselves and ate with their eyes on their food. When they looked up they made a point of not seeing the rest of us, and soon looked down again. They finished their meals and left early. The first sergeant was one of these. As he walked past us a man at my table shouted 'Blanket party!' and we all laughed.

'I didn't hear that,' the first sergeant said. Maybe he was telling us not to do it, or maybe he was telling us to go ahead. What he said made no difference, because we could all see that he didn't care what happened any more. He was already in retirement. The power he let go passed into us and it was more than we could handle. That night we were loopy on it.

I went looking for Hubbard. A man in his platoon had seen him walking towards the parade ground, and I found him there, sitting in the stands. He nodded when he saw me, but he did not make me welcome. I sat down beside him. It was dusk. A damp, fitful breeze blew into our faces. I smelled rain in it.

'This is where he went through my wallet,' Hubbard said. 'It was down there.' He pointed into the shadows below. 'What I can't figure out is why he kept the letter. If he hadn't kept the letter he wouldn't have gotten caught. It doesn't make any sense.'

'Well,' I said, 'Lewis isn't that smart.'

'I've been trying to picture it,' Hubbard said. 'Did you ever play "Picture It" when you were a kid?'

I shook my head.

'It was a game this teacher of ours used to make us play. We would close our eyes and picture some incident in history, like Washington crossing the Delaware, and describe what we were seeing to the whole class. The point was to see everything as if you were actually there, as if you were one of the people.'

We sat there. Hubbard unbuttoned his fatigue jacket.

'I don't know,' Hubbard said. 'I just can't see Lewis doing it. He's not the type of person that would do it.'

'He did it,' I said.

'I know,' Hubbard said. 'I'm saying I can't see him do it, that's all. Can you?'

'I'm no good at games. The point is, he stole your wallet and busted your nose.'

Hubbard nodded.

'Listen,' I said. 'There's a blanket party tonight.'

'A blanket party?' He looked at me.

For a moment I thought Hubbard must be kidding. Everyone knew what a blanket party was. When you had a shirker or a guy who wouldn't take showers you got together and threw a blanket over his head and beat the bejesus out of him. I had never actually been in on one but I'd heard so much about them that I knew it was only a matter of time. Not every blanket party was the same. Some were rougher than others. I'd heard of people getting beat up for really stupid reasons, like playing classical music on their radios. But this time it was a different situation. We had a barracks thief.

I explained all this to Hubbard.

'Count me out,' he said.

'You don't want to come?'

Hubbard shook his head. A dull point of light moved back and forth across the metal cast on his nose.

'Why not?'

'It's not my style,' he said. 'I didn't think it was yours, either.'

'Look,' I said. 'Lewis is supposed to be your friend. So what does he do? He steals from you and punches you out and then laughs in your face. Right in front of everyone. Don't you care?'

'I guess I don't.'

'Well, I do.'

Hubbard didn't answer.

'Jesus,' I said. 'We were supposed to be friends.' I stood up. 'Do you know what I think?'

'I don't care what you think,' Hubbard said. 'You just think what everyone else thinks. Beat it, okay? Leave me alone.'

I went back to the company and lay on my bunk until lightsout. The wind picked up even more. Then it began to rain, driving hard against the windows. The walls creaked. Distant voices grew near as the wind gusted, then faded away. There should have been a real storm but it blew over in just a few minutes, leaving the air hot and wet and still.

After the barracks went dark we got up and made our way to the latrine, one by one. For all the tough talk I'd heard at dinner, in the end there were no more than eight or nine of us standing around in T-shirts and shorts. Nobody spoke. We were waiting for something to happen. One man had brought a flashlight. While we waited he goofed around with it, making rabbit silhouettes with his fingers, twirling it like a baton, sticking it in his mouth so that his cheeks turned red, and shining it in our eyes. In its light we all looked the same, like skulls. A man with a cigarette hanging out of his mouth boxed with his own shadow, which went all the way up the wall onto the ceiling so that it seemed to loom over him. He snaked his head from side to side and bounced from one foot to the other as he jabbed upwards. Two other men joined him. Their dog tags jingled and I suddenly thought of home, of my mother's white Persian cat, belled for the sake of birds, jumping onto my bed in the morning with the same sound.

The man with the flashlight stuck it between his legs and did a bump and grind. Then he made a circle on the wall and moved his finger in and out of it. Someone made panting noises and said, 'Hurt me! Hurt me!' A tall fellow told a dirty joke but nobody laughed. Then someone else told a joke, even dirtier.

No one laughed at his, either, but he didn't care. He told another joke and then we started talking about various tortures. Someone said that in China there was a bamboo tree that grew a foot a day, and when the Chinese wanted to get something out of a person or just get even with him, they would tie him to a chair with a hole in the bottom and let the tree grow right through his body and out the top of his head. Then they would leave him there as an example.

Somebody said, 'I wish we had us one of those trees.'

No one made a sound. The flashlight was off and I could see nothing but the red tips of cigarettes trembling in the dark.

'Let's go,' someone said.

We went up the stairs and down the aisle between the bunks. The men around us slept in silence. There was no sound but the slap of our bare feet on the floor. When we got to the end of the aisle the man with the flashlight turned it on and played the beam over Lewis's bunk. He was sitting up, watching us. He had taken off his shirt. In the glare his skin was pale and smooth-looking. The beam went up to his face and he stared into it without blinking. I thought that he was looking right at me, though he couldn't have been, not with the flashlight shining in his eyes. His cheeks were wet. His face was in turmoil. It was a face I'd never really seen before, full of humiliation and fear, and I have never stopped seeing it since. It is the same face I saw on the Vietnamese we interrogated, whose homes we searched and sometimes burned. It is the face that has become my brother's face through all the troubles of his life.

Lewis's eyes seemed huge. Unlike an animal's eyes, they did not glitter or fill with light. His face was purely human.

He sat without moving. I thought that those eyes were on me. I was sure that he knew me. When the blanket went over his head I was too confused to do anything. I did not join in, but I did not try to stop it, either. I didn't even leave, as one man did. I stayed where I was and watched them beat him.

7

Lewis went into the hospital the next morning. He had a broken rib and cuts on his face. There was an investigation. That is, the company commander walked through the barracks with the first sergeant and asked if anyone knew who'd given Lewis the beating. No one said anything, and that was the end of the investigation.

When Lewis got out of the hospital they sent him home with a dishonourable discharge. Nobody knew why he had done what he'd done though of course there were rumours. None of them made sense to me. They all sounded too familiar – gambling debts, trouble with a woman, a sick relative too poor to pay doctor bills. The subject was discussed for a little while and then forgotten.

The first sergeant's retirement papers came through a month or so later. He had served twenty years but I doubt if he was even forty yet. I saw him the morning he left, loading up his car. He had on two-tone shoes from God knows where, a purple shirt with pockets on the sleeves, and a pair of shiny black pants that squeezed his thighs and were too short for him. I was in the orderly room at the time. The officer of the day stood beside me, looking out the window. 'There goes a true soldier,' he said. He blew into the cup of coffee he was holding. 'It is a sorry thing,' he went on, 'to see a true soldier go back on civvy street before his time.'

The desk clerk looked up at me and shook his head. None of us had much use for this particular officer, a second lieutenant who had just arrived in the company from jump school and went around talking like a character out of a war movie.

But the lieutenant meant what he said, and I thought he was right.

The first sergeant wiped his shoes with a handkerchief. He looked up and down the street, and though he must have seen us at the window he gave no sign. Then he got into his car and drove away.

All this happened years ago, in 1967.

My father worked at Convair in San Diego, went East for a while to Sikorsky, and finally came back to San Diego with a woman he had met during some kind of meditation and nutrition seminar at a summer camp for adults. They had a baby girl a few weeks after my own daughter was born. Now the two of them run a restaurant in La Jolla.

Keith came home while I was in Vietnam. He lived with my mother off and on for twelve years, and when she died he took a room in the apartment building where he works as a security guard. He's had worse jobs. The manager gave him a break on the rent. All the tenants know his name. They chat with him in the lobby when they come in late from parties, and they remember him generously at Christmas. I saw him dressed up in his uniform once, downtown, where there was no need for him to have it on.

Hubbard and I got our orders for Vietnam at the same time. We had a week's leave, after which we were to report to Oakland for processing. Hubbard didn't show up. Later I heard that he had crossed over to Canada. I never saw him again.

I never saw Lewis again, either, and of course I didn't expect to. In those days I believed what they'd told us about a dishonourable discharge – that it would be the end of you. When I thought of a dishonourable discharge I thought of a man in clothes too big for him standing outside bus terminals and sleeping in cafeterias, face down on the table.

Now I know better. People get over things worse than that. And Lewis was too testy to be able to take anyone's word for it that he was finished. I imagine he came out of it all right, one way or the other. Sometimes, when I close my eyes, his face floats up to mine like the face in a pool when you bend to drink. Once I pictured him sitting on the steps of a duplex. A black dog lay next to him, head between its paws. The lawn on his side was bald and weedy and cluttered with toys. On the other side of the duplex the lawn was green, well-kept. A sprinkler whirled rapidly, sending out curved spokes of water. Lewis was looking at the rainbow that hung in the mist above the sprinkler. His fingers moved over the dog's smooth head and down its neck, barely touching the fur.

I hope that Lewis did all right. Still, he must remember more often than he'd like to that he was thrown out of the Army for being a thief. It must seem unbelievable that this happened to him, unbelievable and unfair. He didn't set out to become a thief. And Hubbard didn't set out to become a deserter. He may have had good reasons for deserting, perhaps he even had principles that left him no choice. Then again, maybe he was just too discouraged to do anything else; discouraged and unhappy and afraid. Whatever the cause of his desertion, it couldn't have been what he wanted.

I didn't set out to be what I am, either. I'm a conscientious man, a responsible man, maybe even what you'd call a good man – I hope so. But I'm also a careful man, addicted to comfort, with an eye for the safe course. My neighbours appreciate me because they know I will never give my lawn over to the cultivation of marijuana, or send my wife weeping to their doorsteps at three o'clock in the morning, or expect them to be my friends. I am content with my life most of the time. When I look ahead I see more of the same, and I'm grateful. I would never do what we did that day at the ammunition dump, threatening people with rifles, nearly getting ourselves blown to pieces for the hell of it.

But I have moments when I remember that day, and how it felt to be a reckless man with reckless friends. I think of Lewis before he was a thief and Hubbard before he was a deserter. And myself before I was a good neighbour. Three men with rifles. I think of a spark drifting up from that fire, glowing as the breeze pushes it towards the warehouses and the tall dry weeds, and the three crazy paratroopers inside the fence. They'd have heard the blast clear to Fort Bragg. They'd have seen the sky turn yellow and red and felt the earth shake. It would have been something.